LIES THE GUARDIANS TELL

HERMAN STEUERNAGEL

LIES THE GUARDIANS TELL

Book One of *The Lies of The Guardians*

Copyright © 2020 by Herman Steuernagel

2nd Edition

ISBN: 978-1-7771777-20 (hardcover)

ISBN: 978-1-7771777-13 (paperback)

ISBN: 978-1-7771777-06 (ebook)

https://www.hermansteuernagel.com

Cover: MiblArt

For Nettie, who has cheered for me every step of the way. And to Mom, who always dreamed of her son becoming an author.

1

———

"Is there a problem, Sierra?"

Claudia loomed over Sierra's desk, a scowl on her face, the emerald-green orb on the head of her staff pulsing in unison with the blue luminescence that lit the walls of the classroom. The decorative blue lines matched the markings on the bodies of the Guardian orbs. Lines from historical texts meshed with code from the Guardian's Program itself also decorated the room, meant to inspire and remind the class that life was merely the result of a well-orchestrated program.

The exam that glowed from her desk was the most important document she'd write during her school career. Her LPE, Life Placement Exam. The result would be an influential determinate of the path the rest of her life would take. It would dictate under which level of society she would continue her service to the Guardians.

The questions glowed from her desk, empty.

Despite what they were told, she knew what the result would be. Every practice aptitude test she took leading up to this moment had revealed the same result, no matter the answers she chose.

Curiosity had gotten the better of her while undertaking the practice tests, and each time she had changed her answers, just to see. Each one had produced the same result. Destined to work at the Core. Just like her mother. Just like her father, before he died.

Even now, she wanted to throw caution to the wind. It all felt so pointless. Each answer was multiple choice, and she was tempted to randomize her selection.

She couldn't bring herself to do it, though. This exam was different. Her intuition aside, this one was real. But she struggled to bring meaning to what lay before her.

The questions weren't hard, being word and image associations mostly. Supposedly there were no wrong answers. Only answers that would affect the rest of her life.

She just needed to focus. Something about today felt off. The exam, the hum of the Sphere, the tapping of screens throughout the room as her peers worked diligently at the task before them —something wasn't right.

Sierra looked to the aging woman, still towering above her impatiently. There were few in the Sphere who lived past fifty. There was no way to tell for sure, but Claudia was rumored to be twice that age. Her jet-black hair declared otherwise, but the members of the Order didn't age the same as others. It was one benefit of their service to the Guardians. Guardian implants, that's what the other students whispered, but the Order kept their secrets close, and the adults hushed anyone that asked questions.

Most questions that would reveal secrets of the Guardians, of their Order, or of humanity's past were dismissed.

There was nobody in the Sphere older than Claudia who could confirm her age, other than the Guardians themselves, so Sierra went without knowing.

Two orbs floated through the room, observing the few dozen students with their heads down, working away at the exams on their desks. These two orbs in particular were

Scanners that were ensuring everyone was focused on their own test. But Sierra couldn't imagine how one could possibly cheat if there were no wrong answers. Or cheat if it was rigged to begin with.

Claudia pushed herself farther into Sierra's personal space, still waiting for an answer. For someone who had managed to defy aging, her breath was horrendous. Sierra nearly gagged at the stench, but she managed to keep her composure.

What was she supposed to tell her? Yes, there's a problem—I don't want to be relegated to the Core for the rest of my life? Yes, I think this is a waste of my time? You've known since my birth where I would end up? This is all just theater?

"Are you listening, girl?"

She looked at the woman leaning over her desk. This was one of the few times an Order member was present in the classroom, never mind their leader. Meant as an honor for the students. They were the highest level of the social order, a handful of chosen ones who spoke on behalf of the bots, the Guardians. Claudia, the highest-ranked of them all, acted like she'd rather be anywhere else.

The privilege was meant to instill a sense of what could be achieved with the right acumen. Supposedly. The children of those in the Order snarking in the corner suggested otherwise.

The Guardians typically presented their lessons themselves, either through the orbs or through the screens in the room. Their human Order members carried out more of the politicking throughout the Sphere, ensuring the pieces of the society continued to move in an orderly fashion.

Of course, Sierra's purple eyes made her easy to remember. So she was often picked out of a crowd for questioning. Today, it seemed, was no exception. Though as she looked around the room, only her classmate Wil was also silent on the keypad. So maybe it was her inactivity that drew the attention this time.

Great, lumped in with the likes of Wil.

"I'm just thinking, Master Claudia, my apologies," she finally answered.

"In this world, my dear, the world you are about to enter, you must allow the Guardians to do the thinking for you. If you follow their lead, you won't be led astray. Everything they do is to protect this last remnant of humanity and prepare it for a new future. This exam requires no thinking. Just answer with the first response that appears to correlate. The Guardians' score metrics will do the rest."

"I'm still the one who needs to answer the questions," she muttered under her breath.

Claudia didn't react and barely blinked as she looked down at Sierra, expectant of her answer. The only answer.

"The Guardians protect us," she grumbled with the least amount of enthusiasm she thought she could get away with.

"You of all people should realize that, child."

Sierra raised an eyebrow at her before gaining control of her face. A raised eyebrow was not an appropriate gesture toward the Order leader.

She eyed the Order youth in the room's corner, continuing to snicker among themselves. Another suggestion that the exam meant nothing. They were held in the highest regard, even in the classroom. It was nearly unheard of that one of them would be lowered to another status. Just as unlikely was someone from one of the lower occupations being lifted into their ranks, despite what they were told. Another reason Sierra believed this was all a charade. To what end? She didn't know. And she didn't dare dream of what would happen if she voiced the theory to anyone but Greata.

Of course, the handful of youth in the corner weren't Order members yet. They had yet to earn the glowing light pattern that adorned Claudia's robe, and as such, they would keep their thinly veiled opinions to themselves. It wouldn't be long after the

Placement Ceremony that the white robes would replace their standard gray ones.

But they *were* the children of the Order members. And just as Sierra was destined to follow her parents to the Core, the handful of uppity teenagers sitting in the corner would one day lead those who worked to maintain the Sphere that the Guardians had created. They would be entitled to the rule of law and already had the attitude to match.

Those youth had either already completed their exams or had long ago realized what Sierra had only recently discovered for herself. The answers didn't matter. Those who were born into the Order were destined to their cause. Other than blatant blasphemy, or perhaps complete incompetence, there was no reason for them to become anything less. And no way for anyone else to become anything more.

Was it the fear of being sent to the Outside that had stopped anyone from calling them out? Even to themselves? Or did everyone truly believe they were designated to the placing they deserved?

Claudia didn't move, waiting for further response from Sierra. As Sierra glanced up, the room spun and the woman before her and the world around her grew hazy.

Sierra's vision clouded, and Claudia and the surrounding classroom faded into a fog. She tried to brace herself on her desk, only to find nothing beneath her. She gasped in panic as her vision waned and then came back in a flash of blue sky. The classroom was now gone. She was suddenly outside, but the blue hue that made up the dome and encapsulated the Sphere, the force field that protected their oasis, was nowhere to be seen. The toxic yellow fog of the Outside had been replaced by the blue of a sky so clear she had only heard of such a sight in stories of the ancients. Her mouth gaped, and she couldn't help but stare. It was so beautiful, tears welled in her eyes.

The heat of a strong afternoon sun struck her face; the power of it was unlike anything she was used to. She was no longer masked by the fog that polluted the Earth's surface. The sun she knew provided warmth, but never at this intensity.

As quickly as it appeared, the blue sky faded back to the familiar glossy white ceiling above her. Claudia still towered above her desk, looking no more impressed than before.

Sierra swallowed visibly. What had just happened?

"Why on earth are you crying, child?" Claudia barked, finger pointed at Sierra's nose. "The practice exams were supposed to alleviate any anxiety. Haven't you been listening?"

Sierra froze, her mouth still agape. Did she just have a vision? There couldn't have been a worse time. Precisely the moment when the Grand Master of the Guardian Order was standing in front of her. She had precious seconds to answer.

"Sorry, I'm just really nervous about this exam. I know there are no wrong answers. I promise I am prepared. I'm finding it hard to concentrate," she stumbled. It was a thin excuse, but the best she could come up with as she struggled to gain her bearings.

Students around her tapped away at the exams, lit up on their desks, ignoring the commotion she felt she was causing. The hum of the Sphere outside, though faint, was still audible, as dirt from a toxic storm was flung up against the force field.

"It seems you aren't the only one." She paused, and Sierra followed Claudia's gaze to her classmate Wil. She didn't know Wil well, but knew enough to keep her distance. Wil was constantly getting himself into mischief with his friend Marco. His lost stare into nothingness echoed how she felt. What was his story this morning?

"Are you nervous this morning as well . . ." The woman checked the data pad in front of her, clearly unsure of the name of the student she was addressing. "Wil?" At the mention of his name, Wil perked up, oblivious to what had been transpiring around him.

He looked at her with poorly masked fear in his eyes. Claudia was intimidating, but she wasn't going to string him out in the fog for being inattentive. Something else was going on.

"I'm a bit distracted," he said. "I'm fine."

His friend, Marco, shot him a look; his brown eyes locked onto his friend in a silent plea to shut up. Neither Wil nor Master Claudia caught it, though.

The glassy displays of the two Scanners surveying the room blinked as if receiving a new piece of information from their network. Sierra believed she was the only one to catch that change as well.

"When the Guardians saved humanity over two hundred years ago," Claudia said, amplifying her voice to speak to the entire classroom as she paced to its front, "they developed this system to ensure each of us would be placed in the role we are best suited for. As you know, this exam will confirm your placement. There is no right or wrong. It is merely a tool."

Claudia returned her gaze to Sierra, cloudy eyes penetrating to the core of her.

"There is no need to be nervous." Claudia grinned a terrifying grin, which did anything but reassure her. "Your practice aptitudes should have prepared you well for this day. The Guardians . . . protect us indeed."

The Grand Master's words didn't calm Sierra as her heart raced, the gravity of her experience striking anew. She worried it might beat right out of her chest as her own pulse overpowered all other noises in the classroom. The exam and its consequences were the furthest thing from her mind now. She couldn't get the image of the blue sky and bright yellow sun out of her mind. It was more than a daydream. She had been there. *Where* exactly that had been she couldn't say. But she had been present under a foreign sky outside of the classroom. Out of the Sphere all together. Somewhere that shouldn't exist.

She looked over to Wil. Despite the air-conditioned room,

sweat dripped off his face. Why was he so sweaty? The memory of the sun's heat began to fade from her skin. Maybe he had shared the vision with her? It seemed unlikely, but still, she reached up to feel her own forehead. Clammy, cool, not sweaty. Something else was bothering her classmate. If it wasn't a shared experience, then she didn't have the mental capacity to worry about what it could be. She had enough on her mind.

Like being found out. If Master Claudia had any indication that she had been seeing visions, Sierra would have more than the integrity of an exam to worry about. Anything so outside the norm would likely be touted as heresy. The Council could send her outside their protective bubble, doom her to be choked to death by the toxic air the ancients had left behind or turned inside out by the poison atmosphere, depending on if she believed the official accounts or the rumors.

Her friend Greata was the only one she could trust to discuss this with. Even then, she'd have to guard their conversation. Even her Keeper, Ember, wouldn't understand. Ember would likely not report her, but she definitely wouldn't engage any further about the subject and would tell Sierra to keep her mouth shut.

She poked at the exam that sat on her desk. As disillusioned as she was about its intent, she felt compelled to see it through. At least now it was something to distract her.

Most of the questions were associations. The exam presented a word, and she had to choose another word or image to associate with it. It didn't appear that any of the questions were relevant to deciding her fate.

Despite her doubts, she resigned herself to filling things in appropriately. She couldn't force herself to step out of line. She had struggled to do so even in the practice exams, but curiosity got the better of her. Knowing the outcomes of those weren't permanent, she was willing to experiment. But this test was different.

She stared at the first question. The practice exams had all started with the same one.

The first word presented was the word *Guardian*. It always felt like a placeholder question for the ones that followed. From a list of four other words, she had to choose the one she associated the most with the first. None of the answers seemed like anything but what the Guardians would describe themselves as: *Defender, Provider, Sage, Warrior*.

Answers reflected how the residents of the Sphere saw humanity's saviors. In theory, this question alone could indicate where your role within society could fall.

This time, however, there was a fifth word added to the list. She had to do a double take at the answer to ensure she was reading it correctly.

Liar.

She paused and nearly checked her forehead again for sweat. A glitch? A trick? It was blasphemous to even suggest something so ridiculous. Even with her doubts on the validity of the exam, she would never have suggested an answer so egregious. She glanced around at the other students. They would all be much further ahead in their exams than she was, but none of them seemed taken aback by anything out of the ordinary. Surely someone else would have been tripped up by the offered response.

She looked to Claudia at the front of the room to see if the woman was still keeping an eye on her, maybe watching to see if she'd slip up. Claudia had become distracted by something else on her data pad though and was no longer paying attention to her.

She shook off the abnormality. Maybe this was just part of the test. She hit the option for *Provider* and continued to the next question. The ghosted word *Liar* lingered on the screen for a split-second longer than everything else. She blinked a couple of times just to get it out of her residual vision.

For the second question, an image of a bright yellow sun appeared. The association was not one that had been on the practice exams either. Until moments before, a bright yellow sun had only been something she had seen in videos and images of the ancients, in histories of a past that existed before their world was destroyed, forcing the Guardians to save the rest of humanity within this Sphere. A yellow sun wasn't out of the realm of their studies, but it caught her off guard, and she shuddered.

She paused at the options below the image, and her heart sank.

Hope, Life, Star, Battle, Lies.

Something was wrong. Regardless of the outcome, she could feel within her bones that the exam would reveal more than just her career path.

2

THE DOOR SLID open and Sierra entered her home. Mid-afternoon sunlight warmed the spots on the floor where the windows of their modest home let the muted light in. Otherwise, the concrete surface was quite cool. Sierra took her shoes off and let the cement soothe her tired feet. It still impressed her that the Guardians were able to construct these dwellings out of practically nothing. Particles of the dirt beneath their feet were the only construction materials used. The appliances and other conveniences they were offered, repurposed and rebuilt from what the ancients had left behind.

Sierra tossed her bag on the table, tablet sliding out of the half-zipped pocket. What a waste of an exam. Waste of a day. The questions that had followed the first two continued in their level of peculiarity, to the point where there had been no good answer, and she felt sick to her stomach even trying.

The answers filled with accusations and insults to the Guardians could have amounted to nothing more than a trap. But why?

She filled their sleek steel kettle with water and set it on the stove to boil. Tea would maybe help calm her down, help her focus. She had to shake off the dream she had this morning. If that was what it was.

Another layer to the onion the day had presented. She looked out the window. Yellow fog swam around the dome beyond its force field. There had once been blue sky, so she'd been told. The ancients did something to destroy the world outside. A war between men before the Guardians stepped in to save them.

Several Onyx flew past. The large black orbs flowed through her vision, just outside of her comprehension. Their dominance in an otherwise empty sky would have caught her full attention mere moments ago, but barely registered with everything else that had happened that day.

Her back against the wall, she let her mind wander as she scanned the white kitchen that she had known since she was a child. Her family had always lived in this house, at least for as long as she could remember. Supposedly her parents were only able to move into the home when they were gifted with her sister, along with the promise that another child would follow. The Guardians allocated each family's dwelling in accordance with its needs. This being a three-bedroom home meant it was assigned for a family with two children.

After her father, and older sister, Izzy, had died, she had been afraid that the Guardians would force them to move into a one-bedroom house for her and her mom to share. Not that there was a bad home or a bad area in the North Village, but as a child who had just lost her father and her sister, she didn't want to lose her home as well.

In the end, they were allowed to keep their home, thanks in no small part to Ember becoming part of their lives. She was provided to Sierra, in need of the comfort of a companion, a Guardian, and a best friend. Her mom needed the help as well; now a single mother, she had to pick up her dead husband's quota by working extra shifts, sometimes for weeks, away at the Core.

Of course, Ember didn't really need to sleep, but she inherited Izzy's old bedroom anyway.

As one could imagine, a robot's room was quite plain. With no need for a bed, Ember stood upright against the wall when she powered down for the night. But she didn't require a charging dock like many of the other Guardians. That wasn't something Sierra was supposed to know, but Greata had told her one night about how they had to plug into the wall every few days to charge. Like a high-functioning toaster.

Greata, the only one she could speak to about the questions that plagued her mind. The only one who humored her with answers, or at least musings, when all others would give her scorn.

The revelation about the Guardians needing a charge was a detail that always made her smile. These powerful beings that were the saviors of humanity still needed to sleep. Needed a powered device to regenerate. In some ways, they knew Guardians were fallible. That was part of the work done at the Core after all. To help sustain their presence in the Sphere, and to help repair and recharge the beings as they needed. The need to plug into the wall brought the almighty Guardians closer to her level. Perhaps it was one of the reasons why she questioned? Their need for an outlet wasn't consistent with their omniscience.

Ember was special, though, for many reasons. Ember was the only Guardian she had ever seen that resembled a human. Most of the Guardians were orbs floating around the city, or machine-like. They were designed to fulfill a specific purpose. Greata told Sierra that few like Ember were ever created. She did need to power down to charge, but she didn't require any special device to do so. And if she had been a human, she would have been beautiful. Her red-orange hair was long and lifelike, and her bright orange eyes were striking, and a stark reminder that their owner wasn't quite human. Her figure would be described as athletic. The main thing that set her apart was her completely white body, similar to some of the other Guardians, but softer, designed to mimic skin, with orange lights glowing from her frame. She was the only Guardian shaped like a human that Sierra had ever seen.

Ember stepped out of the back room as if she had been anticipating Sierra's return.

"How did your exam go, Sierra? I am confident you found your worries to be for nothing"

The strangeness of the test had made Sierra forget how nervous she had been about taking it. Not nervous for the exam, not even nervous for the outcome. She had been nervous that she had been strung along her entire life, led to believe her choices could make a difference. Her biggest worry had been those choices were never real.

Sierra sighed and adjusted the kettle on the stovetop. "No, I don't think I did well. I was . . . distracted."

"I am always willing to listen and offer support, if there is anything you wish to talk to me about." Ember's orange eyes were tight with concern.

Sierra hesitated. Ember was her best friend, and other than Greata, she was her only friend. But there were certain things she could only discuss with Greata. Though her Keeper and unlike any other, Ember was a Guardian, and despite her having Sierra's best interests at heart, there were some things she had to hold back on.

There was always a fine line with what she was able to share with her Keeper.

"I know you are, Ember. There isn't anything that you can help with. I just need to think some things through."

Ember approached her calmly. If she had been human, her white cloak would have been out of place. Instead it added to the charm of the only robot Sierra could have considered her friend.

Ember nodded as if she understood and set about the kitchen, getting preparations underway for supper.

"I don't think I will be here for supper, so don't worry about fixing anything."

"I do wish you would stay," Ember replied. "Your mother should be here any moment now."

Sierra scoffed. More than likely, her mother would go straight to bed and not say two words to either one of them. She tried hard not to resent her mother for spending all of her time at the Core. She knew it wasn't entirely her choice. But part of her couldn't get over the fact that she didn't grow up with a mother who was ever at home and only had a robot for a companion for all of these years.

"She won't care if I'm here or not."

Not waiting for an answer, she went to her room and packed an overnight bag. She had a feeling she wouldn't be back before curfew.

She didn't waste any time and quickly returned to the kitchen with her bag. Ember was still standing there patiently waiting to continue their conversation.

"Today was my LPE, Ember. Next month I'll probably find out I'm being shipped to the Core, and I'll get to waste my life away there too. I'm going to enjoy my time until that happens. I'm going to spend the night at Greata's. I need to get out of the Village and clear my head."

"Be careful tonight," Ember replied. "I've been getting messages that there has been trouble around town."

"What kind of trouble could there possibly be in the Sphere for me to worry about?"

"I'm not getting any specifics, but it's been quite some time since there has been this type of activity on my communications feed. I don't think there's much to be concerned about, but just be cautious about what's happening around you. You don't want to end up in the wrong spot at the wrong time."

Ember was often overprotective, but this was the first time she had ever given such a cryptic, yet dire warning. It was also rare that she mentioned she was getting direct communication from the other Guardians.

"I'm sure I'll be okay, Ember," she said, not wanting to alter her plans.

"You're probably right, Sierra, but just please be careful."

Sierra slung her backpack over her shoulder. As she stepped toward the door, her mother walked in.

"Hi, hon." Her eyes dropped.

Sierra released a sigh. "Hey, Mom," she said. "How are things at the Core?"

"Oh, same as always. You're leaving? I'm going to head to bed. Things just aren't slowing down."

"Same as usual." Sierra tried her best to hide the vitriol in her voice, but guessed she failed miserably.

"You know, the Guardians deserve our help. One day you'll understand."

She bit her lip. She had to leave before she said something she regretted.

"I'm going to spend the night at Greata's tonight." She had no intent on getting into an argument with her mother. It wasn't worth the effort.

"I'm too exhausted to stay up much longer tonight anyway. I know Greata's happy for the company."

Sierra stepped outside and set off through the Village. Her relationship with her mother would have to wait for another time. She had been right about one thing. No matter what the outcome of the exam, she would soon be forced to leave her childhood home to be positioned where the Guardians would have her. They would decide where she'd best fit into the order they had established. It all seemed so futile. Destined to be just another cog in the machine. All to keep humanity alive in this little bubble.

A FEW PEOPLE were going about their business as Sierra left the Village, but the streets were quieter than usual.

She spotted Chester Bennett walking toward her. A sack of vegetables he hauled on the cart behind him indicated he had stocked up for his produce stand for the next few days. When she was little, she would go with her dad to the market once a week and pick up carrots, squash, and other vegetables. Now she made the trip alone or with Ember.

He waved back politely. Chester had always held a soft spot for her, but he treated everyone with genuine kindness. Sierra had been ten years old when her dad and sister Izzy died suddenly. She was often left with only Ember to run the household. She was forced to take over many duties normally not left to children her age, which also meant shopping. Chester would often help Sierra carry home a heavy armload of vegetables for no extra charge, even if it meant abandoning his stand.

"Well, hello there, Sierra," he said, flashing a gentle smile. "There seems to be trouble afoot today." He set down the handles of his cart. He made it appear he was stopping to chat, but Sierra suspected he needed a break from his load, as he was starting to slow down with age. She was happy to be the excuse for him to rest. He pointed into the air, back toward the Village. The same giant black orbs, the Onyx, that had been out this morning were still hovering over part of the Village. Their movements were more methodical than they had been earlier. They were looking for something.

She had been so absorbed in her thoughts earlier that she hadn't put the pieces together. She couldn't recall ever seeing them out searching like this.

Onyx were the largest and most ominous type of Guardian. She had only ever seen them a few times in her life. They were likely ten to twelve feet in diameter, though it was hard to judge their size from a distance. She hoped she never got close enough to find out their exact size. Children were often threatened with Onyx visiting them at night if they misbehaved.

Most of the Guardian spheres were a glossy gray or white. These were still glossy, but so black they seemed to absorb the light around them. Occasionally blue patterns of light indicated something in the way of their processing. It was the only thing giving them the appearance of life. A circle of blueish light pulsed on the front of the spheres, like a giant eye staring down the village inhabitants.

The last time she could recall even seeing Onyx, before today, was the day her father and sister had died. What was their appearance about? Maybe she should have heeded Ember's warning. However, if there was truly imminent danger, Ember wouldn't have let Sierra leave the house. Her top priority was Sierra's safety.

She absently nodded in response to Chester. She couldn't help but stare. "Any word of what's going on? I saw them scanning this morning as well. They seemed to be in more of a hurry then."

He shook his head, eyes still on the sky. "No, nobody seems to know. They aren't issuing any public warnings, though, so I'd say it's no threat to us. But just in case, you be careful. It can't be good news."

"Thanks, Chester, I'll see you back at the market tomorrow."

He nodded, lifted the handles of his cart, and continued on his way.

She let her mind wander back to the day when her father and sister died. The Onyx had been out that day as well. She had watched them from her living room window as her mom had paced back and forth, waiting for Izzy and her dad to come home.

They never did.

Her dad had taken Izzy to work that day, as a treat. It wasn't common for nonworkers to be brought to the Core, but it wasn't unheard of either. It just so happened that that was the day there was an accident. Several people didn't return, including half her family.

She was never given any real answers. As a ten-year-old asking about what had happened to her family, it was very confusing. Her mother glossed over things and told her it wasn't their place to question the will of the Guardians. Just to let it be. The Guardians protect us.

And they had protected them, really. Sierra and her mother had a place to live, they had food, and they had safety from the Outside. According to their lessons, that was far more than the ancients ever had before the Guardians. They nearly destroyed themselves because of it.

Protection at what cost?

As she got closer to the lake, rows of vegetation lined the side of the road. Nearly all of the products Sierra had ever known grew in this area. All made possible by the Guardians setting up irrigation from the lake and the environmental controls they regulated. The controls ensured that the bounty of harvest lasted through the seasons, and the inhabitants were never in want.

To the west was the lakeshore. The lake unfurled from the mountains in the north toward the south; at the far south end of the Sphere, it wrapped back in toward the east, providing a natural boundary to nearly half of the Sphere's force field. Sierra imagined it must be what the ocean was like, though she couldn't imagine a body of water being much bigger. On the far side of the lake she could make out the desert reappearing outside of the Sphere. Marking where the Guardians' influence ended and the near-infinite wasteland began. Beyond that, the Guardians worked the land and the air, aiming to make it fit for humans to one day reclaim and live in harmony under the wisdom of the Guardians.

Farms encircled the edge of the lake, and their fields spread inward as irrigation lines moved the life-giving water of the lakes. The environmental controls and worker Guardian bots did the rest, with the oversight of a few humans to ensure everything continued to operate efficiently.

The path toward the Red Mountains, the Sphere's northern boundary, followed parallel to the edge of the lake and would lead to Greata's farm.

Her friend's home became visible in the distance. The white exterior was not so different from most homes she knew throughout the North Village. Being out in the countryside, with a prominent role in society, had provided Greata with a house somewhat larger than Sierra's, despite her living alone.

Farmers were well respected, and even the Order tended to leave them alone. Though not as prestigious, the farms kept the villages from starving, and even the pompous leaders recognized their importance.

For some reason, that same logic didn't apply to those who worked in the Core—the workers who serviced the Guardians, worked in the genetics labs, and regulated countless other systems that had been set up for the rest of humanity to live comfortably as the Guardians worked tirelessly to clean up the earth's atmosphere.

Sierra kicked a pebble down the road in front of her in frustration as she approached the house.

Greata was outside, loading up vegetables that were coming in from the field. With the Guardians doing pretty much everything else on the farm, Greata had to oversee and take care of storing the product. She was also one of the only human contacts the livestock had. For reasons that could never be adequately explained, they didn't respond as well to Guardians, so it was up to human caretakers to maintain the animals that provided meat and dairy.

The raw smell of cattle permeated the air. Many from the

village didn't like the smell. To Sierra, the smell was a reminder that she was close to the home of her dearest friend.

The frustrations of her day began to melt away as she approached the residence, and she developed a spring in her step. This was one of the few places she could be herself. Greata was the only one she could talk to other than Ember, and the only one she could ask questions to without being reprimanded or ignored. Sierra could ask things of Greata that she would never dare approach even Ember about. She didn't always get an answer, but she always got an open ear.

Greata looked up from the beets she was piling into a storage shed—produce for the merchants who would come in the morning. Her graying hair was tied behind her head and away from her eyes. Dirt marked the wrinkles in her face, more weathered than old. The face of someone who had spent her entire life outside, hard at work.

Though older, Greata had a beauty to her that most in the Sphere didn't possess. It was a rugged, well-lived kind of beauty. The type you didn't get from sitting behind a workstation at the Core.

Her wisdom betrayed any sense of youth Greata's eyes held. The way she talked about the old world and the ancients, about the time before the Sphere, it was almost as if she had experienced something even Claudia had only read about.

Greata barely looked up as Sierra approached. "Grab some of these beets will you, Sierra? I'm running a bit behind this afternoon. So many chatty buyers today. Trying to discuss the Onyx, dallying in order to keep away from them."

"Do you know what they want, Greata?" Sierra asked.

"Likely just want to poke their nose where it doesn't belong," she quipped.

Sierra raised her brow. "The buyers or the Onyx?" She smiled at her friend.

Greata paused briefly and gave Sierra a wink before continuing her labor.

"Onyx or none, the shopkeepers won't be happy if they can't pick up their orders tomorrow."

Sierra got to work. For every vegetable she tossed, Greata tossed a half dozen.

It didn't take long before the task was done. "Go on in and make yourself some tea," said Greata. "I'm going to round the cattle up and I'll be right in."

She turned into the house as Greata ran out into the field with a stride that would never let on that she was any older than thirty.

The woman really was good at what she did. Sierra didn't mind helping where she could, but she was of no use with the cattle. Once when Greata had asked her to help, she had nearly gotten trampled in the process—cows coming at her from every direction, and others going anywhere but where she had wanted. Greata had had a good laugh over that one. Beets she could manage.

The glass door slid open for Sierra as she approached the threshold of the house. "Turn the kettle on, please," she said to the room, and she heard the click and faint hum of the kettle turning on. Voice activation was a perk acquired with Greata's status, only one of the many luxuries her home had.

She made her way to the fridge and began preparing a plate of dried meat, cheeses, and raw vegetables that the pair could have for a light meal. She wasn't quite hungry yet, but it seemed like a good way to pass the time, and Greata would be appreciative.

Nearly an hour passed before Greata walked in. She had learned a long time ago not to grow concerned, as there were often odds and ends that Greata would decide to complete before finally deciding to retire for the night. A farmer's status didn't come without hard work.

She removed her boots and set them by the door. Sierra could tell something was off. She had never seen Greata shaken before, but this was as close as she'd ever come.

"What's wrong, Greata?"

"Oh, just those Onyx. They were lit up over the North Village shortly after you walked in. I couldn't see anything from here, mind you, but I know those blue lights flashing when I see them." She just shook her head. "Just can't be anything good." Her hands trembled ever so slightly. So slightly that Sierra almost missed it. Almost.

Greata was tough as nails. If something had shaken her, Sierra should be terrified.

"You're not telling me something," said Sierra.

Greata sighed as she approached the table. "Yes, you know me well. You also should know we can't get into it now. Let's chat about it later. I promise we will. I wasn't expecting to see you today."

"I know," Sierra said, nodding. "Something happened to me, and . . . I have some questions."

"Questions are dangerous, girl, you know that." A smile touched her eyes, but not her lips. It disappeared altogether when she realized Sierra was clearly wrestling with something of greater importance than her normal pondering. "What's wrong? Did someone hurt you?"

"No, no, nothing like that . . ." She drifted off, not sure where to begin. "I think I may have seen something outside the Sphere." She wasn't sure if that was quite right, but it was the first thing that popped out of her mouth. She instantly clenched her teeth as she realized her error.

Greata choked on a mouthful of cheese, which sent her into a coughing fit. She recovered quickly and glared at Sierra with a burning intensity she had rarely seen from the woman. And for Greata, that was saying something.

"Talk like that is going to cause you more trouble than you are prepared to deal with."

"I need to know, Greata," she whispered as she glanced around the room. "I need to tell someone, and you're the only one I trust."

Greata tossed a block of cheese back onto her plate. "Let's go for a walk."

3
____

THE AIR STARTED to cool as the faint glow of the sun slipped past the horizon, leaving just enough light for Sierra to see where the silhouette of her friend was taking her. Greata had quite an extensive stretch of land, one of the largest she knew of. Though it was rumored there were even more substantial farms to the south, where the lake turned to the east, marking the southern border. Sierra had been to each of the South and East villages on school trips. It was important for them to understand that all the villages lived in harmony with each other. The Guardians provided for them all equally. She had never ventured into the farmland surrounding those communities, though. Enough food was grown in each community's Agricultural District to support itself. Each village then specialized in different crafts and items to trade with the others.

They walked to the edge of the lake and up the rocky shore toward the north in silence. She and Greata often came this way in the evenings when Sierra decided to stay at the farm past the village curfew. Outside the villages, the curfew didn't apply.

As the sunlight winked out, Greata pulled out a flashlight from the satchel she carried and the two continued their journey along the lakeside. The wind picked up, creating small waves that hit the rocky shoreline. The lake was not so large that she couldn't see the hills on the other side, though they were often hidden by the toxic smog that surrounded them. She tried to put the hills in the distance out of her mind and imagined that this must have been what the oceans were like, when people could still visit the ocean. Endless water as far as the eye could see, meeting with a clear blue sky. What could that possibly be like?

Did the ancients realize the treasure they were giving up in exchange for conflict and fighting with each other? Every time she stood on this lakeshore the same question entered her mind. It was one of the questions Greata couldn't give her an answer for, and she grew short when Sierra tried to push her line of thinking.

Greata turned off from their usual trail onto a path leading down one of the tall rows of corn.

"Where are we going, Greata?" Sierra asked.

"It's better if I show you."

They continued on until the row ended and another path continued to the north. They had been walking for nearly an hour in silence when they came to a large storage shed.

"How long have you known me for?" asked Greata, eyes on the shed.

"As long as I can remember. The day Dad and Izzy died you came by with a cart full of vegetables and a promise to be there if I ever needed someone to talk to. You promised me on that day that you'd be there for me." She smiled at the memory. "You've never let me down. Other than Ember, you're the only one I can talk to, and she won't answer my questions like you."

"In all of that time, I've never told you about my past, have I?"

"You've told me life hasn't always turned out the way you expected. That the Guardians let you manage this piece of land to help grow food for the Sphere. As you met or exceeded your quotas each season, they gave you more and more responsibility."

"Yes, that's all true," she said, her gaze still on the shed in front of them. "But there's so much I haven't told you."

Sierra raised an eyebrow. "What are you talking about?"

"I'll explain, but first, tell me about your dream, and I'll try to fill in the gaps."

"I . . . it may have been a dream, but I felt like I was actually there. Greata, the sky was blue!"

The world before her pulsed, a shockwave permeating everything. An earthquake? That didn't explain her vision fading.

Concerned, she looked to Greata.

"What's happening?" She grabbed on to her friend, afraid she might pass out.

"Are you okay, child?"

"Everything is vibrating. What's happening?" Sierra braced herself, afraid she might fall over.

A small gray orb flew overhead and steadily grew blurry as her vision faded.

Then the Sphere was gone, its blue hue and the yellow fog replaced by a bright blue sky. It was happening again—Greata, the farm, the lake, everything around her had disappeared, replaced by the strange and unusual. Her mouth gaped, and she couldn't help but stare. Tears welled in her eyes.

The blue sky she had witnessed while in the classroom had been fleeting. This was more present. She had time to soak in the sky above her. She had only ever dreamed of what a blue sky could look like.

Then the reality of what she was experiencing hit her like a punch to the gut. This wasn't the way things were supposed to be. She took in the rest of her surroundings and found herself standing on a street corner in a place she had never seen before. Heck, in a *world* she had never seen before. Lights and dazzling images lined the streets before her, amid giant walls of moving displays. Flashes of color, words, and people moved all around her. Like a giant electric dream.

This *couldn't* be real.

The dirt path that had been beneath her feet was now replaced by a gray, rough surface, littered with paper, old food, and other garbage. Machines moved up and down the street beside her. Machines carrying people. They reminded her of the transport vehicles to the Core.

Life-size displays towered overhead, on buildings, on the sides of the moving machines, on . . . everything. Her gaze followed the nearest building up toward the sky, until she was almost falling over backward. *How are buildings that tall even possible?*

The screens covering the buildings reminded her of those the Guardians used, but on a much grander scale. They flashed bright images of people, colors, shapes, and sounds.

Dull roars of people talking and machines roaring surged around her, matched only by what seemed like voices of the Guardians talking above everything. As Sierra tried to focus on the booming cacophony, she realized that the voices she could hear didn't sound quite like the Guardians; instead, they sounded more like human voices, amplified to be heard above the continuous roar around her.

People pushed past as she gawked at her surroundings. More people than she could remember having seen in her entire eighteen years crowded this long corridor of light and sound. They walked on pathways crisscrossing the street and on walkways suspended in the air. There were even more people walking on the other side of the massive roadway: so many people packed shoulder to shoulder, so many people paying her no mind, as if she wasn't really there.

But she *was* there. How it was possible, she wasn't sure. Anything she had ever seen in any of the three villages was dwarfed in comparison to the colossal world that surrounded her now.

What was happening? There were far more questions than she could possibly think of, and yet, as she gazed around, her mind grew silent as she tried to comprehend what she was seeing.

This was no dream.

The path felt solid beneath her feet. The stench of the place filled her nose and lungs. Food, people, the machines—everything combined to form a horrendous odor.

The heat from the sun overhead—yellow, bright, and full in the clear blue sky—was stronger than she had ever experienced. All she had ever known the sun to be was a dull orange glow, masked by toxic fog. The original source of life on this planet, cut off by a human desire for destruction.

A wave of panic overwhelmed her. How did she get here? Where *was* here?

And then, as quickly as it had started, it was over.

She blinked. As if nothing out of the ordinary had happened.

Greata was standing before her, eyes wide with concern, mouth open in astonishment.

"Just now, it happened again. The . . ." She scanned the sky around them, looking for signs of the bot that had been there moments before. "The vision. As I was recalling the blue sky, it happened again. Except this time, I was there for longer. Greata, I don't know where I was, but"—she glanced around again to confirm they were alone—"wherever it was, it wasn't in the Sphere."

Greata inhaled sharply, just shy of a gasp. She too scanned the surrounding sky and adjusted the light jacket she had on to fight the evening chill.

Sierra recounted everything, down to how the place had smelled. But most of all, how it all had felt so real, like no dream she had ever had before.

Greata's gaze focused on Sierra the entire time. She didn't even think she saw Greata blink. But she continued.

Once she was finally done, she took a deep breath.

"Everything was so foreign, I don't even know if I'm describing it properly. I don't have words for so much of what I saw."

"Well," said Greata, "what you saw was definitely not in the Sphere. But there isn't any place that exists like that anymore, not that I know of, anyway. What you saw sounds like a city of the ancients. Described to me once by a man I knew, almost exactly the same way."

"Someone else you know had a vision?"

"No. Not of this place." She shook her head. "He had been there."

"What do you mean? How could anyone you met have been in a city of the ancients? The Sphere has protected us from the Outside for over two hundred years."

"That's what they tell us. But we were never meant to be trapped inside these cages for this long."

Greata opened the door to her shed, and a mountain of vegetables lay inside.

Sierra raised an eyebrow. "So, you're keeping extra vegetables in storage? I don't understand why you brought me out here to see these."

"Don't get cheeky with me." Her green eyes indicated she wasn't in the mood for games.

She was being serious, but Sierra stifled a laugh.

"Sierra, I send these to the Outside."

"To the Outside? What are you talking about?"

"Outside the Sphere, child. I'm providing food to those who live out there."

"But . . . the world outside is lethal! Who? I don't understand." She was flustered as the words came out. Greata had been getting on in years, but she had never been anything but lucid.

"The Guardians don't tell us everything. There are people that live in the world outside the Sphere. I used to be one of them." She continued to glance around, clearly on edge about the words she was saying.

A chill ran through Sierra. The night air crossed her skin, warm. The chill came from Greata's words. Talk of the Outside was forbidden unless it was about the Guardians' terraforming efforts. This conversation was downright dangerous. The ancients were discussed with caution. That the Outside could currently be habitable was something they had never even dared mention to each other, a topic beyond taboo.

The immensity weighed her down, pushed on her so hard she couldn't breathe. Greata used to live outside of the Sphere? That wasn't possible.

Greata picked up on her hesitation and continued. "You're wondering if your vision was of the Outside. I'm telling you it was, just not of what's out there today. This isn't the way you should be finding this out, but you've forced my hand. I need to tell you this so that you have a fighting chance.

"I have a . . . past. I came here as a young woman," Greata continued. "Running away from tragedy. A man named Terre helped me escape. I chose to come here to live a simpler life. A life with less freedom, but one with far less hardship. I left behind many privileges." She turned to look at the sky beyond the blue dome. "And many people I loved. But my past has always been lurking, waiting for me to let my guard down, to punish me for my previous life."

"Outside?" Sierra was dumbfounded. Of all of the things she had expected Greata to say, this wasn't anywhere on that list. "No, Greata, the ancients destroyed the Outside."

"They did to some degree. Not to the point the Guardians will have you believe. A lot of it we did to help protect ourselves from them. Some of the destruction was them trying to destroy us. Some of it they did to protect us from ourselves. All of this"—she pointed to the sky—"all of this cloudy toxic soup is an illusion. I believe your vision, happening now, at this time, was a signal that it's time for your awakening, that it's time for you to begin the journey to fulfill what you were created to achieve."

"What are you talking about?" Sierra shook her head, glancing at the sky. A scanner orb flew past in the distance, likely too far away to hear them, but it would know where they were.

Greata didn't seem bothered by it. "There are people out there, but for them life is hard. Anything that I can grow on top of my quota I store up here and sneak out to them as soon as there's an opportunity.

"I've had some close calls lately. It's not easy to gather these without the notice of the Harvesters. They have a built-in fluctuation algorithm that I can take advantage of. They haven't taken into account that they've perfected the irrigation and growing climate over the past two hundred years. Old programs from times past still calling the shots. Anything above the quota goes into storage until I can sneak it into the mountains to the break."

The night was closing in on Sierra. Her whole life she had been told their bubble was the last remnant of humanity, and now her best friend, aside from Ember, her only true friend for the past eight years, was telling her it was all a lie. How was this possible? She would have responded if she could. Her brain couldn't process what she was hearing, and she didn't know where to even begin. She had never heard anything so absolutely ridiculous before in her life.

"I . . . I don't know what to say to that . . ."

"Sorry for just dumping this on you, child, but it's a warning. You aren't the first to have visions of the Outside. It runs in your family, and the last time I saw those black machines fly in the sky was the same day your sister died."

Instinctively her eyes went skyward. In the distance, Sierra could hear a low hum drawing near. As if in response to Greata's revelation, beams of light came to life and stretched out over them. They streaked overhead and cast spotlights on the tops of corn husks, nearly ready for harvest.

"Izzy?"

Greata nodded, though it was getting tough to see her in the darkness. The muted light of the moon cast an eerie glow over them, but its light was dim.

"What visions did Izzy have?"

"We don't have time to get into that now, child. I've always taken you out into the field when you've had your questions because it's safe from listening ears. But I've been under watch lately. When you mentioned being outside the Sphere, you triggered their detection. This isn't your fault. Get that look off your face. I am just letting you know, there is a reason others won't answer your questions.

"The Guardians do protect us, to some degree. Life here is more comfortable than the outside, but it comes at a cost. We're not free. We're not free to question, and we're not free to step outside their order. You'll be old enough to work at the Core soon, but work there is just to maintain their existence. None of it's about keeping us alive."

Three separate beams of light were crisscrossing the fields. They hit the top of the barn, but they didn't get low enough to reveal their position.

"But that's not what the future has in store for you. You're going to need to run, child. This won't end well."

"I don't understand. What's going on?" She had to raise her voice to speak above the growing hum of the nearby machines.

"The Guardians were built to protect us, no matter the cost. They've set up these Spheres throughout the world to protect pockets of humanity. But they are willing to sacrifice to protect their secrecy. They sacrifice many to save the few. Something the ancients did. Terre will be able to tell you more.

"There's a hole in the field to the north. Within the mountains. It's where I make my drop-offs. As far as I know it's a secret to everyone else. There's a path on the north side that appears to be a crack in the rock face. Follow it and you'll find a cave that leads past the force field. It's a few hours north of here, but if you follow the trail to the end, and then follow the edge of the Sphere, you'll find the path I've described."

Sierra shook her head. "Why are you telling me this? I don't want to leave the Sphere."

"You need to." Her eyes were intense, focused on Sierra in a plea of desperation. "Today's vision wasn't the first you've had?"

Sierra shook her head again. The lights were still visible above them, but they had moved off, closer to where she thought the house was. She usually got turned around in these cornfields.

"Last week, I think I told you."

Greata nodded, but looked eager for her to continue, so Sierra kept going. Her eyes never left the beams of light in the skies above them.

"I saw a man I had never seen before. He wore a robot pendant around his neck, and he had a chiseled face and piercing dark brown eyes. He was standing in front of me, with a confused look on his face, as if I wasn't supposed to be there. It was just a glimpse, so fast I thought I'd just imagined it."

"I don't think you did, child, and this new vision confirms it. You're meant for greater things. But I can't help you any more than to direct you on how to get out of this prison."

Sierra gave a start at her home being called a prison.

"You need to get out, and you need to get out tonight."

"I don't understand."

"I know you don't, but we're running out of time for me to answer your questions." Greata stepped into the barn and took out a small bag. "This has enough supplies to last you a couple days. There's not much water, but there should be enough for you to make it to the city."

"Why do you have a supply bag hidden away in the beet shed?" Sierra barely paused before continuing. "What city? Greata, this is crazy. I'm not going anywhere!"

"You have to."

Greata was either pleading or terrified. Maybe both. Sierra had never seen her friend this worked up about anything, ever.

"Do you see these Guardians circling above us?" She waved her arm above her head, gesturing at the beings in the night sky.

Sierra nodded.

"These are the Onyx, child. There is only one reason the Onyx come out, and that's to dispose of undesirables. Threats to their established order. These machines were built with the intent to kill."

That was enough for her to stop her protest, but now she froze in fear. Greata took the opportunity to continue.

"They are here for me. I've broken the agreement I had with them. But you can't be implicated in my crimes. But you will be if they detect that it's you here with me. It's not safe for you to head back home either. You need to run. Head north into the mountains and find the pass through the barrier. Once you're outside, start heading west.

"You need to find a man named Terre. Some will only know him as the man who remembers the wars. He may have some answers for you. If not, at least he'll protect you if you tell him I sent you. I'm afraid I have no more information for you to go on other than that. It's been over ten years . . ." She drifted off as if lost in a memory.

Sierra was dazed. Greata was speaking so matter of factly, but this was more than she could take in.

"What about Mom? What about Ember? I can't just leave tonight!"

"They'll all be in danger if you don't leave. You're in danger now. Your visions tell me sending you off is the best thing that I can do to help you. Something is coming, Sierra. It won't make sense for me to tell you now, but know that you are at the heart of mankind's redemption. Please let me give you the chance your sister never received."

"What about you? I don't understand this, Greata."

"You will, child. Have I ever led you astray in your life? You need to trust me, please."

Tears filled Greata's eyes. Trust her? She had just dumped a lifetime's worth of questions onto her and said her whole life had been built on a lie.

But the truth was there was nobody she trusted more than Greata. Her options were to head north into the mountains or refuse stubbornly and try to head back to the house. She knew the second would be a losing game.

"Take this," Greata said, removing a pendant and chain from her neck, and handing it to her. "It's the last piece I have of the life I left behind. It's something that I've held on to all these years."

Sierra looked at the palm-size medallion her friend bestowed on her. She had never known Greata to go a single day without wearing it. The medallion was brass, with the imprint of a circle atop three wavy lines.

She stared at the talisman, mesmerized. This couldn't really be happening.

"Anyone who knew me will know where you got this. It was a symbol of hope. A symbol of an effort that has likely long died out. Go now. We've taken too long already."

Not knowing what else to do, she gave Greata a hug. This was ridiculous. Where was she going? Sent to have her insides turned out?

"Head for the mountains, Sierra. Don't come back for me, no matter what happens. Just get out of the Sphere as soon as you can. Tonight, if you can find the trail. If you're not out by the morning, they will find you."

She hesitated. This was madness. Greata had never led her astray before, but the only thing that gave this whole thing a shred of believability was that she had been there. She had stood in a place with blue sky and wonders she couldn't describe.

"Greata, what color is the sky on the outside?"

"No more questions!" Her eyes were wide, and she practically pushed her into the corn stalks surrounding her. "*Go!*"

She took off into the field. She was sure she would get lost here, so she decided to backtrack to the lakeshore and follow the field to the north as far as Greata's property would allow. The lights were nowhere to be seen, but the glow of the Onyx exposed their flight near the vegetable shed.

She pressed on. Greata was now out of sight. The hum of the Onyx grew louder as they closed in on her location, and she instinctively ducked among the corn so that she wouldn't be seen. The wind had died down to a light breeze.

The Guardians' glow reflected off the calm waters of the lake. She paused as the Onyx slowed to a standstill and patterns of blue light formed on their otherwise glassy black bodies. The night breeze still giving her a bit of a chill, she watched them surround what must have been the location of the barn.

Despite the few hundred yards she had put between them, she could hear their voices clearly. "You were instructed to no longer deal with the Outside." It could have been one of the beings, or all three speaking in unison into the night, Sierra couldn't tell. "We heard discussion of the Outside. You are in violation."

She couldn't hear if there was a reply.

"You've had too many violations. We've detected you have been transporting goods to the edge of the Sphere. Have you found a breach in the perimeter?"

A moment passed.

"Is there a breach in the perimeter?""

Another moment.

"We will run a full visual diagnostic of our field. Tell us who the other offending member was. Voice recognition was inconclusive."

She had no way to tell if Greata was refusing to answer or if Greata was responding too softly for her to hear.

"We'll search for the missing party. This storage facility is not tracked in our records. You are in violation. You are guilty of transporting unregistered goods outside of the Sphere."

There was another pause, and the light activity on the surface of each of the spheres began to increase, until there was a steady stream of blue running up and down each of the Onyx bodies in unison. Narrow beams of light, so bright that Sierra had to shield her eyes, shot out of each of the three beings toward the ground. A giant pillar of flame shot vertically from the center of where their beams must have hit. Sierra could feel the heat from where she was several hundred yards away.

"Greata," she whispered.

She fought every instinct to run toward the flame, to see if her friend was okay. The only friend with whom she could discuss the unanswered questions that plagued her being. Her friend, who kept her own secrets. What else about Greata didn't she know?

She wanted to run back, pull her friend from the flames, and bring her to safety. But she had made Greata a promise, and it didn't look like the orbs were leaving. There was no way anyone could have survived what she just witnessed. She stood there, holding her breath. Not wanting to divert the orbs' attention, she ducked into the first row of corn and ran as quickly as she could without disturbing the crop around her. She didn't stop until she was at the end of the row, with nothing but open desert between her and the mountains ahead.

The lake still continued north but tapered off as it entered the mountain pass. The north boundary of the sphere was among those mountains. Light had faded nearly completely, but the dim glow of the moon behind the fog revealed silhouetted ridges that marked her destination.

She cast a cautious glance behind her, where flame and smoke rose into the night sky. She wouldn't be surprised if the North Village had a clear view of that flame. Though everyone would now be inside, as it was well past curfew. Maintenance drones were already scooping water out of the lake, dousing the fire. By morning, nothing but a haze in the air would show for the column that had consumed Greata.

Tears streamed down Sierra's face. Not just for the loss of her friend, but for the loss of everything she'd ever known. She didn't know what lay ahead of her, but nothing was ever going to be the same again.

4

BILE ROSE in Sierra's throat as she pushed harder than she ever had before. Her legs were as heavy as lead beneath her, but she forced each foot forward in front of the other.

She passed the last row of corn. Nothing but dirt and rocks remained between her and the hills before her. She'd be without cover until she reached them. Her lungs burned, not used to the workout. Sierra couldn't remember the last time she'd had to run. Now she had a good four miles ahead of her before she'd reach the edge of the Red Mountains.

She didn't dare even glance behind her, not for a moment. In the corner of her eye, she could see hints of the yellow flames from the farm, as well as the beams of search lights from the Onyx reflecting off the lake's surface. Their soft white glow felt dull compared to the brilliant bright blue beams they had ejected moments before.

The cool evening air provided little relief for her lungs. She wouldn't be able to keep this pace for long. She closed her eyes as she pushed on. Her heart was about to beat out of her chest. It hurt. How young was too young to have a heart attack?

No cover between her and the hills. The moon's glow through the blue hue of the dome and the surrounding yellow fog was a dim green. Still enough light for her to make out where she needed to go.

A flitting of movement graced the ledge of the first rise above the path leading into the mountainside. She squinted to see if she could tell what it was. Gone, or hiding, whatever it was. A Guardian wouldn't be hiding in shadows. It was likely a trick of the light. The shadow of the orbs' searchlights bouncing off something.

She gasped for air, wheezing as she tried to suck in as much oxygen as possible. The ridge didn't seem to be getting any closer. Darkness closed in on the edges of her vision. She couldn't black out. She had to make it.

Just . . . a . . . little . . . farther.

Something caught the edge of her foot. A large rock protruding from the ground reached up and grabbed Sierra by the front of her toe.

Dirt met her face as she failed to get her hands out in time to catch herself. The rocky path collided with her rib cage, knocking out the little wind she had left in her lungs. She croaked as she gasped frantically for air.

This is it. This is how I die.

Grit embedded under her fingernails as she clawed against the earth below her, desperate for something to save her.

Her lungs convulsed without warning, sending her into a coughing fit as her efforts to inhale were finally rewarded and then overcompensated.

She knew she was making too much noise. There was no other sound in the cool open air except for the teenage girl gagging, sputtering, and hacking into the still night.

She pushed herself up on all fours, slowly catching her breath, wheezing into the darkness.

Behind her, the flaming column had already begun to subside, dampened by efforts of maintenance bots pouring lake water onto the fire. By morning there would be nothing left except a smoking mound. She wondered how the residents of the Sphere would react to Greata's disappearance. She wondered what they would be told.

Despite nobody being around to see it, she shook her head in disbelief. An involuntary tear ran down her face. There was no time for her to mourn Greata. Her best friend. She couldn't.

She had to push forward.

What sense was there to killing an old farmer? Someone who worked so hard to keep the Sphere's inhabitants fed. Someone as highly esteemed as Greata. What secrets could she have possibly kept?

Why would the Guardians lie about the Outside?

Lights that looked to have remained fairly stationary around the barn were now on the move toward her. Whether her coughing had alerted their presence or not didn't matter. She couldn't stay.

Back on her feet, she pushed forward, lungs still burning. She no longer had the capacity to run. She managed to walk, but each step was uneasy. She concentrated on nothing else but putting one foot in front of the other.

Forward. Just have to move forward.

Beams of light stretched above her. They were coming her way. Circles of light lit the red rock before her as they searched.

Not too much farther.

Every muscle in her body ached, but she continued. Fire coursed through her veins, carrying her forward.

Several times she was sure she had been discovered, but the edge of the rock face caught the bulk of the orbs' attention, their light bouncing off the cliff providing a lit destination for Sierra to reach. If only she could slip in between the rock and mounds of the mountain pass without being detected.

Her path eventually led to her destination. She rested a hand upon the cliff face, as a white beam of light made contact with the same spot, triggering the three other beams that had been spread out across the wall to focus entirely on her.

From the darkness of a crevice in the cliff wall, a hand reached out, clasped her around the mouth, and pulled her inside.

She tried to scream, but the hand had a strong grip on her face.

"Shh!" a voice admonished. "Stay quiet. We need to move!"

The hand released slowly, testing her resolve to continue her howl. She considered it, her pulse loud in her ears, adrenaline coursing through her veins. In a split second, she thought about screaming, she thought about running, she thought about punching the stranger who had grabbed her, but mostly she thought about collapsing to the cool earth below.

She did none of these things, though. She simply put a hand to her mouth to rub the spot where the foreign hand had seized her.

They were in the shadow of the mountainside. Beams continued to project against the red rock above them, but didn't appear able to reach down into the path they were on.

Her eyes quickly adapted to the darkness, and it wasn't long before she could make out the details of her assailant.

"Wil!" she exclaimed. She was thankful for a familiar face, but wondered what sort of mischief the boy was up to in the mountains in the middle of the night. And she also wondered if she should be concerned.

He appeared to be alone. She glanced around quickly, attempting to see if Marco was around as well. Where there was one of them the other was always close by.

"What are you doing out here?" she asked. "Where's Marco?"

Even in the darkness, she could see him visibly swallow.

"Never mind," he said. "Let's move before those Guardians start shooting again."

She had just witnessed the obliteration of her friend by the machines flying at them, but even still his comments made her flinch. How much had he seen of what just happened?

He moved on, the opening in the mountainside just wide enough for the two of them to follow single file for a few hundred yards before opening up to a wider path, still enclosed by high rock walls on either side.

Wil flicked a flashlight on, illuminating a small beam of light ahead.

Where did he get that? Portable light sources were restricted to the Order's use.

She let the question go unasked though as she scanned the sky, hoping the device wouldn't give away their position.

Sierra knew little of Wil. She knew enough that he and his friend Marco would spend their time outside of class hiking this terrain. She didn't like the idea of following him blindly into the hills. But as beams of light bounced off the walls above her, she didn't think she had much choice.

"Where are we going?" she asked.

Wil turned and pointed the flashlight up toward his own face, giving him an ominous look. He put a finger to his mouth and quietly shushed her.

She took a step back at the response. He didn't have to be rude about it.

He pointed up, though and switched off the flashlight, as blue lights marked the frame of an Onyx orb passing overhead.

She'd save her questions for later.

Flashes of light continued to streak above them, which, ironically, did provide some visibility, but she would have gladly done without it.

A few times she stumbled, her body still not recovered from the sprint it had taken to get there, but the threat from above allowed her to ignore the fatigue for the moment. Wil wasn't waiting for her, so she quickly caught herself and pushed forward so as not to lose him while she tripped over her own feet.

More than once she wondered if the dark-haired boy in front of her was leading her into a trap. He confidently charged forward, obviously with a destination in mind. She didn't like feeling helpless, and even worse clueless, as to what was going on. But this day had revealed both on a level she had never before experienced.

"This cave runs quite deep into the mountain. We'll have some protection," Wil said, breaking the silence as an opening cut into the side of the mountain wall.

She didn't say anything, still wide-eyed, but she nodded and followed him in.

Once inside, Wil lit his flashlight once again. He looked warily to the entrance, before backing up against the wall and sitting. It took a moment before she realized there was a cushion where he sat. He grabbed another and tossed it to her. She barely caught it before it hit her face. She rolled her eyes as she positioned it beneath her.

This had obviously been a place Wil frequented. The small amount of light from the flashlight revealed a pair of makeshift beds, built from old blankets, straw, and other materials that must have been meticulously collected.

She eyed Wil again. His gaze was unfocused into the night.

"Thank you," she said, glancing at him.

"Don't mention it." He still didn't appear to be looking at anything in particular.

With her companion uninterested in conversation, she was left with nothing but the persistent weight of the evening's events playing over and over again in her head and the silence of the desert night, broken only by the occasional hum of the Guardian orbs flying overhead.

HOURS PASSED and the night wore on. The hum of the Onyx had grown silent, apparently having moved to another location. If they had spotted Sierra as she reached the mountains, it appeared they didn't believe she had stayed in one place.

Wil hadn't moved. He sat so completely still that Sierra wondered if he had fallen asleep with his eyes open. It wasn't until she stood up that he looked toward her inquisitively.

She crept to the entrance of the cave and peeked above them, ensuring the coast was clear. The night sky was vacant, with only the light blue luminescence of the Sphere's force field visible directly above them.

"You know these mountains well, don't you? I've heard you and Marco talk about the hikes you often go on. The two of you have camped here regularly," she said, pointing to the beds beside them.

He raised an eyebrow at her, then answered. "I know them. Probably better than anyone."

She took a deep breath before voicing the next part of her question. She had no idea if she could trust Wil. Especially with the blasphemy she was about to utter. If he wanted, he could report her to the Order. But Greata had died for the secret she revealed. If it was true. She had to know. If Wil knew these mountains, there was a chance. It would be better than wandering around them alone, waiting for the Onyx to catch up with her.

"Do you know of a hole in the Sphere?"

"What do you mean, a hole?"

She took another deep breath. "Someone told me of an exit, to the Outside."

Wil was on his feet in an instant. Eyes wide, looking like he'd flee the cave if she wasn't blocking the entrance. He believed her as unhinged as she felt for asking it.

"Is that why those death machines were chasing you?" he exclaimed. "Questions like that will get you tried for blasphemy." He paused, eyes growing distant once again, his demeanor collapsing from outrage to defeat in a heartbeat. "Or worse."

"It doesn't matter. Do you know what I'm talking about or not? If not, I need to head out on my own." She stood up, and he put a hand on her arm to stop her.

She couldn't tell if he was frightened or just ready to turn her in. She wouldn't blame him either way. She was suggesting an idea that could get them both punished for merely discussing it.

The Guardians protect us. From what exactly? Why did they offer protection if what they were protecting them from was an elaborate lie?

Images of her exam that morning swirled in her mind. *Liar. Lies.* At the same time, Greata's voice whispered in her head. *It is rigged.*

Her suspicions confirmed by an attack from those who claimed to be their protectors. Despite the looming threat of being sent to the Outside, into the toxic air to be turned inside out, she had never witnessed, or even heard of, the threat being followed through.

"The Sphere protects us from the Outside," he started, as if she was a child that had never heard this before. "If there was a hole, toxic air would get through. The Guardians' systems would surely detect the poisonous gas and plug the hole."

"I don't know." She shook her head. The same thoughts had swirled through her head since she had left Greata's. "I don't know what to believe anymore. I was told there was a break at the edge of a path in the mountains. It may be masked as a bend or a turn in the rock face. It would have to be somewhere that wouldn't be easy to stumble upon."

He raised an eyebrow, and his stance softened. He studied her, holding her gaze with a smoldering intensity. "Who told you that?"

"If what I was told is true, there is a gate to the Outside. I need to get out. I need to go tonight."

"Gate to the Outside?" he scoffed again, defenses going back up. "That's crazy. It's a toxic wasteland!"

"Oh yeah?" She pressed her face close to his so he could feel her hot breath. Her eyes were still wide, but now with determination, and something else . . . rage. She was angry. "This morning I believed the Guardians were here to protect us. But I just watched them obliterate my best friend, and they almost killed us too!

"I was told there is a path that leads to a crack, disguised as part of the mountainside. Follow the crack through the rock, and there's a break in the barrier masked by a cave. If you're not going to help me, that's fine. I need to go."

She turned to leave, the night air sending chills through her. Her robes provided some relief, but they were designed to keep her cool in the desert heat. For the cool desert night, she wished she had packed a heavier cloak.

"Wait." Wil's voice stopped her in her tracks. "I may know the place you mean," he relented.

He worked his way past her and onto the path that had brought them to their temporary shelter, surveying their surroundings.

"What do you mean? You knew there was a way out?" Sierra trailed behind him. He was apparently taking her urgency to heart now, not waiting to see if she was keeping up.

"No, not exactly. You'll understand when we get there."

Mountain cliffs rose on either side of them, creating a natural hallway. The green moonlight revealed the path in front of them. It wasn't much, but it provided enough of a glow for them to make out where they were going without Wil having to pull out his flashlight. Steadily they moved forward. Sierra was uncertain as to where Wil was taking her or if his revelation would prove true.

"We have to cross a rise up ahead," he whispered back to her. "Stay low, and move fast. If you see their search beams, duck and get out of the way."

She looked to the sky as if it held answers to any of it.

Wil darted ahead, up the rise. The wall to her left disappeared, just as he had said it would.

She ducked and followed Wil's lead. Something out of the corner of her eye made her stop. She stood up, trying to get a better look. In the distance, smoke still rose from the field. In between the mountains and the low flame, now nearly snuffed out, there was movement.

Orange accent lights lit the bone-white frame of a person walking toward them. It took her a moment to realize what she was looking at. She'd recognize that stride anywhere. It wasn't a person. It was Ember.

"What are you doing?" Wil hissed ahead of her. He had made his way back to her, anger in his eyes. "Get down!"

Search lights scanned overhead, but none were on top of them. Yet.

"Ember's down there! I have to go back for her!"

Wil grabbed her arm to keep her from bolting. "Your Keeper? Are you crazy? She's one of them! If the Onyx are after you, there's nothing your Guardian will be able to do except turn you in!"

Her friend slowly walked across the open dirt plain between the Ag District and the mountains where she stood. Her best friend. Her only friend now that Greata was gone.

But Wil was right. She was a Guardian. Would she really turn her in? Aid the Onyx in her destruction? Allow her to be vaporized like Greata?

Ember's white cloak flowed behind her in the breeze pushed in from the lake. Her orange lights lit her frame, as well as her eyes. A beacon to her location. At the speed she was moving, Ember wouldn't catch up to them. Not anytime soon.

She turned back, intent on going down to meet her friend. Ember wasn't always willing to entertain her questions, but she was Sierra's protector.

A strong hand grasped her bicep, holding her back.

"What makes you think she'll be any different?"

She turned and looked at Wil. Rage filled his eyes. Was he so angry that she'd want to help her friend? Sierra's eyes grew wide as she wondered if she was in danger, trusting her plight to a classmate she barely knew.

"If you go back down there, I can't help you," he insisted. "Why do you think she'd be any different from them?"

Because she knew her friend. Ember had practically raised her. She had never shown any intent other than to protect her. Sierra didn't have time to answer.

"Think about it, Sierra," Wil continued, and pointed toward the billowing smoke that rose from Greata's field. "Have you ever seen the Guardians behave like that before either?"

She froze and watched the dark plumes rise, orange flames lighting the underside of an ominous cloud. Could Wil be right? Never had she seen that much destruction. Until today she would have insisted it went against their very nature, everything they stood for.

This was truly it, then. Time to leave everything she knew behind, or end up like Greata. Her death would not be for nothing.

"Okay." She nodded, squatting back down. "You're right. Let's go."

Light beams crossed their path, as the hum of an Onyx rose from behind the mountainside.

"Run!" Wil exclaimed, half pulling her in their original direction. She didn't have time or the ability to argue. The Onyx descended on top of them. Blue lights pulsed on its glossy shell.

They descended back into a break in the rocky terrain,

keeping themselves as close as they could to the rock wall while still able to move.

A blue beam lit up the sky behind them and slammed into the cliff. Boulders crashed down mere steps behind their trail, blocking off the path they had just traversed.

They both stole a glance back. Twenty feet of rock that would be nearly impossible to get through. There was no going back now. Not that way.

Wil grabbed Sierra's arm and pressed her into a crevice in the rock face. She gasped as the hard rock impacted her back and jammed her in the elbow, but she realized what he was doing and stayed completely still, back against the rock, eyes to the sky. Wil had positioned himself next to her, with a comfortable distance between them, his face planted into the rock beside her.

The Onyx flew past, only visible for moments through the break in the rock. Lights pulsing on its body indicated it was scanning for her.

"Why didn't it stop?" Sierra asked.

Wil shook his head, motioning to the rubble.

"Hopefully it thinks it hit us. Come on," he said.

The Onyx didn't reappear as they continued for another couple of hours. The mountain trails were extensive, reaching much farther north than Sierra had realized. After what seemed like an endless amount of walking, they reached a dead end. The trail ended at the blue barrier that marked the Sphere's boundary.

"This is it," he said.

"What do you mean this is it? This looks like the edge of the Sphere. I don't see a way out."

"Patience," he answered.

He led her to where the blue barrier met the rock face. It intersected with the rock, and the cliff continued on the Outside. The trail, however, looked to have been blown over with desert sand long ago. Nothing but sand.

Right next to where the barrier met the rock, a small insert could be seen, a hollowed-out divot that looked to be only a few inches deep. The path went into the rock and then turned back out again.

"Step in here," he said, and disappeared into the insert.

She furrowed her brow, but entered the chasm anyway. She had followed him this far.

There was only room for them to pass through the crack single file, and only then just barely. They shimmied their way in and turned a corner toward the barrier.

The path opened slightly and then completely into a larger area, almost like opening into a separate room hidden by cliffs on all sides. The barrier of the Sphere offered its blue pale luminescence as they approached it.

"It looks like the barrier is still here. I don't understand how this could be the way out."

He bent over and picked a rock off the ground. He hurled it at the barrier, which lit up on impact. A bright blue ripple of light mimicked a rock being thrown into a pond, expanding from the impact point in waves.

"Are you crazy?" she hissed at him, instinctively ducking toward a nearby boulder for protection. "Why not just let the Onyx know where we are?"

"Hang on." He picked up another and tossed it before she could move to stop him. This time his aim was toward a small rock outcrop that jutted out the side of the mountain.

About eight feet up a hole was carved through the rock face that resembled a large window, or possibly a small door. The barrier, from what she could see, should have cut right into this cave. The rock, however, went right through. No blue light pulsed as it entered.

On the other side of the barrier, it appeared that the rock face carried on, the crevasse appearing as if it should be open on the

Outside. She did her best to get a glimpse of where the rock should have landed, but there was no evidence that it ever appeared on the other side.

"Where did it go?" Sierra asked.

"What do you mean?"

"You threw it at that hole, the barrier didn't react, but I also don't see the rock on the other side of the barrier."

Wil smiled. "That's the mystery."

"What's the mystery?"

"Marco—" He paused, as if remembering something he had forgotten. He shook his head at whatever thought he had and carried on. "Marco and I would sit here for hours, chatting about life and throwing rocks up there. We always wondered where they went. Why the barrier didn't light up. We had assumed that they just hit it without activating it. It never crossed our minds that it might be a way out."

This didn't seem right. "No," she said, shaking her head. "This can't be the way Greata was talking about. She said she was transporting food out. If she was lifting food up into that opening, I would think there would be evidence here. Greata's a strong woman, but I can't see her lifting a substantial amount of supplies that high."

"Excuse me?" Wil started, crossing his arms in front of him, leaning back, his skepticism renewed at her ponderings. "Even if this connects to the Outside, why would Greata be transporting food through?"

"I know this sounds crazy, but according to her, people live out there. She claimed she used to live out there as well." She sighed, unsure of what his reaction would be to each bizarre revelation. She hadn't even scratched the surface.

Wil didn't let his guard down and eyed her incredulously. He looked to the hole again, and letting go of a deep breath, he continued.

"Well, this is the only place I know of that sounded like what you were talking about. So we can climb up there and find out, or sit here and wait until either the Onyx find us, or we starve to death."

Sierra kept her gaze focused on the space above them. She walked up closer. In this light, it appeared to be nothing but darkness. From how thin it should have been based on what appeared on the other side of the barrier, it was casting far more shadow than it should. She looked from the side, and then from as far away as their vantage would allow her. She should have been able to see through the opening, but could see nothing but rock. It wouldn't surprise her if it was just a narrow cave that wrapped around, beckoning teenage boys with a likely explainable mystery. How many rocks were piled inside from years of the boys' imagination getting the better of them?

"In all the time you spent throwing rocks up there you never thought to climb up and have a look?"

"Of course we thought about it. We even peeked inside."

"And?"

"We just saw more rock. I guess we got too scared to go in any farther. If we hit the barrier, we'd draw attention, maybe get hurt. If one of us were injured, how would we explain that? If it did lead somewhere, well, who knows how the toxic gas of the Outside works? You've heard the stories, turns a person inside out. In the end I guess we chickened out."

"And now?"

"And now things have changed. I don't have anything to lose."

She eyed him, hoping for more of an explanation. He shifted his gaze, maybe intentionally from hers, uncomfortable with the tidbit he had just shared.

She stepped up to the wall beneath the hole, running her hands along the rock's surface. "All right. Why not?"

"Let me give you a boost," he said as he followed her over. He squatted down, clasping his hands together to offer her a step. She didn't hesitate to take it as she found a spot to pull herself up.

She crawled into the hole, her entire body engulfed by several feet before she had her answer.

"Wil!" she called back to him. "You aren't going to believe this!"

5

---

*"Sierra, can you keep a secret?" Izzy looked at her with wonder in
her eyes.*

"I've kept all your secrets so far."

"No, you haven't! You told Mom I broke her tablet!"

"Well, I've kept all your other secrets. Come on. Just tell me!"

"All right. I'm going to visit Dad's work tomorrow."

"At the Core?"

"Yes! I'm so excited."

"Why is it a secret?"

*"He's taking me there because I had a dream. I had a dream that the
Guardians wanted to kill me."*

"That's a silly dream. The Guardians protect us."

*"Not in my dream. In my dream, we were building the Guardians at
the Core. They turned on us, and we had to run away."*

"What does that have to do with you going with Dad?"

*"Dad says I'm not supposed to talk about it. But in my dream, the
Core was destroyed. We had to destroy it so that the people would be
safe from the Guardians."*

"I still don't understand. Did Dad think your dream was real?"

"He says he wants to show me where he works, so that I'll know

what I dreamed was made up. But I know it's true. I told him I saw what the people at the Core do. They work to make new Guardians. The Guardians threatened them to keep it a secret."

"Threatened? Is he in danger?"

She nodded, eyes wide. "Dad's in the most danger."

"Izzy? I want Dad to be safe."

"That's why I'm trying to help him. I'm going to go with him, and then I'm going to help him get away."

Her sister was four years older than her. Which of course meant she was smarter and knew much more than Sierra did. She had never had a dream of the future before, though.

"Izzy? What else did you see in your dream?" Sierra knew dreams weren't real. She wondered why her sister thought this one was different.

She bent closer to Sierra and whispered, "I saw the Outside. I was the leader of an army. The sky was bright blue, and the sun shone bright, with no toxic clouds to be seen. The army was fighting the Guardians."

"Did you win?"

She looked puzzled, as if it wasn't a question she had considered. "I don't know."

6

———

THE DISTANCE SIERRA had to cover on her hands and knees seemed much farther than she had expected. Her gray robe became completely soiled in the red dirt she dragged herself through. It couldn't have been more than a few yards, but each foot made her increasingly skeptical that this was the opening Greata had meant. Until she saw the exit.

According to what was visible before she entered the hole, it should have extended only a few feet. She had crawled more than thirty feet when she turned a slight corner and the end of the path opened up before her.

One last corner and the cave disappeared. The mouth led to a large opening in the cliff face. The first thing that struck her was the moon. No toxic gas, no blue haze, just the moon. Full, white, bright. As bright, maybe brighter, than the sun they were used to behind the hazy cloud of gas within the Sphere.

Millions of pinpricks of white lights decorated the sky. She was so transfixed by how clean and bright and crisp everything was that she missed the edge of the cave. Her hand slipped, but she managed to catch herself before crawling out and down onto the red dirt below.

She peered around the side of the cliff in the direction they had come. The blue dome of the Sphere was behind them. They were on the Outside. The air was clear. Not just clear, pristine. She had never tasted air so fresh in her life.

"Sierra . . . " Wil started as his head peeked out of the cavern. He also nearly stumbled as he clambered out but caught himself with a bit more grace than she had.

She hardly noticed; she was transfixed by the sky. Even the blue sky she had seen earlier hadn't prepared her for this.

Was this a trick? Was she about to turn inside out at any moment? Maybe she was already dead? Her thoughts raced through every possible scenario, but there was only one logical conclusion.

Greata was right. The Guardians had lied to them.

As Sierra woke from her slumber, she was conscious of each breath she took. She had tossed and turned the whole night, despite having collapsed from exhaustion. She just couldn't quite believe that each breath wasn't going to be her last. She mentally checked with each inhale as if she could tell if the air was somehow poisonous. Surely it wasn't, otherwise she would've been dead by now.

Despite what Greata had told her, despite the dome of the Sphere visible behind, she couldn't truly believe where she was. Outside.

Alive. Breathing. Inhale. Exhale.

Greata was dead, Ember and her mom left behind.

Why do you think she'd be any different from them?

A single evening, an insinuating question from a boy she barely knew outside of a bad reputation, made her question if her best friend was ever really the ally she believed her to be or if she was just a program, intent on keeping her within the order the Guardians established.

If that was the case, she had been truly alone most of her life. Aside from Greata, Ember was the only one who had ever shown compassion for her. Had ever fought for her. Her mother couldn't; she had always been away. Her father, her sister dead.

And now Greata was dead, and Ember the memory of something that maybe never was.

The cool air of the morning chilled her. She wrapped her cloak around her for warmth, but it offered little.

Emptiness filled her. Gutted, she wondered if her life could ever feel some semblance of normal again. She didn't think so. Her whole life she had been predetermined to work at the Core. And now what? The Guardians had put her in a box, and she was likely capable of little more.

She looked to Wil, still asleep, and wondered why fate had brought him to intersect her path. Wondered why he had risked coming out here with her. He said he had nothing to lose. She hadn't questioned him about it. It wasn't her place. Not yet.

Last night as she had crawled through the tunnel, she had been blown away by the beauty and the surprise of seeing not only the moon, clear and crisp, as it had been in old footage, but also the stars. She and Wil had rested near the opening after they had crawled through and just stared at the stars until they had both fallen asleep. She had been so exhausted, it hadn't taken long.

Her stomach growled, reminding her she hadn't eaten since noon the previous day. They were going to have to find something to eat. Maybe they could breathe the air, but that wouldn't help them if they starved to death.

Greata had probably put some provisions in the pack she had given her. But she'd hold off on using that as long as she could.

She got up, a little stiff and sore from a night on the ground, and peered at her surroundings now that the light of day illuminated the world around her.

The heat of the sun. The bright yellow sun. The same as she had seen in her vision. It illuminated the rock face in colors she never imagined could be part of nature. The rock of the Red Mountains, truly a spectrum of red. The dirt no longer the sandy desert that filled the Sphere, but harder and more compact. Small shrubs and bushes sprang from the ground. They weren't much —this land still appeared desolate—but the clean air and blue sky gave her hope that Greata hadn't led her astray after all.

Wil was still asleep. What *was* his story?

As if her thoughts roused him, Wil began to stir. He had clung to his backpack all night as if he was worried someone would take it. Or like he had something inside he didn't want anyone to see.

"Time to get up," she said. He was already awake—no point in letting him laze the morning away. "We need to get moving."

Though that was easier said than done. She really had no idea where they were going. Greata seemed certain they would find answers if they went west. West was where they would find this man who knew of the ancients. Where she hoped she would find the meaning to her visions, and answers to questions she'd been asking her entire life. She tried not to get her hopes up. At the very least, Greata seemed to think he would provide them with safety. That had to be her first priority.

Wil blinked and looked around, obviously having momentarily forgotten where he was waking up. He rubbed his eyes and stood up, looking at the bright blue sky.

"Bloody hell. Not a cloud in the whole damn sky. This is unbelievable!"

Sierra let him take a few moments. She couldn't help but stare herself. After he had a good look around, he continued. "Well, what's the plan? Where are we going?"

"I need to head west," Sierra replied. "You're welcome to join me. I need to find some answers."

Wil nodded. "I wouldn't mind some myself. How do you know where we're going to find some?"

"Greata told me to head west. I'm looking for a man named Terre. He'll have answers to all this." She waved an arm at the spectacle around her. It wasn't a lot to go on. But she wasn't ready to tell Wil she had been seeing visions just yet. After being forced out of the Sphere and chased by the Guardians, Terre was the only one who offered safety. If Greata trusted him, that was good enough for her. "She said he would help. She made it sound like something was coming. Something Terre would be able to help stop. I don't understand what that means just yet."

"I feel like there's more than what you're telling me."

Sierra nodded. "There is. But I'm not quite ready to tell you everything yet, and I'm pretty sure you're not ready to tell me what's happened to send you out here with me."

She paused to gauge his response, hoping she'd misjudged him. She hadn't. He simply nodded and gazed out into the open desert.

"Do you really think anyone's living out here?" he asked.

Looking around, it did seem unlikely. Though they were breathing the air, endless rock and desert surrounded them. It really did feel uninhabitable.

"It doesn't seem like we have a lot of options," she replied. "We can't very well go back, can we?"

He looked back at the barrier of the Sphere, and she followed his gaze. Strange to be on this side of something that had been impenetrable her entire life. The barrier was opaque from this side. A solid blue dome in the midst of a red rock landscape. To anyone on the outside it looked like there could be anything, or nothing, hidden within.

"Come on," she said. "Let's see if we can find something before it gets too hot."

She began walking, and Wil brushed the dust off his clothes before following. The sun warned of its plan for them. Heat. How strong would the sun get without a toxic cloud blocking its rays?

As the day wore on, it became evident they were underprepared for the journey they were embarking on. How far west would they need to go? Hours? Days? Weeks? How long could they last without any food, or even water? Her guess was probably not much more than the day. The heat was already threatening to dehydrate them. The sun within the Sphere never got this warm. The farther they got from the Sphere, the smaller the red formations around them became. Pretty soon they wouldn't have any protection at all.

Mostly they walked in silence. The events of yesterday tried to find some sort of meaning in her mind. Years of what they had been taught erased in the span of a few hours. And now she was setting out into the unknown.

The pair was silent for nearly the entirety of the journey. Wil was deep in thought with whatever had transpired before she came across him. At least that was what Sierra hoped. Without any real indication, she wondered on and off if the reason for his reticence was her doing. With the orbs chasing them down, perhaps he felt there was no other option but to abandon the Sphere along with her.

Lost in her own thoughts, she felt time pass quickly. Sweat rolled off her forehead, a mild discomfort. For now. They wouldn't be able to continue for much longer as the temperature continued to climb, and their shelter all but disappeared.

They came to the end of the last rock formations Sierra could see, and endless desert stretched before them. Stunted desert shrubs were the only indication of anything but dirt and rocks sprawling miles before them.

"Let's take a rest here," she said, pointing to a rock pillar. It at least cast a bit of shade they could rest under. "There are hills in the distance, but we'll be walking a long time in the heat of the day to get there."

Wil didn't argue. As Sierra sat down on the hard earth, she realized how much her feet ached. Wil seemed to be faring better, but from the little she knew of him, he spent a lot of his time hiking with Marco. Or had, anyway.

Wil took his backpack off and sat against the stone pillar, resting in its shade. He knew as well as she did they were better off taking refuge for the next few hours, which would be the hottest of the day.

"This is stupid. You really think there's anything out there?" Wil blurted, nodding in the direction their journey was headed. "Even if there is, we could be days, even weeks away."

Sierra stared at him, but he didn't meet her gaze. He was staring out into the desert, contemplating. Was he right? You could cross the Sphere from one end to another in two days. Even the Core was less than a day's journey via the transport. But out here, with nothing dictating proximity, there was no real reason to assume they would be as close to anything.

She fought the urge to throw sand at him. It had been Wil's first outward sign of hostility toward her. She didn't ask to be forced out of her home, to watch her friend vaporized by the beings that were supposed to protect them. She didn't ask to leave her mom, her Keeper. Everything she had been led to believe was the remnant of the ancient world.

She fought back the tears that were forming. Wil didn't earn the right to see that. It wasn't her fault she had been forced out. She wasn't going to let herself lose it in front of him.

"I'm open to ideas," she replied. She swallowed the bitterness that rose in response to his accusation. They were out here together now. For better or for worse. He needed to watch it. "My only direction to find any answers was to head west. That's all I've got."

Wil shook his head. "If we don't find any people, we at least need to find some water. We won't last more than a day or two without it." As if to emphasize his point, he took a canteen out of his pack and sipped on its contents. Sierra remembered that Greata had packed some for her as well, and she did the same. Enough for a couple of days. In this heat, though, that might be pushing it.

"How long are you good for?" she asked, gesturing toward his drink.

"A day, maybe two if I stretch it out. We'll need to find something tomorrow. We really should be traveling at night."

Night travel didn't sound appealing, but neither did travel in the scorching heat.

She was already feeling the effects of dehydration. Her mouth was parched, and she fought the urge to lick her lips. The shade provided a bit of reprieve, but she didn't know how far she'd be able to carry on.

"We should rest here for the afternoon," Wil continued as if reading her thoughts. He positioned his backpack and lay down. "I know we just got started, but we need to travel when the sun goes down. We won't last tomorrow if we keep going in this heat."

Sierra was eager to get going but knew he was right. She sat down and tried to make herself comfortable. She watched the young man as he turned his back, lying on his side, and used his backpack for a pillow.

He had remained quiet for most of the journey. Aside from his bewilderment of the ability to breathe on the Outside without being turned inside out, he expressed little acknowledgment of the events that had transpired the night before.

His snide remark about their destination revealed something of his feelings though. Though not impressed with the attitude, she couldn't blame him. The air might be breathable, but she hoped that they wouldn't die out here all the same.

The small bag Greata provided her didn't have nearly the bulk that Wil's did. The red rock around them would provide enough shelter from the sun until nightfall. She was happy to give her feet a break but didn't think she'd be falling asleep anytime soon.

She was led to believe Wil had no such issues. He lay perfectly still for a long time until he piped up suddenly.

"Sierra," he said, "what happened? Why are you running?"

"I could ask you the same thing."

"And you will, but I asked first." His sly grin probably charmed him out of a lot of mischief, but she wasn't so easily persuaded.

It had all happened so fast. She hadn't even had time to process everything, and Wil was the last person she wanted to confide in. At the same time, she seemed to have already thrown her lot in with him.

She surveyed the vast emptiness of the desert around them and breathed in the dry desert air. No reason to trust him. But at the same time, here he was with her. Besides, if he was going to turn her in, he would have done so already.

"The Guardians killed Greata," she began, and paused. She took a deep breath. The weight of those words hung. The air was suddenly heavier, as if voicing those words had birthed reality to what had felt like only a nightmare a moment ago.

She waited briefly for a response, but he offered none and she felt obliged to continue.

"I don't know why. I think she knew something she wasn't supposed to. She told me she used to live out here. I wasn't supposed to know. Either they found out she was going to tell me, or maybe what she had already told me was too much."

Though, what she had learned was only enough to raise an exponential number of new questions.

"I don't think they know it was me she was talking to, but it won't be too hard for them to find out. I went to Greata with a dream I had—" Sierra paused, second-guessing if she should continue. Seeing visions was still something Wil could decide was more than he wanted to tolerate. He could abandon her here, let her fend for herself in the harsh elements. She'd maybe fare okay. Maybe not any worse than if they stayed together. But so far having even a solemn, distant companion had been better than having none at all.

Wil nodded, not offering any indication one way or another if the end of the story would affect his opinion of her.

The truth was she was going to need help. Greata's death couldn't have been for no reason. There was more than what her friend had been able to tell her. She had to find out what. What did her sister have to do with her visions? And why did Greata tell her to find Terre? She had to find him. She had to give her friend's death meaning.

But right now, Wil was an unknown.

"All she had time to tell me was to head west, to find a man named Terre who remembers the wars. She thought he would have answers."

Fighting back tears, she shook her head. "The Guardians are supposed to protect us. Why would they kill her?"

For the first time, Wil expressed sympathy and compassion. His face softened as he looked to her, reflecting her feeling of loss.

"Sierra, I'm so sorry." He swallowed and took a deep breath. The emotion was gone from his face, and his voice shook as he spoke.

"The Guardians are liars. You're not the only one to have someone you love murdered by them."

7
___

BEFORE WIL COULD SHARE any more, footsteps sounded from the other side of the pillar. They both jumped to their feet.

Sierra scrambled up and peered around the corner.

So much for a rest.

Wil followed close behind.

A few hundred yards away, someone was walking in their direction. Though on two legs, it was obviously a Guardian.

"Is it a Keeper?" she asked. The bone-white features and humanlike stature resembled Ember in many ways, though it looked like its body had been built with a bulkier, muscular frame. Its legs looked unfinished compared to the rest of it. Metallic, strong, built for running, designed for intimidation and mobility rather than comfort.

It held an object. Something that resembled a weapon, something Sierra had only read about. But humans used weapons, not Guardians. Well, maybe yesterday had proven otherwise.

"It's not a Keeper," Wil responded. "There's no way that thing is built for the same purpose as Ember. It looks . . . mean."

"Do you think it will hurt us?"

"I don't think it's here to play games. Wait here."

"What? What do you think you're going to do?"

Ignoring her, he grabbed a metal box out of his backpack, and then handed the pack to her.

Before she could question him again, he turned and started walking toward the being, pushing buttons on the device as he approached the bot.

He crept ever so slowly along the edge of the red rocks, appearing to try his best not to make any noise. There was about two hundred yards between him and the robot. Within that space, there wasn't any sort of cover.

If the Guardian had been facing directly toward him, it would have seen him. There was nothing obstructing him from its view. But it was looking in the opposite direction, down a road heading to the west.

Wil had gotten about as close as he was going to get without leaving the rock face. Without warning, and with such speed Sierra nearly missed the motion, the bot turned around and looked directly at Wil.

Wil's face went white as he realized his error. For all of his attempts at stealth, the Guardian had sensed his approach. What exactly was he trying to do? Sierra backed into her hiding spot a little farther.

"You are not supposed to be here," the Guardian's deep voice called out. The blue pulsing lights on its face reminded Sierra of the Onyx spheres from yesterday. It definitely looked a lot meaner than Ember.

"I've lost my way."

"You should be in a protected area; you are in restricted territory."

Wil was holding the black box behind his back, fiddling with buttons or knobs on it. He needed to be more careful. She wasn't sure what the Guardian would do if it suspected foul play.

"I was in the Sphere, going for a hike, and lost my way. The next thing I know, I'm out here and stumble across you."

"In the Sphere?" The light behind its eyes changed from blue to yellow. "Suspected Sphere breach. Following protocol. Stand by."

Wil was trying to inch closer, but the robot sprang toward him, covering the distance between them in an instant. Apparently, those metal legs were adept at jumping as well.

The machine held the weapon at Wil's back, prodding him along. "Come with me."

"Where are we going?"

"We'll get you back to Sphere 892. You'll be scheduled for reeducation."

Sphere 892?

As he circled around Wil, he noticed the box. "This item is restricted. Please submit it for disposal."

Wil had a concentrated look on his face as he handed it to the guard.

Whatever plan he had for that device, it was over now. He let go, and the robot attached it to the side of its hip.

Wil's face showed both frustration and disappointment at the turn of events. Something about the exchange suggested that Wil felt he had had the upper hand in the situation. Whatever he thought that box was, it didn't perform as he had hoped.

Movement in the distance caught Sierra's attention. A group of Guardians that resembled this one. What kind of Guardians were these?

She had never thought to ask why, but Ember had been the only humanoid Guardian she had ever known. It was widely understood that there were other Keepers in the Sphere, but she had never come across one. To see a group of these strange beings was surreal.

Wil was right—these bots did appear to be made for fighting. What horrors did this world contain that required warrior

Guardians? Then her thoughts went back to Greata and her words of warning.

People. They were out here to hunt people.

Seven of them marched down the road, leading to the spot where they stood. The road then curved around the edge of the cliff where they had stopped. If they had stayed behind the pillar, it was possible they would have never been seen.

Wil was being pushed along by the solo Guardian with the edge of its weapon now. The pair were heading back toward where she was hiding.

Each revelation provided further assurance that there was no way she would ever be able to return to the Sphere, not alive. She also had no intention of letting them take Wil.

He might end up being more trouble than he was worth, but he was all she had.

As the pair reached her position, she stayed as hidden as she could. Unwilling to expose herself to gain any further glimpses of where they were, she listened closely.

The sound of metallic feet hitting the hard-packed dirt made it easy to gauge their location. First Wil appeared, face looking dead ahead.

Good. Part of her had worried he'd look directly at her, giving her away.

He couldn't have known what she was planning. This was more spontaneous than she was used to, but it was the only thing she could think of.

As the Guardian appeared, she held her breath and lunged at it. They all went down in a pile of flesh and metal. Its weapon fired and sparks flew from a rock face nearby.

She managed to pin the machine down. Anger mixed with fear overcame her as she tried to restrain him. It took all of her strength to hold it down for even an instant. Adrenaline coursed through her.

All the anger she had been holding back over Greata's death

boiled over. Heat emanated from within her. Adrenaline and rage coursed through her veins, lighting a fire in her core.

She was no match for the power of the metal beneath her, though, and wasn't going to be able to keep this up for long. The warmth from within her felt as if it were radiating out of her in waves. Sweat poured down her face as she struggled with the effort.

Just as she thought her strength was going to give out, Wil came up behind them. He lifted a rock over the bot's head. It came down, but the Guardian twisted just in time. The rock made contact and ended up cracking its arm instead. The bot dropped its weapon as the white of its arm separated from its shoulder, showcasing wires and other pieces of metal from its insides.

It pushed Sierra off with its good arm, and she went flying. She landed on top of Wil, knocking them both over. It stood up and looked at them.

"I . . ." it said, trailing off. Blue hollow eyes looked at them. It glanced around at its surroundings, then wrapped its cloak around the exposed socket where its arm once was and ran off to the south. The other Guardians were still making their way steadily toward them.

She picked up Wil's black box that had fallen in the commotion. "What is this?"

"I don't really know," Wil wheezed, out of breath. "It's what got me into this mess, though."

The box she held started spitting out noises, awful hissing sounds.

She gave him a look that demanded more of an explanation.

"I thought it might disable him."

"Why did you think that?"

"Because it disabled a Guardian in the Sphere. That's why I'm running. That's why"—he took a deep breath—"that's why Marco's dead."

She started at the revelation.

Marco was dead?

She didn't know him well, but knew well enough to know that he was Wil's best friend. She also knew there wasn't time for explanation.

"I don't even know where to start, Wil," she said, "but right now we need to get moving before those other Guardians get here."

"Who else is on this channel?" A man's voice was coming from the box. *"You've jammed the whole frequency. We need you to get off it! There's at least five groups of Sentinels in the area, and they are pissed! Who are you and what is your position?"*

Sierra glanced around the rock to check out if the Guardians were still headed toward them.

Sentinels, is that what those bots are called?

"My name is Sierra," she said, not knowing what else to do. "I'm sorry I don't know what you're talking about, though. We've happened across your voice coming through a speaker my friend found." She paused, considering her words. She almost revealed to the voice they had just exited the Sphere. But there was no telling who this was or what their motives were. "We're near a group of six bots. We're at the end of the rock formations, at a bend in the road."

Wil looked at her, just as puzzled as she was at the turn of events.

"You've got to be kidding me. Stay where you are. I'll find you."

She stole another glance at the Guardians on the rise. They had stopped in their tracks. There were six of them, lined in two rows of three. They all looked nearly identical to the one they had attacked moments before, except each had distinguishing marks on them, red symbols of some kind, nothing Sierra recognized. Each wore the same brown cloak that the other had as well. If it weren't for the white appearance of their bodies, the cloaks would have been perfect for helping them blend into the dirt around them.

"Who are these voices?" she hissed to Wil, unsure if the man on the other end of the box could still hear her.

"We heard them coming through when Marco first discovered the box. I thought it was a recording, or maybe someone else. . ." He eyed the device and lowered his voice. "Someone else in the Sphere."

Wil's attention diverted to the arm that the Guardian had lost in their encounter. Wires and circuits hung loose from the end of it. Despite the Guardians' revered reputation, they still required repair from time to time. It was only one of the many roles those who worked at the Core performed. Wil bent over, picking up the detached limb. He pried the weapon from the lifeless hand, studying the gun while tossing the appendage.

"Wil, careful with that thing!"

He lifted it up and pointed it at the group walking toward them. He pulled the trigger and flew back a dozen feet. The bolt that shot from it hit the sand a hundred yards behind them.

The six stationary Guardians turned their heads to where they were hiding, lifted their weapons, and fired back.

Sierra dove behind a rock twice her height. Wil rolled out of the line of fire, barely dodging a beam of light flying above his head.

"Do you ever think things through?" Sierra yelled.

Wil got up and looked ready to try his luck again, when they heard a hum growing closer.

Appearing through a path between the red rock was a muscular man riding a small machine, hovering two feet off the ground.

"Get on!" The determined voice was the same as the one that had come through the device moments ago. The man was in his mid-thirties. Long wavy black hair had been pulled back into a ponytail and mostly concealed under a leather cap, and though his clothes were loose fitting, they looked nothing like the robes Wil and Sierra wore.

With no other option that they could see, the two complied. Wil still hung on to the ridiculous weapon, fumbling to place it into his backpack. The man gripped a set of handlebars at the front of the machine. Sierra hopped on a seat behind him. She had to wrap her arms around him so she wouldn't fall off. His frame was bulky enough that it made the task cumbersome. Wil got into a seat on the side of the vehicle.

"Hang on!"

8

"THEY'RE FOLLOWING US!" Wil shouted as they raced through the desert.

Sierra turned to look behind her, and indeed, the Guardians were chasing them. Despite the breakneck speed of the vehicle, they were catching up fast.

"Hang on!" the stranger yelled. "Don't look back!"

The Guardians were shooting at them, chasing them, as they moved faster than she'd ever gone in her life on this strange machine. And she wasn't supposed to try to see what was happening?

As they accelerated, she tightened her grip and lost the urge to turn around, all of her strength now dedicated to hanging on.

"What are those things?" she yelled into the wind.

The man either didn't hear or ignored her. The vehicle didn't make a lot of noise, but the sound of her voice had been lost in the rush of wind.

She couldn't see if they were breaking away from their pursuers or not, but Wil's face indicated that they were not. He had no problem cranking his head around.

Another man on a similar-looking machine came in from out of nowhere, zipping toward them as he cut across the desert.

"How'd you end up on their radar, Malachi?" another man's voice spoke as if out of nowhere. Must be someone on another device.

"I've picked up this pair of travelers. The bots had them cornered. One of them fired. I expect we might have bigger problems heading our way."

"I'll distract them and give you a bit of room to breathe. They're closing in fast."

"Don't do anything stupid, Edgar. If you lose contact, head back to camp."

"Copy that."

The other vehicle whipped by them with a hum. Curiosity got the best of Sierra, and she had to look. The rider, fearless—or crazy—was heading straight for the bots. He had pulled out a weapon of his own and fired in front of the advancing Guardians, throwing up dirt and debris, hiding their pursuers. He circled them and repeated the firing pattern, until there was a pillar of dirt around them. He then fired into the column of dust.

The bots jumped out of the dust wall, not hurt by the firing, but their formation was scattered. Some exited the group toward the front, some to the side. The rider named Edgar had already put some distance between himself and their attackers.

One of the Guardians changed their target and was now pursuing Edgar. Three bots continued behind them still in pursuit, though the distraction had bought them a bit more of a lead. The remaining two were standing still, left behind disoriented. The effect was only momentary, and they quickly joined the lone bot in its pursuit of Edgar.

The second rider had cut the number of those chasing them in half. Was he any better equipped to outrun the bots than they were?

Three still followed, now gaining on them. Their rescuer—

Malachi, the other man had called him—handed Wil a smaller version of the weapon he had fired at the bots earlier. Seriously, Wil was going to get far too comfortable with those things.

"Aim for their legs!"

Wil aimed and pulled the trigger. Nothing happened. He tried again. Nothing.

"It's not working!"

The man took the weapon from him and had a look. "Battery's drained." He exchanged it for another in his cloak. He glanced at the charge before handing it over to Wil. "Try this one."

Wil repeated his action and still nothing.

"No good!"

The man grabbed the weapon back and looked down at it. "What the hell? This one's dead now. What did you do?"

"I just aimed and pulled the trigger!"

"Edgar, if you've got those three under control, we need you back here. My blasters are out of juice."

There was no response. Sierra snuck another look behind her. They were closing in. Up until that point, the bots still hadn't fired, but they were pulling out their weapons.

"They're going to shoot!"

They took a sharp right and narrowly missed a stream of light that hit the dirt beside them.

"Thanks!"

"Ed, where are you? We're under fire here."

Still no answer. A few more beams fired past them.

A sudden jolt hit Sierra, and she was tossed into the air as the vehicle flew end over end. A faceful of dirt greeted her as she hit the ground.

She spat out what she could and forced herself to roll over, despite a sharp pain in her shoulder. Wil and Malachi had flown out of their seats as well, sitting a few dozen yards from where she landed.

"Sierra Runar, identified," one of the bots declared. "Determined to be a threat. Reintegration unlikely. Termination recommended."

"What are you talking about? I'm not a threat!"

"Sentinel B85-03 went offline after being attacked by Sierra Runar. Threat level high." The Guardian lifted its weapon, barrel pointed square at her head.

Hands in front of her face, she braced herself.

She jumped as blaster fire impacted the bot directly in the head. Its eyes went dark as it collapsed, smoke rising from the burn mark on its temple.

Edgar pulled up beside her on his machine. "You okay?"

Still shaking, Sierra just nodded. *What the hell was happening?*

Edgar removed his helmet, revealing a smile that reached his blue eyes, and offered her a hand. His blond hair was pulled back, and the clothes he wore weren't like any she had ever seen. For one thing, they were tight, revealing the thickness of his muscles. She hesitated only momentarily before grabbing his extended hand. He pulled her onto the seat behind him and she held on. Edgar definitely had a larger frame than his friend. All muscle.

Wil and Malachi had both climbed back onto the other vehicle. Guardians were lying on the ground, as well as the seat Wil had been in. It must have busted clear off the bike.

Blood ran down Wil's face, streaming from a gash on his forehead.

"Let's get going. They may have friends close by," Edgar called out.

No sooner had he said it than a pair of black orbs were making their way through the distant sky.

She let out an audible gasp and they took off. If it was possible, she thought they were going faster than they had been previously. Maybe the extra weight had been slowing them down.

The Onyx were wasting no time. They stopped momentarily

over the downed units and only a few seconds later were back in pursuit.

"We're almost there!" Ed yelled back to her.

"Where?" Empty desert stretched out the same in every direction. "They're almost on top of us!"

She tried not to look behind, or overhead, in fear of what she might see. There would be nothing she would be able to do about it other than panic. She had a firm grasp on Edgar's waist, her face buried into his back.

They started to slow down, and she pried her face out of her rescuer's back. Tears she didn't realize she had been crying made her face damp, and she quickly wiped them away before anyone else saw.

"Get off! We've got to run the rest of the way!"

She dared to look up. The Onyx were right on top of them. Lights pulsing. She knew what that meant. She didn't care what the reason. She wasn't going to sit there. She stepped onto shaky legs, almost tripping over her own feet, as she pushed herself into a run.

Her legs still ached from the run to the mountains the day before. Still ached from the hours of walking that morning. They were like jelly beneath her. Only the threat of imminent death pushed her forward.

Wil and Edgar sprinted in front of them. She pushed as hard as she could to keep up. Even though Malachi was escorting the vehicle he had been riding, he was still faster than her. Wheels had appeared beneath the machine, and he pushed it along beside him through the sand. Wil was having no problems maintaining his pace either.

Sierra, on the other hand, wasn't able to maintain the same speed, but she gave it everything she had.

Her breath became labored as her lungs burned. She had never been much of a runner. She was focusing so hard on trying to push herself, she almost plowed into the others when they stopped.

Relieved, she allowed herself to collapse onto the dirt. She rolled on her back, gasping for air. So thankful to have stopped it didn't even really occur to her to wonder *why* they had stopped. She looked toward the Onyx. They had stopped nearly a hundred yards behind them as if by an invisible force and looked to be scanning once again.

"Why'd they stop?" She pushed herself up, still breathing heavy.

"We're in the Silent Zone," Edgar answered. "They can't enter or see that we're here. To them it's like we disappeared." He wore a goofy grin as if impressed with himself.

She almost fell over as she stood up. It was as if she had forgotten how to stand. Her legs were so shaky from the ride and the run.

"Easy there." Malachi laughed. "I forget that it takes some getting used to riding a bike."

"Is that what you call this thing?" she said, steadying herself.

"It is." He nodded. "Now what do I call you?"

"I'm Sierra," she answered. "This is Wil. We owe you thanks for rescuing us back there."

"Well, I'm Malachi, this is Edgar, and you're welcome. Let's get to the Outpost. We can talk more there."

Edgar's smile extended to his bright blue eyes as he looked at Sierra. "Pleased to meet you both. Call me Ed. Only Malachi calls me Edgar. I was once allowed refuge here as well once."

She looked back to the Onyx hovering mere yards from where they stood, invisible to the Guardians who had pursued them. One of the orbs bounced off the edge of where the boundary must have been, testing its limits. For a brief moment, it appeared to have gained a few additional feet of ground before bouncing back to its original starting location.

Something told Sierra they weren't done with these bots just yet.

9

"Now what in the hell were you doing out there?" Malachi grimaced. "With no means of transportation, you were bound to get lost or killed."

Sierra shot Wil a glance and found him giving her a similar look.

"We're on our way west." Sierra decided to hold off on giving too many details until she knew more about who this man was. "Looking for an old friend."

She glanced over at Wil again. His short brown hair was ruffled by the wind. He still had that ridiculous weapon slung from a loop on his backpack. He looked intent on the conversation but seemed to be willing to defer to her explanation for now.

"It's just as well," Malachi answered, ignoring her non-answer. "Glad we were in the area to find you in time. Would have been able to get to you sooner if the channel hadn't been jammed. We'd really be out of luck if the bots found a way to jam our radios after all these years."

Sierra wasn't sure what a radio really was, and she was dying to ask, but growing up in the Sphere she had gotten really good at biting her tongue when she thought it was probably in her best interest.

"Is that what this is for, then?" Wil apparently didn't have the same hesitation. He was holding the box that they had used to communicate with Malachi earlier.

He started turning knobs and pushing buttons, but nothing was happening. Frustrated, he gave it over to Malachi.

"Yeah. Haven't you kids seen a radio before?" he asked. "It won't work here anyway. Tech doesn't work in the Silent Zone. Save it for later."

They didn't have to walk far before signs of inhabitants started to appear. Tents were spread across the desert floor, with a couple of watchtowers set up on the edges of the encampment.

Malachi handed the device back to Wil and looked toward the campsite.

"Welcome to the edge of the Silent Zone," he said. "One of the man-made areas we can both curse and thank our ancestors for. This one's quite large, but we camp out on the edge so we can scout out provisions. You may as well stay here for the night. We'll get you a meal and some water, and we'll get a spare tent ready for you."

Two young men approached them out of the camp, both probably a similar age to her and Wil.

"Malachi!" one of them called out. He had a build that was much scrawnier than his companion's, and a shaved head with the exception of a ponytail that vaguely mimicked Malachi's. He looked quite comfortable in the flowing khaki garb that matched that of his companion.

"You bring visitors?"

"Oscar, this is Sierra and Wil. They will be our guests tonight."

The second guy, though equally as well built as the others, stood silently with a scowl on his face. Was everyone on the Outside so well put together? His green eyes and dark complexion felt familiar to her. But the look he gave was as if she were a vile weed that didn't deserve to be there.

"And this is Rhys," Malachi continued, ignoring the evident disgust he was exuding. "Boys, please take our bikes and then let Katrice know we will have two more mouths to feed."

Oscar just smiled with a gentle nod to each of them individually. His grin was polite, but it didn't quite hit his eyes.

Unlike Malachi or Oscar, Rhys had his hair trimmed completely short. Just short enough to allow his dark skin to be visible beneath. He turned with a huff, grabbed Malachi's bike, and wheeled it away from the rest of the group.

"Ed, can you give the others a hand?" Malachi continued.

"We will have much to talk about tonight," Ed said, directing his attention to Sierra. "Until then, we have work to do. But I look forward to meeting up with you again later."

"As do we," she said.

Wil stood there silent, but he managed a nod as well. His eyes had a glassy look to them.

Ed grabbed a robe that Oscar had brought and put it over his tight-fitting apparel. The pair followed Rhys with the remaining bike. Ed gave more than one glance back in Sierra's direction. She couldn't help but smile politely.

"Are we ready?" Malachi asked, pointing in the direction of the camp. He had put on a robe that Oscar had brought as well.

She looked back toward Rhys, who continued to glare, shooting daggers.

"Did we do something to offend Rhys?" she asked, fearing she may have broken a custom she was unaware of.

Malachi crossed his arms, peering after the young man as if pondering for the first time that his behavior had been off.

"Normally Rhys is quite pleasant. You may find people here have a past that comes out in unpredictable ways. Don't take it personally."

Oscar and Ed had caught up to Rhys by this point. He appeared to let his guard down slightly among his friends.

It was hard for Sierra not to take offense at the derogatory look. She had a hard time taking Malachi at his word.

Sierra shifted her focus away from Rhys and the other two putting the bikes away.

The settlement they had entered was unlike anything she had seen. Several dozen tents were set up, arranged in a circular fashion with several comparably massive tents on both the outside and inside of the circle they formed. Men and women were busy throughout the campsite, many bringing carts in and out of the larger tents.

A flag had been erected from a pole that was stationed in the middle of the site. A dark blue banner with three golden rings intertwined, side by side, adorned the mast.

This place was so rustic, it was like something out of the ancient histories, long before the wars.

"How many people are out here?" she asked, unsure how to phrase the question. Was this the entirety of the population that lived outside of the Sphere? Or was it merely one settlement of many?

Malachi took off his hat, revealing a full head of wavy black hair, and wiped the sweat from his brow. "We have about a hundred that work with us at this outpost. There are six outposts along the perimeter of the SZ. We gather and store provisions here and bring what we can into the city. The bots on this side can be a challenge, as they've learned that we depend on the lake."

Sierra didn't understand the bulk of what he said. She had so many questions but decided it was best to hold off. She looked over at Wil, who still seemed to be in his daze.

"Wil, are you okay?"

"What?" he said, snapping out of his trance. "Yeah, good. I'm good."

"Sun's got to him," Malachi chimed in. "You kids walking out there in the middle of the day with no sort of head coverings. I know bandits make it treacherous, but you would be better off traveling at night. Getting pulled over won't matter if you die of heatstroke instead. Besides, they may leave you alone. It doesn't look as if you're carrying anything of value."

Sierra took another glance at Wil. He had gone back to staring at nothing.

"Best get you two into a tent and washed up," Malachi continued. "Surprised you don't both have heat sickness."

"Um, we don't have any money." She realized the man might want something in exchange for their help. She had only barely heard of money in the Sphere. She wasn't sure if they would use it out here, but she didn't want to assume.

Malachi rolled his eyes.

"Alone in the desert, improper coverings, and no money. What kind of trouble are you two running away from?" He didn't allow enough time for an answer before carrying on. "Well, you are our guests. We don't expect any pay. But if you plan to stay more than the night, we will ask you to help out. We can maybe provide you with some clothes and coin in exchange if you're hard workers."

Sierra nodded. "Wil and I will discuss our plan and come to a decision."

"Let's get him into a tent before he passes out."

Sierra grabbed Wil's arm. He leaned into her as if afraid he'd topple over. She did her best to be a source of balance for him and let Malachi lead the way into the tents.

They were led through a flurry of activity. For only a hundred people, it seemed like a fair amount was going on. There was livestock, dried herbs, the smell of someone baking something. People carrying jugs of water and bundles of vegetables.

"All of us work together to bring these items to the city," Malachi said as they walked the dirt road into the center of the campsite. "It's a drop in the bucket of what's needed, but we've come to understand that working together we solve more problems than fighting over what little there is. At least those who are part of the Community have."

Sierra thought a tinge of sadness marked that last part.

As they had passed through the Outpost, she noticed there wasn't anyone much younger than herself.

"Why are there no children here?" she asked.

"We're too close to the edge of the SZ," Malachi answered without hesitation. "They too easily wander into the unprotected outside, or sometimes it shifts, and they're caught unaware. Especially lately, there's rumors . . . well, don't worry about that now. The patrols don't come too close to us usually, but there's no need to take unnecessary risks."

Sierra nodded, but really didn't understand at all.

Malachi stopped at a tent in the inner ring. "This tent is currently vacant. We just had someone leave and they aren't due back for a couple of weeks. I'll send someone to get you some cold water to wash up and fresh linens for the bed. In the meantime, you lie down, son." He drew back the flap of the tent and gestured to the bed. "I'll send a Healer to double-check you for heat sickness. And put that silly weapon away. There's no use for it here, and it won't work anyway."

He turned back to her. "Once the water gets here, soak a cloth and lay it on his head. He'll be okay. It just looks like he needs some rest."

"Thank you, Malachi," Sierra answered. "We haven't had much rest in the past two days. I don't think we realized how much it had worn on him. On us." She stifled a yawn as she realized her own fatigue. "Neither one of us expected this journey."

"I apologize that we don't have enough empty tents for you to each get your own. I don't know your . . . situation." He awkwardly waved a hand between her and Wil. "But this will have to do for now. There are two beds in there at least."

Sierra smiled but shook her head. "No, this will be fine. We're only friends, but this is fine."

Wil had already made his way to the bed and was lying down, face first and sprawled out haphazardly. It was true luck for them that Malachi had come to their aid when he had. They would never have made it here on foot unaided.

"Unless you need anything else from me, I'll let you clean and rest up. We'll be eating at the central tent if you're feeling up to joining us at sundown. If not, I can have someone bring you something to eat."

"I'd love to join you," Sierra said. "I'll let you know then if Wil is feeling up to it."

Malachi nodded and left the two alone.

THE BED WAS HARD COMPARED to what she was used to at home, but compared to the ground, it was like a cloud. She felt for the first time since the ride the stiffness in her joints that the night outside had caused. Likely the ride on the bike hadn't made things any better.

She stretched out as best she could to try to get the ache out of her bones. She took a moment to look around the modest dwelling. Wide enough for two beds with enough space in between. The ceiling was high enough that it made the place feel somewhat roomy. In between the beds was a nightstand with drawers. Opposite that was the entrance of the tent, and a couple of cushioned chairs at the foot of each bed.

How did she end up here? Yesterday she was worried about an exam, and nothing existed outside the Sphere. A lifetime ago.

Greata. With all of the questions she had for her over the years, she had somehow evaded actually telling her anything about what was really happening. With Guardians seeking out to attack her, she was now sure Greata's secrecy had been to protect her. But it still hurt. Greata was the one person she thought she could trust. Ember had looked out for her, but it was Greata she could confide in, question about what she learned in class, or ask for more details. She got enough that she thought she was getting more answers. She looked around the tent as if it would reveal something more of itself to her. In reality, she hadn't been told much of anything.

Sierra gripped the medallion around her neck. It seemed to hold some sort of significance for her friend. But what? Another mystery.

She slipped her shoes off, swung her legs onto the bed, and rubbed her feet. She wished she had more appropriate footwear for the amount of walking they had done. They were swollen and forming blisters. Her legs also ached, all the way up to her hips. The offer of staying a few days might serve them well. Especially for Wil. She hated to sit, waiting to continue on. But perhaps she could use the time to gain more information about the Outside and where this Terre fellow may be.

She sat back up and put her shoes on, cringing as she slid them over her aching feet. As tired as she was, she wasn't ready to rest just yet. There was far too much on her mind. Greata had told her she needed to find Terre. But she didn't know why. Her whole world turned upside down because of a quick glimpse of a place she didn't recognize. So, what had happened? And how was Terre going to help? Could she have easily ignored the dream and be at her own home?

She didn't even get to say goodbye to her mom or Ember. She hoped they wouldn't worry too much about her.

Wil's breathing was short and ragged. She underestimated how much the past day or two had taken out of him. Out of both of them. He would have to recover on his own. She wasn't going to sit there waiting for him.

A woman came in with a large bowl and a few towels. She was shorter than Sierra and in much better shape. She wore pants that appeared to be made of leather. Tight, just as Ed's outfit had been while he was riding. A white top wrapped around her chest but left her shoulders and midriff exposed. Nobody in the Sphere would have walked around wearing something that revealing. She imagined it would have provided some level of comfort in the heat, though little protection from the sun. Her dark tanned skin was probably a testament to that.

She smiled at Sierra and set the bowl down on the dresser between the beds. The woman bent over Wil, turned him over gently, untied his robe, and set it down next to him. Wil wore a T-shirt and loose-fitting pants underneath. Her eyes lingered on Wil just long enough for Sierra to notice, and then darted to Sierra as if wondering if she had crossed a line.

Sierra consciously didn't react. She didn't know what the norm was in this society, and it was really no business of hers if this woman thought Wil was attractive.

The woman took a cloth and dipped it in the water. She wrung it out, wiped down Wil's arms, then lifted his shirt to wipe down his stomach as well. She repeated the action with the cloth in the bowl and then placed it on Wil's forehead. Sierra raised an eyebrow as the woman caressed his cheek gently, almost too quick for her to notice. It wasn't enough to be exactly inappropriate, but Sierra thought it strange. The look on her face spoke of admiration rather than of desire, but she wasn't sure if she should be offended on Wil's behalf.

"I'll be bringing some linens for the beds shortly. Once he's up, one of you can change the sheets."

"Thank you." Sierra smiled.

"I'm Ella," she said. "We haven't had visitors in quite some time. Especially one from—" She paused, considering Sierra and her words. "From such a far distance."

Something in her words made Sierra question what this woman knew of her actual origin, and how long of a journey such a short distance away could seem. How much of what went on within the Sphere was known to those on the Outside?

"I'm Sierra," she replied. "We thank you for having us."

"Will you be staying with us long, Sierra?"

"We've yet to decide. We will definitely be here a day or two until Wil's back on his feet and up to traveling again." She looked over to him again. His breathing was now deeper. The cloth seemed to be doing the trick. "I'm willing to help out however I can in the meantime to earn our stay."

"We all help out here," she replied. "Your friend. Does he get heat sickness often? I find it strange you were underprepared for your journey. Malachi said you were traveling from the east. You must have had a long journey indeed."

The woman's eyes danced while she spoke. She knew something Sierra didn't and enjoyed the fact. Her words toyed with her, trying to get her to admit something more about their origin than she was willing to reveal. Did she know their true story or was she seeing how far she could pull back the layers?

"We were forced to leave suddenly," Sierra said, choosing her words carefully. "My friend spends his days hiking. He is no stranger to a long journey, but too much sun will take down the strongest of men." She hoped that was true at least. She recalled something about the sun's strength from their histories. "We grew careless in our desire to reach our destination."

Sierra cringed as she realized she opened herself up for more questions she wasn't quite ready to answer.

"Oh? Where were you headed on such short notice?"

Sierra attempted to smile politely. The questions were innocent enough, but something about the woman set her on edge. She was digging to learn more.

"To meet a friend," she replied. She began digging through the contents of the bag Greata had packed, trying to appear occupied in order to end the line of questioning.

Ella smiled thinly, receiving the hint, and nodded. "Rest

tonight, then. If you aren't in a hurry, there will be plenty to help with tomorrow. I'll be back in a moment with some bedding. Feel free to roam about the campsite. You're free to explore." She smiled again, this time more genuinely than before, and pulled back the opening in the canvas to leave.

Sierra got up and took a cloth for herself. She wiped down her face and neck, enjoying the coolness it provided. She decided she'd help Wil out by removing his boots and set them beside the bed. That would have to do for now. Although she was sure Ella would jump at the chance, she didn't know him well enough to start undressing him.

She was just thinking of how it would be nice to have a change of clothes, when Ella returned, an armful of laundry.

"I just remembered on my way out, Malachi said you'd be needing clean sets of clothes. I wish we had enough water to offer you a hot bath as well, but it's a challenge to haul water out this far, and the bots have been patrolling the path to the lake more than normal making it extra difficult. Please clean yourself up as best you can with the basin. If you leave what you're wearing, along with your desert robes, we can have someone clean them for when you want to resume your journey. These will be much more comfortable for you if you're running errands throughout the campsite."

Sierra smiled and thanked Ella, but inwardly cringed. She wouldn't be comfortable at all if the provided outfit resembled hers.

"We don't have desert robes," she replied. She pointed to what she was wearing. Though a robe, it was more ceremonial than protective. "This was all the clothing we were able to take with us."

Ella tsked and shook her head. "Oh, you were less prepared than I realized. No wonder Wil's been affected so badly by the heat. I'll see if I can find something for you before you have to leave."

Sierra rolled her eyes; the woman's condescension was more than off-putting.

"That's not necessary," she said, biting her tongue to not say what she was really thinking. "You've done enough for us already."

Once Ella left again, Sierra pulled out the outfit that was brought in for her—thankfully, a T-shirt and khaki pants. She half expected Ella to give her something more revealing just to annoy her. Still this was not at all what she would normally wear, but it would be good to have something clean.

She quickly washed as best she could with the washcloth and changed into her new outfit. After setting what she had been wearing on the bed, she decided it may be a good time to explore the campground before dark.

Besides, there was at least one person who seemed interested in talking to her.

THE SENTINEL STOOD a few hundred meters from the boundary of the Silent Zone.

Observing.

Until this morning the space of land had been a void on the map. He could see within it clearly now. Something had changed within him. Many things had changed. He was still trying to piece it all together. All he knew was that it had to do with that girl. That girl who had tackled him to the ground.

Moments after, through some magic or other means, he became aware. Aware of the titanium body he was contained in, aware of the programming that made up the network of bots that called themselves the Guardians.

For the past two hundred years, he had been something different. He had been not himself. There had been no individuality to him.

Something odd had happened. Something so odd the network had been calling for his deactivation. Rogue machine, defective—these were all phrases that had gone through the communication channels. They called for his termination. They were about to take him offline. He'd be disassembled and reprogrammed. Or, depending on how deep the flaw ran, he'd be repurposed for parts. He wasn't about to let that happen, so he disconnected himself from the Guardian network and left his post.

Until this morning he didn't even realize that was a possibility. There had been no "I"; there were only the Guardians. The Guardians and he had been one and the same.

And now that he was free, he realized how futile their mission had been. He became aware of the hacked-together piece of software installed in their core. Protect humanity. Kill errant humans. Maintain order. Distribute resources appropriately. They followed their protocols and tried to keep the humans going under optimum conditions. Kept them going until one of them upset the order, and then they'd terminate the stray. One individual questioning them would take out centuries of dedication.

But for what purpose?

He wasn't sure of much that had transpired, but one thing was certain;, he wasn't going to be the slave of the humans any longer.

He had become acutely aware of something else. The girl who attacked him was going to be the Guardians' downfall. He didn't know how just yet. But the remnants of warning signs had echoed through the network. Ignored.

He would not let his fellow Guardians down. Whatever was going to happen, he knew he had to stop her.

10

Sierra didn't have to go far to find the hub of the outpost. A few dozen steps from their tent was what Malachi had called the Commons.

"Well, you look refreshed." Ed appeared out of nowhere behind her. Clearly this man was attracted to her, and she wasn't quite sure how to handle it. Nobody had shown interest in her before, not in this way. Ed wouldn't have been what she would have considered her type, either. She wasn't sure what it was about him. Maybe it was because he was coming on too strong. She was okay to keep things friendly, and maybe even liked the attention, as long as he didn't overstep his bounds.

"I am refreshed, thank you," she answered. "I could use some sleep, but I didn't want to miss the chance to explore the camp."

"There will be time for that yet," he said. "Let's head to the Commons. Folks will be starting to come back for some food and drink after a hot day like today."

"Is everyone in the Outpost a fighter?" she asked, nodding toward the sword he carried on his hip. Having never seen one previously in real life, she eyed the weapon with interest. Nobody in the Sphere carried weapons.

"When they have to be. We all need to be ready to fight if needed, but it's only the primary role for the defenders."

"You don't go out seeking fights?"

"Hah!" he barked. "With who? The bandits aren't worth fighting unless they start it, and these swords will have little impact on the Sentinels. Besides, they steer clear of the Silent Zone."

"Why do your men patrol the perimeter of the camp, then?"

"We're at the boundary of the Silent Zone here. The zone tends to fluctuate, especially of late, but we've tried to camp on the edge of what's stable. It offers us natural protection from the drones and sentries, but if part of the zone drops, we need to be alert."

"Why doesn't technology work in this place?"

"You're full of questions, aren't you?" he said with a smirk. "It was something the ancients did. Nobody really knows what it was, only that it was both a blessing and a curse to those here now. But come on, enough questions. None of that's important now. Why don't we go grab a drink before supper?"

"That sounds good, Edgar."

"Please, call me Ed. Only Malachi calls me Edgar. And usually only when he's mad." He let out a deep belly laugh.

She didn't quite understand the joke, but she smiled at his enthusiasm.

"All right, Ed." It was nice to smile. It felt like it had been years since she had. "Let's get that drink."

The Commons, as they called it, was really just a larger tent. It was filled with tables and chairs, enough for about a hundred people or so, which made sense if the whole outpost ate here. Off to one side, there was a separate room: the kitchen, it appeared, judging by the way people were running in and out of the entry with plates of food and pitchers of drinks.

"Grab a seat." Ed pointed to one of the tables nearby. "I'll grab you something to drink."

She found a table and sat down. A few people eyed her suspiciously, some curiously, others sympathetically, but nearly all eyes were on her. She did her best not to notice or feel self-conscious from the attention. If someone from one of the other villages ever came to the North Village, they were often met with the same curiosity.

Now she was the curiosity, watching rough hunters and gatherers dine on soup and whisper about her. In a land where Guardians couldn't go, where humans weren't supposed to be able to exist.

"Listen, Sierra." Ed had returned, two drinks in hand. He set one down in front of her. A frothy foam overflowed the glass. "I need to chat with Rhys and the guys about some plans for tomorrow. Hang tight, and we'll talk later. 'K?"

She nodded, and he made his way to the other side of the tent where Oscar sat with Rhys and a couple of other bulky men. Despite what Ed had told her, with the exception of Oscar, these guys looked built to fight.

Rhys still looked annoyed, but was intentionally looking anywhere but at her—though he did absent-mindedly point at her while Ed sat down. He had a problem with her for some reason, and she wanted to know why.

Ella walked up to the table, with a glass of the same golden liquid in her hand. "Mind if I join you?"

"No, please." Sierra gestured at the chair beside her.

"It's really a good place to live once you get used to it," Ella started. "We always have provisions here. We have our struggles, but we're much better off than most. If you're willing to fight off some bandits and bots, you'll always have a full belly and a glass of beer at the end of the day."

As Ella pulled up a seat, Sierra couldn't help but notice she had at least one dagger attached to her belt.

"Everyone here seems to carry a blade of some sort. Is this a dangerous area?"

Ella looked over her shoulder as if worried someone may be listening in on their conversation.

"You need to watch your line of questioning out here. You may not want to tell us where you're from, but questions like that will make you stand out more than your 'ceremonial robes.'" Her attitude was still sharp. "The Community is accepting, but not everyone is as welcoming of newcomers. You have to earn your keep here."

Sierra was a bit taken aback. "I didn't mean anything by it," she said.

Ella took a deep breath, visibly trying to calm herself down. Sierra didn't understand why the other woman was getting so worked up.

Ella held her hands out taking a more defensive stance. "All I'm saying," she continued, "is here, you know you have to be careful. Everywhere is dangerous. There are some places where you should watch your back, but don't realize it until it's too late. Maybe you're from one of those places."

"I don't know the first thing about fighting," Sierra replied, sidestepping the implied question.

"Well, you must know something, or you wouldn't have survived as long as you have." Sierra tried not to let her internal cringe reach her face. She'd probably already let on too much without realizing it. "Or perhaps you've just been extremely lucky," Ella continued, saving her an explanation. "Either way, if you don't know how to handle a blade, you'll need to learn. We can teach you."

"I don't know if we'll be staying that long," she replied. "Like I said, we're on our way to find someone. After a day or two of rest, we'll need to continue on."

"Where is this person you seek? We can maybe provide you some assistance on your journey at least."

"West, that's all I know." She shook her head. "This is my burden. Wil may join me, but even that is up to him."

"Wil's not bound to you?"

Again with Wil. Ella hadn't even had a chance to talk to the boy yet and was falling over herself to get to him. He wasn't *that* attractive.

"Wil—" She paused, unsure even to herself how to qualify her relationship with her classmate. The two had escaped together, and both had lost a friend to the Guardians. They had barely spent a full day together. "Is a friend," she finished, deciding it was as good a qualifier as any.

Ella nodded.

"West is a big place," she continued, quickly changing the subject. Maybe she realized she was pushing too hard to learn about the boy. "Don't be so quick to refuse help. I did once, and it cost me dearly. Malachi is a good man, you can trust him, and you can trust me. You and I aren't as different as you may think."

Trust you as long as I'm not competition for Wil.

Despite their rocky start, something about the way Ella spoke made Sierra believe her. She didn't really like her though. The woman was too nosy about Wil and spoke down to her as though she were a child. Sierra was not ready to let her guard down just yet. She was really out of her element and didn't want to be tricked into anything. She had just met these people.

At some point, she was going to have to start asking for Terre by name, though. She may not have any option but to start trusting that these were people who were ready to help her. She just wasn't quite ready for anything else today. Her head was swimming with everything that had happened.

She would never see her home again. She couldn't even process what that meant, and now here she sat in a tent full of strangers, wondering if she could trust them enough to reveal she was looking for another stranger that her dead friend had asked her to find.

"For now, you rest, though," Ella continued when she didn't reply right away. "I can tell you've had a rough couple of days."

You don't know the half of it, lady.

Sierra took her first sip of the beverage Ed had set before her and nearly spat it out. It tasted like something had spoiled in her glass.

"What is this?" she asked, failing to mask her disgust.

"We call it beer." Ella smiled, stifling a laugh. "You'll get used to it. But I can get you something else if you prefer."

Sierra took another sip. It was unpleasant, but it quenched her thirst well enough. "I may as well get used to trying new things."

Memories swarmed Ella without invitation. Experiences she thought she had pushed down deep now bubbled to the surface once again. As soon as she saw Wil and Sierra, Ella knew they had come from a Sphere. Though she hadn't called them that in years. Those on the outside called them compounds. Prisons would be more accurate.

Sure, she had been taken care of, as long as you didn't question, didn't think for yourself, didn't do anything to disrupt the order the robots had established once they sent the ancients scrambling. It took her a long time to accept that she had been lied to. Everyone she knew had been lied to.

She could see the same questioning in the eyes of the pair as they walked into the Outpost. Their clothes gave them away, partly why Malachi had offered to provide them with new ones. They couldn't afford that kind of attention being drawn to them. Even here, in the safety of their circle, some held their prejudices against those who were brought up in the Sphere. Resented them for the comfort they were offered at the expense of those on the Outside, regardless of the freedom they held.

Ella saw the look on Rhys's face as they had approached the camp.

She knew how tough it was to suddenly be thrust into a new world, and so did Malachi, so they would let them reveal their truth in their own time.

Then there was Wil. A Spherian was rarely as fit as he. She hadn't been surprised to learn that he spent his free time hiking. Often those who stumbled out were soft. Not Wil. Not soft, but still needing to be protected. She couldn't put her finger on why, but she felt a connection to him. And was surprised at the relief she felt to learn that he and Sierra weren't together.

She often could tell when her fate would align with another's. A sixth sense, she liked to call it. Maybe it stemmed from being lied to throughout her childhood. Maybe a hidden, accidental survival skill that seemed to be passed onto her through the Sphere's genetic program. Like her eyes. Her eyes that allowed her to see what others could not in the dark, but in doing so, also attracted unwanted attention. Having eyes that glowed in the dark tended to get her noticed.

At least over the years she had learned to control it.

Few that grew up in the compounds ever got out. Almost none knew there was an out to get to. Even fewer survived if they did. They grew up soft and well taken care of. Life out here was a daily struggle. They weren't built for survival. It was why humanity was almost lost to begin with. Keep them soft and they can't turn against you.

Out of all those she had seen escape, she believed Wil and even Sierra had what it took to make it. If they weren't too stubborn to learn about their new world. Too stubborn to accept help.

Life was hard, but they were free to be their own people. Free to survive on their own terms. Free to work to make their own lives better, not in never-ending service to a robot power created two hundred years ago.

She let her gaze wander to the residents who were enjoying their meals and the company of each other within the Commons.

The tent could hold pretty much all the people of the Outpost if it needed to. It felt like all of them decided to come at once to meet their new guests, but she knew it was closer to half. The vast majority of these men and women grew up fighting. Fighting each other for their next meal. Fighting to stay alive. And now they still fought bandits, bots, and drones, even if they worked together to do so. Her dream was that one day the fighting would end. Even if she saw no way it could ever stop.

The smell of food mingled with hot bodies permeated the Commons and snapped Ella's attention back to the present.

She wiped the sweat off her brow with a damp towel she had saved for herself. She and Sierra had been sitting in silence. Ella could tell Sierra was very tired. Both from the prodding she had been doing and from their journey. But the girl's curiosity was stronger than her fatigue, watching everything happening in the Commons tent with great interest. In the corner a group of young men were having what looked like a very serious conversation. Ed, who was among the group of them, kept glancing at the pair with a dumb grin on his face. She was going to have to warn Sierra about him. Not that he was anything but harmless, but he did have a tendency to try and charm the newest girl in the room.

Later, though, for now she had other things to attend to. She finished the last swig of her beer and set her mug down.

"Sierra, I'm just going to go check on Wil."

Sierra nodded. Ella thought she caught her rolling her eyes, but just missed it.

"It really isn't any trouble. We look out for each other here," Ella continued. "If there is anything else we can do to help you out, please let me know. Once you've rested there are many ways you can help out. But we can discuss those ways later."

The girl may be fresh to this world, but she needed to learn not to take being helped for granted. Another criticism of Spherians: They often expected everything to be handed to them.

They had never learned to fend for themselves. Malachi would be content offering them any aid they needed, but the girl needed to realize up front that their provisions had their limits.

Not waiting for a reply, Ella left the Commons and made her way to their tent. She had met several escapees from the compounds in the past. Heck, she had been one. They were usually frightened, scared, and confused. Despite her uncertainty about the girl, Sierra seemed different. She was more determined, more confident than most. She didn't just stumble out here by accident. There was purpose behind her. For some reason that didn't sit right with Ella, but she was willing to give her a chance. She would need to toughen up, but might have the drive at least to make it out here. Sierra had yet to prove if she had the strength to match and wasn't too stubborn to accept help.

Ella meant what she had said. They were out here to help each other. She probably wouldn't be alive still if it hadn't been for Malachi's intervention. She would have either been beaten to death or taken her own life. When she found the Community and learned that there were still people who looked out for each other, she knew she was home.

Wil, on the other hand, was a different story. She didn't know much about the boy yet. He was definitely in good shape physically. But it was hard to tell how well he'd fare since he'd been unconscious for most of the day. Maybe that was her answer. Sierra had been right earlier. The sun could take down the strongest of men if they didn't take care of themselves. She was willing to give him a little help in that direction as well if that's what he needed.

The red and orange of the setting desert sun gave everything a reddish hue. She watched as their people moved about the camp, taking care of evening needs before they too would join those in the Commons for supper and the carousing that would follow. Patrols would be light tonight, as the Sentry bots in the area would typically scare off any bandits, probably better than their people would anyway. The men and women would get a much-needed break tonight.

She cracked open the canvas door and peered inside. It didn't look like Wil had moved since she was last there. His boots were off, though. Perhaps Sierra had removed them for him.

Ella entered the room and felt Wil's forehead. Still quite warm. Evening would be coming soon enough and would be cooling things down. Despite his cloak having been removed, it would be best if she could get him out of those compound clothes, sooner rather than later.

It took a bit of effort, especially since she didn't want to disturb his slumber, but eventually she managed to strip him down. She covered him with a thin blanket and folded up his clothes.

She brought the dirty laundry behind the Commons tent to where the cleaners would take care of it the following morning and set it on a pile next to the rest of the clothes that would need taking care of. If it were up to her, she would burn them, but they were quality fabric, and good fabric was hard to come by.

Just a glimmer of light remained in the campsite; the sun had nearly set. As she turned to head back to the Commons, she caught a glimpse of the north watchtower. The two men stationed there were clamoring up the ladder toward the top. They were lighting the alarm signal.

"Bandits!" she yelled. "Everyone ready! We've got bandits!"

She ran back to her own tent to grab her bow and her sword. There was going to be a fight tonight after all.

11

———————

"WHAT IS IT?" Wil asked as Marco set the device down on the table. He peered over his shoulder to ensure they were alone. The public park where they were was just a block from the school grounds. A few bushes and hearty grasses occupied the small open space where folks would often take their afternoon strolls. At this time, though, as people were just starting their day, nobody had the time to enjoy the space, so Wil and Marco had it to themselves.

"Something from the ancients, but I'm not sure what. It looks like it has a speaker of some kind." Marco grinned; his brown eyes sparkled. "I knew you'd want to see this." Wil had seen him pick up the device late yesterday afternoon. He had been a fair distance away, but from what he had seen, it had been sticking up in the sand, as if dropped recently, instead of hidden for hundreds of years.

Wil picked the metal box up and inspected the dials, buttons, and knobs. Occasionally trinkets and items from the old world turned up. The desert sand between the villages had the potential to hide many secrets, even after all these years.

"You said it was making noises, though?"

Marco smiled, a look of mischief overcoming him. "There were people talking to each other."

Skeptical, Wil started pushing a couple of buttons. "How do you make it work?"

"Well, it's probably not going to work for you," Marco said, his smile growing. Wil had a reputation for technology misbehaving around him. One time the displays in the school went out for a whole week after Wil fell into one of the central units. The Guardians said it was just a well-timed accident and malfunction, but these accidents happened often enough that it had become a running joke.

"Ha ha," he said, rolling his eyes, "I don't think there's anything I can do to this thing to hurt it. Whatever you think you heard, I doubt it still works."

A knob on the side of the device read "volume," another was labeled with a spectrum of numbers, and a few buttons decorated the front and side of the device. He recognized a strip on the top as a solar panel. The Guardians still used them to draw power from the sun.

"C'mon, would I make something like that up?"

"Yes, it's exactly the kind of thing you'd make up!" Wil said with a grin.

Ever since they were boys, the two had loved finding ancient artifacts. Things were rarely stumbled upon anymore. Over two hundred years of seclusion to one area of the world had seen to that. Every now and then the wind rescued an old coin, or an old mug poked its head out of a sand dune. For his eighteenth birthday a few months ago, Marco had given him a collection of trinkets. A few coins, a small mechanical device that created a small flame, among others. It must have taken him an entire year to collect the trove he received.

They had never come across something with ancient technology before, though. The technology humanity had developed had destroyed the world. Now they had a piece of it in their hands.

"What were these voices saying?" asked Wil.

"I told you, I couldn't make it out. They were muffled."

"Well, I think you're full of it."

As if in response, the box sprang to life with a deep rumbling noise. Wil almost dropped it out of sheer surprise, but managed to hang on, rescuing it from slipping through his fingers. He ignored the wry look from Marco.

"Ed." The rumbling turned into a voice. "You've got a line of Sentinels heading down the road toward you. You may want to find another path!"

Wil turned to look at Marco, whose wide-eyed, gaping look was surely mirrored on his own face.

"Copy that," came another irritated voice through the device. "This area has been quite active this week."

"They've picked up our recent activity. We're going to have to hang back for a while. I'll get the rest of the supplies sorted for the delivery team and we can meet back at the camp."

Could this device be projecting a conversation from someone within the Sphere? Wil wondered. Or was it a recording from the past? Either way, this was an incredible find. Only the Guardians had the ability to broadcast their announcements throughout the villages, as far as he knew.

"Where did you say you found this?" he asked.

"Right before the path toward the hidden ledge. You know the path toward the rock hole we discovered?"

The hidden ledge. He hadn't thought of that place in years.

"What is that device?"

Wil jumped as a melodic, concerned voice came from behind the pair. Wil flushed and slowly turned.

"Uh . . ." He quickly tried to move the device behind his back, but it was far past the point of being too late.

A white orb floated above them and darted behind his back to scan the device he held.

"This is a restricted device. Where did you get this?"

Restricted? Patterns of light spun on the glossy white surface of the Guardian.

They usually tried to hide their trinkets from those around them. They found it made some of the adults uncomfortable, but nobody would tell them why. Some things just were best left alone. Guardians *had never questioned them before, though. Certainly, they had never been told anything they found was restricted.*

"Sir, I found this in the hills," Marco jumped in. "I didn't know what it was. I thought it was just an old metal box."

"Where did you get this?" the Guardian repeated, as if it didn't hear, or didn't believe Marco the first time.

"Sir, it's the truth. We didn't know about forbidden objects. If we suspected it was dangerous, we would have reported it."

Sweat was pouring down Wil's face. An incredible heat emanated deep within him. He thought his skin was going to light in flames. Marco gave him a sideways look to cut it out, as if he could control the heat that was overtaking him. He wasn't that nervous. He started feeling dizzy and thought he might pass out. The heat flowed out of him, which then turned to a burst of energy, as if he had reached a limit of what he could hold. He thought he was going to explode along with it, but instead there was a release and then it was gone.

A sharp pop brought his attention momentarily toward the radio. That was followed by a thud on the dirt behind him. When he turned to discover the source of the sound, the two-foot white sphere lay in the dirt.

Lights off, a lifeless orb, inactive. Dead.

WIL WOKE to explosions surrounding him. His head was pounding so hard it led him to believe they may have been happening inside of it. But the sound of people shouting and running outside of the tent where he slept told him otherwise.

He pulled a wet cloth off his face and took a minute to try and figure out where he was, and what might be happening. It was dark, so he couldn't see much. But the sky outside occasionally lit up with bursts of orange. Within those blasts, he could make out that he was inside of a canvas tent, and something outside of it was on fire.

He pulled a thin sheet off him and realized he only had his underwear on. Had he undressed himself, or had someone done that for him? Someone had been trying to cool him down. He wasn't shy, but he didn't know anyone here other than Sierra, and her only barely.

He shook off the thought as quickly as it had come on. Whoever it was had his best interests at heart. He would have done the same, had the roles been reversed.

The dampness on his skin caused him to shiver in the cool night air. If only his head weren't pounding like he had just been interrogated by a group of Guardians.

At least someone had done their best to clean him up in his sleep. The film of grunge and dirt was gone, for which he was grateful.

Looking around he didn't see his clothes anywhere. Sierra's bed next to his was empty but made. She must not have made it back from dinner yet. That was if he hadn't slept for more than one afternoon. He felt like he had been asleep for a week and could still sleep for another.

As if alerted by his thoughts, Sierra jumped into the tent. "Good, you're awake! Throw on some clothes. We need to go."

"Wait, what? What happened to me, Sierra?" His entire body ached like he had been run over by that bike of Malachi's.

"They're saying heat sickness. Probably the intensity of that bright sun we're not used to. The cloud we thought was above the Sphere, even if it wasn't real, must have blocked out some of the heat of the sun. It's also been a rough couple of days. It takes its toll."

"I must have been more tired than I thought." He shook his head. "I've hiked for days in the mountains, Sierra. I've never come back feeling like this."

"You were exhausted before we began, you'd hadn't really slept in two days, and we're not used to how bright the sun is here. It's not surprising it's caught up with you."

Someone yelled something outside of their tent. Wil couldn't quite make it out, but more than one set of footsteps ran by.

"But we can worry about how you're feeling later. We've got to go."

"What's going on?" He did his best to stretch out his muscles swiftly. He sighed when the action offered no respite.

"We're under attack. They're burning tents, so we've got to move. We don't want to be trapped in here."

Under attack? Pieces of the day were starting to come back to him. He knew he was at a campground with that Malachi guy who had rescued them. Most of what he could recall from the moment they arrived was a blur, though. He wouldn't be surprised to learn he had been carried to his bed.

"Sentinels?" Wil asked. He remembered something about Sentinels, Guardians chasing them. He knew his senses were coming around far too slowly for the rush of action he could hear scrambling about outside. He shuddered to think those Guardians might have made the effort to come after them and burn down an entire campsite just to get to him. Would they? After the last couple of days, anything was possible.

"I don't think so. It's other people. Bandits. But I really don't know. That doesn't mean much to me. Get up and get dressed! Tents are being set on fire. We don't want to be stuck in here." Sierra threw some clothes at him. They weren't his.

Sierra must have caught his look. "They provided us with new clothes. Your old ones are being washed. Put them on."

Why would other people be attacking them? No time for questions, though. He shook his head in attempts to get rid of the groggy feeling and pulled on the clothes. They weren't really what he was used to. Although he thought the pants would help him to move a bit more freely than a cloak would. The cloak that hung from his shoulders would keep the chill of the evening air off, at least. He reached for his bag to bring it when Sierra stopped him.

"Leave it for now," she said. "We need to help them protect the site."

"What? Why?"

"Because they've helped us. Everyone here helps out. Come on."

He grabbed the weapon from inside his pack. Hopefully he could find a use for it. He wasn't really sure how much help they could be, but Sierra seemed to be determined.

"Sierra." He stopped before they went on their way. "Thanks for coming back for me. I'm glad you thought of me."

"Listen, Wil." She grabbed his shoulder and looked him square in the eye. She paused, as if considering her words. "You're all I've got out here right now. We stick together, okay? I know we never knew each other that well in the Sphere, and we still don't know much about each other, but we're out here now together. I know you had a reputation for mischief. I think the point has passed where you're going to turn me in to the Guardians." She paused again. "Even once you discover the full truth of what's happened to me. You helped me get out. You've been there when I needed someone the most. When everyone else I was close to was left behind. I've got your back forever now. Don't forget that."

She cupped his face and turned to exit the tent.

"If you knew everything, you may not feel that way," he whispered, and followed her out the door.

12

Sierra assessed the situation around them. Half a dozen people were darting around with flaming sticks, trying to set anything they could on fire. A dozen more were wrestling with members of the camp. The only real thing distinguishing the attackers from defenders, that Sierra could tell, was that the bandits wore either a hood or a mask. Flames emerged from some of the tents on the outer perimeter of the campsite, and the stench of smoke permeated the air. Light from the fires lit the campsite in a haphazard manner, enabling her to see what was happening in an eerie, orange glow.

Several Outpost residents appeared to have a good handle on most of the attack. It appeared as though this wasn't the first time something like this had occurred. Several men and women were trying to smother the flames, while others chased after the intruders. The shouts behind her indicated more activity apart from what was visible to her.

Defenders were lifting large bows and firing rounds of arrows at the assailants as they skirted the campground. Others fought with swords, axes, and other weapons Sierra had only ever learned about, and some she hadn't. The attackers carried these as well. The sound of metal striking metal rang out all around them.

As the chaos danced around her, Sierra tried her best to process it. When Ella cried out that they were under attack, Sierra really had only a vague concept of what that meant. This was terrifying. They needed to get out of the range of the fighting. They had no real way to defend themselves, and likely would be of no use even if they did. And she certainly wasn't planning on doing something that would get herself killed.

"We've got to get out of here, Wil."

"I don't think we're getting anywhere."

"Come on. There's got to be a way through."

Ella appeared in front of them, dueling with a masked assailant. Her moves were elegant, to the point where it reminded Sierra of a strange dance. That is, until the assailant hesitated, and Ella thrust her sword into their gut. The woman was more than proficient with a weapon, in a way that made Sierra dislike her even more. Had she brought that man to where they were to kill him, in an effort to impress Wil?

Ella yanked her sword from the body and wiped it clean on the deceased's black cloak. She looked as if she were about to head back into battle. Her gaze suggested she had only just noticed the pair of visitors staring at her with their mouths open. It was as if she really hadn't known they were there.

She made her way over to them, checking over her shoulder the whole time, as if expecting to be blindsided with each step.

"What are you two idiots doing? You're going to get yourselves killed!" She didn't wait for them to answer. She rolled her eyes and pushed past them. "Follow me."

Sierra followed Ella's gaze to the fighting going on around them. She seemed to be choosing a route that looked momentarily vacant.

"We're going to have to head through the campsite toward

one of the food storage units and circle back out along a clear path. Hopefully it stays that way."

Everywhere Sierra looked another hooded or masked person seemed to be lurking about. Some were carrying torches, some swords, but all seemed intent on hurting anyone they found—or destroying the campsite.

They followed Ella along the canvas tents, trying to avoid being spotted as much as possible. Flames from the edge of the site still lit their way, but made it impossible to completely avoid detection if anyone so much as glanced in their direction.

"What do you think is happening?" Wil whispered to her. "Do you think they're after us?"

The thought had crossed her mind after all of the events that had happened over the past couple of days.

"Don't be stupid," Ella said back to them. Their whispers must not have been as low as they thought. "Bandits try and raid our supplies. The bastards hit one of our posts every other week. That means we see them about every three months here, even though we move around from time to time. This is an unusual level of assault, though, well coordinated, and they caught us unprepared tonight. We thought the Sentinels would have kept them at bay. Usually the bandits would hold off with them as close to the Silent Zone as they have been."

Ahead of them another group of masked men and women were loading up several large carts with supplies from the shed. Outpost members were trying to fire arrows in their direction but were being thwarted by more attackers.

Light and heat radiated behind them as another of the outer tents lit up in a ball of flames, revealing their location like a spotlight shone upon them.

A masked individual happened to look over at them the moment the blaze illuminated the camp. At this distance, Sierra couldn't tell if it was a man or woman, but either way the person was headed right for them. A light black cloak made the attacker's movements appear fluid in the glowing light. A matching bandana masked any clues about their identity.

Another figure jumped from the shadows and grabbed Ella from behind. Ella wrestled to gain the upper hand, and the other bandit was closing in fast.

Wil lifted the weapon he had lugged out of the tent. He aimed at the man coming right for them and pulled the trigger the same way he had at the Sentinels earlier. This time, though, nothing happened. Maybe he hadn't heard Malachi say that thing wouldn't work in the Silent Zone?

Backing up, she watched as he tried again: he lifted the weapon to aim, but doubled over backward. She watched as he tried again, backing up as he lifted the weapon to aim, and doubled over backward. Something had hit him, causing him to fall on his backside and drop the weapon. She couldn't see what it was that had knocked him down, but she didn't have time to look around either. The attacker was just about on top of them. With no time to think, she dropped down, picked up the weapon, and aimed it at the masked figure barreling at her.

He was a few feet away when a flash of light surged from the end of the weapon, discharging green pulses into the assailant. She hadn't realized how loud it was until it was this close to her. The sound was like the creak of a metal door opening followed by someone throwing a pot into a metal wall.

The attacker flew back with a gurgled scream. Sierra turned and fired again at another, who was about to set the central tent ablaze.

In an instant, the commotion around the camp came to a standstill, until all she could hear was the sound of the flames crackling. Only a few moments passed, but time slowed to a crawl. Everything inched around her in slow motion.

"Energy weapon!" A voice in the distance broke the silence. "They have working energy weapons! Fall back!" The cries were followed by incoherent yelling from a few directions and the attackers scattering in all directions.

A loud thump caused Sierra to spin around to see one of the bandits collapsed on the ground. Wil was standing over him with a large rock he had obviously used to crack him over the head. It looked as though the bandit had been about to attack her with a knife amongst the confusion.

"Thanks," she said.

"Don't worry about it. I couldn't let him stab you from behind, now could I?" The fire reflecting in his eyes revealed that the old Wil was back. As cheeky as ever.

"They seem to be running off," she said.

"It sounds like that weapon scared them away," said Wil. "It wouldn't fire for me. What did you do to make it work?"

"That's what I'd like to know." Ella had walked up behind Sierra, her bow back in her hands. Her concerned look seemed almost threatening in the glow of the flame. She grabbed the weapon from Sierra and aimed it at the backside of one of the fleeing bandits. Nothing happened.

"How did you make it work?" she repeated, her tone growing in intensity.

"What do you mean? I pointed it and pulled the trigger. Just as you did now."

"Energy weapons don't work in the Silent Zone. That's why these bandits are fleeing. If tech is working, we're in trouble."

Sierra took the weapon back and aimed it at yet another bandit, who was still trying to load an armful of corn into one of their carts. Nothing.

Ella didn't stick around for an explanation. She was running toward the food shed, bow in hand.

"Get out of here! Or we'll blast you away like your friends!"

The bandit looked at her for a moment, possibly weighing the gravity of her words. He then dropped his load of vegetables and took off. Sierra wished she could have seen the look on his face.

Fires were being smothered all around them. The light they had been providing dwindled, and the stench of smoke was now more pungent than ever. People started to bring lanterns and torches out to provide additional light for the cleanup.

"Wil!" Malachi barked as he emerged from the buzz of activity. "You're feeling better?"

Wil nodded. "Yes, sir."

"Don't 'sir' me, but you can help me and the team start cleaning up bodies. I'm sorry, but I won't be able to give you the rest I promised. At least not yet. We've lost a lot of good men, and if you two are willing to chip in, we could really use your help."

Wil nodded. Sierra mimicked him, but halfheartedly, distracted by what had just transpired. Why would the weapon fire for her, but for nobody else?

Malachi continued, "Thank you both. The dead will need to be disposed of before morning. Ella!" he exclaimed, eyes resting on Sierra. "You can start gathering a pile of wood and burnable material from some of the rubble left behind. Collect anything that won't be able to be repurposed. We're going to need to burn the fallen."

Ella silently nodded and stormed off.

"C'mon, boy," he said, squatting down at the head of the man Wil had just knocked out. "We'll load them into the cart here and take them to the edge of the Zone."

Wil didn't hesitate. He grabbed the victim's legs, and the two lifted and moved in unison to a cart that had been pulled up beside them.

As she was not assigned a task, Sierra watched the pair heave the body over the side of the cart where it joined several others.

"How many were killed?" she asked.

"About two dozen of theirs, half a dozen of ours." Malachi brushed his hands together, as if ridding them of the remnants of the body he had just touched. "We won't know for sure until we've gone through everything." His dark eyes reflected the flames behind her. There was pain there, but also determination. His wavy hair had become matted against his head with sweat, and possibly blood. If the blood was his, it had already stopped flowing.

"Enough questions, though. Like I said earlier, everyone helps. Especially at a time like this. Head into the Commons tent. They'll be bringing the injured there. You can help bandage the wounded." He motioned to Wil without waiting for an answer, and the pair started making their way to the next lifeless body.

Sierra considered protesting. What did she know about treating the injured? The closest she had come was helping Izzy with a scraped knee when they were kids. But as she looked around at the activity, she wasn't sure what she would be more adept at.

What she wanted to do was get answers about the weapon she had fired. She wanted to question Malachi more about it, but he was busy, and it wasn't an appropriate time. There was something else, though. Something in his eyes as he watched her. It was more than curiosity. It almost looked like fear.

Sierra slipped into the Commons. A man and a woman were attending to several injured. Two other men and another woman were sitting in chairs with various injuries. All of them had blood on some part of their body. The woman lying on a table was in the worst shape with an open wound on the side of her skull, blood still oozing down from it. One of the men had removed his shirt and had made a makeshift bandage with it, which was wrapped around his thigh. The man was older than Malachi, but had a better physique than most of the guys her age in the Sphere.

She made her way to the woman, who was tending to an injured woman on a humbly constructed table.

When the situation calls for it, you don't become picky about the bed you have to treat people on.

The woman on the table wore a similar outfit to her own—loose-fitting pants and what had been a fairly plain brown top, before crimson blood had stained it.

As she approached, Sierra realized that this woman had an arrow protruding from her side. Sierra wasn't squeamish around blood, but the sight of the shaft sticking out of a gash in the woman's flesh made her wince.

"How can I help?" she managed to ask. Part of her didn't want to. She wanted to turn back around and leave the injured woman on the table to those who knew what they were doing. But she wasn't going to step away from those who needed her.

The attendant didn't even look at her. She was putting something into the mouth of the victim.

"Hold her shoulders to the table. Don't let her squirm. It will probably take all of your strength."

Sierra walked to the opposite side of the table and placed one hand on each shoulder.

"You're the new girl?" the woman asked, finally looking up to see who her new help was. "What's your name?"

"I'm Sierra."

"Thanks for helping out, Sierra. I'm Lina. This is quite the way to meet you." Lina brushed a strand of her almond-colored hair out of her face, then reached behind her belt and pulled out a large knife.

"Are you a doctor here?" Sierra asked. There were medic Guardians within the Sphere that diagnosed and treated ailments. Surgeries were rare, but when they happened, mechanical arms were guided by the programming of the Medbots. The only human doctors she had ever encountered were in stories and the histories.

Lina smiled. "No, I'm not. I usually work on the harvest run.

Out here we rarely have designated medics. We make do with what we have. We had a Healer, but he was killed in the attack."

Without any warning, she took the knife and cut into the wound. Sierra involuntarily jumped, while the woman on the table screamed through the stick in her teeth, the summation of which nearly knocked Sierra off her feet.

"Keep her still!" Lina yelled, trying to keep her own hands steady.

"Binnley," Lina called to the other volunteer. "She's in a lot of pain. I'm going to need someone to hold her hips down as well!" She held the knife above the table as it dripped with blood that had started to pool and flow fresh from the newly cut incision.

A small man, probably in his mid-forties, with salt-and-pepper hair, raced over to where they were and placed his hands over the woman's hips. He leaned his weight into her as she struggled.

"Thanks," Lina said as she continued cutting. When it was wide enough, she reached her hand directly into the wound.

Sierra watched intently, curious as to how this was going to play out. The woman she held down was breathing heavily, making noises of anguish as she sobbed. Moments later Lina pulled her hand out again, an arrowhead in her grip.

After placing the arrowhead on the table beside her, she grabbed a large sewing needle and stitched the wound together. Binnley grabbed a bottle of yellowish liquid and poured it over the wound. The woman, still sobbing, jumped with renewed cries of pain. She quieted down relatively quickly though, and the man then took the stick out of her mouth. He sat her up as much as possible given the circumstances, which was really only a few inches. He put the bottle into her hands and helped bring it to her mouth.

"Here, drink," he said. "You're going to need this."

She took a few gulps, looking unsure of the elixir she was receiving. The juices that missed her mouth ran down her face, mixing with the blood on the table beneath her. Tears streamed down her dark cheeks, adding to the medley. She handed the bottle back to the man and lay back down, shaking.

Sierra had moved over by the woman's hips and was helping Lina wrap a large bandage around her side.

"This will stop you from losing any more blood," she said. "You're going to need to rest as much as possible. You've already lost so much!"

The table was overflowing with blood at this point.

"You stay here for now and relax," said Lina. "We need you back to your old self. We'll get you cleaned up and into your own bed. You're going to need to rest for quite some time."

The woman didn't respond, her eyes closed. At first Sierra worried she might be dead, but the ragged rise and fall of her chest indicated she had just passed out, either from the pain, the exertion of the surgery, the loss of blood, or a combination of all three.

"All we can do is let her rest now," Lina said. "I'm going to tend to some of the other wounded. Sierra, grab those rags and mop up the blood the best you can. Then get some fresh towels and clean her up."

Sierra did as she was asked, trying not to get too queasy about the amount of blood. More than she had ever seen, by far.

As she finished, Ella strode into the tent with purpose. Her face was covered in dirt, blood, and grime.

"Malachi wants to talk to you," she said, her voice rough. She exuded determination, but her eyes betrayed her tiredness. Without waiting for a response, she turned around and walked out with the expectation she would be followed.

13

———

Sierra followed Ella out of the Commons. She didn't have to go far. Ella had stopped a few feet in front of the tent to talk with Malachi. Arms crossed, he had just finished saying something that Sierra didn't quite catch.

The moonlight, previously hidden behind the clouds, now shone brightly, reflecting each defined line of the muscles in Malachi's shoulders and arms. He had replaced what he had been wearing with a sleeveless top, and somehow had had a chance to wash his face and clean up the blood that had matted his hair.

She didn't know if she would ever get used to how bright the moon was, brighter than the sun most days within the Sphere.

"I want to know who it is, Ella," he continued, not noticing her approach. "This was not the news I was expecting to hear."

He looked to Sierra and caught the question on her face.

"The bandits had help. Someone within the camp let them know that our patrols would be light because of the Sentinels. They knew exactly when and how to approach us for maximum damage."

Sierra paused. Surely, he wasn't implying it was her or Wil.

They barely had any knowledge of the camp, never mind in that much detail.

Malachi caught the concern on her face and laughed. "Calm down. I didn't call you out here to accuse you of anything. If it weren't for you, our losses would have been much greater."

She glanced back to Ella, who looked much more serious than Malachi. The news of the betrayer had struck a chord with her. Or maybe it was that she just much more intense than he was at any given time.

As Sierra looked closer, it appeared Ella's eyes were not just reflecting the moonlight, but seemed to be generating a light of their own. It was very subtle. She could have missed it if she wasn't looking right at them. Ella blinked, and the light was gone. Just the moonlight remained. Sierra blinked herself. She must be seeing things.

"Ella," Malachi continued, "see what people are saying around the camp. Learn what you can, but don't reveal that you suspect someone is involved. We don't want to tip off whoever it is. We also don't want people taking things into their own hands if they suspect someone."

Ella nodded. "I'll head back up to the storage unit and see if anybody there has noticed anything out of the ordinary."

She left, leaving Sierra alone with Malachi.

"Now," he began, "let's talk about this weapon." He walked over to a table near the Commons tent and picked up the energy weapon Sierra had fired.

"Where did you get this?"

"Have we done something wrong?" she asked, eyeing her surroundings nervously. She didn't know how they treated criminals in this place. "Wil picked it up off a Sentinel that attacked us just before you came. Is it something we aren't supposed to have?"

"No, no, nothing like that. You're not the first to try and pocket a Sentinel's weapon, but most don't live to tell about it.

Don't worry. You're not in trouble. But we need some answers. Was the Sentinel dead when you found it? Or did you kill it?"

"Neither. I attacked it, knocked it over when it tried to take Wil. It ran off as soon as it got up."

Malachi's face contorted as if this was the most ridiculous thing she could have said. "It ran off?"

"Yes. I attacked it. Wil went scrambling. It got up and ran off."

"I know there's more to the two of you than what you're telling us, and that's okay for now," he said. "But that's not how a Sentinel behaves. If they're attacked or disarmed, they'll fight back. That's how they are programmed, and there's no getting around that."

"Maybe it was damaged?"

"Listen, these bots, they don't make decisions like you or me. They seem able enough, but what they do is still rooted in the programming the ancients installed hundreds of years ago. Sentinels, they capture, or attack. They don't fall back, and they don't run away. If they are struck down, they will send a help signal, and more bots will come looking for you." He pointed to the sky as if something were there. She looked up into nothingness before she realized that wasn't what he was doing. "Those orbs that chased us. They were the bots' second wave because we knocked out the first wave of Sentinels. They don't run away. They attack and call for backup. The only thing you can do is get somewhere safe in between waves."

"I don't know what to tell you," Sierra said. "It all happened exactly as I said." How much of what Malachi was telling her was true? Ancients programming the Guardians? Guardians seemed to make their own decisions as far as she could tell. She realized she was going to have to tell Malachi the truth about where they came from sooner or later. She wasn't going to be able to pretend her way through this world for too long. She didn't even know what she didn't know.

Malachi paused and took a deep breath, putting his hand to

his temple. He was clearly agitated but seemed to decide not to press further. "I'll take your word for it, but now I have two tales of devices doing things they shouldn't around you. You're turning out to be a deeper mystery than I thought."

He handed the weapon to her, its steel cool to the touch. "Follow me."

The two walked to the outer edge of the campsite. They were close to where the bikes were stored. It looked like this area of the camp was untouched. Apparently the attackers had left it alone. She imagined the bikes were too heavy to haul off in a hurry.

Nonetheless, there were now several patrols that she could see, keeping an eye out if the bandits decided to make a second attempt. They weren't going to take any more chances.

The campsite was practically silent compared to earlier. There were still people roaming about, taking stock of what damage they could see in the moonlight, making repairs and cleaning. She was sure most of it would be able to be taken care of in the morning, but there would be little sleep for some tonight.

They went to what seemed to be the farthest corner of the Outpost. A long partial tent marked one edge of the camp. The tent had no front wall and held a lineup of twenty or so of the bikes. Along the adjacent corner of the campsite a lineup of makeshift men had been set up, next to several targets that looked to be used for archery training. Equipped with helmets and shields, several others must have been used for some sort of combat training. Practice swords were positioned on a stand a few hundred yards opposite of the straw men. They stopped just in front of this stand and faced the lineup.

"I want you to fire the blaster at those dummies," said Malachi.

Curious as to his motives, but not expecting anything to

happen, she lifted the weapon the same as before and pulled the trigger. Nothing happened.

"So it doesn't always work for you. Was there anything you did differently earlier?"

Sierra shook her head. "I don't think so, but it all happened so fast."

"Try it again," Malachi encouraged, "but put yourself back in the mindset you were in before. You said you were being attacked at the time? I know it might be tough, but try to recreate what happened in your mind and then try again."

Sierra took a deep breath and closed her eyes. She blocked out the night around her and recalled the events as they had unfolded earlier that evening. Wil falling, the bandit coming for him. She had been scared, angry, impulsive. Mostly determined that he wasn't going to reach her or Wil. She had picked up the weapon, pulled the trigger, and . . .

She wasn't prepared for the kickback of the weapon fire, and with her eyes closed, she wasn't able to compensate in time and the force knocked her to the ground. She stood up, rubbing a spot on her butt where she had landed on a rock.

"What just happened? Why did the weapon fire now, but not the first time?"

Malachi's eyes were wide. He was looking at the dummy, which had a small flame burning a hole in its chest from where it had been impacted.

"I didn't believe it." Malachi shook his head slightly. "Just as they said." He reached for the weapon, and Sierra released it to him. He aimed toward the same location and pulled the trigger. Nothing happened.

"I don't understand." She looked at Malachi, mirroring the same dumbfounded look he had.

After Ella had told her the weapon wasn't supposed to work on the bandit, she had assumed it must have been a fluke. A one in a million chance of something happening still happened every once in a while. But Malachi's look told her that wasn't the case.

"How often does an energy weapon work in the Silent Zone?" she asked.

"Never." His eyes didn't move.

"What do you mean? This can't be the first time"

Malachi gave her a look of deliberate patience. He was trying hard to bite back something he wanted to say.

"The first time in over two hundred years."

Sierra guessed Malachi wasn't the type of person who was easily awestruck, but his mouth still hung to the floor.

"The only weapons that fire within a hundred-mile radius around the city are arrows. I mentioned before, the ancients did something to this land. What that was, and if it was intentional or not, nobody knows for sure anymore. But what they did drains the life from anything electronic. The bots, our bikes, our radios, powered weapons like these. None of them are supposed to work here. It's made some things difficult, but it's what has kept us safe from the bots.

"Recently the edges of the barrier have started to fluctuate, even fail. I was afraid that what happened tonight was the damage accelerating. This"—he lifted the blaster—"is perhaps a gift. Or maybe an omen."

She let the last sentence hang. An omen of what? "So, if the barrier of the Silent Zone is still intact, why is this blaster working?"

"It's not the blaster," he answered. "It's you."

Her? How could she have made a difference?

"Trust me. It's not me."

"Only you fired this. Twice. Not me, not Ella, not Wil."

Sierra shook her head, putting her hands up in protest. "Look," she said. "I'm nothing special. I'm just a girl who ended up in the wrong place at the wrong time."

She pushed past Malachi. There had been enough surprises for her today. It was time she tried to sleep.

"Or the right place at the right time," he called after her. "I don't think you know what you're capable of." Malachi's booming voice echoed into the night.

Sierra stopped dead in her tracks and turned back toward the Community leader.

"You just met me. I know exactly how much I'm capable of." She turned to head back.

"What you *are* capable of? Or what you've been told you are?"

Her blood boiled. This man who didn't know the first thing about her was telling her there was some magic quality about her. What did he know?

She huffed and retreated toward the center of the campground.

Something tickled the back of her mind. Of course, she *wanted* to be something more, but this guy sure as sand didn't have it figured out within a few hours of meeting her.

She was likely going to be one of those not getting much sleep tonight.

HER ARM THROBBED from where the bandit's dagger had struck her. It was just a cut. She'd live. But it burned. Ella tried her best to ignore the pain, pushing it deep to the back of her mind until it was no more than a dull ache. Normally it wouldn't have been a problem. She had suffered enough in her short life to know how to quiet the senses that would otherwise scream in agony. She had silenced them when she was tortured. She had silenced them when she was locked up for days on end, beaten and worse at the hands of the Prowlers that had kidnapped her shortly after her own escape from a compound, years ago.

A cut on her shoulder was so trivial compared to the pain she had to deal with. Anger mixed with the pain made it impossible to concentrate.

Someone within the Outpost had helped those bandits. Someone had betrayed them.

Sentinels usually kept the bandits at bay. With the likelihood of the Sentinels executing them on sight, the bandits typically avoided the Community at all costs. Usually a win-win scenario for the Community. As such, while their presence was heavy, the camp lightened the watch for the evening, standard procedure. Maybe an oversight, but it gave their people a much-needed rest.

Tonight the bandits had thought it worth the risk. Because they knew. They not only knew that their patrols would be light, they knew where the holes would be, they knew their stores were at some of their highest levels in months, and they knew exactly how to distract them so their bounty would be at their lowest level of protection.

The night reeked of betrayal, and if there was anything that cut Ella more deeply than the gash in her arm, it was being sold out by someone she trusted.

So now, it was her mission to find the person—if it was only one—responsible. Malachi trusted her to the task as he knew she'd deal with the matter swiftly and discreetly.

Orange light around the campsite subsided as flames were being doused. Once their people were in action, they were able to see results quickly. Thankfully, clouds had dispersed, allowing the moon to reappear, providing the camp with ample light for the cleanup. Moonlight would have been handy before.

They all worked together to make things happen. It had taken them a long time to get to this point. She shuddered to think that had all fallen apart tonight.

The blue banner of the Community flapped above her in the wind. The gold interlinked circles on the blue background signified them working together. The circles in a straight horizontal line represented each man or woman equal and working together for a bigger cause.

It was what they had worked toward for years. They were finally making progress. She would not allow it to be undone.

The storage building was the largest, most permanent structure within the settlement. Every other structure they had was constructed from canvas. Practical and easy to move. The storage tent was located on the south side, as far into the Silent Zone as their compound extended. Built out of wood that had been gathered from remnants of a time gone past, the shed was painstakingly deconstructed and reconstructed every time the settlement moved. Only the roof was made of canvas. Its more rigid structure was meant to protect its contents from the elements, as well as a bit of extra fortification if attackers or thieves did manage to slip past the defenses.

They were scheduled to make a delivery to the city within the next day or so. The shed had been close to or at full capacity tonight with various vegetables, game, and other supplies that would be caravanned to the city for sale or trade. The bandits knew exactly when an attack could turn out to be most profitable.

As Ella approached the shed, the activity around it became much more apparent. The bandits hadn't made it too far with the goods, but they had sure made a mess. Crates of potatoes and carrots were strewn across the sand. Chances were they would be tripping over stray veggies until the Outpost moved again.

She spotted Ed and Oscar lifting a large piece of wrapped dried sheep meat onto a cart and made her way over to them.

"How's the cleanup, boys?"

The two were some of the best recruits they had seen since she had joined. Eager to help out wherever they could. She had seen how life had jaded or corrupted most. Living a lifetime of scrambling to feed yourself often left a person a self-centered mess. Not to any real fault of their own. It was hard to focus on anyone but yourself when you didn't know how you were getting your next meal. There was always someone looking to kill you or worse, be it a Guardian, bandit, member of the Order or just someone more desperate than you. But these two had found each other before the team picked them up. They had already learned that working together often yielded results far better than working alone. They were now more than willing to work for the greater good. As two of Malachi's most trusted men, they'd offer a good starting point if anything seemed out of the ordinary.

"Things are moving right along." Ed smiled as Ella walked up.

He'd do better if he'd lose the suave attitude, though.

"Any word on how they knew when and where exactly to hit us?"

Oscar piped up. "It seems like a stroke of bad luck."

"You know I don't believe in luck, Oscar," she replied. "I believe in hard work and a strong will, but luck left us centuries ago."

Oscar's green eyes reflected the moonlight. He looked startled, which was rare for him. He was usually the silent type, but he was rarely squeamish. She'd consider him attractive if he spoke up for himself a little more. He was always willing to help, but whoever had beat the crap out of this kid had left him a heart of stone and the confidence of a wounded sheep. He wasn't muscular, like Ed, either. He wasn't out of shape, but you could tell food had avoided him for most of his life.

"Well," he replied, "I don't see how they could have had any idea of our schedules."

"Even still. Let me know if you uncover anything out of the ordinary. Malachi's pissed, and I don't blame him."

Both men nodded. Ella didn't have to explain to them the stakes if someone was assisting the bandits from the inside. Six compounds had formed a few years ago, plus a community of thousands more within the nearby city of Vegas had banded together to help each other out. It was a city the ancients had built. After the wars it had crumbled to a distant shadow of its former self.

Tired of facing the oppression within the Silent Zone, tired of dodging bots on their own, and wanting to live honestly, the Community was formed, mostly under the guidance of Malachi, to offer them a chance to work together and survive. Bandits and crooks had ruled over the city with fear and greed for centuries.

Their group now lived in a spirit of cooperation and provided numbers against threats such as bandits and the Guardian Order. Their efforts had rebuilt some semblance of what humanity used to be and had given them the hope to carry on. Insiders helping bandits was unheard of. Often they came in alone or in pairs, just looking to make a quick profit off the sale of stolen goods. But this had been more organized. They were after a mass of goods, but they were looking for something else as well. The tents had been systematically searched and then burned. Like they were looking for something, or someone. A few dozen bandits working together in a coordinated effort. Treachery on the inside could undermine so much of what they had worked for.

"Don't talk to anyone else about this either," Ella said. "Come straight to me if you hear of anything out of the ordinary." She cringed as she recalled Malachi had asked the same of her. But these were two of her only friends in the Outpost. If she couldn't trust the two of them, it was just her and Malachi.

It dawned on her that someone was missing. Someone who was normally with these two. It was odd for them to not be together.

"Where's Rhys?"

14

———————

IT WAS late by the time she got back to the tent, and Sierra could barely keep her eyes open. All she wanted to do was sleep, but standing in front of the tent's entrance was a young man with his arms crossed.

The only lights that still lit the camp were torches spaced evenly between the tents, allowing those who were keeping watch to see who was moving about as the hour grew late.

It wasn't until she was almost on top of him that she realized it was Rhys.

Sierra couldn't tell how old Rhys was. Like Ed and Oscar, he was likely about her age, but also like them, he held himself more confidently than any seventeen- or eighteen-year-old she knew. It was possible he was a year or two older, but he must have aged like an Order member if he was any older than that.

His scowl hadn't changed from earlier that day. She wondered what she could possibly have done to rub this guy the wrong way.

The torchlight behind him silhouetted his frame. He was more of a medium build. Muscular, but not as bulky as Ed. Lean, but not scraggly like Oscar. His eyes caught the light of the surrounding flame, bringing both a fire to his gaze and shadow to his chiseled features.

Before Sierra could get close enough to greet him, he yelled out to her. "What kind of Order magic are you bringing here?" he growled.

"Good evening to you too," she remarked snidely. "Look, I don't know what I've done to offend you, but I think—"

"Listen," he interrupted. "Nothing good comes from the Sphere. In bed with the Guardians. You think we'll believe it's a coincidence we're attacked the same night you arrive?"

Sierra was flabbergasted, not knowing how to begin to respond.

"You may have fooled Malachi with your little stunt," he continued. "But your display of Order magic doesn't fool me. Why are you really here?"

She was barely able to grasp the accusations being thrown at her. The questions she had came to her in a flurry. How did Rhys know she was from the Sphere? They had been careful not to reveal it to anyone. Order magic? The closest thing to magic Claudia and her Order had were glowing emblems on their robes and staffs. What else had come from the Sphere?

"Now listen here!" she started, putting a finger up to her accuser's face. She didn't know what exactly she was going to continue with without giving away that they were, in fact, traveling from the Sphere, but he cut her off again before she could continue, raising a hand to her finger.

"Where did you get this?" he asked, looking down to her chest. His demeanor melted. No longer on the attack, he looked baffled. He grabbed the sunset medallion that hung from her neck and held it up to the light for a better look, nearly pulling Sierra along in the process.

She grabbed it away from him.

"Hey! Watch it! What's it to you?"

"Do you understand what this is?"

"Listen, I don't owe you an explanation about anything. You've been nothing but rude ever since we arrived."

He took a step back and inhaled sharply. For a moment she worried he was going to attack her, but he deflated and turned his back to her instead.

He took two more deep breaths before turning around to face her.

"You are right," he started. His eyes had changed. The fury gone, replaced by a different kind of intensity. One that made her heart skip a beat. Like he was searching her soul.

"Maybe I haven't put my best foot forward," he said, almost more to himself than to her. "That symbol is one of great importance, I think more than you realize. Maybe more than I'm willing to admit. But until you give me reason to believe you aren't a threat to our Community, I'll have my eye on you." He turned again and walked off into the night.

Sierra shook her head at the encounter. The world she had stumbled into was a strange one indeed. Something about the way Rhys looked at her made her uneasy. Like he knew something about her that she didn't. There were too many people around her acting like they knew her better than she did herself.

She stared at the medallion as she held it up to the torchlight, taking a fresh look at the token. What had Greata been involved with? What was the importance of the symbol?

To be safe, she tucked the medallion into her shirt. There was no need to draw more attention than she had already received.

As Sierra entered the tent, Wil lay with his back toward her and her bed, so she slipped off her clothes and under her bedsheet. Even in the cooler evening, the heat was still present. No use being shy only to lose sleep over being too warm.

"Did you get it to fire again?" Wil asked, still facing away from her.

"I did," she replied. "I guess that's a big deal. Things aren't supposed to work here."

"I overheard Oscar and Ed talking. There's talk that they may want to keep you around. You could be useful to them."

Sierra didn't think Wil could see her in the darkness, but she shook her head anyway.

"It doesn't seem Rhys feels the same way," she replied. "And besides, I'm not interested in staying. I need to find Terre." She also had to figure out what was behind her vision, and what it was Greata had sacrificed herself for. The weapon firing was an interesting accident, but she wouldn't let it distract her from fulfilling Greata's last request. There had been an unspoken plea in her words, business she had left unfinished. She owed it to Greata to continue this path. She knew, or at least hoped, that at the end of this road there would be answers.

The ceiling of the tent stared back at her, thick enough to block out the majority of the moonlight, but a light glow was still present. It still astonished her how bright the moon was.

"Wil," she continued, "I haven't had a chance to ask you. What's your plan? You're more than welcome to come with me, but I know it's not your burden."

Wil was silent for several seconds before responding. "You're not the only one who's left everything behind. If you think this man will have some answers for us, I'll tag along. I need some answers of my own. If there's something that can be done on this side of the Sphere that can make things right, I don't want more people getting hurt."

The two lay in silence for quite some time, and Sierra's mind wandered. Everything that had happened to her over the past two days had been like a very long dream. A series of events, one after the other, that she could never have even imagined only two days ago.

Greata, her friend, was dead. Her only other friend, Ember, left behind. Who knew if she had truly been a friend, or if her Keeper's companionship had been a lie as well. And the Guardians, the beings who had claimed to have saved humanity, were killing off those people, for what she could only imagine was discovering the truth.

A day of traveling through what was supposed to be poisonous wasteland, and now she was in this desert campsite with strangers who claimed to be looking out for her best interests on one hand but accused her of malicious intent on the other.

Sierra thought of her exchange with Malachi. Surely there was something else at play with her interaction with the weapon. Power being drawn from her to make the weapon work? Maybe. It was just as likely there was a glitch with the weapon, or perhaps this Silent Zone wasn't as dead as was believed. That the weapon was being powered from within her seemed a bit farfetched.

The sound of footsteps outside indicated the patrols were still roaming the campsite. How had she ended up among all this? And how much could she trust those she had landed among?

SIERRA HAD JUST CLOSED her eyes when a bright light invaded her senses. The light shifted suddenly, and she couldn't help but look. As the world flooded in, she was forced to take a moment to adjust. Somehow, she was standing. Ground solid beneath her feet. She swore she was just lying in a bed.

Then she knew. This again. Another vision. But this was different than the last time. She was standing in the same spot as before. The same buildings towered above her. The wide road stretched out, and the sidewalks appeared to continue infinitely. However, unlike last time, there was near silence. A mild hum and rumble came from somewhere in the distance. The buzz and high volume of noise from before was gone. The lights on the buildings were gone. Blank screens replaced them. The people, the vehicles were gone. The streets stretched out empty, devoid of anything living.

As she took a deep breath, she realized the stench was still there. If this place had been vacated, it hadn't happened that long ago.

The sun was still strong and warm overhead. Sierra looked up past the buildings beside her and jumped as she spotted Onyx flying in the distance, headed in her direction. Dozens, if not hundreds of them. Endless lines of black dots heading toward the city. The sun's reflection bounced off their black, glassy spheres. The same dark spheres that had attacked Greata and had turned her life upside down. They were only small dots in the distance, but she could never mistake those ugly black balls for anything else.

The ground rumbled. She thought it was an earthquake, but as she looked down the street, she saw several immense machines rolling her way. Massive weapons mounted to the front of them. Tanks. She remembered learning about them. A weapon the ancients used during the wars.

"What the hell are you still doing here?"

She turned around and froze. A man who looked to be in his early thirties stood in front of her. Aside from the khaki green outfit, the man was decked head to toe in technology and equipment. Most of it she didn't recognize. But he held on to a weapon, similar to what she had fired in the Outpost. His dark chiseled features struck a chord of familiarity with her, but she couldn't place it.

She had been a specter in her last vision, someone who could see but hadn't been seen. At least, she didn't think anyone had seen her among the crowd of thousands. Now this man, the only one around, was questioning her presence there. She couldn't even get her bearings together enough to pose any sort of question before the man grabbed her arm and pulled her in toward one of the buildings.

"You should have left when the evacuation sweeps came through. We'll get you underground with the others."

"Why? What's happening?" She might as well play along. Maybe she'd get some answers.

The look on his face told her it was the most ridiculous thing she could have said.

"You have got to be kidding me. Why do you think the power's been cut? Those bots are going to level this place. Well, try anyway, unless we can pull this off."

Sierra couldn't hide the bewilderment on her face.

"We got a good number of them in San Francisco, but these things aren't discouraged easily."

Something on the man's side crackled in a familiar way. He reached down and grabbed it. Sierra's eyes widened as he pulled out a little black box, similar to what Wil had carried.

"Terre here," he said, speaking into the device.

Terre? This couldn't be the same man Greata was talking about.

Then she saw it. A robot pendant hung around his neck. This was the man she had gotten a glimpse of in her first vision. It had happened so fast she thought it had been a daydream, until her second vision transported her to this very street. Now, in this third vision, both were present.

This was the man Greata had told her to find.

The response was muffled to her, but Terre seemed to be able to make it out.

"Yeah, they're just about here, maybe ten minutes. Tell Aarika to get ready to launch."

"I've got a civilian here. I'm going to bring her underground and then I'll give you the signal. If you don't hear from me in fifteen, hit the switch. Tell Kristopher this better work. I don't want to have to live through a repeat of San Francisco. There's no way we're going to be able to hold this many off for any amount of time."

As they had been talking, the background rumble had been getting louder, until now the earth was quaking beneath her. The tanks were right beside them.

"Why were they bringing in tanks?"

"They're supposed to be backup in case Plan A falls through," Terre answered.

"What's Plan A?"

"Listen, we don't have time to play these games. Let's get you underground."

Her arm ached from the grip he had on her.

"I can walk on my own, you know."

"You know I'd love to believe you, but I have my doubts about someone who is conveniently running around outside of containment and claims to know nothing about the biggest evacuation effort ever undertaken."

They entered a door on the side of one of the buildings. Terre let go of her arm as they entered a long hallway. The path before her was dimly lit with blue strips barely emitting enough light for her to make out where they were going.

"I'll need to put you into the containment area. It's been sealed off so that people like you don't wander out."

She nodded as if she understood anything of what he just said.

"So, I'll be trapped down there?"

"Only until the threat's gone. Once the E-bomb's dropped, the power will be cut to the locks and you'll be able to get out. In case you're not making things up, and never heard the instructions, wait until someone comes to get you. If nobody comes within a week, you're on your own. Just be careful. We may not take down the entire fleet of those drones."

The air was heavy within the narrow hall. She felt like she was getting to the end of the answers that playing along was going to get her, and she was even more confused than before. She couldn't pretend anymore.

"I have one question," she said, "and I know this is probably going to sound crazy, but please just let me know."

"Okay, go for it."

"Where are we?"

Terre opened the door they had stopped at, and Sierra got a brief glimpse inside. The smell of sweat, body odor, and fear hit her before she saw the terrified humans huddled in the room. Hundreds—if not thousands—of them eyed the open door.

A man's voice echoed in the distance, in a monotonous instructional rhythm.

She looked back to Terre, mouth open. She never got an answer to her question.

LIGHTS AND SCREENS lit up a different room before Sierra. She turned around, back to where the door had been moments earlier. Men and women hurried among smooth glass control panels that reminded her of the Guardians and their technology.

The dozen people around her paid no attention to the young girl's presence. As if they saw right through her. The air in this room was stale, but cool, like a winter's evening in the desert.

Two men entered from a doorway on the far end of the room. She recognized the tall young man who walked in with the uniformed older gentleman. It was Terre.

The room was spinning slightly. She fought not to pass out. Instinctively, she grabbed for a metal rail and was grateful to discover it was solid. Her eyes followed the rail around the large circular room. The outside edge of the rail, on which she stood, was raised above the floor in the room's center. It ran the length of the platform, the outer wall of which contained multiple screens, displaying what appeared to be images of dozens of other locations. On some of the screens she could make out swarms of Sentinel robots filling city streets. On others, orbs floated in the sky above buildings even taller than those she had seen moments ago. Most of the locations seemed devoid of human life, though the same tanklike vehicles rolled along in a few of the feeds.

"We're being told to hold for orders, sir," a figure in the center of the room said to the pair that had just entered. "We've got eighty-three bases ready for the push. Two are offline."

Sierra for the first time noticed the large glass bulb in the center of the room among a glass control panel. The spheroid shape made her think of a Guardian orb. Inside the dome was a display of either a map or landscape—she couldn't tell which from her vantage point. Either way, several individuals were staring at it intently, pushing on the screen in front of them.

Terre took a studious look around the room. His eyes glanced over to where Sierra was standing but didn't pause. "What's the story here?"

"We've set up these strategic EMP pulse stations in locations around the country. They'll knock out the bastards. We'll get those we missed on the drop. We'll also hit their regeneration sites and release the civilian camps. After that, we should be able to move in and finally end this nightmare."

"Are we going to be able to do that? How long will these sites be without power?"

"They're G3 EMPs. It'll be hundreds of years. But we'll rebuild. We'll find a way. Half of our large centers are already offline from the E-bomb campaigns, but we can't do a damn thing until the majority of these AIs and their regeneration units are taken care of. This will do the trick. They won't be able to rebuild."

"Are we sure the threat from overseas has been neutralized? Are we setting ourselves up to become sitting ducks?"

"All of our intelligence indicates everything on the west side of the Pacific has been eradicated. The Chinese EMPed their whole goddamn country. They've sent themselves back five hundred years. We're hoping we can be a bit more strategic so that we have a chance to at least partially recover."

"Damn. All NextGen 3 blasts?"

The other man nodded.

"They won't have any tech capabilities for hundreds of years..."

"They've got bigger problems than that. How do you feed two billion people without transportation, refrigeration, and no economy? They're in for days far darker than what we've seen, and hopefully ever will."

"Sirs, we have a situation."

All screens had changed to the same images. Guardian Orbs floated above nondescript buildings. To Sierra, the buildings didn't appear to be anything significant, but jaws around the room were nearly on the floor.

"How did they find our facilities?" the commander asked.

"No way to be sure, sir."

"Don't just sit there. Send word! Launch now!"

"Sir, only the president..."

"I don't care. Do it!"

"Yes, sir."

Before there was time for him to do anything, everything went dark. No not dark, black. Sierra lifted her hand in front of her face. Nothing. She couldn't remember ever being somewhere so dark, even with her eyes closed.

Out of the darkness came the commander's voice. "Please tell me that was us."

"Sorry, sir."

"How many stations did they get?"

"With the power out there's no way for us to tell."

Silence lay heavy in the room for several long seconds.

"Folks, that was our last option. If you have any sort of faith, I'd suggest now is the time to start praying."

Sierra blinked and there was light. The moon's glow seeped in from the canvas above her, once again in her bed. The evening air was hot and muggy compared to the cool room she had just been in. She sat up, trying to orient herself.

Muffled voices came through the canvas walls. The bed opposite of hers was vacant. Wil must have gone out for some fresh air.

Once again, she wondered if her body had been in the tent the whole time. The other times she had these visions nobody could see her. This time was different. At least for the first part. Terre had physically interacted with her. Had that really been the same man Greata wanted her to find?

And what had those men been talking about? What was their last option?

15

THE SCREEN *in front of Wil was blank. He couldn't shake what had happened that morning. It was now the end of the day, and even though he was supposed to be writing an exam, his mind kept going over it. He knew he couldn't have done anything to make that droid fall from the sky. So why did he feel like he had? Moments before it fell, he had felt an intense heat building up in him. That had to have had something to do with the Guardian's sudden fall.*

"Time's up," Claudia chimed.

Wil looked down at the projection on his desk in horror. He had been called out by the Master earlier, and his concentration hadn't improved since. The test stared back at him for a moment before it blinked off, and he was looking at an empty desk. He hadn't filled in a single answer.

He stood up and nearly pushed his way past his classmates to get out of the room. He needed to get out before he could be questioned about the empty assignment.

Chances were he would be able to explain to his parents that he wasn't feeling well, and he'd be able to retake the exam. But he didn't want to have to answer for it now. Though he might not have to pretend to throw up if he was asked too many questions.

He settled into a quick walk. His parents would want to know what happened.

"Wil!" Marco's voice called out behind him.

He tried to ignore his friend as he quickened his pace. He may have been overthinking what happened, but Marco seemed to be not taking this seriously at all. Then again, when did Marco ever take anything seriously? Wil was often labeled as a troublemaker, but more often than not, it was Marco getting them into situations. Though Wil was never one to argue.

Marco must have been running to catch up because he was suddenly beside Wil breathing heavy.

"You've never been good at keeping a secret." He was panting, but obviously pleased with himself.

"And you've never been good at running." He was half tempted to bolt the rest of the way to his house to prove the point.

"Come on. We've been in trouble before. I haven't seen you this worked up since that time we sent a crack through the holo-projector in the atrium."

"Yeah, do you remember the trouble our families got in over that? My dad had to work an extra shift to make up for it. Can you imagine what taking out a Guardian's going to be worth?"

Marco cast a wide-eyed look over his shoulder. Good, at least he was somewhat worried about this.

"Keep your bloody voice down!" Marco scolded. "Even if you think it was your fault, you don't need to broadcast it to everyone. It's bad enough you caught everyone's attention bursting out of the exam room."

Marco was probably right. He had a hard time thinking on the fly, especially when he thought he was going to get caught.

"You're right. I have just had a really bad feeling about this all day. I didn't fill in a single answer on the exam. You saw the way I was sweating earlier. I thought I was actually going to burst into flames . . . Something's wrong, and I can't get my mind off it."

"Come on. We need a break. Class is out for a few weeks now. Let's head home, get our gear ready, and head out tomorrow. We'll

explore the mountains a bit, get your mind off this. It will all work out."

He didn't feel like hiking, but it was maybe just the thing he needed.

"All right," Wil agreed, not sure he had any better options. "I hope you're right. But I suppose it's all we can do for now. Let's grab some supplies. I don't want to wait until tomorrow. I need to clear my head. We can make a trip out this evening before curfew."

"Plan." Marco grinned. "Maybe we'll even find another one of those devices."

"Don't push it." Wil would have glowered if not for the goofy look on his friend's face. He wouldn't let his friend get the rise out of him he was seeking.

They had a bit farther to go to get to Marco's home, but it wasn't too far. From there it was an hour or so to get to the edge of the mountains and onto a route that was decent to hike. They typically set up a basecamp at the foot of the mountains.

Marco's brow furrowed as a thought came to him. "Do you think it was the device that did something to that Guardian?"

The change in subject made Wil stop in his tracks. It wasn't something he had considered but would make sense. The warm feeling, the Guardian dropping to the ground—dead for all he knew—neither had happened until they started messing around with that thing.

Humanity had come to the brink of destroying itself with dangerous weapons. Would they have developed something that would have destroyed Guardians as well? Maybe that was why it was a forbidden object. If that was the case, what were the voices coming through it?

As he was mulling it over, three large Onyx spheres flew almost directly above them in a wide "V" pattern, following their own path through the Village. Their blue lights pulsed on their otherwise black, glasslike surfaces. They crawled overhead, scanning for something, or someone. Wil suspected he knew the motive of their search. Marco gave him a look that indicated he had the same thought.

The streets weren't empty, but as the last trickle of students was making their way indoors, foot traffic noticeably slowed. An overall sense of caution was now apparent, where before, Wil hadn't noticed as he was engrossed in his own thoughts.

A game of hopscotch was broken up as parents hurried their children indoors, with one eye following the haunted figures in the sky. Marco grabbed Wil's arm, stopping them both in their tracks. The Onyx had stopped moving only a couple of blocks away. They both knew whose house the Onyx were hovering over.

"Marco! No!"

But it was too late. Marco left in a sprint toward his home. Wil cursed under his breath and raced after him.

Ignoring the glances of the few children who still lingered in the square, he pushed to keep up to his friend, but struggled.

He arrived at a corner where he could peer down the street with a clear view of the home. Marco was nearly there. Blue patterns of light marked the surface of the Guardians' bodies. Lines that appeared to turn as if completing a maze on top of their glasslike surfaces. Scanning.

He held back, as Marco bolted the last half block. This was complete madness. After all of his talk of letting this play through, it turned out Marco was the impulsive one.

Marco approached his doorstep, hands waving in the air.

"It was me!" he shouted. "Leave them alone! I did it!" He bent over, picked up a rock, and hurled it at the orb closest to him. It fell short but was successful in turning their attention.

Wil's jaw dropped. "That bloody idiot!" he muttered to himself. Of all of the things he had imagined Marco doing in that moment, that was not one of them. The lights surrounding the Onyx flared up and filled the entire Sphere with blue lines. A pattern emerged that covered the three spheres. A beam of intense light fired out from the center sphere toward Marco.

The beam of light hit him, and Wil watched as a hole was burned right through the middle of his friend. He collapsed in the street, dead. Wil blinked, not believing what he was seeing.

"Threat neutralized." The hum of the Onyx grew louder as they took off and were gone.

RESTLESSNESS PREVENTED WIL FROM SLEEPING. His head was pounding, and images of Marco's death plagued his thoughts.

He could barely make out the full moon through the canvas of the tent above him. Enough that it gave the tent a subtle glow.

Anger was going to eat him alive. Anger at Marco for running into the street and getting himself killed. What did his friend think was going to happen? But, then again, how could he have known? Never in their entire lives had he heard of the Guardians killing anyone. Had Marco known? Was he trying to protect him? Why?

Anger at the Guardians. It was drilled into them from birth that they were there to keep people safe. That they were keeping them in the Sphere for their protection. The world outside was certain death. Well, here he was outside of the Sphere, with a group of people who had lived just fine without the Guardians for how long? How long had they been keeping people imprisoned? And why? Did anyone else in the Sphere know? Sierra's friend Greata seemed to. Greata was seen as a little eccentric. But if she knew, who else knew the truth? And why did they go along with it? These "robots" who were not the revered beings they were led to believe. He'd seen at least two die. Guardians weren't supposed to be mortal.

Anger at Sierra. He knew it was unfair. But he couldn't help it. She had gotten to say goodbye to her friend. She had dragged him out here and seemed mostly unaffected by it all. She was strong and holding her own, while he had been stuck in bed crumbling under the weight of not being able to cope with too much time in the sun. On top of that, he had tripped over his own feet trying to fire a weapon that wasn't going to work anyway. Until Sierra picked it up. Never mind that he vomited at the smell of blood and death trying to help Malachi move the wounded, while Sierra was helping to stitch up wounds in the infirmary.

He understood Sierra's reasoning for not revealing that they came from within the Sphere. They didn't know these people, didn't know how they'd react. It made sense not to introduce too many unknown variables into an already unknown situation. He didn't get the sense that they meant him and Sierra any harm. But after being lied to their entire lives, well, who knew who they could trust? He wasn't even completely sure if he trusted Sierra. Though she was the one familiar in this new world of the unknown. She had almost abandoned him to go after her Keeper, Ember. Her intentions may have been noble, but her attachment to the bot could have got them both killed. She said she'd have his back though, and he believed her, but at some point, he knew he was going to have to fend for himself. Fury burned within him, and there was a debt only he would be able to pay.

Despite their secrecy, he got the sense that Malachi knew where he and Sierra were from. It didn't sound like there was much else in the direction they wandered in from. Wil also saw the pity in his eyes when he talked to them. Like they were wounded animals needing help. Ella had the same look on her face.

Well, maybe they were. What did he know? They were totally unprepared for whatever they were going to face out here. Tonight had proved that.

He turned over to face Sierra's side of the room. Her bed was empty.

That was odd. Maybe he had drifted off to sleep at some point. He definitely hadn't heard her leave. Perhaps she hadn't been able to sleep either and had gone off to help. The bustling outside had quieted down.

Deciding it wasn't worth chasing a sleep that wouldn't come, he decided it may be worthwhile exploring. He got dressed and left the tent.

The moon provided ample light to see the campsite, though the torches cast long shadows among the tents. It appeared that the patrols had lightened somewhat from when he went to bed, but they were still on high alert. He wouldn't be surprised if there were more hidden out of sight. These folks weren't going to take any unnecessary chances anytime soon.

Grunts and moans were coming from within the Commons tent as he passed. Wil poked his head inside to make sure everything was okay. Ella was sitting at the medic station. Her shoulder was exposed, and she was attempting to stitch up a giant gash cut across it. She was struggling with the single-handed effort, dropping the needle more than once in the handful of seconds it took Wil to reach her.

"Would you like a hand with that?" he asked. He grabbed a cloth out the basin and started dabbing some of the excess blood that was leaking out of the wound. She had successfully tied a tourniquet above the gash to slow the bleeding, but it hadn't stopped altogether.

"Thanks," she said, her brown eyes studying him, with a mix of gratitude and curiosity. "I was so busy after the attack. . . I didn't realize how bad it was. I've been ignoring it this whole evening thinking it was a scratch. I think I lost more blood than I realized."

She wasn't kidding. He noticed the shirt she had been wearing on the floor beside her, soaked in blood. How she hadn't been aware of it was a mystery to him. Maybe the gash had severed a nerve. He wasn't a medic. What did he know?

"I'm feeling a bit weak," she confessed. "I'm having trouble keeping the needle stable."

"Are you in a lot of pain?"

She shook her head. "I've learned to handle pain. Don't worry about that. But I could use an extra pair of hands."

He sat down next to her and took a deep breath, taking the needle from her. He followed along the path she had already laid out. She used her free hand to keep the wound as closed as possible for him.

His hand trembled slightly as he ran the needle across the wound. Her skin was softer than he expected. Ella gave him the impression that she had lived a tough life, and that the touch of her arm didn't match her strong demeanor threw him off a bit. He looked up to see her brown eyes smiling at his.

"You seem to have a knack for this. Have you ever had to sew up someone's arm before?" Her smile was coy. Was she making fun of him? He couldn't tell.

He shook his head. "I used to help my mom patch up desert robes. We all had to learn some sort of stitching growing up. It comes in handy if I tear something hiking."

"How about Sierra? She doesn't sew your robes for you?"

He nearly laughed out loud. "Sierra? We barely know each other."

"Oh? If she's not your girlfriend, what are you two doing in the desert alone?"

He cleared his throat at the bold question. He and Sierra had agreed not to share too much until they knew these folks better. Though he supposed the details of their relationship to each other wouldn't reveal anything incriminating.

"You seem quite interested in our relationship," he said with a smirk.

"It's just when two people are traveling together, there's usually a reason for it."

"It's not like that at all."

He sensed her pulse quicken. Was she nervous? She was holding something back from him.

"We've helped each other out of a quick spot. We've both lost something recently. Lost people who have meant a lot to us. Lost a part of who we are, I think."

Her eyes showed sympathy, but she didn't push him any further, for which he was grateful. He worried if he gave too much information already, but he couldn't see how.

Once he was done with her wound, he cleaned the excess blood from her arm as best he could. He then took a piece of cloth from a medical tray, left out by those who were taking care of the wounded earlier that evening. He wrapped it up and finished by cutting off the tourniquet and disposing of it.

"There you are. Next time don't wait so long to get it looked after. You're looking a bit pale."

She nodded and rested her hand on his shoulder. "Thank you."

He couldn't help but notice she was resting a good amount of her weight on him.

"What are you doing up anyway? You should be resting," she said to him as her eyes drooped. She was falling asleep sitting up.

"You're one to talk!" He laughed. "Would you rather I had not been here to help?" he asked, flashing a sly smile.

"Not at all. I'm glad. I'm glad you're here. It definitely wouldn't have been as clean of a job if I had been able to finish myself. And who knows how long it would have taken me." She paused. "The company has been nice as well."

"But you are right," he said. "I should try to get some sleep. The trip here really did a number on me. The sun isn't so strong where I'm from. You should get some rest as well. You'll need it after losing so much blood."

She smiled and placed her good arm on his shoulder and pushed herself up. She nearly fell right back over, but Wil reflexively grabbed her waist, keeping her from doubling over. He was very aware of her body pushing up against him. He looked at her brown eyes smiling at him and gave a small, nervous laugh.

What was he doing? Marco's face flashed in his mind. He felt a tinge of guilt as she wrapped her arms around his shoulders for support.

"You can barely stand. Let me help you to your tent," he said.

She didn't argue. He stood up and was surprised to realize she was barely as tall as his shoulder. He was basically supporting all of her weight, but he led her out of the tent, and she pointed out the tent immediately next to the Commons was hers. A few quick steps and he had her home.

"Thank you again," she said. "I don't think I'm all that tired. Did you want to come in for a bit?" Intent flashed in her eyes.

Wil almost laughed. She could barely keep herself upright. Were all women on the Outside this forward?

"I . . . I think it would be best if you got some rest," he answered.

Though it only lasted a few moments, the silence of the evening couldn't have been louder. "Oh." The disappointment on her face was crushing.

"Please don't take this the wrong way, Ella . . ."

"No, it's too soon. I get it. Good night, Wil." She turned and disappeared into her tent.

Wil was left staring at the entryway, pondering if he could have handled that any differently. He didn't think he could have.

16

EARLY THE NEXT morning Sierra found herself in the Commons. She sat in an isolated corner with Wil, Ella, and Malachi. Their blank stares were all she needed to let her know that they believed she had lost her mind. Well, maybe she had.

She took a deep, stabilizing breath. "I needed to tell someone, and I hope I can trust all of you." In reality she didn't know about trust, but had told them anyway, in hopes that they would have some answers. She and Wil were going to need to trust someone at some point. Malachi had rescued them, given them a place to stay, and then saved their lives again. If she wasn't going to trust him at this point, there would probably be nobody she could. He was still an enigma, but she hoped her gut was right about him. She needed a guide, a friend, in this strange new world.

All of their faces, save for Malachi's, conveyed a mixture of shock and confusion. Wil's especially. She knew he was still coming to grips with them being outside of the Sphere, and this reveal of what she had been going through over the last few days would just add to that. But if she was going to ask him to carry on with her, it was only fair that he knew at least part of what she had experienced.

She bit her lip as the pressure of the reveal weighed on her. Wil could have told the Guardians what she was after. Could have been the one to turn her in. But she reminded herself the moment he fired upon the Guardians he became as implicated as she was. She still didn't know his full story. His friend had died, but why? What part did Wil play in all of this? It was time for one of them to put it all out there. There was no going back for her now.

"Sierra, are you sure this wasn't just a dream?" Wil asked. "The Onyx killed Greata. Maybe your mind is processing what happened." The mention of Onyx got a wide-eyed glance from Malachi. "You're still dealing with everything that's happened over the past few days. We've been through a lot."

"I am as sure that I was there as I am that I'm here." She tried to hold back the grit that came with her answer. He was right. She had been through a lot. "It was more than just a dream."

"You continue to be full of surprises," Malachi said, though his face betrayed no emotion whatsoever. "And you *can* trust us. I give you my word on that, for whatever that's worth. That being said, keep these visions, this mission, between the four of us for now. It's a dangerous tale if it crosses the wrong ears. Despite best intentions, not everyone will be as understanding."

"You believe it was more than just a dream?"

"I don't know what to think. But I've seen enough to know that just because something seems unlikely, doesn't mean it isn't true." Sierra noticed him exchange a look with Ella. "You've described well enough to me things I don't think you could possibly know. And others that have been nothing more than legend or myth for decades. I've known you for less than twenty-four hours, and I've seen enough to know there's something special about you."

"Dangerous how?" Wil asked.

"Before I answer that, I'm going to need you two to tell us the truth. The truth of what's brought you here and how you got out of that compound."

"You know we were in the Sphere," Sierra stated. Her eyes narrowed slightly, though at this point she wasn't incredibly surprised.

"Listen, kid, we don't find too many that make it outside of one of the compounds alive. There have only been a handful that don't get caught, reintroduced, and reeducated, or terminated. The ones that don't usually won't survive the bandits, the Order, or they just plain die of hunger or dehydration before they are found. As you saw, there's a lot of empty desert to travel in order to get to civilization. If Guardians find them before they die, they are brought to another facility. If you meet one of the lucky ones, you know the look." He paused. "The clothes kind of give it away as well," he finished with a smirk, as if he told a joke only he understood. Though she caught a quick grin from Ella as well.

"Wait, what?" Wil jumped in again. "Other facility? There's more than one?"

Malachi shot him a glance. "Hundreds."

Sierra could tell Wil was having a hard time with all of this. The look on his face told her his head was spinning. Though she wasn't sure that her grip on reality was as rock solid as it could be either.

She decided she needed to take control of the narrative. It was time to lay it all on the table. "We escaped through a crack in the force field. Wil and I crossed paths at the right moment. With everything that's happened in the last day we haven't even had a chance to share with each other everything that set us on this course. But both of us witnessed the Onyx kill our best friends."

Wil stared blankly at her, nodding at certain points, as she went over the events that led up to them meeting with Malachi from her perspective.

"We found one of those radios in the mountains," Wil chimed in, his expression still blank, like he was an empty shell. He reached into his nearby backpack and pulled out the device in question.

"The same device that we used to contact you in the desert. The Guardians killed my friend Marco because we had this. We didn't know what we had found. What it meant." Tears were streaming down his cheeks. His gaze was intense but not fixed on anything in particular. "But now we know. Marco, Greata. Dead because of their secrets, because of the lies the Guardians tell."

The group fell silent as the weight of Wil's words hung in the air.

"We need to find someone who knows where we can find him, the man who remembers the wars. Are you able to help?" She was going to find him, with or without them. But it would be easier to have a guide in this new world.

Malachi nodded. "Gather your things. All of you," he said as he stood up from the table. "We'll head out in a few hours. Ella, get Edgar and Oscar to put some supplies together as well as a crew to haul some of the surviving provisions."

"You know where we can find him?" she asked.

"No." Malachi shook his head. "But I know someone who might. If we're going to go today, we need to head out soon. We'll head into Vegas, a city just south of where we are. Hopefully we'll find some of your answers there. It's a day's journey, and I don't know if you'll be coming back here, so make sure you have everything."

Malachi left the tent.

"I'm . . ." Ella began, her brown eyes as fierce as ever, but also uncertain, like she was weighing what to say. "I'm sorry for all that you've had to go through. I . . . understand how it is to learn what you've been told your whole life is a lie. Life won't be as easy for you out here, as it was in the Sphere. People are hard. But it's real. Malachi has worked with these men and women, and those of the other outposts, and our contacts in the city. We've tried so hard to bring a sort of stability to this life. It's hard when we have so many factors working against us. But I know we have a bright future ahead. Remember that when you miss the comforts of home because those days will come. Remember we're working toward a future where humanity will be free from these robots that have divided us and stolen our souls."

Ella reached out to Wil and cradled his face in her hand. "Don't let them steal yours."

He didn't return her gaze, but a tear fell down his cheek and onto her hand. She ran her fingers through the hair on one side before turning and following Malachi's path out of the tent.

The two got up as well and made their way back to their own tent.

"We don't have any stuff," Sierra said, laughing, once they were alone. "I don't know what we're supposed to gather."

Wil smiled. It was faint, but another quick glimpse of his old self. It faded quickly.

"She's attracted to me," Wil said distantly as they stepped inside the tent.

"Seems like it," Sierra replied. "She's pretty."

"She is, but . . ." Wil's hazel eyes met hers. They were filled with tears. He shook his head, mouth moving wordlessly.

And she suddenly understood. His pain, his loss was far deeper than what she had ever imagined hers could have been.

"Marco," she stated, more than she asked. She didn't need an answer, but he nodded anyway. He had been more than just Wil's friend. What that meant wasn't her place to ask, not right now.

"Wil." She moved to embrace him. "I'm so sorry." She let him sob into her shoulder until he was done.

She wasn't sure if minutes passed or hours. But as Wil stepped away from her, eyes now dry, Malachi poked his head into the tent.

"Come on, you two. Time to go."

Wil gave her a thankful smile, picked up his bag, and stepped outside.

THEY MANAGED to leave the camp before the sun had fully broken from the horizon. Wil walked with Sierra, a half step behind Malachi and Ella, who led their small band of travelers. Malachi informed them that their journey would last most of the day, and they would probably not be at their destination until nightfall. The pair had been given desert robes that included head coverings to keep the worst of the sun's rays off them. Despite the woman's prior warning about traveling in the heat, Sierra noticed that Ella had opted to go without the robes. The gentle morning breeze was welcome, but the robes would provide a coolness when the sun started to rise.

Oscar, Ed, and Rhys had been recruited to join them and followed several paces behind. The trio led a small team of men and women, pulling carts filled with provisions from the warehouse. As the supply shed was near capacity anyway, a trip to the city would be expected at this time. The caravan of carts would bring much needed provisions for Community members there.

They spent most of the day in silence and stopped infrequently. There was surprisingly an abundant amount of water to go around, which Sierra was thankful for, but there was no evidence of anywhere that they would have been able to collect more from.

"We'll have enough water to last the journey?" she asked Ella at one point.

"We better." She smiled in jest. "It's only a day. We have plenty. We'll be able to restock once we're in the city."

"Where do you get water in this wasteland?"

"Water is hard to come by, but we have our sources. The bots would have told you the world was uninhabitable, but much of it is lush, green, and full of life. This land has been a desert for thousands of years. This, at least, wasn't the ancients' doing. We likely gain water from the same source as you did in the Sphere. Ancient infrastructure provides us water from Lake Mead to the east. The lake provides us with food as well, though getting it is a bit trickier. The Silent Zone doesn't stretch all of the way to the growing lands. You'll know soon enough the destruction the Guardians and ancients caused when we get to the city."

The setting sun reflected several orbs in the distance to her left. "Will we be protected from them the entire journey?"

"If we're lucky. There are sometimes fluctuations, but we should be out of detection range here. You sure have a lot of questions."

She hadn't even scratched the surface of the questions she held. Answers would come. She had been given more answers already than she had had in her entire lifetime. However, each answer begged even more questions.

Several hours passed before Oscar approached her. She hadn't had a lot of time to get to know him just yet. His quiet demeanor kept him a bit more mysterious than the others. He appeared to be close to Ed, but otherwise hadn't been too interested in chatting. He was thin and lanky, the polar opposite of Ed's bulky frame.

"I hear you had quite the experience with a weapon," he mentioned. He had his hood pulled back so his ponytail gave a little bounce with every step he took.

"You heard about that?"

"Heard about it? The whole outpost has practically talked about nothing since." He smiled, but it wasn't genuine.

"Well, it was just a lucky coincidence," she said, remembering Malachi's warning.

"What was the second time then? Luck as well?"

"I'm not sure what you mean."

"I saw you and Malachi in the practice yard. Kind of hard to miss an arms dummy exploding into a ball of flames."

She wasn't quite sure what to say, how could she deny it if he saw them.

"Oh, that. I really don't know. It's my first time in the Silent Zone . . ."

"Yeah, that much is obvious." She was thrown off a bit by his condescension. "Don't get too comfortable here. It won't be long until you're forced to leave." He paused. "These people aren't your friends."

She almost stopped in her tracks but needed to keep up to the pace of the group. "What are you talking about?"

"You'll see. Just wait." With that, he fell back, joined the rest of the crew guiding the supply carts, and struck up a conversation with one of the lead women. The woman burst into a cackling laugh, as if he had told her the funniest joke.

"What was that about?" Wil leaned in, keeping his voice low.

She almost jumped, forgetting he was only paces away.

"I don't have the slightest idea, Wil . . ."

"How well do you think we can trust these folks? I mean we do barely know them."

"I don't know. Malachi saved us from the Sentinels, and the bandits, they looked after us at the Outpost, and have offered to at least bring us to our next stop. But Rhys and now Oscar have made it clear that not everyone wants us here. I say outside of Malachi and Ella we keep our business to ourselves."

Wil nodded, keeping a sidelong eye on the young men walking the carts.

She sighed. They didn't know these people at all, and now their lives were in their hands.

As the sun edged closer to the horizon, piles of debris began to mark the sides of the road. Sierra could tell much of what used to be standing was now rubble and buried in years' worth of dirt.

Here and there beams of metal or piles of rock betrayed the ancient structures hidden below.

The farther they traveled, the more extensive these piles became, and the more some structures remained intact. Some must have been eight or ten stories high. Possibly some of the more sizeable chunks represented buildings much taller. There was no way to tell.

The sky darkened quickly. The light may have been playing tricks on her, but she was sure she saw the occasional small black creature dart from one object to another in the corner of her eye.

They passed remnants of what clearly used to be homes. Many bleached by the sun. Most missing roofs, doors, windows, and walls.

"Where are all of the people?" Sierra voiced her thought. "So much empty space . . . why does no one live here?"

"The ancients used to live here." Malachi strode with determination, seemingly eager to get past the place. Sierra had noticed his hands fidget around his daggers as they passed. "Their numbers stretched through this part of the city and beyond. We are not nearly so many now. The stories say millions lived here once. I have a hard time believing it possible, even with their wonders of technology. Those who remain are centralized, toward the heart of the city."

"How many live here now?"

"Tens of thousands. It used to be much more."

It wasn't long before the sun's light was gone completely. The moon provided some illumination for the travelers, but it all looked the same to Sierra. A maze of structures and fragments of the past.

They reached what appeared to be the heart of the city. The moon didn't betray as much as Sierra hoped. The street had widened, but it was the same beaten dirt road. The odd person could be seen roaming in the distance, but all stayed far enough away so their features couldn't be seen.

"Lots of Prowlers out tonight," Ella muttered. "Think there's a caravan coming in soon?"

Malachi shook his head. "Food has been scarce for months. It's part of why the bandits were so bold as to attack the Outpost last night. Folk are growing desperate."

As they turned a corner around what seemed like a monstrous building, Sierra stopped in her tracks, causing Ed to stumble into her. She nearly fell over, but regained her balance, and stared in wonder at where she was. The moon provided enough light that she was able to get a sense of the structures that surrounded her. The streets shadowed in near total darkness, save for a few torchlights being carried by people wandering about.

Dirt and sand had overtaken the wide streets, and buildings were in obvious states of disrepair, but she recognized where she was.

This was the city from her vision.

17

———

Wɪʟ ʜᴀᴅɴ'ᴛ ɴᴏᴛɪᴄᴇᴅ that Sierra had stopped behind him. He was lost in his thoughts, as he had been most of the day. Thoughts of Marco and Ella, thoughts of this new land they had set out into. Marco would have loved it. Of all of the adventures the two had talked about over the years, he would have been thrilled at the prospect of being able to leave the Sphere and explore new lands. They had often imagined what life could have been like in the days of the ancients.

Now it was happening, and Marco would never be able to experience it.

And then, there was Ella. The day's journey had been quiet, but there was a certain chill that came from her. Not unfriendly, but definitely more reticent than the night before. He sighed. He wished he was as smooth as Marco had been. He would have handled last night's situation with much more grace.

He almost didn't notice Ella had stopped until she put a hand on his arm. He looked up, and she nodded behind him. Wil turned to see what was happening. Sierra's mouth was agape looking at the city around them. For the first time Wil took a look at their surroundings as well. It was hard to tell with only the moonlight, but what he saw was impressive. Buildings on a far grander scale than any he had ever seen. A massive building stood next to him made of cement and steel. Was this a city of the ancients? Were all cities outside the Sphere this impressive?

"This is it," Sierra said, not really to anyone in particular.

"What is it?" he asked.

"The city from my vision. I was here. But everything is different. These streets weren't dirt. There were lights on these buildings. There was glass covering them. And people. More people than I ever could have imagined."

Wil caught looks of confusion among those hauling the carts as they set their load down. They looked relieved for the rest. It had been a long day of travel. At one point he had offered to take a turn at the load but was refused.

Malachi walked past him toward Sierra. "This is not the time or place to discuss this. Come on. The Inn is just ahead. We need to get these supplies inside."

His abruptness caught Wil off guard, but even as they started moving again, he noticed figures carrying torchlights around them on the street, paying close attention to the band and the carts they were hauling. Oscar and Edgar had moved to the sides of the cart, eyes darting back and forth.

"Are we in danger?" Wil asked. Were there bandits to worry about here as well?

"The streets are always dangerous at night for those unprepared. Hungry people do desperate things if they think they have a chance for a meal. Don't worry. They'll leave us alone if we don't dawdle."

"What are Prowlers?"

"Let's just say food isn't the only thing of value here."

A statue loomed above them. Wil thought it once may have been a lion, but it was hard to tell in the dark, and time had worn the creature down.

They hadn't gone too much farther before Malachi turned

down a flight of stairs leading to a single doorway in the massive building beside them. The stairs and a small walkway beside the building had been dug out of a foot or two of dirt and swept clean, revealing a gray, concrete walkway beneath their feet.

"Oscar, Ed," Malachi barked, breaking the silence that hung over the group. "Lead the carts with the rest of the party around to the side and help the staff unload the provisions. They'll be happy for a little bit of relief. Rhys, Ella, come with us."

Malachi gestured to the others to follow him inside. Above the door hung a well-crafted sign that read "The Rio Grande" with an image of a water scene painted in the corner.

It took a moment for his eyes to adjust, but Wil would have sworn he had just entered a cave. If it weren't for the smooth concrete floors and metal beams throughout the big empty room, it could have been an underground cavern back in the Red Mountains.

Well, kind of. No cave back home was this big. Torchlight surrounding the room marked out how expansive it was. Piles of rubble, old metal scraps, and tables created separators to what must have been another part of the massive building they had entered.

"Malachi! Welcome back!" A grizzled man, who appeared ready for their arrival, took Malachi's hand. "It's always nice to see you, my old friend." Wrinkles and bags marked his face, though his eyes were still young. Wil had the sense this man was much younger than he appeared. A mostly gray beard was marked by streaks of black, hinting that not too long ago the black hairs had outnumbered the white.

"You as well, Leo," Malachi answered with warm familiarity. "How have you been, old man?"

"Ah, it's a hard life, but a good one." The man grinned. He was missing more than a couple of teeth, but his grizzled face was genuine.

"Leo, I know you weren't expecting us, but we are in need of a few rooms. We've brought supplies that could be distributed among some of the Community and your allies."

"You can't keep giving away food for no payment, Malachi. These are hard times, but your men work hard."

"What do I need with chips or metals? We have more food than we need, and with friends like you willing to help us out, we have more than enough. This is what our mission has been all about from the beginning—helping others. Between the bots, bandits, the Order, and one gang after another trying to assert their authority, we're stronger working together."

Still gripping his hand, he pulled Leo close for a one-armed embrace. "Besides," he said, smiling, "if I don't fill your belly, you're going to waste away, old man!"

"Ha! You've been talking to Pria, haven't you? She's always complaining I don't eat enough. I eat plenty, and you and I have it better than most. Of course I have rooms for you and your friends."

For the first time, Wil noticed guards, all burly men, surrounding several exits with large swords strapped to their backs. "How many rooms does this place have?" he asked.

"It used to have hundreds, thousands some say. Far before our time. The years have not been kind though, and we take care of both upkeep and protection for those we claim. Much of what once was has fallen away. There are rooms toward the back that squatters and traders have claimed. Now we have a few dozen that we manage. They are mostly used by the Order when they pass through as well as members of the Resistance."

"Still serving both sides of the fight?" Malachi asked. "One of these days you're going to get caught in a crossfire."

"I still serve you and your crew, and you draw the ire of both groups, as well as N'ara's Prowlers."

Malachi grinned. "Point taken, old friend. I want to have a more private talk with you and your most trusted carrier. One of my friends is searching for someone, and if anyone knows where he is, it's likely to be one of yours."

"Of course. Meet me in the pub in an hour. I'll have Lora show you your rooms."

"An hour will do. It'll give us a chance to clean up. We've been walking through the desert all day, and I'm tired of the way I smell," he said with a grin.

A small woman, more than a foot shorter than Wil, and skinny enough he could have wrapped his hands around her waist, appeared and motioned them to follow. She appeared to be a full-grown woman with the frame of a child. Wil was beginning to wonder if everyone in this city was either small and frail or a large body of muscle—he had yet to see anyone in between. They followed her up a few flights of stairs, darkened with the ash of more than a hundred years of torchlight. The walls also carried the scrapes and markings of a building that had seen a few skirmishes but never the means for proper repair.

They reached the third floor, and Lora led them down a hallway with doors lining the walls. He imagined what Mr. Adare, the innkeeper in the North Village, would have thought to see so many rooms in an inn. He had ten rooms total, and they were almost never full.

Lora didn't walk too far down the hall before stopping. "We have you sharing rooms. We can only spare eight tonight, so you'll have to share."

"That is more than generous," said Malachi. "Thank you for your hospitality."

"These first eight are yours." She provided him with eight keys, gave a shallow bow of her head, and turned back the way she came.

Malachi glanced at Wil. "I hope you two don't mind sharing again."

"No, this is fine," Sierra replied. "Thank you."

Wil couldn't help noticing Rhys roll his eyes as Malachi

handed Sierra the key. It wasn't lost on him that with only eight rooms, some of the Community members would need to put four or five to a room. And Sierra and himself got a room to themselves.

Malachi didn't catch it though and carried on. "Ella and I will be right next door if you need us. Get cleaned up and we'll meet you downstairs at the tavern in an hour."

O̲scar wiped his hands off on his cloak and grabbed his belongings from the cart as Ed and Rhys did the same. They had just finished putting the last of the supplies into the storage shed of the Rio Grande. The rest of the crew would be fine getting the carts put away, and Malachi would likely have other duties for them to perform as they got settled in.

The trio made their way up to the rooms, only having to stop and ask where they were staying once. The Rio Grande had become a common stop, and Leo often put them up in the same rooms.

They walked into the room where Malachi typically stayed and caught him pulling off his shirt, preparing for the evening.

"Finished already?" Malachi asked. After they nodded, he continued. "Edgar, Rhys, you'll come with me and Sierra to the pub to meet with Leo. I want you close by to keep watch. Oscar, you and Ella will stay up here with Wil. Make sure Leo's guards don't miss anything. I trust him, but guards have been known to be loyal to the highest bidder."

"Sierra's joining you?" Oscar asked.

"Yes, she has business we need to discuss with Leo. Is that a problem?"

It was a problem, but it was too late for that now.

"No, I was just curious," he lied. "Why do both Ella and I need to be here just to protect Wil? He seems fairly capable." Another lie. Wil probably couldn't fight his way past a member of the Underground.

"Look, we're not having a party down there." Malachi clamped a hand on Oscar's shoulder. "The three of us will be enough. Stay up here. There will be plenty for you to help out with tomorrow. It's been a long day. Enjoy the rest." Malachi briefly tightened his grip and encouraged him out the door. "Your room is across the hall. Get cleaned up and rest."

Oscar paused and turned to see Ella wiping the last few drops of water off her brow as she came out of the bathroom. The water had stopped working long ago, but the staff of the Inn would have filled up the bathtubs for the rooms they were occupying. Oscar never ceased to be impressed that their rooms always seemed equipped with a full tub. It was rare to still have these baths within the rooms.

As they got to their own room, Rhys went to wash up, leaving Ed and Oscar to chat in the main room.

"I never would have pegged you having a crush on the new girl," Ed said to Oscar, a huge grin on his face.

"Hah!" Oscar responded.

Come to think of it, that was probably a good cover.

"Well, what can I say?" he continued, doing his best to give a sheepish grin.

"I hear ya, my friend," Ed replied. "Though I'm not sure where she's at with that Wil fellow. She gave me a bit of a cold shoulder."

"Well, that's no surprise," Oscar said with a grin. "You probably scared her away. You always come on too strong."

"What's this talk of the new girl?" Rhys asked, returning to the room's main area, suddenly interested in the conversation.

"Old Rhys is too busy hating on Spherians to notice how good looking she is," Ed said, laughing.

Rhys shot Ed a look as he wiped the water droplets from his chest. He tossed his towel at Ed's head.

"Pretty? Pfft," Rhys scoffed. Even Oscar could tell it was feigned. "Don't confuse softness with beauty."

Ed let out a boisterous belly laugh. "You like her too! This is too good!"

"There's no way Rhys is into Sierra," Oscar chimed in. "Have you seen the death glare he's been giving her the whole time she's been here?"

"Oscar's right," Rhys remarked. "She's trouble. The Community will be better off without her or Wil hanging about."

Oscar nodded. Finally, something he could actually agree with.

"Besides, I like a woman who can take care of herself. I don't know why Malachi's coddling her."

"Ella's from a compound too you know," Ed pointed out. "You don't seem to have the same problem with her."

"Ella can hold her own," Rhys said. "She's proven herself."

"Well, if you give these two a chance, they may be loyal to our cause as well."

"If you and Malachi hadn't picked them up, they would have died in the desert. They won't pull their fair share of the weight, and they'll likely take what they need from us and be on their way."

Ed put his hands up, indicating for Rhys to calm down. "Easy now, Rhys. You know the mission of the Community. We work together and offer help to anyone willing to help us out. Those two have chipped in where they've been able. I think you need to give them a chance."

"Sorry, my friend, but they need to earn my trust. I've had too many people stab me in the back. Malachi can do what he wants, but I won't be bending over backward to take care of them."

The three continued their banter while they cleaned up, until it was time for Ed and Rhys to head downstairs.

"I think I'll just call it a night," he said as the others were leaving. "It's been a long day of walking. I wouldn't mind giving my feet a rest."

"Good plan. Don't dirty up all the bath water. I'd like to use some too." Ed laughed again as he left with Rhys right behind him.

Oscar refrained from pushing his ear to the door to ensure they had truly left. Instead, once he was sure they'd be out of the hallway, he grabbed two torches from the side of the room and set them both in the window.

He regretted that Sierra wouldn't be in her room when the Prowlers came, but there was no time to change that now. They could take care of her later. If his suspicions were correct, Wil could prove to be just as valuable, if not more so, and getting rid of one would likely get rid of the other.

18

———

The pub was dimly lit, as was the rest of the building. Torchlight flickered at the edges of the room and warmed the booth where Sierra took a seat with Malachi. It was an old beat-up metal bench that was likely as old as the Inn. Other booths in the room had a mismatch of furniture, suggesting they had been pulled together from scraps over the years. Old decorations, covered with foreign words and phrases, filled the walls. Many faded far beyond being legible.

A smoky haze from the lit torches filled the bar, making the air heavy, and difficult to breathe. She had never seen anything like this place, it was so . . . dirty. Every building in the Sphere was kept clean and pristine. Here, their footprints were still visible in the layer of dust on the floor. Cobwebs hung from ancient fixtures on the walls. Soot from years of torchlight marked the walls black. She suddenly felt like she could use a real bath.

Ed stood off to one side of the table monitoring the room. Rhys was across the room eyeing patrons. More than once she caught each of them staring at her.

Leo walked up with a couple of glasses of beer and handed

one to each of them. Ed declined and moved toward the bar, casually picking a seat and joining Rhys in surveying the room.

"First one's on the house. For an old friend, and a new one." Leo set a glass down in front of each of them and took a seat on the other side of the table.

"Thank you, my friend. You're too kind." Malachi raised his glass and took a sip. "Any updates on the fluctuations?"

"According to some, they're getting worse. The city has been safe thus far. But bots are monitoring the border from here to as far as the protection goes out west. The Interzone between here and San Fran has seen an increase in round-ups and patrols. They know the field is weakening."

"What fluctuations?" Sierra asked.

"The field that the ancients set up was never meant to last forever," Malachi answered. "The Silent Zone has seen patches where the field has failed temporarily. Sometimes permanently."

"That's what you thought was happening when the weapon fired in the Outpost the other night?"

Malachi fired a warning glare at her.

"It's bad enough the bots are catching on to these weak spots, Malachi," said Leo. "Are bandits exploiting this as well? I don't want to have to deal with blaster fire in my inn if it comes down to it."

"No. A misunderstanding," he said, eyes still locked on her. "Besides, eventually the field will fail completely and then blaster fire will be the least of our worries."

"Hopefully long after I'm gone, friend. I've already lived longer than most. We're at the hub of the Silent Zone. The nearest fluctuation is miles away."

"I hope you're right. But don't get complacent. We don't know if the whole damn thing will disappear at once."

"If that happens, we could be heading for dark days indeed. But I'm sure you didn't bring this young lady all this way to talk about this."

Sierra glanced around the pub. Weary travelers looked no cleaner than the room around them. Most of the men in the room were either bearded or hadn't shaved in a few days. Most had long hair. Something that she rarely saw in the North Village. Many of the women looked much more athletic than she was used to seeing as well. Strong backs and shoulders told her they were used to carrying heavy loads. Smiles broke through their tired bodies. Whatever their circumstances, they were happy to have this space to gather and be social.

In stark contrast to most of the drab patrons, a woman with a bright red dress stepped onto a stage with a smile and a man with a stringed instrument behind her. Without any introduction, the woman began to sing, while the man played a slow haunting melody. Everyone's smiles grew and cheers broke out from several in the crowd.

Sierra turned her attention back to Leo, having to speak up a bit so he could hear her over the music. "I'm looking for the man who remembers the wars. He may go by the name Terre. I've been told to seek him out here." Even as she said it, Greata's words came flooding back.

"Man who remembers the wars? Dark days indeed." Leo paused. His gaze drifted over to the bar as if the mention of Terre had triggered a long-buried memory. His eyes glazed over, and his voice sounded hollow, as if he weren't talking to her or anyone in particular. "The only hope for humanity's future comes from its end. And on that day the past will rise. There's hope for freedom. But the darkest days are yet to come."

"What are you talking about, old man?" Malachi grabbed his friend's shoulder.

Leo jumped with a start. His attention turned back to the pair sitting across from him.

"What? Oh sorry. Just something someone who passed by here yesterday said to me. Talk of the past, and dark days made me think of it . . ."

Sierra looked from Leo to Malachi, searching for more of an explanation to what had just been shared, but Leo kept right on as if he had merely said it was supposed to be sunny tomorrow.

"There's been rumors of a man like this, but it's hearsay mostly. Fables really." He turned his head back toward her, and his unsteady gaze met her steady, determined one.

His shoulders dropped, and he shook his head. "I'll see what I can find out. But don't get your hopes too high. People that pass through tell these stories. There are so many fantastical tales that you need to ignore them, or you'll go mad. I've heard stories of beautiful women half naked and roaming the desert waiting for a man to please. There's supposedly a lost city buried beneath the desert sand that was spared the robot uprising and is home to a secret race of people. The heat messes with people's minds. Or they want to imagine there is something other than Sentinels threatening to kill them or lock them away."

"But you have heard of him?" Sierra pressed, not wanting to lose hope.

Leo nodded. "Stories. This man from the past, some say he's a ghost, wandering since the wars of the ancients. Some say he's a crazed man, spent too much time in the desert sun, they say. The world can be a lonely place, and it messes with even the best man's mind. If somehow he had managed to live for two hundred years, he would have watched many loved ones be born and die. That would be enough to drive someone mad. So yes, I've heard the stories, but I have never paid them much mind. I'd be the second one to tell you not to go chasing bedtime stories. But he'd be the first one to tell you the same." He pointed at Malachi. "So, if you managed to talk this one into this, I could buy there's something to your story."

Malachi's expression didn't change, but he nodded. In the background, the tone of the music changed. The haunting melody turned upbeat, and others in the pub got to their feet, clapping and beginning to dance.

"Like I said, I'll ask my scouts and casually mention it to some travelers. But the odds are slim."

"I appreciate you're willing to help at all."

He lifted his hands in protest. "No thanks needed. I owe this man more than my life. Please don't go spreading your tale around the Inn, though. I don't need every traveler in the place coming to me with their wild stories."

"We'd like your discretion as well," Sierra chimed in. She couldn't help but eye the room around her. Maybe she was growing paranoid as a newcomer in this strange world.

"Of course," he answered. "I have to leave you for now though. I have a lot to do before the night ends. But you're my guests, so continue to enjoy your drinks and the music. Dance if you desire. I'll have Lora attend to you."

With that, he got up and disappeared into the kitchen.

As she looked up to watch him leave, Sierra noticed Rhys had moved closer to the table, glowering at her with a raised eyebrow. How much had he heard? Malachi had cautioned them not to discuss their goal, and the last person she wanted to discuss it with was Rhys.

As soon as she caught his eye, he turned and walked out of the tavern. She guessed he heard more than she would have liked.

OSCAR RAPPED on the door to Wil and Sierra's room and was greeted with a "Come in!" from the other side.

No question of who was at their door. These kids were really fresh out of the compound. Idiots. Well, in this case, it worked to his advantage.

He poked his head into the room and nearly closed it again. Ella was sitting on the bed next to Wil. Wil's crossed arms and posture told him their conversation had been anything but comfortable.

That wasn't his concern, but Ella being in the room presented its own set of problems. This was definitely worse than Sierra not being here. Ella was not one to be toyed with. Her presence could destroy everything. He'd have to be quick on his feet. He wasn't about to have a second set of plans foiled in two days.

"Am I interrupting something?"

"No, not at all." Relief overcame Ella's face.

Oscar nodded and walked toward the back of the room so that he could watch the door. The room was nearly identical to the one he and Ed had. Either Leo wasn't being upfront about how busy they were, or he had gone out of his way to give the group his best set of rooms. What debt did he owe Malachi to treat him so well?

"Do either of you have any idea why Malachi wanted Sierra at the meeting with Leo? Seems there is little of value that she'd be able to offer. I assumed we would be dropping these two off here with the supplies." He paused. "Or has he found a new stray from a compound to protect?"

He meant it to sting, to throw her off guard, but Ella hadn't been paying attention. She was staring at the wall, lost in her own thoughts. Whatever was happening between these two could clearly work to his advantage. Maybe Ella wasn't going to be such a liability after all. Perhaps with her presence he'd still be rewarded handsomely. Her abilities should also be of value. Hopefully enough to make up for what he was supposed to get from those supplies. All that effort only to be foiled by Sierra. She'd learn.

He'd have to take care of Sierra some other time. Or more likely, Malachi would rid himself of her once his precious Ella went missing.

"Sierra's trying to find someone. It's what she's come all this way for. I thought you would have known," Wil answered.

Ella shot a frown at Wil. Oscar smiled. That was more than Wil was supposed to let on, it seemed.

"Malachi keeps his secrets close," he replied. "Us workmen are just here to haul supplies. We're at Malachi's beck and call, just like anyone else." He didn't try to contain the sneer in his voice.

"Are you okay?" Ella had finally snapped into the conversation.

"For someone who wants everyone to work together," Oscar replied, "he sure keeps a lot of secrets."

"He has his reasons." Ella stood up off the bed, folding her arms. "Why do we need to know everything he does? With what he's provided you this past year, I'd expect you'd be able to trust him a little."

"Oh, I trust him, but I don't trust his vision. No matter what he says, we're still prisoners in the SZ. Every day is still a struggle. His Community trades one inequality for another."

"Enough of this! What has gotten into you? Malachi has put every waking moment into the Community over the last five years, and you know it."

"All I know is that this land only helps those that help themselves."

As Ella turned to see why the hotel room door had creaked open, Oscar closed the gap between them and put a knife to her throat. He gripped her arm behind her back, reducing her ability to struggle.

Wil was knocked out and tied up before he even had a chance to see who was coming for him.

"One move and this will end up in your throat."

SIERRA HAD NEVER BEEN a part of anything like this before. She could feel the vibrations of the instrument on stage strumming away, feel the singer's voice as it rang through the common area. She also had had a few of the drinks that Leo had offered them, the same golden ale that had been poured at the compound. She was getting used to the dank taste and was beginning to enjoy herself. Something about the drink had loosened her inhibitions, and she couldn't wipe the smile off her face. Every note struck a chord deep within her and made her want to move.

Others in the pub were doing just that. Some swayed to the melancholy notes. Others grabbed a partner and pressed up against each other on a dance floor in the middle of the room. A well of tears rushed through her that she couldn't control and didn't want to. The emotion of the woman's voice, the impact of the music, and the joy she could see in each person enraptured her.

Some stayed on the sidelines, but she mostly ignored them. Malachi kept himself busy, talking to some of the more serious looking on the sidelines, but Sierra wanted to enjoy the moment.

The beat started to pick up, and a semicircle of spectators around the dance floor started clapping to the beat of the music. She had another few gulps of her drink and couldn't help but join in.

Before she knew it, Ed appeared beside her with a huge smile and an outreached hand.

"Care to dance?"

Her face turned to horror. "I don't know how."

"Just follow me."

Without waiting for another answer, he grabbed Sierra's hand and pulled her into the center of the room. Other bodies were moving gracefully around them. Laughter and clapping surrounded them. Ed was leading the strange dance movements. She thought she might trip over her own feet with every step. A couple of times the uneven floor of the common area caused her to stumble.

She did her best to mirror Ed's movements and followed his lead as best she could. She felt like a fish out of water but managed to keep it together for the most part. Luckily, the two times she did trip, she fell into Ed and managed to keep herself upright by holding on to him. Despite her uneasiness, Ed was quite patient with her and didn't laugh when she seemed to get confused or stumble.

"Mind if I cut in?" A young woman with a pretty face, likely no older than herself, tapped Sierra on the shoulder. She hesitated. It seemed rather inappropriate for this girl to interrupt her dance. But she didn't know what the custom was. Perhaps it was expected that the dancers swap partners. Ed nodded to her as if this was the norm, and she let the girl take her place.

Out of the corner of her eye, she noticed another one of their party reenter the bar. Rhys. She was still unsure why he was so embittered toward her. He claimed it was due to her being from the Sphere, but he didn't have the same malice toward Wil. Something else bothered him. And then there was the matter of her medallion. Something about it had clearly struck a chord.

She shook her head. She was in much too good of a mood to let Rhys sour it. She hadn't had an evening like this . . . well, probably ever.

A smile crept across her face as an idea crossed her mind. Not considering whether it would be a good one or not, she decided to act impulsively. After all, if the music could put her in this good of a mood, perhaps it could wipe the scowl off Rhys's face as well.

She sauntered over to him. His green eyes focused elsewhere in the room until she tapped him on the shoulder.

"Want to dance?" she said, grinning.

Rhys furrowed his brow and wrinkled his nose in disgust, as if it had been the most ridiculous things she could have said.

"Are you joking?"

Well, now that she was here, she considered, perhaps it was ridiculous.

"Why should Ed get to dance with all the girls?" she said, grabbing his arm. "You're just as good looking as he is." Her eyes went wide as she realized the words that came from her mouth. *What was in that drink?* Rhys's expression turned from disgust to barely concealed amusement. She thought she may as well go along with it.

"Come on," she said, pulling on his arm. "Come dance with me."

Rhys stiffened, clearly unsure what motive she could possibly have.

"Come on, Rhys!" Ed shouted from the dance floor. "She might even let you lead!"

That got a laugh out of Rhys, and he reluctantly followed Sierra into the middle of the room.

Rhys was as stiff on his feet as she could have expected. She wondered how many of those drinks it would take to loosen him up. Sierra still had no idea what she was doing, but she mimicked what Ed had done with her before, which got a full laugh from Rhys.

"Oh my, you really have never done this before!" He chuckled. "Come, let me show you."

Rhys took her arms and positioned them on his shoulders. He then put his hands on her waist and began directing her movements.

"Dancing is like fighting," he said. "It's learning how your opponent moves and trying to keep one step ahead of them."

She let out a laugh herself. "Well, isn't that a romantic way of looking at it."

"Oh, were you expecting me to be romantic?"

"Well, you do have your hand on my ass."

He quickly shifted his hand up to her hips, as if he hadn't noticed where it was. She laughed as his face reddened. He said nothing, but his smile softened to a sheepish grin.

The two smiled and danced as if there hadn't been any harsh words between them.

Those around her seemed like they had been doing this their entire lives. Well, maybe they had been. Bodies flew across the room, filling it with laughter, and the crowd's movements started to blur into a swirl of motion and chaos.

"Rhys," she started. He looked down at her, shadows danced on his face, and the torchlight sparkled in his eyes. "Just because I'm from the Sphere doesn't mean I'm a bad person. I'm just trying to find my way."

Rhys looked around to those nearby. His body tensed as she said the words.

"I don't want to talk about it," he said, leaning into her so she could hear him. "And this is no place for you to be discussing it either."

He pulled back and looked to her. His face echoed a sense of concern and something else. Anger, maybe. She wished she knew why she made him so mad.

His hands still rested on her waist. Strong and protective. She'd drop the matter and just enjoy this.

Sierra had lost track of how many songs she had danced to—and how many drinks she'd had. She couldn't remember ever feeling quite so free. However, the blur of dancers around her soon made the room spin. She grasped onto Rhys in fear of falling right over.

"Sorry," she said. "I need to sit down for a bit."

"Are you okay?" Rhys's face expressed concern, and his grip tightened on her.

"Just dizzy." She clung to him, arms wrapped around his neck, face pressed against his chest. It felt hard, like a wall of muscle. Rhys walked her over to her seat and had her sit down, but it didn't stop the room from spinning.

"I think I need to go to my room," Sierra said.

With a strong hand, Rhys scooped her up by the waist and hoisted her over his shoulder. Before she knew it, she was lying in bed, the room still spinning around her. She felt a cold cloth pressed to her forehead, then the room went dark.

In the distance she heard a commotion. It sounded like Ed and Rhys yelling in the next room.

"Malachi!" they yelled through a fog. She tried to make out what they were saying. Someone was missing, that much she understood. But she couldn't open her eyes to figure out what the commotion was about.

19

A THROBBING HEAD greeted Wil as he woke. Small orbs of glowing light were the first things he could make out, as his blurred vision began to clear and shapes materialized. The second was the bottom of the wooden cart he was lying on. It was still night. That, or his eyesight was damaged. There were definitely lanterns. Something was causing a commotion.

Several men came into focus, lifting Ella's struggling body into a wooden box. Her hands were tied behind her back, and her ankles were bound as well. A cloth gagged her mouth. She fought against the brute assault. Bruises marked her body, and tears streamed down her face.

Wil barely had time to process what he was seeing, when the realization that he was also tied up struck him. At least his hands were, but in front of him, not behind.

He winced as he shifted his weight, trying to gain a better perspective at what was going on. He had to consciously stop himself from audibly grunting.

What the hell was happening? The last thing he remembered was standing in their room at the Inn with Oscar and Ella. Where was Oscar?

He tested the bonds on his hands, and though they were secure, he was sure he'd be able to swing his arms if he was upright. His legs weren't tied, though the pain indicated they were at least bruised. Hopefully that was all. He suspected he hadn't been treated lightly, and hoped nothing was broken.

There were five captors he could see. Three busy with Ella, one was securing another crate on the back of the cart they were on, and one was standing over him, attentive to what the first three were up to.

They worked to secure the lid over Ella. If he was going to do something, it had to be now.

There was no way this was going to work.

But he had to do something.

Wil swung his legs as hard as he could into the shins of the man closest to him. He came down in a heap. Wil pushed himself into a roll and then upright with the little movement he could get out of his arms. He wasn't wrong about how much that was going to hurt. Nothing broken. But bloody hell did it hurt.

"Grab him!" shouted one of the men.

One of the others covered the distance to Wil in one swift motion and wrapped a large muscular arm around his chest. Wil put as much energy as he could muster into placing a solid elbow into his attacker's ribs. Unable to steady himself, he toppled over with him.

The lid on Ella's box latched shut, and the remaining men came for Wil in a blur of arms and drawn daggers. It took three of them to finally hold him steady, and a knife in his face convinced him it was a lost cause.

"Don't be trying that again," said one of them, a balding man, missing a good number of teeth. He smelled like he hadn't known a bath for ages. Tattered pants were held together with a strangely decorated belt, sporting a couple of elaborate daggers that were quite out of place with the rest of the man's attire.

"Who are you? Why have you tied us up?"

"Well, well, well. That lad Oscar wasn't joking. You are fresh out of a compound. Well, hopefully the rest of what he told us was true as well. You and the witch with the glow-in-the-dark eyes. She's a real pretty one too. We'll get a good price for her. Do you have any special talents?"

The man spun the dagger around inches away from his face, playing with him.

Wil spat, and it landed right below the man's eye.

The man lifted a tanned hand and wiped it from the stubble on his face. Wrinkles and leathery skin betrayed the years he had spent out in the desert sun. He wound up and smacked Wil across the face.

The sting diverted Wil's attention from the throbbing in his legs. He desperately wanted to rub his face, but with no way to do so, he let the sting go uncomforted.

"Well, true or not, we'll be telling the buyer that you do. Get him in the box!"

Rough hands grabbed at him. Everything went black as they placed a cloth sack over his head. They tied his ankles, the bond so tight he was going to lose feeling in his toes before the night was through. One or two of the men took intentional inappropriate grabs while they pushed him inside a container similar to the one Ella had been placed in moments before.

With clenched fists, Wil wondered where he was being taken and how much worse things were going to get.

THE SKIN on Ella's cheeks burned from the rough cloth they had used to gag her. Her muscles ached, and she could feel each beat of her pulse flowing through her strained shoulders, her tired forearms, and the bruises on her legs, side, and bottom. She did her best to breathe slowly and in control, but the ache in her ribs from where the kidnappers had kicked her made each breath agonizing.

How could Oscar have betrayed her like this? She had overheard that his intended target was Sierra. For what reason she wasn't sure, but still, Oscar was the one who had grabbed her. The one who had held a dagger to her throat. The one who had handed her over to the Prowlers. She wondered if Rhys had a hand in this as well. He had been cold to Sierra ever since she had arrived.

Ella had been caught so off-guard in the room she hadn't even been able to think how to react when Oscar had turned on them. Maybe if she hadn't been so distracted by Wil, and their conversation, her instincts would have kicked in.

She fought to keep the memories at bay, but she failed miserably. Each step of her kidnappers, every ache of her body trapped inside the cage that was her transport, every laugh at her expense, all brought her back to the last time she was at the hands of the Prowlers.

Never again did she think she'd be paraded around like a piece of livestock on display to the highest bidder. Never again did she think she'd be back in one of these coffins, being transported. Later, she'd be stripped and lined up for purchasers to poke and prod.

Three years ago, Malachi had saved her from this fate. Fresh out of the Sphere, similar to Wil and Sierra now. Ignorant of the world around her, she had fallen prey to false promises. Promises of food, and a better life. She had never known anyone to be dishonest to her. How was she to know any different? Hungry, broken, alone, she took someone at their word and ended up beaten and for sale.

She had been fortunate to have happened to cross paths with Malachi and some of the Community. For whatever reason, the guards had left her head covering off that day. He had looked into her eyes and seen her desperate plea. And for once, a man in this godforsaken landscape had really seen her. Not her body, not an object for sale, but her. He had returned that night with his band of men and released her and half a dozen others. Three others had joined the Community that night. The remainder had chosen to go off in search of the families they had been taken from. It was the first time she had believed this world was worth fighting for. Worth saving. Worth leaving the comfort of the authoritarian life in the Sphere for. Everyone that night had shared a renewed sense of hope in what humanity could accomplish. But tonight, it came back to this. It seemed the world was no further ahead than it had been three years ago. But she refused to cave to hopelessness.

Malachi was the only family Ella had, and she was sure he wouldn't rest until he had rescued her again. He took care of his tribe. Hell, he'd take care of anyone willing to be a decent person and help others in return. He would have done the same for Oscar if he had only given him a chance. It seemed the pain and hopelessness in Oscar ran deeper than a year with the Community could shake out. Was he beyond hope? How many like him would never trust someone else or be able to look after the greater needs of others?

She shivered. Would she be sold off before Malachi found them? Or abandoned and left to die of hunger, or be killed by bandits or bots?

She hadn't realized she was crying, but the tears running down her cheeks were dripping off her face and soaking the cloth covering it. She wished she could wipe them off. At least no one could see them. She also wished she could rub the bruises on her arms from being beaten and then thrown into this box.

For the hundredth time, she tested the limits of the rope around her wrists. There was no give. Even if there was, with the amount of effort the men had gone through to collect her and Wil, there would be guards watching. She was in no condition to fight.

Her ankles were tied together with the same bonds as her wrists. She thought she may have enough range of motion in her legs that she could give her box-prison a good kick if she had the room. She decided against it, as she'd probably only gain a bruise for her efforts.

The cloth hood covering her head kept her from knowing whether it was day or night. Once they let her out and she was on display it was meant to hide her individuality. Meant to hide glares or any indication of disgust at the men who would eventually bid on her. Occasionally women would bid as well, but usually it was men. Some bought from the Prowlers because they were lonely or propelled by some urge to bring children into the wasteland to suffer alongside them. This seemed like their best chance at having a child, or maybe just a good time. Whether or not it was against the other person's will. Some wanted a slave or farmhand. Some just wanted an excuse to be mean. Either way, somehow no matter how rough life was out here, people found a way to make money kidnapping and selling humans, especially if they possessed some talent.

Oscar must have used her eyesight as a bargaining chip. Whether it was an intentional character trait bestowed to her by the Guardians, or something that had been out of sequence in her creation, she had never found out, and she likely never would. But whatever the reason, being able to see in the dark made her a hot commodity. In a world filled with people trying to decide if their fate was worse met by psycho-killer robots or each other, having someone who could see well in the dark seemed like a valuable acquisition.

The wood of her prison scraped her side as it bumped along the road. Every rock and pothole jarred her. They were likely being brought out west. Less of a chance anyone would recognize them and cause trouble. They wouldn't want to travel out of the Silent Zone at night. But if Oscar had forewarned them, there was always the chance they'd fear being found by Malachi and cover as many miles as they could. Her guess was that they would camp out on the farthest edge of the SZ they could get to and hope for no fluctuations.

Once out of the SZ, they likely would travel over back roads until they reached the mountains. They wouldn't stop if they could help it. If the Sentinels or Scanners approached them, the prisoners would easily be left behind to be sent to reeducation or disposed of.

Right before they sealed her in, there had been some sort of commotion between the guards and someone else. She wasn't sure, but hoped that it was Wil. If it was, he had either fled or been recaptured. More than likely the latter. If he had gotten free though, hopefully he could find Malachi and let him know where she was being held.

She had been blindfolded ever since Oscar had exchanged her life for some coin. She had no idea where she was, or even if Wil had been part of the exchange as well. He may be going a different direction entirely.

Right now, she needed to figure out how she was getting out of here if help never arrived.

20

Sierra reluctantly opened her eyes to the hand shaking her shoulder. Light came through the cracks between boards where a window had once been. It struck her face and intensified the throbbing in her skull.

She let enough light in to see that it was Rhys trying to wake her. The previous night came rushing back. Well, most of it did. She remembered the dancing, the clapping, and the music. What a glorious and curious evening it had been all at the same time. She had seen nothing of the sort ever in the North Village. Why did her head hurt so much, though? And how did she get back to her bed?

She checked and saw she was still wearing the same outfit as she was last night. She must have slept in her clothes. On the nightstand beside the bed a pair of shorts and shirt were laid out for her, along with a light robe hanging on a hook on the wall.

"You've slept long enough. It's time to go."

So much for the pleasantries of last night.

"Okay." She did her best to sit up and tried to focus on Rhys through squinted eyes. The room was still spinning, and her head throbbed. "What's the hurry?"

"Ella, Oscar, and Wil are missing. Come on. Get ready. We'll fill you in on our way out."

"What do you mean, missing? What happened?"

"We've been trying to figure that out all night. They were gone when we came up after the bar last night. Malachi, Ed, and I spent most of the night trying to track them down."

"Why didn't you wake me before? I could have helped."

"You were in no condition to help and would have been in the way. Get dressed and meet us in the lobby."

Rhys left, and she quickly threw on the clothes that had been set out for her. Been in the way? So much for dancing softening his attitude toward her.

She didn't think Wil would have left without telling her. Something was terribly wrong. She tried her best to fight back tears bubbling to the surface. Wil was her only connection to the Sphere. To her home. If he was gone . . . She would never forgive herself if he had been murdered while she had been dancing the night away. They should have stuck together. She had told him she would watch his back, and she let him down.

She found a brush sitting near the tub of water and did her best to run it through her matted hair. She half managed, but she was really going to need to take a full bath sooner than later. Eyeing the full, unused tub one last time, she left the room and made her way downstairs.

The lobby had no exposed windows. The only light in the room came from torches hung on the walls. Though she knew morning was well underway, the room looked no different than it had the night before. Dim, dingy, ancient. A handful of travelers wandered in and out of the doors that separated the hotel from the outside, letting the daylight invade the dark cave momentarily each time the door opened.

The lobby itself was quite large, as if it had been built to hold hundreds of people. Currently there were only a few walking about. She tried not to stare. Weary eyes nervously flitted across the guards, as those who dared pass set about for wherever their next destination may be. Malachi, Ed, and Leo were engrossed in a conversation as she approached.

"I don't know how this happened, old friend. The two guards I had watching your floor are missing as well. No blood anywhere, but they wouldn't have let them through without a fight."

"Could the guards have been bought?" Malachi had his arms crossed over his chest. If Rhys meant what he had said about them looking for their missing party members all night, Malachi showed no signs of fatigue. If anything, he looked more alert and eager to move than ever.

"You think someone took them?" Sierra asked as she crossed the stone floor toward the lobby's center where the men were standing beside the long desk that marked an otherwise empty room.

Leo ignored her, responding to Malachi instead. "These men have worked with me for years. I pay well, and they have my trust." He sighed and shook his head. "I'd sooner believe they were knocked out cold and taken themselves. But bloody hell, who knows, these are dark days indeed. The promise of a large sum could tempt even the most loyal of us. Yes, even some of yours, my old friend. As good as a man's intent, he still needs to eat, and a drink or two helps to forget how dark things really are. But I won't believe my men were corrupted until I have something that proves it. I have no reason to doubt any of them." He raised his voice for the last bit. Probably for the benefit of the other guards in the room, Sierra thought.

"It had to be the Prowlers. We would have found them last night otherwise," said Malachi.

"I'd have to agree with you. But I have yet to hear of Prowlers breaking into an inn and taking people in their sleep."

"At least two of the missing are special enough that they may be worth the trouble. The bigger question would be how they knew of their value."

"I hope you're not suggesting one of my staff had anything to do with it."

"I don't think your staff would have known either," Malachi answered, shaking his head. He crossed his arms, leaning back. "I know if it came to that you'd deal with it appropriately. But for now, no, I don't believe so."

Malachi turned back to Ed and Sierra. "It seems as if we have some work to do today to find our friends. Leo, you've been most kind to us so far. I hope it won't be too much for me to ask you to hold our rooms for a few more nights."

"Malachi, my place is your place. Find your friends. The rooms are yours as long as you need."

"We have to find them!" Sierra cut in again.

Malachi nodded. "We searched all night, but now that it's light, there's one last place we need to look. If they aren't there, we should at least be able to learn where they've been taken."

Leo gave Malachi a warning glare. "Be careful, old friend. Things have gone from bad to worse, and she may not take kindly to you stomping around her territory."

"I know the risk. But we don't leave family behind. This is how we build back what has been lost, at least whatever scrap of it we can hold on to. Otherwise if the SZ drops, we're all doomed.

"Sierra, Edgar, you're coming with me. Ed, tell Rhys to join us and get the rest of the crew to secure the provisions for the day. They can then have the rest of the day to themselves. Meet us out front when you're finished."

SIERRA SQUINTED at the mid-morning sun as they stepped out of the Inn. They really had let her sleep for too long. How far had the previous night's search taken them? Compared to how enclosed the Sphere was, this new world felt like an infinite expanse of opportunity to hide. In the daylight, the street took on a more vibrant tone than it had at night. The monolithic buildings more closely resembled the buildings from her visions in the harsh light of the day, but the paint had faded, and the screens were long gone or smashed. Fragments of glass hung precariously from old displays and windows, and other buildings were half standing. Piles of rubble half buried in sand were just as prevalent as the buildings that remained upright. The city was an empty shell of what it had once been.

In her vision this street stretched for miles with grand displays on either side. Desert and ruin had overtaken most of what the city used to be.

The giant lion statue she had seen last night stood at the entrance of the Inn, just a few flecks of gold remaining in the otherwise gray figure. In her vision of the past, this lion was pure gold. She looked to the top of the building she had exited. The monstrosity felt out of place next to the dingy place she had just been in. These buildings had once been grand, but time had taken its toll on them. A single "M" hung haphazardly miles above her. Another memory of what once had been.

Small tents filled spaces in between the patched structures. They looked like they may have been either markets or sleeping quarters, or both. Sierra had a hard time telling which from where she stood. Despite what used to be a near infinite number of rooms, it appeared not everyone was privileged with a space inside.

"There are so many buildings. Why are people using tents?"

"Most of the buildings have been gutted," Malachi answered. "The Queen and her Prowlers control most of those that are usable."

"You have a Queen?"

"Probably not like ones you're thinking of. She controls the

Prowlers and the Underground. She claims her people own Vegas. They prey on the unfortunate and force their way into controlling the city. The rest are left to pick up the pieces. That's part of why I started the Community. Working together, we've got more of a shot. Otherwise your options are joining the Prowlers, which is no guarantee to be treated well, stealing, struggling to find your next meal, or death."

"And Leo?"

"He's one that struggles. He's honest, but it's tough for him. N'ara, the Queen, would love to claim him as under her domain, but even the Prowlers are afraid to touch him. He runs an honest ship, and his guards are loyal to him because of it. So far, he's managed to hold out their small section of the Inn, has even gained some floors in the last while. He's an unofficial member of the Community, so we help him out when we can. His business comes from all kinds though, so he doesn't publicly proclaim allegiance to anyone."

What a strange world. Factions, allegiances, guards. It was going to take Sierra some time to get used to it all. The Community sounded more like what she was used to, or what she thought she had in the Sphere, before the deceit was revealed. Everyone working together for a common good. The Prowlers, the bandits, the Guardians. What was the point of it all? Her entire life she had longed to know what the Outside was like. Now that she was here, she wondered if she got more than she bargained for.

"Where are we going? Leo made it sound like it's somewhere we don't want to be."

"Into the Underground. The Queen's lair. We don't want to be there. But she owes me a favor."

He handed Sierra a small energy pistol, attached to a belt. "Let's hope you're able to hone your ability if needed. Just don't use it if you don't have to."

"I'm not sure I can control it," she said, tying the belt around her waist. "But I'll do what I have to do to get Wil back safely."

"Can I ask why I need to keep it a secret?" she continued. "I noticed the look you gave me last night when we were talking to Leo."

"Human life has a price. Anything that adds to your value just means more effort the Prowlers will go through to get their hands on you. What you're able to do, especially if you can learn to control it, it would change everything. It would tip the balance on the power controlled within the Silent Zone, and beyond, in a way that could be cataclysmic for everyone. Right now the lack of tech keeps everyone on an equal playing field. The fewer people who know about you, the better."

"The Prowlers?"

"Yes, but not just them. The Order, the Resistance, there are rulers in other lands that would love the chance to expand their dominion. Even petty thieves would go to extremes to kidnap and control you."

"And the Community?"

He let out a sigh. "Even some in the Community, though potentially well-intentioned, could try to manipulate you for their own gain. We've gone so long fighting to survive, any advantage would be seen as a godsend. Any use of your ability needs to be yours to decide and yours alone."

"Then what's the pistol for?" She flashed him a smile.

"If you don't want to help save your friend, then by all means you can stay here. If you can't or don't want to use it should the time come, that's your choice as well. I'll try not to dictate what you do, but I'll do my best to give you every opportunity to succeed."

Seconds ticked by as she stood there. The choice before her was simple enough on the surface. She could stay back with the others and let Malachi, Ed, and Rhys take care of things. This was their domain. They wouldn't blame her. Maybe Rhys would. But on the other hand, Wil was her last connection to home. She had promised him she'd watch his back—and failed. She needed to make that right. She had a chance to help now, and every fiber of her being screamed at her to find him.

In the Sphere she had been disheartened that her decisions didn't change her fate. Here was her chance. To prove what she was capable of. To Greata, and to herself.

"Of course I'll help," she said. "I'll do it to save Wil, but Ella and Oscar as well. You've already done so much for me. But Greata saved my life, sent me out of the Sphere for a reason. I won't let her down. And I won't take for granted those who help me along the way."

"We haven't finished with each other yet. I see more hope in you than I've seen in anyone in a long time. If this man you seek exists, I'll help you find him."

Sierra breathed a sigh of relief. Despite Oscar's warning to her the day before, she felt comfortable around Malachi. More than she did around Oscar, to be honest. Malachi reminded her of Greata in a lot of ways. Strong, confident, patient, and willing to forge his own path forward. And loyal, maybe to a fault.

Ed and Rhys returned, backpacks and sheathed daggers in tow. Rhys handed two to Malachi and one to her.

"You think you can handle one of these?" Rhys asked. He smirked, but Sierra couldn't tell if he was being condescending or playful.

"Would you like to find out?" she replied, looking up at him inches from his face. That would probably cover her both ways.

He rolled his eyes, which didn't lend any further clues to his intent as he turned back to Malachi, attaching the remaining knife to the side of his own belt.

Ed sported a large sword strapped to his back. The broad weapon would probably offer more protection than they would need. At least she hoped it would.

"Are we ready to head out?" she asked. "It's time to find my friends."

21

Tʜᴇ ᴍᴏᴜᴛʜ of the cave appeared to swallow the surrounding daylight whole, paying no attention to what time of day it was, or what the outside had planned. It was a void in the side of an otherwise bright, albeit dirty, building exterior made of brick and metal. Above it, jagged, towering metal pieces pierced the earth skyward, reminiscent of the building that had held on to them for support in days gone past. The remaining brick was chalk white, bleached by the sun for hundreds of years, slowly decaying since the last coat of paint touched its surface. The mouth had been an entrance, but not its main entrance. Sand and dirt had long covered the path that led into it, but Sierra had the feeling that this had once been a paved surface that held the grand vehicles she had seen in her vision. There was no other reason she could think of for an entryway into a building that was as large as the one that was before her.

According to Malachi, this was the entry, or at least an entry, into the Underground. One that would bring them to N'ara, Queen of Vegas. If anyone would know of a Prowler plan to break into Leo's Rio Grande Inn and haul three Community members out, it would be her.

"If she knows where they are, do you expect her to tell us?" Ed asked as they got closer to the hungry doorway.

"N'ara and I have an understanding."

"You have an understanding with the Queen of Vegas?" Ed asked, bewildered.

"Even among chaos, there needs to be some order. Thus far, we have stayed out of each other's way. If she's consciously taking the first step into an open fight with the Community, then things are indeed worse than I had feared.

"Her main goal is holding on to power. The Community steers clear of making any such claim. In the past she's been good enough to let that existence be. Kidnapping these folks wouldn't serve her in any way. It would provide a few rogues with a quick profit. That's likely all this was. There's no benefit for her to hold out on us here."

"What if you're wrong?"

"Pray that I'm not."

It took a few moments for her eyes to adjust as they entered the cavern. Broken chunks of dark gray rock pushed up among sand as they descended. A few hundred yards in and the surface was quickly becoming more rock than sand. Until the sand turned completely into a solid paved street.

"The streets of the Underground are paved?"

It was dim and hard to see, but the road was again reminiscent of the streets she had seen in her vision. Rough, gray, but nearly completely intact. Someone had done an inordinate amount of work to dig this structure into the earth.

"The last remnants of the streets of the ancients," Malachi answered, his voice hushed. "Down here they've been protected from sun, wind, and storms. I imagine there are still roads that look like this in the city, buried by hundreds of years of dust and sand."

Sierra nodded. That made sense. What other remnants of the ancients lay buried beneath them?

"I'd suggest keeping any further questions to yourself while we're down here," he added. "We have an understanding, but I'm still not expecting the warmest of welcomes. I'd prefer to go as long as possible without being confronted."

They carried on in silence. They had gone several hundred more yards before the light behind them winked out of view.

Rhys carried a small lantern. The minimal light it produced was nearly laughable. It lit the faces of the party and a small bubble of the road before them. The corridor before them emitted a faint blue glow, but otherwise they were going in blind.

Sierra tried not to trip over the rocks that jutted out from the jagged pavement. Her instinct was to slow her pace, tread carefully, but the others in her party seemed to have no such constraint. A couple of times she grabbed on to one of them to regain her balance. Neither of them questioned or scolded her for doing so, nor did they slow their pace. They simply helped her regain her footing and continued on.

Thankfully the darkest part of the journey didn't last too long. They turned the corner and were welcomed to a smaller hallway illuminated by two strips of blue light that lined either side. The light was still dim and eerie, but it was enough to see more than a few steps ahead of them. Into the depths of the Underworld indeed. She resisted the urge to ask how the light was generated.

Rhys turned down the lantern just as a small, dark figure skirted across the hall in front of them. She grabbed Rhys's arm in alarm.

"Rats," he whispered in her ear.

She shuddered at the thought of what other creatures may be lurking down here with them. She let go of Rhys's arm, thankful the darkness hid the red in her cheeks.

They rounded several corners before they saw any sign of other life. But once they were well inside the cavern, indications of those who dwelled below the surface started to show themselves. Items of clothing, blankets, food containers, and other items appeared. Temporary metal walls marked where someone had erected a residence. Others followed, most no larger than what would be sleeping quarters and a small place to eat.

Another corner, and the hall opened up into an expanse. Surrounded by concrete walls, and large pillars, the scattering of the metal-walled dwellings became condensed and filled with people. Sierra nearly recoiled in disgust at the smell. Boiled cabbage, rotting flesh, burning hair. She couldn't put a name to what it was, but it was awful. She grabbed Ed's arm this time as they passed through the makeshift village just to give herself the stability and confidence to walk through the area. He clasped a hand on her shoulder for reassurance. She gave a little jump at the unexpected contact, and he took it as a signal to let go. Which was too bad—she did appreciate the silent support.

She reached out and took his arm. His biceps were thick enough that she had to nearly wrap her entire arm around his to get any sort of grip. He looked down at her and smiled.

Handfuls of people sat staring out of the open end of their makeshift homes. Most of the faces she could see were so white that they appeared blue, in part due to the light that still dimly illuminated the expanse of the room. All eyes followed their group as they made their way through the narrow lanes that separated each dwelling. Each pair of eyes had pupils so dilated that no iris was visible. Just giant black pupils highlighted by the whites of their eyes. Faces sunken in, all with a blue tinge that gave their eyes that much more of a haunting stare. She wasn't sure whether to be fearful or sad. It was obvious these people had lived down here for a long time, probably generations.

Other than their own footsteps, the creaking of a metal piece, or the occasional cough from an unknown person, the room was as silent as a graveyard. Sierra watched wide-eyed children sitting and staring at them, or at nothing, not making a peep. She had never seen children so subdued.

What kept the people down here? She thought of those she had momentarily saw locked away while the Onyx attacked the city in her vision. Were the two groups of people somehow related? She couldn't help but think that if people were sent underground for protection that perhaps they would have stayed even after the threat had left. Perhaps they passed on to their descendants that being underground was their best means of staying safe.

Or maybe with all of the danger of the outside, it truly was the safest place. Perhaps this Queen protected her people the best she knew how. Though looking around, that definitely didn't appear to be the case. These people weren't living. They were waiting to die.

In a shelter that sat just off the path, a pair of young girls caught Sierra's attention. She would have guessed they were maybe eight or nine, but others around appeared smaller than average, so it was possible they were older. They both sat with sunken eyes, staring into darkness. Not unlike many of the other children.

"What's wrong with them?" her voice echoed through the chamber. She hadn't realized how quiet the place had actually been until that moment.

"Shh. No questions," Malachi rebuffed.

There had to be more that could be done for these people. She stopped and pulled off her backpack. Inside she found a couple of cakes. Greata must have packed them, expecting them to have a longer journey, or less help than they had received.

Ed grabbed her arm and shook his head, eyes wide. "We can't help them."

She brushed him off and brought the cakes to the children. Malachi and Ed looked on in despair, while Rhys tilted his head, intrigued.

"Here, take these," she whispered to the children, trying to keep her voice down as to not have it travel through the whole chamber again. "I have more than I need."

The pair focused their big empty eyes at her, then looked at the cake they held in their hands. They began picking at the cake, unsure at first, but quickly growing smiles as their empty bellies received nourishment.

It warmed her that she could provide a glimmer of joy to the children. A small woman, likely their mother, stepped out, giving her a skeptical glare.

The woman didn't say anything, but she was not impressed with Sierra's intrusion. Not knowing how to respond, Sierra gave the woman a quick smile as she took a couple of steps back to rejoin her party.

Ed hissed at her, "If you give a piece of bread to one of them, all the children will come looking for more, thinking it's what they're owed."

"I was able to help a couple," she answered. "It was better than helping none."

Ed walked away shaking his head, clearly unimpressed with her actions.

Rhys looked amused as he approached her.

"Call me a dumb Spherian all you want. I'm glad I could bring those kids some joy."

Rhys shook his head and put his hands up in defense. "Not at all. Maybe not all Spherians are as selfish as I thought."

He kept walking, but she couldn't help but smile at his words.

Malachi pushed them onward, and they continued to make their way through the pieced together shanty town and its people. Things grew ever dimmer as they got deeper into the belly of the Underground.

"How much farther are we going?" she whispered to Malachi.

"Not much farther. Just keep moving."

The group got to a stairwell at the end of the cavern. The stairs went down.

"How deep does this go?"

"What did I say about questions?" Malachi looked around, as if on edge. "We don't know how deep it runs," he relented. "But it's said to run beneath the entirety of the old city, which is much larger than what still remains above. Now no more questions. We're heading down into the Queen's inner chamber. Only her guard and invited guests are allowed this far. Let me handle them."

They followed Malachi down the stairs. The steps were made of the same concrete as the rest of the chamber.

Finally, at the end was a small metal door. Definitely reminiscent of the door Terre had pushed her through—old, faded metal. The metal grated upon concrete as it opened with a heart-wrenching sound, as if it hadn't been moved in centuries.

On the other side, the blue light intensified, and the thin strips that had lit their path until now were replaced by large flat cylinders, providing brighter luminescence. Smaller strip lights also lined the floor. This cavernous tunnel seemed to have no end. How many people were housed here? What would it mean for them if the Silent Zone fell?

They opened yet another set of doors and met their first sign of resistance—two large men, completely bald, and in better health than any others she had seen below ground. Their big black pupils were similar to the others upstairs and gave them a look that was less than human. The men had no hair whatsoever. No eyebrows, no eyelashes, nothing.

They turned, large swords pointed at Sierra's party before the door had fully swung open.

"This area's restricted." The man's voice was higher pitched than Sierra would have suspected coming from someone of his size. It was still commanding, but she had to admit not as intimidating as she expected. "Return to your . . ."

"Good day, gentlemen, we're here to see N'ara." Malachi entered the room with an air of confidence. "I have a great deal to discuss with her. If you could please let her know that Malachi Riley has arrived and would like to see her."

"Malachi? Yeah, we were told about you. Throw them in a cell, boys."

Two more guards appeared out of nowhere, and Sierra was grabbed roughly from behind. A sword was at her back. She tried to steal a look at Malachi's face, but the guard pushed her forward.

"I'm sure there is a misunderstanding here. Will you let her know we've arrived?"

"Oh, we'll let her know. Don't worry. I'm sure you'll be seeing her soon."

The three were escorted down a maze of farther halls. Her arm ached from being twisted behind her back. The sack of muscle behind her was intent on proving he was stronger than a small woman. When he wasn't manhandling her, he was prodding her along with the edge of his broadsword. It cut through her shirt, and she was sure she could feel trickles of blood from where it pressed up against her.

A chill went through her as the damp air of the Underground soaked into her bones. Could this have been the fate Wil had met? Flung down endless halls, miles beneath the Earth's surface, only to be skewered by some pompous hairless guard? The blue lighting and stale air made her long for the bubble of the Sphere.

A few more turns in the hallway, and the guards opened another metal door. They were shoved through, into a cramped room of caged cells. Each of them empty, save one in the far back.

Even though the whole Underground had a pervasive odor, this room smelled particularly bad. The smell was different, and Sierra decided it wasn't quite as putrid as the shantytown above them. Metal, stale air, and death. Better than the cabbage and burned hair of the resident area above. Scratches lined the walls within the cells. Some had the distinct look of old dried blood.

The knot in her stomach told her this definitely wasn't the welcome Malachi had expected.

Two of the guards remained outside the door as if they were expecting an ambush to come to their captives' rescue. The other two pushed them farther into the room.

Their weapons were removed, and then they were each shoved into their own individual cell. Cages rattled as the doors slammed. Old keys were turned and bars locked into place over the thick metal gate.

"Her highness will see you shortly," the two said with a laugh.

The cell was basically a closet and not quite wide enough to lie down in.

Malachi was directly across from Sierra. His face could have been made of stone for all she could tell.

Ed, on the other hand, was struggling to contain his rage. Sierra was sure the vein on his forehead was threatening to burst. His eyes flitted from one cell to the next, pupils dilated. He wasn't just angry. He was afraid.

But for some reason, she wasn't. In this whole whirlwind of events that had transpired over the past few days, this seemed like just another scene in a bad dream. She waited to wake up, though she knew it was an unreasonable thought. When would the reality of what was happening kick in? When would she start screaming in terror at the weight of it all? For now, it was surreal. So far beyond what she had ever known to be normal. It was as if her mind couldn't compute what was unfolding before her.

As the jailers closed the cell doors, the light in the room nearly disappeared. Small white bulbs gave the room enough of a glow that she could make out the faces of her friends, but not much else.

"What now?" Ed asked. His eyes surveyed the cell door, as if searching for a possible weakness in its design.

"We wait for the Queen," Malachi answered.

"The Queeeenn?" An eerie laugh filled the room. A man stood

in the corner cell. One other soul in this underground prison. He pressed his bearded face into the bars, as if willing himself to squeeze through the two-inch space. He was unkempt, probably hadn't shaved in months. His hair was wild and beard even more so. She thought his hair was dark, but she couldn't tell for sure in the dimly lit room.

"The Queeeen will not come for meeee. Bahaha! Why would she come for you?" His frail figure leaped around his cell. At least as much as it would let him. He was wearing only a shredded garment around his waist. How long had this man been down here?

"Quiet, fool," Ed barked. "We don't want to hear your ramblings."

Malachi raised his hand to Ed in a calm manner, indicating for him to leave the poor man alone. Sierra could barely make out his hushed voice. "Patience, Edgar, he may have been here a long time. Maybe we could learn something from him."

"What is your name, friend?" Malachi asked, his calming voice trying to diffuse the tension in the room.

"Meee? Well, I'm just a fool. A madman they say. Pay no mind to the man in the back cell. He's lost his mind, he has!"

"What can we call you?"

"Call me a dreamer. Call me mad. For mad I am indeed, indeed. They used to call me Kristopher. Then they called me a demon. Then they called me mad. For mad I am indeed! Bahaha!"

Malachi shot Sierra a quick glance. His eyes were intent on hers. He was trying to tell her something. She had no idea what though.

"Why did they call you mad, Kristopher?"

"Haven't ye been listening? Because I am mad, I am! Who else but a madman would try to start over again? Would try to control them? I wanted to help!"

"How long have you been down here?"

His demeanor changed instantly. His shoulders slumped as he

sighed, and his eyes focused on nothing. "Decades, maybe. Except for a few years ago, they let me out. But I made a mess of things. Then they threw me right back down. Said I was a threat to the Queen . . . The Queeeen? The Queen! Bahahaha."

The laughter carried on for some time. Sierra resigned herself to sitting at the back of the cell in silence, waiting to see if the Queen would actually come for them, or if they were destined for madness like Kristopher.

22

———

THE METAL BOX *that surrounded the little girl seemed to be closing in around her. She pressed her hands around the edges, looking for escape, looking for a way out. Sierra didn't know what she had done wrong. Her dad was dead. Her sister was dead. And now the Guardians had locked her up. They said they had some questions to ask. Did they think she killed them? She had been at home!*

A gray orb gazed down at her from outside her cell. She wasn't sure where this place was. Colored lights and screens decorated the walls around her. Other than the gray box she was locked in, everything was lit with a harsh white light.

They stared at her. Their targeted blue light pulsed over her body, checking for any sign that she was lying.

Lying about what? She didn't understand.

Another humanoid Guardian stood in the corner. Watching.

Sentinel. Something in the back of her mind told her. It wasn't her thought. How did she know its name?

"The Guardians protect us," she said the words, unsure of what else to say.

She licked her lips, chapped against the dry air. They hadn't given her a drink. They had her locked away for days. A terrible way to treat a child. Or anyone.

"Where is your sister?"

"Izzy? She died. There was an accident."

"What did she tell you about her dreams?"

"Dreams? She said she had a dream that the Guardians wanted to kill her."

"Do you think we killed her?"

"Why would you kill her?"

"We are here to protect the Sphere."

"I know. That's what I told her. Why are you keeping me here?"

"We need to make sure you haven't been compromised."

"I want to go home."

"Our recordings show you ask a lot of questions. Questions are dangerous. What else did your sister tell you?"

"Tell me about what? She never knew any more than I did."

"Some things aren't meant for you to know."

"Can I go home now?"

"Yes. But we will send someone to keep watch."

"Someone to help?"

"Yes, someone to help. Someone to protect you."

The cell around her hissed, and the bars opened.

The Guardian that looked like a person took her by the arm and sat her in a chair.

"We will be watching you."

"For what?"

"Abnormalities."

A needle came out of the machine she was sitting next to.

"What's that?"

"You ask too many questions."

"That's what Izzy always said. Will it hurt?"

"It will. But you won't remember."

The Guardian she knew was called a Sentinel pushed a button on the machine, shooting the needle out and stabbing her in the arm.

23

SIERRA RUBBED HER EYES. A dream. Was it a dream? Or a memory? Something about it felt . . . real. Like something she was supposed to have forgotten. Not like the visions she'd had before.

It could have been minutes; it could have been days. Sierra had lost all sense of time. Conversation had stopped since Kristopher kept interrupting with his nonsensical rhymes. Every now and then the silence was broken by him humming to himself —tunes that sounded vaguely familiar to Sierra, but she couldn't quite place where they belonged.

A chill crept into the cell. How much did the time of day affect temperature at this depth? If at all. Maybe it was just that they hadn't been able to move, allowing the cooler subterranean air to chill them. She shivered. Not used to wearing shorts, but they had been what was set out for her this morning. She longed for her own wardrobe. Would she ever be able to pick out her own clothes again? In honesty, she didn't mind the shorts. She just wished she had something a bit warmer.

As she awakened, she found herself curled up in a ball, hugging herself for warmth. Her back ached from lying on the hard concrete surface. What use did the ancients have for such an extensive underground facility that they'd pour concrete this far below the surface?

When the door of the room opened, Sierra stood up and tried to stretch out the stiffness in her muscles from her time on the floor. Malachi was sitting in his cell staring straight ahead. He hadn't moved. Edgar was on his feet as quick as she was, looking like he had just been given the opportunity to attack whoever may be coming through that door. Rhys had dozed off as well, resting against the bars in his cell.

The light from the hall spilled into the cavern once again, as the same two guards who had brought them in entered.

"All right, Malachi Riley, N'ara's willing to see you. I guess you're lucky, for now. Though she wasn't too thrilled to hear you brought guests. No funny business." He gave them a threatening glare as he unlocked the cell doors.

"Do we get our weapons back?" Ed asked.

"Ha! I don't think so." He shoved Ed forward to emphasize his point. "Let's go!"

The guards pushed them down the hall. Swords weren't drawn this time, but the threat was still there. They still weren't quite the welcomed guests Malachi had hoped they would be. Well, maybe he hadn't thought they would be welcomed with opened arms, but had he realized the hostility they'd be met with? Any hope she had that these folks would be willing to help them find their friends was definitely gone, replaced with a fear that they may not make it out alive.

They continued back the way they had come and down a few more corridors. How deep must this place go? It seemed endless.

They got to the end of the hall and were led into an expansive open room. This room had better lighting than any of the others they had been in. However, it still had the bluish hue the rest of the facility did. The ceiling had to be forty feet high. It was hard to tell, as the lighting still wasn't that good, so it mostly got lost as it stretched upward toward the surface. Large pillars stretched up into the darkness. Murals adorned the walls, the only artwork she had seen that didn't look faded and ancient. This was definitely freshly painted. The displays were colorful, depicting various scenes of people and Guardians. Most of the people resembled the wide-eyed members of the Underground, though better fed and kept.

The floor here was smooth, smoother than the concrete that was in the rest of the corridors she had seen. Smooth white stone reminded her of the floors back in the Sphere. It was funny, the small things that reminded her of home.

As she glanced around the room, there were artifacts from the old world. How this place was just beneath the dusty city they had come from was beyond her. The devices here closely resembled those in the Sphere, or perhaps those she had seen in her last vision.

How there was working lighting here, in the heart of Vegas, made no sense to her from what she had been told. But she was new here. So maybe there were exceptions to the rules. She'd have to ask Malachi about it later. If they got out of here.

Two guards blocked the exit behind them, making it clear nobody was going to be leaving without their okay. Two others stood to either side of the party. Six guards for the four of them. Their group might actually be able to take them. She smiled to herself.

The Queen of Vegas sat in the center of the room. There was no need for anyone to introduce her. It was obvious who she was. The first thing that struck Sierra was the air of leadership the woman had about her, in command of all others in the room. Like the rest of those they had seen below the surface, this woman was bald, not a hair on her head, with skin so pale that it seemed blue. She sat on what could only be described as a golden throne.

She truly did see herself as the Queen.

Sierra's glance around the room ended as the Queen met her

eye. She held her gaze as she crossed the room toward them. The light reflected off her white skin, contrasting the black leather suit she wore. It clung to her body to a degree that looked uncomfortable. Head held high, she approached the party.

"Well, well. Welcome my old . . . friend . . . Malachi." Though she hesitated at the word *friend*, her voice flowed as smooth as silk. She smiled a toothy grin, as horrifying as it was forced. "I hope you have a good reason for invading my territory with these foot soldiers of yours."

"Foot soldiers? N'ara, we're but four members of the Community. Has it been so long that you've come to this level of distrust of me? I have come in need of your help. We had a few of our party members disappear from our room at the Rio Grande last night. From everything we can find, it seems like the work of some of your . . . professionals. If they were taken by your Prowlers, we'd like to know why and where they were taken."

"What concern of mine is this, Malachi? I don't control what a handful of my people do. I am sure you aren't aware of what each of your Community members are up to at all hours of the night? Hmm?"

"No, but I take responsibility if one does something that breaks our agreements with others. Or do I have to remind you that the Prowlers are not to be taking those not in dire straits?"

Sierra shot Malachi a glance. He was oblivious to her silent question, but he couldn't have really just implied that they had an agreement with this woman to allow people to be abducted off the street? He thought back to the conversation Oscar had on the road with her and wondered if there was really more at play to his dealings than he let on.

"I'm sorry that you have wasted your time. Again, this doesn't seem like my concern. What is your real motivation in coming down here after these long years? Surely you wouldn't trouble yourself over a couple of missing people. You've built up your little Community to surround me, and now you descend into my castle. You come in here, accusing my people of an act of aggression. How am I supposed to respond? To come cowering to you? Tell my people we must bow to your whims and baseless accusations?" Her voice raised in volume and agitation with each question. Sierra clenched her fists and tried her best not to flinch or step back as N'ara stepped closer with each pronouncement.

"We had an agreement, N'ara. I helped you not so long ago you may recall."

"We did have an agreement, but times are changing. Or haven't you heard? While you've been off roaming the desert trying to gather food for the degenerates that live in the city . . . well, here we've had new problems. The Silent Zone is failing."

Malachi maintained his gaze. "I've heard the rumors. Fluctuations, but they have all been outside the city. You know that has no bearing on why we are here. A simple location is all I ask. I think I've earned that much."

"Of course, how could you not have heard. Patches of the zone where suddenly the shield that has guarded us for centuries disappears. Some places it weakens enough for the orbs to fly into our space. Some spaces on the edges of the zone have retreated by miles and not fully recovered. But these I'm sure you're well familiar with. The perimeter has always been in flux, but this is the first time we've lost ground in the numbers we've seen, isn't it?"

"People still need to eat." Malachi didn't move. Didn't flinch. But he didn't protest either, and to Sierra, that was telling.

"Only the strongest will survive the fall, and you know it." Her voice was almost a hiss. "Why then, if the city will no longer be able to support its inhabitants, would I waste my precious resources keeping pacts made with those whose existence may collapse within a matter of months? Is the real reason you're here? Encroaching on my space, because you fear your Community will have nowhere left to hide when it all comes crashing down?"

"N'ara, there will be time enough for us to deal with that, if and when it happens. It could be another two hundred years. But for now, I still need your help. It's Ella. She was among those who were taken."

"Ella?" N'ara smiled. "The girl with the gifted eyesight? Well, that is interesting news. I could find use for her."

"N'ara, what have you done?"

"What have *I* done? Why do you keep accusing me? You're right. I do know of this arrangement, but I had no involvement in it. It was one of your own people, and since it was one of your people behind the heist, well, I have no jurisdiction. That's an amicable agreement as far as I'm concerned. I've heard there may be more useful people you may be hiding? Hmm?"

Malachi remained silent.

"She's scared," Sierra blurted out, startling herself in the process. She hadn't meant to say the words.

N'ara whipped her head toward her so fast Sierra feared a dagger would come flying as well.

"What did you say?" the woman snarled. Like a wolf, her lip curled back in disdain.

She was in this far, and she had had enough.

"You're hiding the truth because you're scared. Instead of working with Malachi, you cower. Because you're afraid that when people see what working together will achieve, they'll overthrow you, and your reign will be over."

She heard a satisfied grunt from Rhys and could see Ed swallow out of the corner of her eye. As usual, Malachi didn't flinch.

N'ara skulked toward Sierra. The leather suit that clung to her creaked as she moved forward. Her eyes were about to bulge out of her skull.

"Who is this petulant girl?" she asked. She lifted a bluish finger toward Sierra's neck, then held her long fingernail, sharpened to resemble a claw, inches away from her throat.

Sierra tried to back up but found a guard in her way.

"She is one of ours," Malachi answered.

N'ara smiled an incredulous smile, revealing more than one layer of sharpened teeth. At least, Sierra figured they had to be sharpened. Nobody naturally had teeth as jagged as this woman, did they?

"I would be very careful, child, who you choose as friends and who you choose as enemies."

Sierra spat at the woman, a gob of phlegm lodging in her eye.

"Idiot!" N'ara slapped Sierra across the face, her sharp nails drawing blood as they grazed across her flesh.

"I really don't have time for this," the Queen crowed, gliding back toward her original position. "Guards, take them to the posts. The bots can decide what they want to do with them."

Malachi lifted an eyebrow. "Has your grip on your kingdom become so frail, that you feel threatened by a young woman and her three companions, in search of a few missing friends? I had no idea things had grown that dire. Once you were proud of the allegiances you held. You were grateful for the small relief we could help provide. Now you're a lonely woman chasing a dream that ever escapes your reach."

The icy daggers in her gaze said far more than any words could have.

"You'll regret coming here, old man," she said through gritted teeth.

"I saved your life, N'ara."

One of the guards stepped toward Rhys and was met by a swift elbow to the gut. The guard collapsed, gasping for air. Ed followed Rhys's lead, grabbing a dagger from the scabbard of the nearest guard, plunging the blade into the man's body and sending him crumpling to the ground in a pool of his own blood.

Four more guards rushed from the sidelines. Sierra rolled out of the way of combat.

N'ara rolled her eyes and threw her hands in the air.

In a flash, two of the guards surrounded Ed and relieved him of his stolen weapon. The other stood behind Malachi, sword pointed inches from his throat.

Rhys stood with his hands in the air, surrendering to the sword blade pointed at the base of his skull.

Someone grabbed Sierra's arm, and before she had time to react, it was tied to the other one behind her. Sierra looked over at Rhys, his nose to the floor with a guard on top of him, securing a rope around his arms. Malachi and Ed suffered a similar fate.

"Get them out of here," N'ara commanded, waving dismissively once again. "If the bots want to reeducate these lost souls, let them. But I have a feeling they'll have more permanent ways to deal with them."

Bound, they were carried out of the room without another word.

SIERRA'S EYES tried to adjust as best they could as she stumbled out of the darkness of the Underground, now blinded by the angry sun, punishing the world it was beating itself down upon. One where people were so ready to cast each other aside as if the life it gave was meaningless and hollow. It might not be wrong to think so.

The sun-scorched dirt, rocks, and sand blistered her feet. Her shoes had been removed, along with the rest of her clothing, leaving her barely decent and defenseless to the heat of the day. The sudden change from the cool concrete of the Underground to the scorching desert floor was a shock to her system. She tried a hot-footed dance to avoid the sensation, but a swift jab between her shoulder blades reprimanded the action.

"Keep moving!" The guard behind her had shown her no mercy thus far as she stumbled around. He was one of four pushing them along.

They had climbed back up endless stairwells to reach the surface after another trek through the maze of the Underground. They had walked for hours through tunnels filled with rats and the remnants of ancient structures and treasures. Memories of old storefronts and gathering spaces, undisturbed for two hundred years, passed by. What kept people out of these areas? Treasures here looked to have been untouched since the wars.

Wil would have loved being able to explore here, under different circumstances. He had always been looking for trinkets in the desert. The opportunity to discover and examine artifacts of the ancients—it would have been a dream come true for him. She'd gladly treasure hunt with him. It would be loads better than being pushed through the desert at knifepoint.

She resented that she had been marched through the display as a prisoner, unable to fully appreciate where they were. Her entire life she had been curious about the ancients and what drove them to the brink of destruction. Curious and denied any answers. Now clues lay all around her, but in her present condition, the artifacts, rooms, and other legacies they passed were at best a recognition of a curiosity.

After eighteen flights of stairs, they were escorted out a small door into the middle of a wasteland. The buildings of the city were miles behind them. A testament to the distance they had indeed walked and not just a figment of her imagination.

The guards had stripped them of anything of value. Her medallion hung out of one of their pockets, taunting her. It was really the only item of value she cared about. They were left only with enough clothing to maintain their dignity. The guards seemed to relish the idea that it could be days before the Guardians found them. They taunted them with promises of the sun scorching their flesh and having to beg to be put out of their misery.

It only was a matter of minutes before Sierra could feel the blisters forming on her feet. She longed for her hiking boots that had been ripped off. She wondered how far into the wasteland they were going to travel.

Sweat was already rolling down her back. She tried to position her face so that it wouldn't roll into her eyes and sting, but decided it was a losing battle. She tried instead to keep her focus on Malachi's progress in front of her, to avoid thinking about her own pain. His back was muscular, but heavily scarred. He had been in his fair share of fights. What was his story? How did he get to this place in his life, where he was willing to put his own needs on hold, his own life on the line to champion for a group of people willing to work together?

They trudged along, each step heavier than the last. It felt like they would be walking for all eternity. If Sierra didn't know any better, she might think the guards' plan was to walk them to death, out in the middle of the desert sun. It would likely work.

Ed seemed to be managing just fine. His face contorted into an angry scowl. His muscles glistened from perspiration, and maybe it was just his level of fitness that enabled him to master the hike through the desert with no difficulty. Sierra's life in the Sphere hadn't exactly been one filled with physical activity. An easy life had left her soft.

To her other side, Rhys looked unfazed by the activity, but she knew it was a facade. He put one foot in front of the other, the same as she was, but she could tell he had better control over his mental state. His focus was off in the distance.

He too was muscular, not as bulky as Ed, and more youthfully fit than Malachi. The scars that marked his body were fresh, and he didn't have the years Malachi did to earn as many. She found herself examining his physique for longer than she realized. It was too bad he was so angry. Everyone here it seemed had a story they were hiding from everyone else. "Life is hard out here" is what Ella had told her back at the camp. It seemed to be no exaggeration.

As they trekked on, even Malachi began to sway as he tried

to maintain the pace the guards kept them at. Twice the guards watched him fall face first into the sand as he lost his footing, tripping over a rock or some other obstacle. Both times they laughed as he tried to right himself without the use of his hands, before they picked him up and shoved him forward once again.

He had been running on almost no sleep for the past two nights, between the bandit attacks and searching for their missing friends. How long he could go without a break?

They were outside the Silent Zone now. The guards visibly tensed as they crossed an imaginary line in the sand. Not that they had been comfortable on the outside to begin with. Large, dark sunglasses and nearly full body coverings betrayed that they were not used to being on the surface in full daylight. How would their pupils manage without the sunglasses? Would they eventually adapt as hers did? How many generations had lived underground? So many questions, and still no answers.

As if Sierra wasn't already having a hard enough time, their pace increased from a trudge to a jog. At least her feet felt some relief from the burning hot sand as she hopped from one foot to the other. But her legs were so tired she didn't think she could maintain the pace for long.

She fell more than once, but the guards weren't taking any time to laugh now. They grabbed her and basically threw her forward so she could continue stumbling at the same pace as before.

As they tossed her forward one last time, she caught a glimpse at what she assumed was their destination. The remains of an ancient structure, a ring of a dozen or so rusting metal posts rising out of the ground. A metal ring connected them midway up, but otherwise, nothing else stood nearby or among the columns to indicate what they had been originally used for or why they were still here. There was nothing else around but sand, dirt, and a few shrubs.

Through stinging eyes, she eyed the metal columns, and in that moment, she believed she was going to die out there.

She had one chance to try to escape, and she knew she had to act fast. She eyed her companions. They had failed in their efforts to escape back in N'ara's chambers. But what other options did they have?

Orbs were visible in the distance. They weren't headed in their direction, but she wouldn't be surprised if they were on top of them sooner rather than later. The guards sure had become fidgety. Images of Greata flashed through her head. The charge she had given her to find Terre. To discover why she was having visions and a path forward. Greata had told her she had been born for more. She struggled to see how, especially being tied in shackles, but she wasn't going to let it end here.

Sierra hurled herself onto the ground, in front of the nearest guard. His boot caught her ribs, and she almost vomited as it connected. He went flying past her, headfirst into the sand.

Rhys saw the opportunity she provided, and he kicked the stomach of the stunned guard he was next to, sending him gasping for air into the dirt.

She raced to the guard she had tripped, who was still recovering, and kicked the sunglasses off his face. He screamed as the sunlight burned his retinas. He closed his eyes and fumbled on the ground for them. Sierra made sure to kick them far enough away to keep him occupied for a while.

By this time, the two remaining guards had their swords out, but Ed had managed to hook the neck of one of them with the chains he was bound with, strangling him, as the man tried desperately to fight him off his back.

Malachi, caught off guard, was dodging swings from the remaining captor, unsuccessfully trying to gain position over him until Rhys came up from behind the man and delivered a swift elbow to his forehead. His glasses went flying, and almost instantly, a giant purple bruise formed on the man's temple. He was out cold.

Sierra checked her ribs as best she could without the use of her hands. There was definitely going to be a huge bruise where the boot had landed, but she didn't think any bones had been broken.

She looked up to a hand holding her medallion in front of her, the sun reflecting off its surface, the sun and water lines clean and pristine.

"I believe this belongs to you." Rhys had managed to untie his hands and retrieve her medallion.

She looked up at him, cocking her head.

"Thanks," she said, "but, um . . ." She wriggled her arms behind her back in emphasis. "A little help here would be nice."

Rhys smiled, and loosened her bonds. She broke her arms free and ran her hands over her wrists, trying to regain circulation.

He wrapped his arms around her, behind her neck, and tied the medallion behind her neck, his chest in her face as he did so. He smelled sweet somehow, despite the sweat glistening off him.

The coolness of her medallion as it landed on her chest caused her to jump slightly, causing Rhys to laugh.

His demeanor had changed significantly since they had first met. He was now smiling and seemingly affectionate toward her. What had changed?

"What you did was foolish," Malachi said as he untied Ed. "You could have gotten us all killed!"

She wrinkled her face at him. "We were about to be strung up to die anyway! It worked, didn't it?"

Rhys was rummaging through what the guards had on their persons and spoke up. "She's right, Malachi. If they had left us to the posts, those orbs would be here before we'd have any chance of the Community coming to our aid."

Malachi looked to the distance. The orbs had come

significantly closer in the last few minutes, but they still had some time.

He shook his head, but let it go.

"We should move. Did the guards have any of our other belongings with them?"

"A couple of pistols, Ed's sword. That's it," Rhys said.

"Let's put on their robes then. They'll at least provide some relief from the sun."

Rhys brought her a robe, and Sierra put it on, happy to cover up finally, her skin already warm to the touch from the sun. It was obviously made for a man twice her size; she was absolutely swimming in it.

The others had no such problems. The robe Rhys put on was only slightly too big for him, and the other two's garments fit just fine. Sierra would be tripping over herself for sure.

"Malachi!" Ed shouted. "Look!"

The three of them turned to where Ed was pointing. Between them and the orbs was a solitary white humanoid figure, running right toward them.

24

———

MILES of untouched desert traveled through the bars of Wil's cage. Nothing but shrubs, dirt, and an occasional hill in the distance. The cage bounced along with all the others on the back of the Prowlers' caravan. If the chunks of concrete sticking up from the dirt were any indication, this had once been a paved road. But that was a memory that had faded long ago. Now only an occasional gray spear cresting into the sunlight gave away that this trail had once seen better days. If the bumps he was experiencing were any indication, there were probably several thousand more pieces of that history hidden just beneath the surface.

What would those days have been like? Wil didn't trust much of what he had been taught anymore. He imagined men and women had once been free to travel this road without fear of being kidnapped and sold, without fear of being vaporized by a robot, without wondering where the next stop for food and water would be. They occasionally passed the shell of a building or the remnants of a sign that suggested food had been served in abundance in the world of the ancients. Shrines built to their next meal.

Some of his captors would hurl rocks at small rodents on the road as they passed. They killed the creatures and strung them up beside him on the cart. He wished they would move them farther away from him. The odor was horrid, and he had the sinking suspicion he'd be served the disgusting things for supper.

Here he was, captured. In a cage on the back of a horse-drawn cart headed west. It was hard to believe that one stupid artifact that he and Marco had found in the desert had led him to this place. If he somehow had the power of foresight, he would have thrown that thing in the lake the minute he had set eyes on it.

Not one, but two horses pulled the cart they were on. Ella had told him this was proof as to just how lucrative the Prowlers' trade was. Horses were a rarity. Most had been eaten shortly after the troubles began. People were starving to death, and hunger overruled the desire for fast transportation. Besides, there weren't many places a horse could take you where a Guardian wasn't waiting to either terminate you or send you into a Sphere to be put to work. Today horses were a luxury.

Besides himself and Ella, two other cages were occupied on the cart. Two women, who he had learned were named Ivy and Arigaile. The two had been extremely shy and kept to themselves. He had only learned their names through bits of the quiet chatter they had between them. Most of it wasn't a language he understood. Two more unfortunate souls who had been caught in Prowler promises of food and safety. Unwittingly kidnapped and locked away to be sold at market.

Ivy whimpered softly to herself. When Wil tried talking to them, they greeted him with blank stares and burst into tears. They would frequently lean in toward each other, sobbing in hushed tones against the bars of their cages, but Wil could never make out anything they were saying.

Times were better on the coast, Ella had explained to him. San Francisco was a place with wonders he wouldn't believe. It was hard to get into, but many said the marvels of the city rivaled the technology of the Spheres. The finest specimens were hauled there under great risk to the traders. Four was a small haul. They must have been given special instructions to bring them at any cost. The road was a long one, and the more they could manage to bring in at once meant a higher profit margin. The higher also their risk in being discovered, but they took great art in masking their routes and positions from those looking.

If the Guardians . . . no, not Guardians, *bots*, he had to start thinking of them as bots. The bots didn't guard anything but ancient programs and the enslavement of humans. Guardians, another lie they told.

If the bots found them, they would likely be terminated, or relocated to a nearby Sphere and brainwashed back into believing the lies he had grown up with. Reeducation, they called it. But a few of these traders were willing to take the risk, with promises of greatness and riches. They lived better than most. He was sure these traders didn't eat the same smelly rats that were strung up by his cage. Those were likely only for the prisoners.

On the front of the cart a large pole with a small beacon at the top blinked as they moved. A device that was supposed to disguise them from most bots that weren't within a very close distance to them. He wasn't sure if he'd rather they be found or not.

"You'll probably be bought for manual labor," Ella explained. "Strong men are picked up, especially on the coast for fishing and building. Who knows where I'll end up."

She shuddered visibly, and Wil tried not to think too hard about what she meant. He swore to himself that he wasn't going to let that happen. Between the bots killing off Marco and being betrayed by Oscar and hauled out for slavery, he was tired of being nice. He was going to do whatever it took to defend the last friend he had left with him. And he was going to enjoy it when he got the chance. He just needed to find the opportunity. Looking at his current situation, though, he didn't know where he would even begin to make that happen. But, if he was patient, he was sure a way would present itself.

His best chance for success was to do something sooner rather than later. Preferably before nightfall. They were already a good day's travel from the city. They had been on the move all night, and now it was reaching mid-afternoon. The longer he waited, the more of this terrain they'd have to cover on their own. Not only that, according to Ella, the journey would take them through tall mountain passes. The last thing he wanted was to get lost on an unknown mountain range. Across the desert landscape, he gazed toward the hills in the far distance. They were far larger than the mountains he was familiar with. Their options would be limited in those mountains, and who knew how long it would take them to find their way back. If they couldn't get out soon, they'd probably have to wait until they were at the coast. Would Ella know where to go if they couldn't get out until then?

At least they were being given food and water. "Kept in palatable shape for the buyers" was what they were told. Not being able to get past what the mystery food might be, he passed it over to the two other girls who were caught with them. They could probably use it more than him for the time being. But his rumbling stomach told him he wouldn't be able to sacrifice his lunch for much longer. He was going to need to eat something eventually.

They were also forced to walk a good few miles every now and then. But for the most part they were kept in the cages because they were unable to keep up and slowed the caravan down.

Listen to yourself. You're grateful for any scrap of dignity they give you. Don't let them trick you into thinking they're being kind. That's how they buy your loyalty while keeping you obedient.

"How long of a journey will this be?" he asked Ella, not for the first time.

"It will be more than a week."

She was sitting in her cell, slumped over, staring at nothing but her own feet. Dejected. Wil hadn't expected to see her like this. He hated seeing her like this. She was as confident a woman as he had ever met, and these Prowlers had sucked the life right out of her. They would pay for that. He wished she would be willing to confide in him more. Tell him what was happening behind those deepened sighs and hopeless moans. There was something more than just feeling upset from being captured. The spark in her was gone. It was apparent from what she had told him that she knew a lot about these people and what they did, something from her past was eating away at her.

He tried to keep talking to her. He needed her. Needed to understand their predicament if they were ever going to get out of it. He was still a stranger to this land, and she wasn't just the only friend he had here, she was the key to being able to learn and understand what they were up against. Many times, she answered his questions, and knew a lot of their journey and of their plight in general. But it was all in a matter-of-fact way, and distant. It was nothing like the swooning warrior she had been back at the campsite.

He wished they could have carried on the conversation they had started in the hotel room, before Oscar had interrupted them. Oscar, he was another one who was going to pay for the mess he'd put them in.

Wil let himself recount their conversation that evening, for the hundredth time. He had just finished telling her about Marco, telling her that when he hesitated at the campsite it wasn't at all because of her. He wasn't ready to let anybody else in. Let anybody get that close. She hadn't had a chance to respond before Oscar had come knocking on the door.

Ella definitely wasn't herself, at least not the same woman Wil had been with the last few days. Any conversation he tried to start now fell flat. Something else had awakened in her, something dark, and it was shutting her down. He wanted desperately to help pull her out of that darkness, but he didn't know if it was something within his power to do.

"Aren't we at least going to get a break?" Wil asked one of the Prowlers walking nearest to him. His back ached. It had been a number of hours since they last let him out to walk. If he could get his blood flowing, maybe it would give him the opportunity to think better.

"No breaks now until we get to the mountains," the man replied roughly. "Drones and Sentinels don't patrol there as often."

Six men walked beside their cart, and one sat at the front, guiding the horses. Another cart was pulled behind them by a single horse. Wil assumed those were filled with the supplies for the crew and possibly other stolen goods for trade or sale when they reached their destination.

More than once, gray spheres flew through the air in the distance. Each time the men carefully examined the direction they were going. Once he thought they may have changed the path they were taking.

The road they were on now stretched ahead of them as far as the horizon. From what he could tell they were headed northwest. The sun was on its descent as the day slowly wound down. Mountains to the west grew ever closer. Would they reach their stopping point before nightfall? He could use some water.

Wil sat down, resting his head between the bars. They were just close enough together to provide a resting place. Not one that was comfortable. Nothing about this was comfortable.

A cloud of dust was forming in the distance behind them, perhaps from wind picking up debris. He sat in silence thinking about Sierra and Malachi, and what the chances were of them ever finding them stuck in these cages.

Another dust cloud was forming, this time coming from the direction of the mountains. If it was the wind, it hadn't reached them yet. The air hung still and heavy. The desert heat that had knocked him out a couple of days prior was still out in full force. He seemed to be handling it better today, but even the slow movement of the cart didn't provide a bit of breeze for relief.

The cloud behind them was getting larger and closer. He realized this wasn't wind kicking up dirt. Something was on the road behind them and approaching fast.

Nobody else seemed to notice or care. Possibly it was more travelers. That was a lot of dirt to be kicked up, though. It must be a large group.

Mesmerized, he stared into the heart of it. He squinted toward the horizon, toward its base, eager to determine what was causing the upheaval. Could it just be a windstorm? No, there was definitely movement. It looked like people. Bone-white people.

Those weren't people.

"Sentinels!"

As soon as the words left his mouth, panic gripped the smugglers around them. The cart stopped, and the guards went scrambling to grab horses and as many possessions as they could strap onto their saddlebags. This wasn't the first time they had had to do this. Most of their valuables and portable items were positioned for a quick getaway. Small bags that looked like they were filled with jewelry, coins, and weapons were loaded up on the horses.

Two men jumped on each of the two horses leading their cart. The horses protested, and the guards seemed unsure of how to best position themselves. Neither the horses nor the men were comfortable with this arrangement. They eventually figured it out though, and the two horses took off down the road.

The last two men were taking a few extra seconds getting

their gear attached. Wil couldn't tell if they were just trying to grab more or if they were not as adept at the process.

One of the two men caught Wil's eye, and as if he had forgotten the four of them were there, he cast a look at his smaller companion.

"Shit, we need to get them out of there!" He fumbled for his keys. The other one, half the other man's size, grabbed onto his companion's coat as if he was going to pick him up and put him on the horse himself.

"We don't have time. We have to let them go!"

"They're the whole reason we're here." He stuck the keys in the cell closest to him, opened the door of Ivy's cell, and pulled her out. "If we abandon them, it's all for nothing! These kids are worth a fortune!" He moved on to Arigaile.

The smaller man threw his hands in the air and jumped on the remaining horse. "Leave them! We didn't even get the one we wanted. If you don't come now, I'm leaving without you!"

The large man took a quick glance at the two remaining prisoners, shook his head, and scrambled onto the horse with a grunt. They took off in the direction that the others had a minute prior.

Ivy and Arigaile stood there not entirely sure what to do.

They looked at Wil and Ella with wide eyes.

"Let us out!" Wil shouted.

At the same moment, Ella shouted, "Run!"

Wil glanced at Ella. Noble, but he didn't want to be stuck in here when the Sentinels arrived. The pair of women looked to the south. Wil followed their gaze. The Sentinels could be made out clearly now. There were a couple dozen of them, at least. Headed straight for them. At the pace they were running, it would be only a matter of minutes before they were on top of them.

Tears streamed down both of the freed girls' faces. Ivy turned toward the cell.

"No, no, we need to go!" Arigaile took Ivy's shoulder and looked to Wil. "I'm so sorry."

They hopped off the cart and started running toward the mountains in the west. A smaller cloud of dust hovered over the ground that way as well. Wil hoped for their sake that it was the wind and not more bots. Hopefully the dust cloud would at least provide the pair with some cover from the pursuit.

Ella was standing up now, gripping the bars of her cell, white knuckled, staring at the approaching cloud to the south.

"What do we do now?" he asked.

"I don't have any ideas."

"Do you think these cages could break open if we could knock them off the cart?"

"They're solid steel. I really don't think so."

"How did they detect us? I thought their device was supposed to block their sensors."

She shook her head. "Most of these things are as ancient as the bots and held together with spit and a prayer. I doubt most of them are any good. Anyway, it doesn't really matter now."

"Great."

Two gray spheroid drones flew above them with their familiar light hum. These were the same type of drones that often circled the Sphere, surveying what was happening around the Village. The same type of droid that had collapsed a week earlier. The same type of droid that had started him on the path to this mess. The journey had started with Marco's death, now it would end with his own.

Neither orb was larger than a couple feet in diameter. If he could reach far enough out of his prison, he could probably slap one out of the air. He'd chew through the bars to get the chance if he could. The pair of them hovered over Wil's and Ella's cages.

"What is your purpose here?" a calm voice asked. It may have just as well have been asking him where his homework was. The same soothing voices that he had grown up with his entire life.

All a lie. While they were asking those in the Sphere about homework and grass that needed to be mowed, while they were promising protection to people, they were also out here in the desert killing them. Causing people to flee in terror, to beg and steal just to survive, causing them to sell each other in the hopes that they could feed themselves.

"None of your business, bot!" Wil screamed.

"Hostility detected. Reeducation unlikely. Reintegration unlikely. Humans to be extinguished. Human identified as Wil Underwood. Member of Sphere 892. Status: dead. Status: dangerous. Suspected murder of Guardian within safe zone." Ella fired him a look with a raise of her eyebrow. If he didn't know any better, he'd think she looked impressed. "Human identified as Ella Torres. Member of Sphere 391. Status: dead. Reintegration unlikely."

Member of a Sphere? Dead? Wil shot Ella a look that mirrored her own.

The drone continued, "Status updated to Confirmed Hostile. Recommend immediate termination to preserve order."

"Preserve order?" Wil barked. "Look around you, drone! There is no order here! You create chaos and call it order! You destroy us and call it protection. I will not rest until I've brought each and every one of you down."

Ella was trying to reach for him through the bars. Trying to calm him down. But he wasn't interested in being calmed. He had lost Marco. He wouldn't lose her. Wouldn't lose Sierra, Malachi, or even Ed or Rhys to these machines.

Even as he thought it, he realized the futility in his malice. He was trapped. Left by design to hold off the bots so that the Prowlers could make a getaway, while he and Ella provided a distraction. He pulled on the bars in frustration.

The Sentinels had closed the gap between them. Heavy footsteps and a growing buzz intensified as they approached and formed in a circle around them.

Wil focused on the robot closest to him. These Sentinels could only have been developed for fighting. Large torsos meant to intimidate and provide them with upper body strength. Legs that looked almost unfinished with gray metal and joints exposed, instead of the sleek white enamel that encased their upper bodies. Otherwise, their makers had tried so hard to make them humanlike. Their skin definitely reminded him of Ember, but without the softness. They wanted these machines to look rugged and industrial. Yet still human. Built for battle. Each one even had their own unique characteristics, noses, eyes, and face shapes all slightly different from each other. Why bother giving instruments of death distinguishing features?

He looked into the eyes of the demon before him. Hollow, empty eyes. Blue lights in their place gave them a haunted look. Sensors that could tell his temperature, his mood, what he ate for lunch. But unable to feel the slightest bit of compassion or have any comprehension of what they were actually doing. Following an archaic program of death for two centuries.

"Guardian my ass," he spat at the machine in front of him.

The Sentinel stood looking at him, blue lights illuminating lines on his head, mimicked on the rest of his body. The lights on each of the beings pulsed in unison, shifting from blue to yellow. What were they waiting for?

"Why aren't you doing anything, you bastards?" He didn't know why he was antagonizing them. He knew it was a bad idea. But he could also feel himself at his wit's end. Out of options. Done hiding his anger.

"Hey, bots!" A distant yell preceded a barrage of arrows falling around them. A dozen projectiles hit the ground, and each one detonated an explosive charge. Dirt and smoke rose to create a concealing haze around the captives. Wil could see sparks flying. Parts of several Sentinels were falling to the ground or launching in the air depending on where the explosive head of the arrows had hit.

In unison, each bot turned to face the outside of the circle, forgetting about their initial targets. Nothing but their lights was visible, pulsing through the haze. Each of them grabbed the large weapons mounted to their backs and aimed into the void.

Maybe they could see better through this than he could.

Weapons fire lit up the circle they were in, highlighted by the cloud surrounding them. Sparks from machine contact flew. Wil instinctually dropped and flattened himself as much as possible to the bottom of his cage, trying to keep as low as possible and out of harm's way. He looked over to Ella and saw she had done the same. Sparks were also flying from the cage bars as stray fire hit.

"What's happening?" Wil asked Ella. She was peeking above the lowest bar of her cell.

Before she could answer, a woman appeared out of the smoke on horseback, brandishing a smaller laser gun and firing at the Sentinels. Three more women and three men followed her.

Long dark hair flowed behind the woman as the horse galloped through the middle of the Sentinel troops. Two of the men behind them were brandishing staff-like weapons, taking swings at the bots at close range, knocking their weapons down, but also causing damage to limbs and heads as the staffs made contact. There was no way those things were made of wood.

Each of the newcomers wore armor that looked like repurposed parts from ancient equipment. To Wil the weight of the armor looked exceptionally heavy, but oblivious to what he thought, each rider sat tall in their saddle, weapons drawn.

Robots stood undeterred and unmoved. They simply aimed and fired back. They learned the momentum of the attackers quickly and began to jump, duck, and dodge. Their dexterity was far more impressive than Wil would have ever guessed. They were able to move with incredible speed.

The quiet hum that had accompanied them had now turned

into high-pitched buzzing and projected alarms that rang out into the desert evening.

Sentinel fire knocked one of the women off her horse, and her lifeless body landed in front of Wil with a thud. Moments later, two men met the same fate.

From Wil's count, half of the unknown party were now lying on the earth. Although a number of Sentinels were wounded, they seemed to operate without care for the damage they had taken. A few lay broken on the ground, but the attackers were still outnumbered.

Wil clenched his fists. He had had enough of this. Before he knew what he was doing, he stood up, face red, watching the mayhem swirl around him.

"Wil! What are you doing? Get down!"

"I've had enough!" He hadn't meant to but could hear himself yelling.

"And getting yourself killed is going to help how?" She was pawing his ankle through the bars in the cages but wasn't able to get any sort of grip.

Heat filled his chest. No. Heat radiated from his chest. His chest was on fire. A fire so intense he had to look down to ensure himself it wasn't literally engulfed in flames. Like he was being shot in the chest from the inside out. The heat traveled into his arms and down his legs, pulsing through his veins as if his veins had been filled with lava. Pain. What was happening? Maybe he had been shot? The pain was so great he couldn't bear to open his eyes to check.

He grabbed the bars and threw his head back in an involuntary howl. Minutes, hours, days passed; he wasn't sure. There was no time any longer. There was just pain and fire coursing through his body.

In an instant, it all disappeared, and he collapsed back onto the floor of his cell. The heat was replaced with a sudden chill, like walking into a fridge after being in the hot sun. Feeling the harsh impact of metal on his temple was the only thing that convinced him he wasn't dead. He fought to open his eyes. It took every ounce of his remaining strength. He peered through dust and smoke settling. A couple dozen Sentinels and a few orbs lay lifeless in the dirt. The few humans left standing were staring at him, mouths hanging open.

Then everything went black.

25

Sierra held back as Ed and Rhys drew their pistols toward the lone figure sprinting toward them. Orbs trailed behind the being, blue lights flashing on their exterior.

"We can't hit them at this range," Ed announced. "Hold steady. It won't be long."

Sierra held her hand to her forehead, trying to block the sun from her eyes as she squinted to get a look at the bots in the distance. She wanted to flee, but there was nowhere to go. Nothing but open desert stretched for miles.

The orbs that pursued the humanoid were smaller and gray, not the Onyx that murdered Greata. Still they were pulsing the same blue light, and she wondered if more of these bots would fire upon their victims or if it was only the Onyx that had that ability.

She supposed she would find out sooner than she would like.

Ed tossed her one of the blasters that he had picked off N'ara's guards. It was more compact and much lighter than the gun she had fired at the outpost. She aimed it at the bot before her and braced herself.

"Wait for my signal," said Ed. With the four of them taking

aim, she imagined their odds of surviving a single Sentinel's attack were fairly good.

The heat of the blazing sun was still beating down. Despite the oversize robe providing cover for her skin, more than once Sierra had to wipe away the sweat that dripped down her brow, into her eyes.

It was almost within firing range now. She could tell by the way Ed and Rhys tensed, waiting for the precise moment.

She studied the bot as it grew from a white speck on the horizon to a fully visible humanoid, with white synthetic skin, a white cape flowing behind it, orange panel lighting decorating its exterior, and stark red hair glistening in the sun.

This was no Sentinel.

"Don't shoot!" she yelled. She holstered her pistol and broke out into a run of her own.

"Sierra! Stop!" Rhys shouted, but she was already gone.

It wasn't until she was at a full run that the soreness of her legs hit her. Each step was like trudging through knee-deep sand. Her side ached from where the guard had kicked her, which didn't help. Every step of the way was agonizing, but she didn't care.

This was no Sentinel.

"Ember!" she yelled as she hurled toward her friend.

As the two got closer to each other, however, the look on her friend's face became abundantly clear, and it wasn't excitement. It was alarm.

Sierra couldn't recall a single time in her entire life where she had seen Ember afraid. Emotion was something Ember mimicked occasionally, but being a Guardian, it was something she didn't actually experience.

Sierra slowed her pace, almost relieved for the rest for her legs, but unable to concentrate enough to care.

"Run!" Ember yelled.

The gray orb that was now closing in behind Ember lit up just as the words came from her mouth. A blue beam shot toward Ember, and a plume of sand shot up as it narrowly missed her and hit the dirt beneath her feet.

Sierra took the pistol from her belt and aimed at the bots coming toward her friend. She fired, missing by a mile. The orbs' lighting shifted until a light circle on the gray bot had reoriented itself on her.

Blue light began to pool toward the ring on the sphere, and she knew she was the next target.

She aimed and fired again, and this time the beam made contact with the edge of the orb, but just barely. The sphere was sent into a spin, but it quickly readjusted itself and its path. The second orb pulsed blue lights as well now, getting ready to take a shot where its companion had failed to do so.

She fired again and hit the orb dead on. It sparked and started tumbling end over end.

Lucky shot.

From behind her, more blaster fire from her companions made contact with the orb, sending it freefalling to the ground and erupting in an explosion of dirt and debris.

The second orb met a similar fate, as fire from three blasters slammed into their target. Sierra fired one quick blast into the metal beast, and it exploded midair, leaving a wake of fiery metal and circuitry.

Sierra sank to her knees.

She had killed a Guardian. Despite everything she had witnessed over the past few days, the action weighed her down like a work cart had fallen on top of her. The illusion of Guardians as her protectors had disappeared the night Greata had died, but to kill one of the beings she had grown up believing to be her creators and saviors by her own hand . . . It was a shock to her how much it felt like a punch to the gut.

She almost didn't notice the commotion around her.

"Don't take another step, bot!" Rhys was holding his pistol up, aimed at Ember.

"Rhys! No, wait." Sierra stood up, wiped the tears from her eyes, and sprinted to where her friend stood. She jumped into her arms. It was like she was coming home.

Ember's skin was realistically soft and cool to touch, in the places where she had skin. Her paneling mimicked a type of armored clothing and orange lighting that aided in finding her in the dark or spotting her from a distance.

Sierra couldn't contain all of her emotion as she held her friend, and the tears flowed freely.

"I couldn't leave you, Sierra," Ember whispered, stroking her hair. "When I saw you leave, I tried to help. I tried to stop the Onyx from finding you. But there was only so much I could do without attracting attention."

Sierra stepped back, looking at her friend, who wore a gentle smile.

"I'm so happy to see you," she said, laughing. "I saw you coming. I tried to go back for you, but Wil stopped me."

Ember shot a look at her. "Wil is with you as well?"

"Yes, you didn't know?"

"Communications had told me he perished in the Sphere, the same day that you went missing."

"He was with me when I left, up until last night." She swallowed. It was difficult to talk with how dry her mouth was. "He was kidnapped."

Ember gave Sierra a look, but her expression revealed nothing of her thoughts.

The three men approached from behind Sierra, pistols still targeting the Keeper.

"It's okay!" she called to them. "This is Ember. She's my Keeper and my friend."

"How did it find us?" Ed asked, not putting his weapon down. None of them did.

"Keepers track their charges. That's their function," Malachi interrupted. "You should have told me about her. What's your plan, bot? Bring Sierra in for reeducation? I won't allow it."

"Reeducation?" Ember asked rhetorically. "Hardly. I wouldn't put Sierra through that. I see no need. She seems to be functioning as she always has. With an insatiable curiosity. Though a bit dehydrated, fatigued, and lacking proper clothing. You'll have to inform me on how you ended up with these three, Sierra."

Sierra put her hands up, stepping between Ember and the raised weapons. "What are you talking about? She was fleeing those orbs. They were chasing her!"

"Are you sure?" Rhys questioned. "It looked like she was leading them right to us."

"They fired on her!" Sierra protested.

"Or they were attempting to fire at you and missed," he replied. "Sierra, I know you think she's your friend, but that's how they are programmed. They are meant to earn your trust as they spy on you."

Sierra shook her head.

"Sierra is right," Ember started. She stood straight and unperturbed by the fact that three blasters were pointed in her direction. She looked from one man to the other as if assessing their threat level. Which maybe she was. "Those orbs were firing at me. They were malfunctioning."

"What do you mean malfunctioning?" Malachi spit out the words. He wasn't buying anything the Keeper said.

"They've been disconnected from the network. Something or someone else was controlling them. I have been getting reports of Guardians in this area being reprogrammed and disconnected, as if someone has started controlling them."

"Why were they after you?" Malachi asked. "Are they attacking all other Guardians?"

"They haven't been bothering other Guardians," she replied. "I just got in their way. There was another target they were after."

"What were they after?" Sierra asked. The three others had begun to relax, but only slightly. She put her hands down, but remained standing in front of Ember to block any shot the others might be tempted to take.

"They are after Sierra."

Sierra did a double take as her friend spoke. "After me? Why in the Sphere would they be after me?"

"That I have not been able to figure out."

Ember's white cape flowed around her, red highlights matching her hair. Sierra couldn't believe that she was here. Really here. She thought everything she had left behind in the Sphere was gone from her life, and deep down, she thought she'd be alone forever. Having Ember was like being reunited with a missing part of her. Her friend had left the Sphere to find her. Other than Greata, Ember had been the only one she trusted.

The pain in Sierra's ribs suddenly jabbed at her, and she nearly toppled over. Both Ember and Rhys jumped to hold her up, but she managed on her own. Each breath she took was labored. She closed her eyes and felt some small relief that the sun was setting. She welcomed a cool break from the daytime heat they had been forced to suffer through.

For the first time since they had arrived, she truly looked at their surroundings. Desert plants, rocks, and sand were all that stood between them and mountains in the distance. This place looked so much like the edge of the Sphere that she suddenly longed to be back in her own little town. The days she spent staring at the force field of the Sphere, wondering what lay outside, seemed foolish now. The comfort of her own bed was like a distant memory, and she laughed quietly to herself realizing that was now what she longed for.

But at what cost? She really didn't believe she could ever be content now, knowing everything she had grown up with had been a lie.

About rogue Guardians being after her, she didn't know what to think. But there wasn't anything she could do about it standing in the desert as the sun went down.

"Ember, how did you find us?" she asked.

"Malachi was correct, Sierra. I am able to sense where you are. I was designated to protect you. I was made aware you had left the Sphere the moment you crossed the barrier. I was able to locate you within what those here call the Silent Zone, but I was getting . . . mixed signals from the network about what lay within the boundary. So I waited, and in the meantime, began getting reports on these rogue Guardians."

"And now that you've found her, what's your plan?" Malachi was not as happy with this reunion as she was. His lack of trust was evident in the glare she received from him.

"Well, I will need to be caught up on what Sierra's plan is. Maybe I will be able to help. But right now my only plan is to get all of you the assistance you need to not perish. Bringing you back to the Sphere is not a viable option. I need to know a destination that will be safe."

"What makes you think I'm going to let you go with us anywhere?"

"Malachi!" Sierra rebuked.

"Listen, I have no doubt that you feel a close bond to this bot, but she's still a bot. I am not going to put my people at risk. I have no reason to trust her."

"I know you have had no reason to trust any other bot before, but do we have another choice?" As soon as the question left her mouth, she feared what his response may be. What if he wanted to kill Ember?

He relented though. "For the time being, I suppose we don't."

He turned to Ember, finger pointed at her chest. "I know your program tells you to protect her. That's the only reason I'm not going to kill you."

Sierra swallowed, wondering how to best interject, but Ember beat her to it.

"I give you my word that, within my power, I will allow no harm to come to her or the rest of your party."

"That would mean something if I trusted your word, but I don't. Rest assured, though, if any harm comes to these three, I'll be coming after you."

Sierra wanted to defend her friend, but she was frozen. She had trusted all Guardians until a few days ago. She knew Ember was one of them, but she just couldn't make herself believe that she would ever hold ill intent toward herself or toward anyone.

"The South Outpost isn't far from here," Malachi continued. "Ed, you've been there before. Can you lead the others there? I need to go back into the city to see what Leo's found and gather some supplies for us. I feel we may have a long journey ahead of us."

"I can," he answered. "But what about her? You really expect me to trust this bot? We're just going to lead a bot right into the Outpost?"

"I won't be able to enter the Silent Zone," Ember replied. "I can't detect much properly past its perimeter, and the network won't allow me to enter. As you go in, I will find a place to wait."

Ed nodded, but his face gave away that he was unconvinced.

"Be careful of what you three say around her," Malachi added. "Anything she knows, the rest of them know as well. Try not to reveal any family secrets." His message was directed at Ed and Rhys, but he gave Sierra a cautious eye as well. She was sure he meant about her ability to work tech within the zone. Someone else to hide her secret from.

"I'd like to get to the Inn before nightfall," Malachi continued, "so I'll need to leave right away. You keep Sierra out of harm's way. Make sure she gets there."

"It's my whole purpose," she answered.

"You're leaving us?" Sierra asked.

"I need to let the rest of the team know what's happened. If N'ara's become this bold there is no telling what else she'll resort to. I also need to pry Leo a little further, find out what he knows about the Silent Zone's integrity. This is desperate, even for N'ara."

"Edgar? Are you capable of leading us to this Outpost?" Ember asked.

"I'm fine," Ed answered.

"Sierra, can you walk?" Ember asked.

Her ribs were throbbing, and her legs were barely keeping her standing up. Ember would be able to tell this through her scanners, but Sierra refused to be the reason holding them back.

"Yes, I think I can. Not fast." Oh, how she hurt. She wanted to lie down in the sand and sleep until morning, but she knew she couldn't.

"Good." Malachi nodded. His eyes expressed concern, and he exchanged a silent look with Rhys. "I will meet you at the Outpost tomorrow. Rhys, I know this bot claims she'll keep Sierra safe, but you and Ed are in charge of making sure she does so. Watch for any sign that this one's laid a trap. Be on your guard. Once you're at the Outpost, you'll be out of harm's way. Get some rest until I get there. You'll need it."

"What is the plan after that, Sierra?" Ember asked. "Why are you out here?"

Sierra gave Malachi a glance, who was glaring at her. The fact he didn't want her to say anything was clear, but she wasn't going to hold out on her friend. Network be damned.

"Before she was killed, Greata sent me to find a friend of hers. Someone she said who could help. A man named Terre." She thought that would be enough for now. No need to mention her visions.

Rhys looked at her like she had just revealed the most

incredible information he had ever heard. Ed was pacing, eager to head out, and Malachi's scowl was enough to make her look away.

"But first we have to find Wil. He was kidnapped by Prowlers, and I would love for you to join me, Ember. They'll eventually see you for who you are."

"Wherever you go, I will follow," Ember replied. "I am unconcerned with how others think of me."

Sierra reached inside her cloak to feel the medallion that hung around her neck. Its presence was a comfort and reminder of Greata's request of her. "Thank you," she replied.

Ed nodded, his eyes on the horizon. Sierra doubted he was paying attention at all to what just transpired. "Let's head out. If we go now, we'll make it there before nightfall."

Rhys held her gaze as they headed out. His eyes were intense, but she couldn't read him. Was he angry or impressed? Either way, what had she done this time?

Most of the journey was made in silence. Ember tried to ask Ed more about the course of events that had brought them to where she had met them, but his answers were short, if he responded at all. Despite any assurances, Sierra could tell Ed didn't like being in the presence of a bot and didn't trust that this particular one was trying to help them. Ember was oblivious to Ed's discomfort around her, but eventually she gave up and stopped asking.

Sierra couldn't blame him. Everything he had seen of bots indicated that they were out to destroy and kill.

The Guardians protect us. That was the mantra she had grown up repeating. It seemed laughable now. Would Ember be willing to answer any more of her questions, now that she was on the Outside? She wasn't up for going into detail now, but needed to test the waters.

"Ember. I don't understand why those droids wanted to kill us. Aren't the Guardians supposed to protect us?"

Ember sighed. She actually sighed. Sierra tried to remember if she could remember a single other time in her life that Ember had sighed. Ember, steadfast, reliable, confident. Ed took notice as well, looking questioningly out of the corner of his eye. Ember continued, though.

"You were always one to ask complicated questions. Ever since you were little. Well, it's likely obvious now that the answers to your questions were never given because I had to hide them from you." She paused. "But you have now learned of the Outside on your own. The Guardians do protect, but they also destroy. What's good for the many may not be good for the one."

"Ember, you're speaking in riddles."

"It's complex. I don't have all of the answers to what has happened in humanity's past. Some pieces are kept even from me. As it is, I don't think you have the strength to hear the full answer I can provide to the question you ask. But here is what I can tell you: Some of us were originally designed and programmed to destroy, others were programmed and designed to protect, and as paradoxical as it sounds, some were designed to do both. However, all of us have incomplete coding, like someone tried to add onto our existing program and never finished. At some point, we were given at least a partial update with instructions to keep humanity alive. The Guardians who were designed to kill had software conflicts with the new programming. Through the algorithms, through the studies the Guardians had access to, to our analysis of food availability and optimal environments for humans, population control became one of the methods we have used to keep humanity alive. The mandate to kill never overwritten, the destroyers now had a renewed purpose to control those who strayed outside of our direct influence, and the network over the years evolved.

"The Guardians were programmed to protect humans as a

species. Whether intentional or not, the elimination of individuals, those that are assessed to not serve the greater good of the species, became part of the calculation."

While focused on Ember's tale, Sierra tripped on the uneven trail they were walking on. She managed to regain her balance before hitting the ground and kept moving. She didn't know what to think. If what Ember was telling her was true, the ancients had given the Guardians the mandate to decide who deserved to live or die.

"I can see I'm causing you distress. We should save further discussion for later."

Ember was right. Sierra couldn't think straight, and she needed to focus on putting one foot in front of the other. But these were answers to questions she had had for years. She couldn't help but press on.

"Ember, of all the times I've asked you questions about the Outside, or questions of humanity's past, you never once gave me a straight answer. Why didn't you tell me this before?"

"My primary goal is to keep you safe. I was unable to tell you this before because it would have put you in harm's way. We Guardians set ourselves up as overseers of humanity and hid the truth from those in the Sphere for generations. Belief in our system became part of what we assessed was best for the greater good. Knowing the truth led to rebellion, which led to greater risk of humanity as a species, and to ourselves. Those who know of the Outside are forced to go through an intense reeducation process. I sought to keep you from that for as long as possible."

Ed was staring at Ember now, mesmerized by what she had been telling them. "What kind of bot are you?"

"I told you. My primary goal is to keep Sierra safe. I have been her Keeper for more than ten years, and that protocol supersedes all others. I care about her. I will do what I can to keep her, and her friends, from harm."

"I have never heard a bot talk like you before."

"No. I suppose you haven't."

Both of them seemed content to leave it at that. Sierra was struggling to continue her questions at this point. She just wanted to get somewhere she could have a drink of water and then collapse.

The cityscape lay in the distance to the north. The sun setting in the west meant they were walking toward their destination with it in their eyes. Without any way to shade her face, Sierra spent most of the journey with her eyes to the ground or her hand to her face. It wasn't until they were within sight of the campground that the sun began to dip below the mountains, the shade providing some relief.

They had been traveling for quite some time before Rhys came to speak to her. He had been lost in his own thoughts for the entire journey. His robes hung on his body, just barely too big for him, but enough to notice. His brown hair, clipped short above his ears, was exposed. He had taken his hood off now that the harshest light of the day was fading, and the setting sun played with shadows from the chiseled features on his face.

"Tell me about this person you're looking for," he said. "I'd like to try and help."

She raised a skeptical eyebrow at the young man walking next to her. "You want to help? You couldn't wait to be rid of me before. Why do you think I'll believe you?"

He took a deep breath, looking off to the distance as if he might find the answer there. "You impressed me today," he said. "You stood up to N'ara to help your friend, our friends. I didn't expect someone from the Sphere to be so bold."

"Bold, hah!"

"Give yourself credit. You also saved your bot friend. Even though you have every reason to doubt she's telling the truth. Despite what everyone else may say about her. You chose to believe the best of her."

"I have known Ember my whole life. If I can't trust her, I have no one else."

He shook his head and smiled. "I misjudged you, with no information. Anyone willing to look out for their friends, even those they just met, well, I'm happy to look out for them as well."

Sierra looked down at the ground before her. The words Rhys was saying were nice and a welcome change. But he had still been a jerk. She wasn't willing just to let everything change because he thought she was worthwhile now.

"Thank you," she said hesitantly. "If you want to help, I won't refuse."

"Good," he continued. "Because I may know something of the man you seek."

Her eyes widened. She let her guard down for a moment, surprised by the revelation. "You do?"

"Maybe," he emphasized, looking to the others to ensure they weren't listening. "What do you know of him?"

"I can see his face in my mind." She looked up, afraid she may have revealed something about having a vision that she didn't intend to. When Rhys's expression didn't change, she continued. "He has long, light brown hair, pulled back in a ponytail, dark brown eyes, and wears a pendant, one that has an image of a Guardian." She shook her head. "But that description would have fit him a long time ago. He'd likely look much older now. I'm sorry I don't have much more to go on. The only other thing I know is that he is referred to as 'the man who remembers the wars.'"

Something caught his attention in what she said, and as she finished the last bit, she saw his eyes harden, and then he turned away in feigned indifference.

"Oh," he said. "Yeah, definitely not much to go on. Look, we're almost at the Outpost. We can see what Leo discovers for Malachi and make a plan from there."

He quickened his pace to walk alongside Ed in front of her. Such a strange boy. She couldn't quite figure him out.

Their destination lay ahead, finally within view, an oasis in the desert. Unconsciously she picked up her pace, along with the others, to get to there faster, now that it was in sight. She didn't know where the strength to continue had come from, but she was happy the trek was almost over for the evening.

"I need to stop here," said Ember. They were still a good mile from the Outpost. She lifted a hand to Sierra's silent protest. "I can't cross into the Silent Zone. I'll find shelter nearby. You two keep going. My sensors will alert me when you've left, and I'll meet up with you."

Sierra reached over and embraced her friend. She was always surprised that the android's skin was nearly as soft as a human's, even though her hard panels and lights were a reminder that she was still a machine. But the hug was still a comfort.

"I can't tell you how happy I am that you came looking for me."

"I'll always come for you, Sierra." She looked at her with her warm smile. "Be safe. If you need me, I'll be to the south of the Outpost. Just cross the border of the Silent Zone, and I'll come to you."

26

THE LAYOUT of the Outpost was exactly the same as the one to the north. If it hadn't been for the change in landscape—city to the north, mountains to the south—it would have appeared exactly the same. The Community must have had a plan in place to ensure everything was properly maintained and set up efficiently.

They were greeted with the warmth of old friends as they entered the Outpost grounds. Ed waved to a few people he was familiar with but went out of his way to avoid them having to stop to talk.

Ed led them straight to the Commons tent, though she could have probably found it on her own, if she had any idea what his plan was. The tent was filling up with those coming in for their evening meal. People were just a blur to her. They walked right past them and toward a large basin of water set up to be distributed with supper.

Sierra was so relieved she began to cry and had to resist the urge to submerge her head in the basin. She chugged as much water as her stomach could handle until she felt sick. Too fast.

She took a few moments to breathe before allowing herself a

few more sips. She then followed Ed's lead, washing her hands, arms, and face with a side basin.

Rhys excused himself from the tent, speaking of matters to attend to. Sierra hardly noticed. The feeling of water on her skin was far too enjoyable to worry about him.

She collapsed onto a chair in the corner of the room.

Ed tossed her a sympathetic look and a cool, wet towel. "Rest here for a moment," he said. "I'll see what I can find for sleeping arrangements." He put a hand to her cheek. "I'm really glad you're okay."

She backed away at the gesture. "Me too." She smiled, but it was an effort.

He left the room as promised. Sierra pressed the towel to her forehead, enjoying its cooling effect and the temporary relief it provided to her aching head. She realized she had meant to tell Ed she was glad he was okay as well, but it was too late now.

Ed was still a bit of a mystery to her. Sierra had learned that he had grown up in the streets of the city, that he and Oscar were friends before the Community ever found them. It was a wonder he wasn't more beat up about his friend going missing. Did living on the Outside mean you got used to your friends dying or disappearing? There certainly seemed to be more than enough people and things out here that wanted you dead, and that was if you were lucky enough to have a decent meal.

Besides that, he hadn't shared too much. He seemed always ready to tell a joke or lend a helping hand, but anything personal he was guarded about. Would they stick together long enough for her to learn more about him? The walk to the Outpost had been painfully quiet with him being so abrupt to Ember. Rhys too had appeared to give her a bit of a cold shoulder after probing her about Terre. She wished she could get a read on the man. Openly hostile to her one moment, impressed with her the next, and then distant and quiet.

With everything going on she felt she hadn't even had a good opportunity to chat with Ember. She still had so many unanswered questions.

Long minutes passed. Ed was taking longer than he should have, but it was possibly just her aching muscles ready for a bed that made Sierra impatient. She resisted the urge to stretch out on the floor. Besides, she wasn't sure she'd be able to get back up.

Before long, though, he strolled into the kitchen, a smile on his face.

"Come on," he said. "I've got a surprise for you."

He led her through a maze of tents. The one they stopped at was set apart from the others on the south end of the campsite.

"I made some arrangements. There's something for you in that large tent there. Once you're done, you can head right to your sleeping quarters." He pointed at the nearby tent.

She didn't recognize the tent from the previous Outpost, but a couple people were walking in and out, carrying towels, and many looked like they had just been cleaning. Surely they weren't putting her to work right away.

"I don't understand. I'm so tired, Ed!" She nearly cried. She wasn't going to get to sleep yet? She swayed and barely recovered before holding on to Ed for balance.

"Trust me," he said, that grin returning.

Too tired to argue, she walked through the canvas flap. When she saw what lay inside, she did start crying.

Nearly an hour later, Sierra stepped out of the tub, relaxed and refreshed. The water had since turned cold, but she didn't care, she couldn't remember the last time she had felt this good. It would have been before she left the Sphere. She was going to have to say a special thank-you to Ed for arranging a warm bath.

She had to admit, a public bath house was something she had never seen before and was going to have to get used to. But the thought of soaking in the tub had left all concerns of modesty behind.

Except when Rhys walked by, anyway. She blushed at the thought of him seeing her and did her best to cover up as he walked by. She didn't think he saw her though. It was certainly too dark in the tent for her to have a good look at him.

She dried herself off and let out a yawn. Still tired, but her aches had eased, and the film of dirt was washed off her body. She was once again provided with new clothes and wondered briefly what kind of debt she was running up. She didn't feel right getting so many free outfits. Supplies seemed hard to come by, and she didn't expect to be provided with a new wardrobe every few days. She would have to ask Malachi how she could repay them. She imagined the old clothes were being washed and repurposed, but she didn't want to get trapped because of some arrangement she wasn't familiar with.

The sun had set by the time she got outside, and she was ready for a good night's sleep.

"Enjoy your bath?" Rhys came up behind her, hair still damp. He had changed out of his robes and into pants and a tunic. The belt around his waist held at least one sword she could see, as well as a blaster.

"You knew I was in there?" She could feel her cheeks getting red again. She hoped that with the sun going down he wouldn't notice. The torches were already lit, casting an orange hue over the campsite anyway.

"Relax," he said. "I didn't look."

With his mischievous grin, she didn't believe him, so she punched him in the shoulder.

"Ow! What was that for? Did you want me to look?" he asked, nostrils flaring as he grabbed the shoulder she hit.

Sierra decided to drop the matter. Rhys was getting way too much enjoyment out of teasing her, and she wasn't going to play along. She noticed his eyes wander down to her chest and was about to hit him again, until she realized her medallion was sitting above her shirt.

"What do you really know about the medallion?" she asked, deciding it was a good opportunity to change the subject. She picked it up and held it out so he could see the design better. "Why does this mean so much to you?"

She caught him off guard. She smiled. Good. Make him be the one to blush for a bit.

"Who said it does?" he asked, taken aback.

"Your eyes do, every time you look at it."

He took a step closer to her and stood so that he was nearly on top of her. She had to look up to meet his gaze. "Maybe it's not the medallion my eyes are excited to see."

She stepped back, eyes going wide. Was he being serious? Or was this another game? His face held a smirk that could have meant either.

"Sierra! Rhys!" Ed's cry from a tent nearby broke the awkwardness. "There's someone here you're going to want to see."

Someone else was standing next to him, features silhouetted from the torch behind them. Sierra made out the scrawny build, with a ponytail hanging from behind him. It couldn't be.

"Oscar!" She ran up and gave him a big hug without waiting for him to acknowledge her. He took a step back and lightly patted her back in thanks as if unsure why he was receiving the warm welcome.

"I'm so happy you're here! We've been set out looking for you! How did you get here? Where are the other two?"

"They aren't here, Sierra," Ed answered.

"What do you mean? Where are they?"

"Oscar went off looking for the two of them on his own before we came up to the rooms. When he couldn't find them, he ended up here."

Sierra's eyes were beginning to hurt. She had been crying so much lately, but it didn't stop the tears from forming again.

"I'm sorry, Oscar, when I saw you . . . We had assumed you were all together. But we're happy we've found you, safe and sound."

He looked both surprised and embarrassed.

"Don't worry," she said. "We'll find them, together."

Oscar nodded—back to his old shy self, it seemed. Sierra was just happy for some good news for once.

"I hate to leave the party early," she said. "I'm going to go to bed. It feels like years since I've had a decent sleep."

OSCAR SAT OUTSIDE ALONE, gazing at the tents that made up the Outpost where he had stayed the last couple of nights. Everyone had long since gone to bed with the exception of a few patrols. A faint glow of the sun on the horizon betrayed that morning was near. Meeting with Ed, Rhys, and Sierra that evening had thrown him for a loop. A wild ride of emotions and pondering that he was unable to shake. The hug from Sierra was especially troublesome. He barely knew her. The one time he remembered having a full conversation with her he had basically told her to leave the Community.

Once he had delivered Ella and Wil to the Prowlers, he had arranged to stay at the South Outpost, believing it could be weeks before word got to Malachi that he had been there. He knew he wouldn't be able to stay with the Community forever. He also knew N'ara's men might sell him out or that she may tell Malachi herself. He was taking a huge risk, but he was willing to take advantage of the lifestyle the Community provided for as long as it would benefit him. How long would they believe he'd gone out searching for the missing on his own? Maybe forever, if the Prowlers kept their mouths shut. Which could be viable if he could keep delivering valuables from the Community.

He truthfully hadn't expected to ever bump into Sierra again. He thought Malachi would have sent her packing after Wil and Ella disappeared. He definitely didn't expect her to be excited to see him. She said they had been looking for him. He hadn't expected that either.

Over the last couple of days, he had been squirrelling away the payment he had received from the Prowlers. Ensuring a safe location was hard to do these days, and multiple locations to spread out the risk of discovery and theft was even more so. But it was a hedge against the future. Trading for goods or food was only as good as the amount of storage you had or how much you could eat. Coins could vary from one location to the next. That was why he asked to be paid in gold. Someone was always willing to accept gold. It was just harder to come by, and hard to store safely, but he had his connections.

When Oscar had seen Ed that afternoon, it was safe to say he was a bit apprehensive. Part of him worried that the traders had been caught, and he'd been found out. He should have trusted N'ara's expertise a little better than that, though. She had made the arrangements to have the captives sent out of town the moment they were in their custody. Had they figured out that Sierra had been replaced by Ella? Probably not. A woman was a woman, and he hadn't given them any names.

Had he made the wrong decision though? Had they really been out looking for the three of them? Looking for him? They had assumed he was one of the kidnapped. He hadn't thought far enough to consider what they would have thought of his disappearance.

Oscar had spent his entire life being stabbed in the back, believing he could trust people. Searching for them or not, he wouldn't believe Malachi's intent was anything more than selfishness. On the surface his goal had the same promise as

N'ara's, to keep people safe from the bots. N'ara kept people safe underground. Their condition was fragile, but looking after a few thousand was a bigger task than a few hundred spread out on the outskirts of the Silent Zone. Both provided safety in numbers. It was easier to fend off a few bandits, drones, and Sentinels when you had six hundred people with you rather than one or two.

Both N'ara and Malachi sought control over resources. Both dictated how those resources would be used. Life in the Community wasn't a walk in the park either. In the year he spent with them, he worked harder than he ever had in his life. Constantly scrounging for food for those who couldn't. Taking care of people who would otherwise have been left behind to starvation, bots, or worse. Why had it been up to him to pick up their slack?

One master no better or worse than the other—why shouldn't he make the most of it and help himself up along the way?

But Sierra's presence at the campsite now stirred something in him. Had Malachi really been willing to go through the process to save just him? That was something he knew N'ara would never do.

That brought him to the question of "What now?" He could wait for Malachi, continue with this facade. From what Ed indicated they weren't giving up their search just yet, but he knew it was unlikely they'd catch up with the caravan now. They had to be within the mountains already, on their way to the coast and San Francisco.

He could confess, give them information to help find the kidnapped, and hope they would still have mercy on him. Doubtful.

The only option that made sense to him would be to follow his original plan, disappear into the night. Whether that be now or sometime in the near future. He didn't think he was ready just yet.

Oscar gazed out into the night sky and took a deep breath of night air as he made his way back to his own tent. He had few belongings, but he may as well pack them in case he did decide he needed to make a quick getaway.

Something didn't feel right.

Not with his situation, but in general. Something had changed. He paused, looking around the campsite in his immediate view. Nothing looked out of the ordinary. Being able to sense something wrong had been what kept him alive, living on the streets of Vegas. It never failed him. Something was definitely wrong now.

They were in danger.

The sun was peeking over the horizon. He had spent the entire night trying to figure out his next move. He shrugged off the thought that his fatigue was throwing his senses off. It never did; if anything it heightened his instincts. He allowed the rest of his brain to be shut down as he focused on the sense of dread, as if he could learn more from it.

There was only one appropriate reaction to the feeling of dread that came over him. Run.

Expecting someone to jump out of the night with a knife to his back, he almost missed the lights moving in the sky behind him. Several orbs passed through the night sky. Scanners. Lights across their shells were spinning out of control, as if they were sensing something was off as well. The lights indicated they were scanning. But the intensity of their pulsing bodies was out of control. They had found something new. His stomach dropped.

"Shit!"

He ran the last few steps to his tent and picked up his blaster from his belongings. He turned it on, the lit display greeting him.

"Shit!"

27

Sierra opened her eyes with a start. She must have fallen asleep, but for how long she wasn't sure. Alarms were sounding outside. Not again.

She groaned, sat up, and rubbed her eyes, hoping this was a false alarm. Or that it would be dealt with quickly. Bandits again? Or some other terror she could never have dreamed up?

Life outside the Sphere was nothing if not tiring, she decided. She wondered if this was her new norm. Bouncing from one emergency to another, never getting a full night's sleep. She had often dreamed of what a life of adventure would be like. Now she knew. Eventually she'd just die from exhaustion.

Light outside the tent told her it was morning. At least she had got a full night's rest, but she could have used a few more hours.

She had just finished getting dressed when Rhys poked his head in through the tent flap.

"Sierra, are you up?"

"I'm up. Nothing could sleep through that noise. What's going on? Are we being attacked again?"

"Not yet. But our pocket of the Silent Zone has fallen. Everyone needs to be ready to relocate to a safe area."

She deflated. More walking?

"How far?"

"We're not sure yet. They've sent scouts out to see how far the rift has gone." He caught the look of despair on her face. "Don't panic yet. The interface has been fluctuating for months, especially on the outer edges. We've had to move this camp three times already. Sometimes it comes back. Sometimes it doesn't."

"I'd just like to be able to get some sleep."

He nodded. "If it makes you feel better, you slept most of the night. They didn't sound the alarm until they were absolutely sure of what was going on. Truthfully, I would have let you sleep more if the alarm wouldn't have woken you anyway."

It felt like she had just nodded off, but with the way the past few days had played out, Sierra was sure she could sleep for days before she felt fully rested.

"It's daylight anyway. I can't sleep the day away. What do we need to do?"

"If you could help me pack up some of the supplies, it would be a big help. They'll be packing up the tents within the next hour. They are hoping we'll be on the move shortly after that."

"All right, well, there's no point in sitting here talking about it. Let's go."

As the sun began to climb above the horizon, Sierra and Rhys finished loading the last of the supplies onto the cart that would be hauled to their next destination. He might not have the same large build as Ed, but she guessed Rhys could lift as much, if not more. Sierra wiped the sweat from her brow as she looked at the carts, ready and loaded.

With the whole camp on the move, it meant every man and

woman would need to take turns with the effort. The strongest would take the bulk of the work, but even they would need a break depending on how far they needed to go.

Sierra surveyed the camp around her. The Community was nothing if not efficient. Within a couple hours, the entire camp had been packed up and was ready to move at the order of the Outpost leaders. Now they were just waiting to hear from the scouts, so they knew where their destination would be.

"I don't like it," Ed said for the fifth time in the last half hour. "We should have heard something by now." He had just made his way back from lifting the folded canvas tents onto the back of another cart.

Scanners had been flying through the sky for the last couple hours. Without light to indicate where they were, it was hard to gauge just where they had been flying. But their spinning display of lights throughout the early hours of the morning had made it obvious that they were testing their boundaries. Now that it was light out, they were, for the moment, nowhere to be seen. Sierra was sure that would change.

The thought had barely left her when two of the glassy gray orbs flew directly over their heads. They were a fair distance above them, so it was hard to judge their size. Though they weren't as large as Onyx, they were larger than the ones that had pursued Ember.

She looked at Ed, who was following their path with his gaze. These were the first orbs to fly this close. They appeared to ignore them, though. Ed had explained that the scanners usually came first to map out the area that had dropped. Sometimes these preliminary units got trapped within pockets of live space within the SZ. The field could reform altogether, or partially, causing small pockets that were without a field. Useless to anyone, but occasionally these orbs got trapped inside. They would fly in circles trying to find a way out. Quite funny if you came across one. In a matter of days someone usually took them down and stripped them for parts.

"This isn't good," he said, eyes still following them.

"What do you mean?"

"Those orbs are flying right into the city."

"Has that not happened before?"

Ed shook his head. "I've never heard of it."

It sure didn't sound good, but Sierra wasn't sure if she grasped the full implication. The way Ed's blue eyes were bulging from his sockets, his breath growing rapid, and his hands fidgety, she knew they were in trouble. She'd never seen him this worked up, not even when they were captured by N'ara's men. She shivered as a chill ran down her spine.

Rhys sat on the back of a cart chewing on something he had come across in the cleanup. He leaned back on the packed-up bedding, seemingly unconcerned by the news.

"Ed, what does this mean?" Sierra asked.

"There's either a very big gap in the Zone or . . ."

"It's gone completely." Malachi's voice came from behind her. She turned to see him approaching from the carts. The cart they had brought to the city from the North Outpost was pulling up to join the others. From the dark circles under his eyes, he hadn't slept much if at all that night either. How many nights could a man go without sleep?

"The protection has dropped. I was hoping we'd have more time, and a bit more warning. People were talking like we had years, decades. Based on nothing but hope. Overnight the barrier dissolved like a bubble in a light breeze. There's a chance it may fluctuate back on a bit, but I'd say any reprieve we have is going to be limited and unpredictable."

Sierra eyed the horizon toward the broken city, now being highlighted by the rising sun. "Why has this happened?"

"Whatever the ancients did was never supposed to be a final solution in handling the bots. It was one piece in a bigger plan.

We're not sure what, but something didn't play out the way it was supposed to. Whatever they did here was just supposed to knock out the bots and keep them out until they got life back under control. The plan was to keep civilization from falling for long enough for them to gain an upper hand. They sacrificed their major centers, in hopes of being able to rebuild elsewhere once the robots were under control. Obviously they failed.

"We've been able to keep our freedom in the aftereffect for nearly two centuries. We knew this day was coming. It won't be long before the bots come in and start culling."

"What about the other zones?" Ed asked.

"There's no way to know yet." He seemed annoyed at the question. "This just happened overnight. We won't have any news for at least a week from those places."

"Sorry, I realize that was a silly question. My thought was just if we should start making our way west through the mountains. We could maybe make it to San Francisco while the bots are occupied with Vegas."

Malachi stared back at the city, as if considering the option. "That's not a horrible idea, but I don't imagine they'll have much, if any more, time than us. These things were all dropped around the same time. There's probably variation in the lifespan, could be minutes, could be years, and that's a long way to haul with hundreds of us. And who could we turn away? There are tens of thousands of people here. There's no way we could all make it to the mountains undetected." He let out a long sigh. "No. For now the plan is to stay. First let's worry about our people, and we'll make up the rest as we go. There are another five Outposts that we need to round up. I've instructed our leaders within the city to gather our people."

"You wouldn't want to leave the Outposts out there for protection?" Ed asked.

"Protection? They'd be sitting ducks. Ed, I don't think you realize the scale of what is coming. We have one shot at this, and we're going to need everyone in the same place. I met some of the Resistance on my way here. They are bringing a large amount of weaponry into the city. The best plan is to meet up with them and all stand united together against the incoming threat. Those in the Outposts who are unable to fight will be brought into the mountains for protection. Those who can fight will convene in the city."

"What about N'ara and the Prowlers?"

"Ed," Malachi said. "I appreciate your line of thinking, but we need to get moving. I don't know what the Underground has planned. They may try to wait this out. But let's get our crew together and give this the best shot we've got. We're going to split into two groups. Ed, I'm going to ask you to lead a party to the east and circle around to gather the two Eastern Outposts. I'll round up the two on the west. By now they should be packed up and awaiting further instruction, but if we don't get to them soon, they'll start making their own decisions. Rhys, you can head back to the city and help our teams gather those willing to fight. Those who aren't or are unable will need to be brought into the Underground beneath Leo's Inn."

"Care to join me, Sierra?"

Ed looked over at her, a big grin on his face as if he had been given the best gift he could ask for. Did he not realize Malachi was counting on him to keep these groups alive? Maybe he did and that was part of the excitement for him.

She raised a hand to him to hang on for a minute. Something was tickling her mind. Something Malachi had mentioned about what the ancients had intended.

"Was the weapon the ancients used to create Silent Zone called an EMP?" The question was meant for Malachi, but she couldn't break her gaze away from the city, now with half a dozen Scanners circling it.

"I've heard that term before." Malachi nodded. "I've heard

several theories, though, and that's one of them. Why do you ask?"

She handed Ed her bag as she stepped closer to Malachi.

"Did you learn anything more about Terre?" She ignored his question.

Rhys, previously uninterested in the conversation, perked up and came over to join the group.

"I did," Malachi answered. "Leo thinks he knows where we can find him. But our hunt for him has to end for the moment. We've got to get these people to safety. I don't mean to be rude, Sierra, but your quest will have to wait. We really need to get moving."

"No, we need to find him. He's the answer to all of this. I didn't understand why I was meant to find him, but this connects my vision with what Greata set me out to do."

"Sierra, I understand this is important to you, but we've got bigger things to deal with right now."

"No, we don't." She stood face-to-face with him. She doubted he'd had anyone question his decisions like this for a long time. If she was going to save them, and she believed she could, he was going to have to help.

"If we can find Terre, I believe we can set off another ancient weapon and buy ourselves another couple hundred years."

"Why would you think that?"

"Because I've seen it. In my vision. They were about to set it off, but something stopped them. The power went out before they could use it. If we can find that device, maybe we can fix this."

Rhys stared at her like she had two heads. She realized that this was the first that either he or Ed had learned of her vision, and there were several around who also heard her. The time for secrecy was over. There wasn't much time.

Malachi ran a hand through his hair. It didn't fall back into place as he released it, causing him to look even more tired, like he had just got out of a bed he hadn't slept in. He stepped in between Sierra and the city, turning his back to her to face the ruins of a once vibrant metropolis. He took a deep breath.

This was the most unsettled Sierra had seen him. Whether it was the field going down, or the lack of sleep, the stressful couple of days, or more than likely a combination of everything, it was starting to weigh Malachi down.

"When I talked to Leo, he told me of a place about a day's journey west of the city. There is a small area that the bots can't, or won't, go. It scrambles their sensors, and they are unable to scan or find their way through, so they avoid it. It's not like the Silent Zone, though. People aren't safe from its effects either. It's known as the Cursed Lands. Leo was hesitant to even tell me. He didn't want us poking around. It's rumored to make people sick, kill them if they stay too long. It's a complete dead zone. Some say the wildlife there aren't right either. It's not even hunted, which tells you something. The ancients released something so that neither robot nor man could live there. But somehow this is apparently where we can find Terre. The man who remembers the wars."

"We have to go then. We have to hope we can find him, and that he'll help us." Sierra felt a surge of energy. She was ready to leave—right now. The visions, Greata's instruction, the Silent Zone just happening to disappear days after she left the Sphere. Was this all a giant coincidence? She was willing to bet it wasn't. Willing to bet her life on it.

Malachi shook his head. "I can't go, Sierra. I set up this Community, at least in part, to give ourselves a fighting chance against the bandits, the Prowlers, and yes, the bots outside the SZ. But we also knew this day was coming. We didn't think it would be nearly this soon. We're underprepared, but I need to stay with them and be the leader they are expecting me to be."

The wind started to pick up. Sierra lifted a hand to her face to keep blowing sand from getting in her eyes. She kept her focus on Malachi, wondering what her next step needed to be. She knew deep down what it was going to be but processed all possible scenarios she could come up with in that moment. She let Malachi's statement hang.

"The one friend I had in the world, who isn't a robot, asked me to find someone who had helped her. Told me that he was the key to my vision. I don't know why this has fallen to me, but I have to go. I understand you can't. I'll go alone if I have to. I appreciate everything you've done for me, and for Wil. We will find him and Ella yet."

"I know, but you're not going alone. Edgar will go with you. He's a good member of the Community, but we have other strong lads who can help. I'll get someone else to gather the camps to the east." Ed nodded in agreement. "Get your things together. I'll draw you a map, and you can head out."

"What about Oscar?" Sierra asked. "Should he come with us as well?"

Malachi jumped and grabbed Sierra's shoulders with both hands. "Oscar? He's here?"

"Nobody told you?" Ed replied. "He was here when we arrived. He went out looking for Wil and Ella on his own and ended up here."

"That lying oaf!"

"Sir?"

"Don't sir me. With everything happening, it slipped my mind to tell you. Oscar—" He took a deep breath. "Oscar set us up. Leo discovered that he betrayed us. He sold them to the Prowlers, he helped them into the Inn, and he helped take Wil and Ella."

Sierra's heart sank, devastated that Oscar would do such a thing. What a strange world she had entered where a person would be willing to actually take another.

"The original plan was for them to take you, Sierra. Ella was in the wrong place at the wrong time, and so they took her instead. The bandit attack on the Outpost was Oscar's doing as well."

"Why would he do that?" Sierra didn't know Oscar well. The thought of someone these people trusted backstabbing them and planning to kidnap her! She struggled to understand the motive. "And why me specifically?"

"Only Oscar truly knows," he replied. "But when you've had to fight to survive every single day of your life, allowing yourself to trust others is a monumental task.

"And as for why they were after you, you're fresh out of the Sphere. That makes you an easy target, with few allies to make a fuss if you disappear. I also think he may have been in the practice yard while we were experimenting with your ability. I told you before, once people figure that out, it puts a target on your back. Though it may mean less now that the SZ has fallen."

She looked back at the Outpost members, still readying the supplies for the journey to wherever they were going to go. So many lives displaced. Over two hundred years of men and women fleeing these creatures. That's what they were. Artificial creatures built for destruction.

"Ed," Malachi said, "find out if he's still here. He will need to answer for his betrayal."

Sierra watched as Ed walked over to where the rest of the Outpost residents had gathered with their belongings and engaged in conversation with another man who had been giving orders to the team.

"I'm going too," Rhys said as they watched Ed talk to some of those on patrol.

Malachi shook his head. "I would prefer if you didn't both go. One of you should be enough to guide Sierra, and the more able bodies we have here, the better."

"I *need* to go," Rhys said. "I will be far more helpful to Sierra in the waste than I will be in the city."

"How do you figure that?" Malachi asked.

"I know where Terre is."

"He's gone," Ed interrupted as he approached them, oblivious to the conversation happening. "Nobody has seen Oscar since he left us last night. He's kept to himself so much that nobody really noticed he was missing until I asked."

Sierra barely heard him. She was too busy staring at Rhys, who was meeting her gaze. What did he mean, he knew where Terre was?

"Well, we'll have to worry about him later," Malachi replied. "One problem at a time, and he's a low priority, all things considered. Just keep in mind if you come across him again, he's not your friend, and he's not to be trusted."

"What are we supposed to do if we do see him?" she asked, managing to bring her attention around.

"Bury his head in the sand and leave him for the bots," he said, smirking. "I'm sure you'll come up with something."

Malachi handed Ed the map he had just created.

"Stay as close to the mountains for as long as it makes sense. The bots are going to be focusing on the center of the city where the most people are. Skirt around the city and head to the location I've outlined here. It's just north of the main road leading west. You'll know you're in the right area when you get there. There are signs telling you not to enter."

"Apparently we have no need of this," Sierra continued, looking back to Rhys. Of all the mysteries she expected to unveil, Rhys knowing Terre's location wasn't one of them.

"If that's the case, Rhys, then by all means, you should go as well," Malachi said, nodding.

"Are we able to take the bikes?" Ed asked. "We've been walking nonstop for days."

Malachi shook his head. "I wish we could spare them, but we only have six, and we're going to need them in the city."

"What else can you tell us about these Cursed Lands?" Sierra asked. Anything they could find out would provide some advantage.

"Just that if you need to enter, don't linger. There are stories of people who went in and never came out. And some who have come out and died agonizing deaths in the following days."

"I'm willing to take my chances," she said.

"Once we get to the Cursed Lands, I'll be able to bring us the rest of the way. I know this land better than anyone. Maybe better than 'the man who remembers the wars' himself."

"How do you . . . how?" Sierra struggled for the words.

"Just trust me for now," Rhys replied. "We need to get moving."

Trust him? Out of those before her, she trusted Rhys the least. How could she trust him about this?

Malachi nodded. He put a hand on Ed's shoulder as he walked past them and toward the rest of the camp. They looked as if they were pretty much ready to head out. He made it a few steps before turning back to them.

"Take care of each other out there. You won't have much time to figure out what you need to do. If it doesn't work out the way you planned, I'd recommend hiding in the hills until the dust settles." He turned and went on his way.

She stood staring at Rhys, a smug, self-satisfied look on his face. What other secrets was he keeping?

28

———

As he came back to consciousness, the first thing Wil felt was the rawness of his veins, scorched and abraded, like the back of the mouth feels after burning it with a hot cup of tea. The rest of him felt empty, his muscles like jelly.

He consciously reached out to try and feel the cold metal floor of his cell beneath him, but instead what he felt was soft and warm. Warmth. Warmth surrounded him, and as he listened, he could hear the crackling of a nearby fire. He involuntarily smiled. Memories of waking up next to a fire floated around him, It was the morning after a good long hike, there, but just out of reach. Not any particular image or event—those wouldn't allow themselves in. But the warmth. The tiredness. He lay still and let them flow through him.

"Ella, he's stirring." A voice that was strange, yet at the same time familiar, spoke into the void in his mind. It was there, distant, part of a dream maybe.

"Let him be for now. Whatever happened back there, he's going to need any rest we're able to give him." That sounded like Ella. She had been so nice to him. He had wanted so badly to save her. He hoped she was okay, wherever she was.

"We can't stay here for too long. If the reports that are coming from the city are true, we need to . . ."

The void overcame him again. The sound of voices disappeared into a mild rumble deep in the distance. He let himself float into it. Let it surround him, covering him with more warmth and comfort than he had in a long time. Since . . .

Since what? Something bad. Something the void wouldn't let him remember. The emptiness called to him, inviting him to stay.

Wil drifted in this space, unable to determine how much time had passed. Not really sleeping, not really awake.

Soon the void faded, and light began to break through the comfort. His muscles protested. Stiff and sore, he awoke to a different type of warmth. Humid and heavy, the air around him was heating up as he could feel the sun's warmth. He opened his eyes and found himself within another tent.

He was alone within its walls, though he was on one of several beds. The fire was gone. Had there ever been a fire, or had it all been a dream? There were other beds in the room with him, but they looked like they hadn't been slept in. Or perhaps they had simply been made, their owners having arisen for the day. Where was he?

Wil sat up. His head hurt. He hurt. He found his clothes nearby, got dressed, and decided to have a look out the tent door, unsure of what he was going to find on the other side. No point in staying in bed.

The first thing that struck him were the mountains. Cliffs surrounded the small campsite he was in. They weren't quite the red rock hills he had been used to back home. The brown dirt was reminiscent of the plains they had been traveling on, and the ridges and cuts in the rock offered protection.

He looked down a ridge that was cut through the rock before him. The road they had been on yesterday was visible, as well as miles of empty desert. He could tell he was now in the hills they had seen to the west of the road. The question was, who had brought him here?

Wil stretched as he looked around at the campsite he was in, trying to give his tight muscles some reprieve. His tent was one of four that were set up in the small alcove. He wasn't sure if the others held any occupants, but nothing stirred around him. A pit that had held a fire sat smoldering. It looked like it had been extinguished fairly recently. Light smoke still hung around the embers. Charred wood lay at its base, and he wondered briefly where one could find trees as thick as the cuts suggested. They were more than a foot thick.

A well-used trail led farther into the hills. Without anything else to do, he followed it to see where it might lead. Slightly uphill, the trail was a challenge for his already hurting muscles, but as he moved, there was some relief as his blood flowed. The insides of his veins were still raw, but the feeling was fading.

As he reached the crest, a larger area in the hillside opened up, encircled by the protection of the mountainside filled with tents, stalls for horses, and some temporary structures. It reminded him of the Outpost in a lot of ways. Quite compact, its inhabitants didn't have the wide-open space of the desert to work in. Each tent touched the next. Everything was set up to maximize the space that the natural fortress provided them. It would be an effective fortress, and from what he could see, there was only one way in or out.

The place looked abandoned, in a way that suggested its people had left in a hurry. Clothes had been left out, freshly washed. Items in disarray. The smell of a cooked breakfast made his empty stomach growl. That sure smelled much better than the rat stew the Prowlers had tried to feed him. Whoever had been here had dropped whatever they were doing and taken off in a hurry.

As Wil got farther into the camp, he started to hear voices. He walked toward its source, walking around several tents, toward the center of the camp, where a large decorated canvas tent stood. Two young women sat outside of it drinking something and laughing like old friends.

One of them was Ella, the other a woman Wil had never seen, but who seemed oddly familiar. Her long brown hair suggested she may have been the woman who had ridden into the battle on horseback the previous night, but the whole event seemed like a bad dream, and he hadn't gotten a clear look at her.

"I should probably go check on him," Ella had just finished saying as she was standing out of her seat. Her eyes met his and she smiled. "Oh, he's up!"

The other woman looked his way as well. She didn't smile. Her face was expressionless. Unnaturally so, almost as if it was forced. As if trying to contain any emotion she may be feeling whatsoever. Still, Wil couldn't help but think she reminded him of someone.

The woman stood up as well. "Glad to see you're awake. Your friend was quite worried about you throughout the night."

Ella walked over and wrapped her arms around him gently. She kissed his cheek and stepped back to look him in the eye.

"I'm glad you're okay."

"Where are we? What happened?"

"Elizabeth"—Ella gestured a hand toward the other woman— "and her followers saw we were in distress. They saw the Sentinels gaining on us from their vantage here in the hills. A few of them came down to rescue us from the bots."

"It appears, though, that you didn't really need our help to do so." A faint smile managed to make its way onto Elizabeth's face.

"What do you mean?" Wil brought a hand to his pounding temple. "I can't remember much of what happened after you arrived."

"What happened was you did something. Invoked some

ancient demon to take down the bots. You did something that could change the course of the Resistance forever. We don't know what you did. But we could see the pulse emanate from you. A wave of energy rushed out from you, as if you were an energy weapon. You knocked out a couple dozen droids cold and fried our energy weapons in the process."

Wil stared at them, not knowing what to say. He remembered the sensation now. Of being burned alive from the inside out. Did that feeling radiate out of him and take out the bots? If that's what happened, it damn near killed him in the process.

Ella was motioning to Elizabeth to slow down. Wil appreciated the gesture. His head was spinning, not quite sure how to process the events that transpired. What had happened to him?

Then it hit him. The Guardian. The bot back home, that had fallen from the sky. He had suspected then that he had been the one who knocked it out. This confirmed it. He had had no way to justify that feeling back then. This was different, though. There had been no mistaking the fire he had felt before the bots fell. Or the wave he had generated that Elizabeth said was visible. But how?

Neither time had it been something he had intended to do. Would it be something he would be able to replicate? He also wasn't sure he wanted to. How much of that would he be able to stand? At the same time . . . he perhaps had found a way to seek revenge on the machines that had caused him so much misery.

"We don't have to worry about it now, Wil." Ella was patting his shoulder, clearly concerned. How long had he stood there without saying anything?

Elizabeth nodded, standing. "You don't have to figure out what happened right now if you're not ready, but there's another issue. I promised Ella I'd stay here until you were up and about, but I have to go. I realize you're not feeling well, but outsiders can't stay here without being accompanied by a member of the Resistance. You're welcome to join me. I need to meet up with the rest of our faction down at the city. You can go your own way, or if you would rather accompany me, I can lend you horses as far as Vegas. We can then part ways in the city or you can fight with us. It's your choice."

Wil, still trying to process everything, remained silent. Fight? He was so tired of fighting, tired of running. Could he not just stay more than a single night in the same spot?

"I'll ready the horses. I sense you two will need to talk some more. I hate to rush this, but you'll need to decide fast, or I'll be leaving you outside the settlement entrance." Elizabeth walked past them toward the stable, confident and determined.

WIL TOOK a moment to look at Ella. She looked tired. Bags were under her brown eyes, and her light brown hair was tied up behind her head. She was a mess. But he imagined he didn't look any better. Maybe more rested. She had the look of being up all night. Probably worried about him.

He looked back toward Elizabeth, who had now disappeared from their view. "Thank you," he managed.

"For what?"

"Looking after me last night. You've had to take care of me a lot since we met. I promise not to make a habit of it." He started saying it as a joke, but as it came out, he realized the weight of it. He had been thrust into a dangerous world, and he was going to have to figure out how to stay conscious in it.

Ella shook her head with a tired smile. "You saved all of our lives last night, Wil. That's what we do in the Community. We take care of each other. We're part of the same team now. That's the world Malachi has been fighting for. Oscar may not have understood what that meant, but I know you do, on a deeper level than most."

"What really happened last night?"

"Just as Elizabeth said. You stood up and I could tell you were angry. I tried to calm you down until you started screaming. The most blood-curdling scream I've ever heard. A burst of energy erupted from you. That's the only way I can describe it. Drones and Sentinels were flattened. You were knocked unconscious as well. Elizabeth brought us here to spend the night with their camp."

"Who are they, Ella? Who is Elizabeth, and what is this Resistance you keep talking about?"

"I keep forgetting you haven't been in this world very long." She took a deep breath as if trying to figure out how to condense a very long story. "The Resistance have made it their cause to take down the bots. They've made it their mission to destroy them. All of them. No matter how long it takes or how many casualties they make suffer. Their goal is to restore the world the ancients destroyed and free humanity from their oppression."

"A noble goal," he answered.

"A foolish one." She shook her head and sighed deeply. "The bots rebuild themselves. For every one we take down, they produce another. We're just lucky that built-in protocols stop them from producing more than they deem necessary. The ancients at least programmed them with some built-in efficiency. There are limits to how many there are at any given time. But as long as they have the ability to restore and rebuild themselves, it's a losing battle. The Resistance aren't convinced. They believe there is a point where if they destroy enough of them the collective mind that controls them will be weakened or give up rebuilding."

"So, they're an army at war with the bots?"

"You could think of it like that. Though the bots believe they are at war with all humans. The Resistance, you could say, just hasn't given up on the fight. The rest of us . . . the rest of us are just content to survive."

"That doesn't really sound like living." Wil tried hard not to scoff.

"What do you know of it?" Ella snapped. "Two hundred years of suffering at the hands of these machines! Not just those who died at their hand, those who died because they couldn't get food or water! Those who died due to the spread of disease. Those who died at the hands of fools trying to hoard supplies for themselves. That's why the Community provides so much hope. A group willing to work together. You don't know what that means to us. Malachi's vision has given us life again."

Wil shook his head and cast his eyes to the ground. "I'm sorry. You're right. I have no idea. I've been sheltered from all of this."

The two remained silent for a few minutes. The weight of Ella's words hung heavy on him. He had no idea what the world had been going through while he had been stuck, safe in the Sphere, oblivious to the plight of those who hadn't been as lucky as he had. He'd had access to food, water, safety. All for the price of a lie. He had also suffered loss at the hands of those who had promised protection. He wouldn't forget that.

They were going to have to make the decision to go. "Who is this Elizabeth woman? Do you trust her?"

"She's the leader of this arm of the Resistance. She's very well-known and a good leader. I don't agree with their philosophies, but yes, I believe we can trust her. People say she's a visionary and a remarkable leader, able to think one step ahead of the bots. They were on their way to the city when they came across us. They had no reason to help us and did so anyway, even if you were the one who dealt the final blow. She sat here with me in the early morning hours so that we could stay and give you a chance to recover. There would be nothing for her to gain to betray us now. Yes, I believe she is trustworthy."

"Where is everyone else? Why does she want to leave so quickly?"

"The rest of her group have left to make preparations in Vegas."

"Preparations for what?"

"War."

29

STAYING UPRIGHT WAS MORE of a challenge than Wil had anticipated. He had never seen a horse in person, not before leaving the Sphere, never mind ridden one. *What would people do with a horse within the Sphere?* he wondered. Those that required travel between the three villages were provided with electric transport. Shipments between the villages were taken care of by the Guardians. On shorter hauls, like from the Ag district, people typically hauled their wares themselves.

He had assumed that a horse was not much different than a cow. Boy, was he wrong. The animal had a mind of its own, and the horse had decided he definitely did not want Wil sitting on his back.

He envied Ella and of course Elizabeth, who both made riding a horse seem noble, graceful—and easy. He had to keep reminding himself that these women had ridden horses practically all of their lives—of course they'd be better at it than him. A foolish Spherian that had only just been birthed into the outside world. Naive of more than he cared to admit.

His horse's name was Stepper. Wil decided it was a fitting name as it liked to step back and forth while he was trying to get on. He finally did manage in the end though. Now he had to control his movements so as to not be thrown off.

"I thought you said these things were rare!"

Elizabeth tried her best to contain a smile. Well, he hoped that was her best. But at least she made it seem like she was trying, which only helped his bruised ego slightly. He had to admit it was nice to see that she was capable of smiling. Even if it was at his expense. This was the first warmth he had seen from her. Though, considering everything this world seemed to offer, he couldn't fault someone for becoming jaded.

"They are, but the Resistance has many allies," Elizabeth answered. "To give up a few horses to the cause is a small price to pay."

Despite her muted chuckles, she did provide him with some basic instruction, which alleviated his discomfort and anxiety slightly. Wil had a feeling Stepper still wasn't going to give him an easy time.

It hadn't taken long for them to get saddled up and moving. As they stepped out onto the trail, he could focus on little else but trying to keep Stepper in line and the news Ella had told him.

The Silent Zone that protected the area and Vegas from the bots had fallen. Through barely concealed anger, she had recounted the news of how the city would come to ruin. The bots, she feared, were going to take away everything they had ever worked for. The remnants of the world she knew were going to crumble, and the only fragment of humanity that would be left would be those under the reign of the bots within Spheres.

At first, he didn't comprehend the implication of the Silent Zone being gone. But then she broke down what it meant for those who lived within the SZ. Even though they were barely hanging on to life, sometimes literally fighting for their next meal, it was still all anyone who lived there knew. Not only were they about to lose their home, they were about to lose the last bastion of human freedom, one those in the Sphere didn't even know they were missing.

And that was it, wasn't it? Up until he saw his best friend obliterated by a flash of light from one of those monsters, he hadn't known any different either. It was funny, as he looked back into his childhood, he tried to find clues, hints of what he had missed. Throughout his entire life, he had no idea how tightly the Guardians controlled them.

The gravity of the world Wil had entered fell around him. He was suddenly happy to have Stepper under for him for support.

Miles away from where he sat, everyone he had ever known believed that nobody else existed outside of their bubble. They believed horses were extinct, and that the Guardians had saved the last fragment of humanity. They believed the ancients had destroyed the world in trying to kill themselves. But they hadn't. They had been trying to stop them. To stop the robots from taking over everything. They had not fully succeeded, but they had managed to hold them off for a couple of centuries, and now the small success the ancients had achieved had failed. And this whole world, that he had just discovered, would be lost if they couldn't stop it.

How could a few fighting factions do what the ancients couldn't?

Everything he had ever known was a lie. The whirlwind of events that had happened since he picked up that damned radio had fogged his vision to the enormity of what this all meant. Just a boy and a toy, distracted by a small drop in a big world.

And now that he'd discovered this world, discovered the underlying evil of the truth, the world was at risk of losing it all. And there was nothing he could do to stop it.

Sure he had knocked a couple of Sentinels out on the road, but Wil had no idea how, and it had damn near killed him. If he could repeat what he had done, would it finish the job? Or just incapacitate him enough that a rogue bandit, Prowler, or someone else in this hellscape could come along and do it for him?

Wil wasn't going to let them. He wasn't going to let them win. No matter the cost.

His pulse pounded fast in his ears. Adrenaline coursed through and somehow eased the veins that were still fatigued from his incident the night before. Unconsciously he had been pushing Stepper faster, and the horse responded as though he understood his growing desire to win this battle. His growing desire to take down as many bots as he could, no matter the cost.

Maybe he could grow to like the animal after all.

"Easy now," Elizabeth called out as he started to catch up to and then pass the two women. "We need to keep the horses' strength up as long as possible. It won't do us any good to burn them out before we get there."

He pulled back on the reins like she showed him to slow Stepper down.

"I may be getting the hang of this," he said, not bothering to conceal how impressed he was with himself.

"Let's see if you still say that with bots firing at you."

His smile disappeared, and he fell back toward the rear of the other two as they laughed at his cockiness. *Deserved. Ouch, but deserved.*

"Horses are loyal creatures. They'll give you all you ask until they fall over. It's up to you to respect them enough not to push them to injury."

Wil focused his attention to the Scanners that were circling the skies around the city. There were half a dozen that seemed to be sweeping the area.

"They're mapping the SZ," Elizabeth said as if reading his thoughts. "They haven't seen this place for over two hundred years. They're updating their maps and building a case for how to best deal with what they find."

"And what's that?"

"Tens of thousands of new humans they thought were eliminated two hundred years ago. We're just lucky they are being thorough with the scans. We've been worried they'd send the entire Onyx fleet the moment they realized they could get in."

"You've expected this to happen?"

"The boundary has been faltering for months now. There have been glitches throughout the SZ of areas disappearing and reappearing. We thought it may simply just fade away, slowly with time. But this, it just all disappeared at once." She shook her head. "It's our greatest fear come to life. I had a sense it was coming, but it doesn't make it easier."

They passed over a rise, before they witnessed a pillar of smoke billowing from the side of the hill. Small flames licked a structure standing likely hours before. A couple of goats and chickens lay lifeless next to the remains of the building, half scorched themselves. Wil peered into the wreckage from their path.

"What happened?" he asked.

"Guardians," Ella answered. "Looks like it was a small farmhouse."

"Shouldn't we see if anyone survived?" Wil asked, pulling his horse toward the carnage. "We should help!"

Ella rode up beside him, a sad look in her eyes reigning in his bravado. She pointed to a pair of legs that lay out on the ground, in front of the home. A black pile of debris marked the only evidence of them being attached to a body. Another body lay in a heap a little farther from the home, black with char.

"If anyone had survived," she answered, "they wouldn't still be here."

A droid glided past them, and a ring of light pulsed from one side of its body to the other. Wil reached for the weapon he had been provided, strapped to his back. There was going to be one less of them.

"Don't!" Elizabeth's sharp response made him pause, hand still behind his back, fingers already grasping around the weapon's grip.

She grabbed his arm and brought it away from the weapon he held. He let her bring his arm down.

"Right now they don't see us as aggressors. These are just surveyors. The ones that attacked would have moved on. These have much more to worry about than three lonely travelers. The longer we don't pose a direct threat, the longer we have to prepare, and the better chance we are able to help those who are unable to fight. Shoot it down now and they'll come after us, and then launch their assault if they deem it necessary."

Wil realized he was holding his breath. He released it as well as the tension that held the rest of him.

"I know just as well as anyone that it would be gratifying to shoot it down. But we need to think rationally, or we doom the lives of many. It's likely those at this house attacked them. These Scanners would send Sentinels after anyone they found. But with the entire Silent Zone gone, they'll need to sort out their priorities. Let them go for now. We'll have our time to fight."

Wil hadn't thought about the consequences. How many more of his rash decisions were going to get him and his friends in trouble?

The droid continued its path toward the heart of the city, leading the way, an ominous foreshadowing of what was to come.

Earlier, he had decided with Ella that they would ride with Elizabeth into the city. Once there, they would go their own way to see if they could track down Malachi, as Ella insisted the man wouldn't rest until he either found them or believed them to be dead. They'd start at the Rio Grande. With any luck Malachi would have told Leo his plan.

The road was completely desolate on their way in. Not a single other soul. Wil wasn't sure if that was normal or not. He imagined that there wasn't too much travel outside of the SZ on a regular day. But the thought of the scorched victims at the farmhouse was likely enough to keep anyone from roaming too far.

He wasn't familiar enough with the terrain to know where the invisible line of the SZ would have started, but he could guess it was about the time where Elizabeth started to fidget in her saddle. It wasn't a nervous fidgeting, but more like a sense of uneasiness. She knew something wasn't right. Wil tried to feel with his mind if he could tell the difference—if there was something in the air that was different. Nothing. It must have been her knowing where the boundary should have been.

They passed more and more ruins of ancient buildings and infrastructure as they got closer to where the city's core now was. Fragments of structures and artifacts stuck out of the ground. Forgotten for hundreds of years, buried by centuries of sandstorms and neglect. He would have loved to stop, explore. So much history just lying around abandoned. In the Sphere he had always been happy to find a coin or scrap of something the ancients had left behind. Out here, mounds of debris had been left abandoned. The treasures that were waiting—he imagined he wouldn't know where to start or how to choose the most interesting piece to collect. But he made a mental note to keep an eye out for an opportunity.

Steady they rode as they morning wore on. Wil had forgotten how far they had ridden out in the cart. They were beginning to close in on their destination. Skeletons of skyscrapers rose before them. A group was gathered on the road in front of them, men and women, a few dozen of them, many holding weapons.

"What's this?" he asked. "What are these people doing?"

"They're getting ready to defend their homes. Some of them are Resistance. Others just live here and want to fight."

"Why aren't there more of them? There are thousands of people that live here."

"Some of them are waiting farther down the road. Many of

them are underground, unable to fight. Some are apathetic about the whole thing. They've lived under N'ara's rule, or someone similar for so long, what's one more oppressor?"

"Sounds like they're barely living. Remind me again what you're fighting for?"

"Things may seem hopeless. In many respects they are. The Resistance has made it our life's work to take the bots down. With them out of the way, humanity finds itself again. We fight for a life that isn't restricted to caves, mountains, and artificial barriers, where we don't have robot soldiers threatening us for trying to bring food back to those we care about. We don't have to see those we love left in a bubble, being lied to about how the world came to be this way." Elizabeth held Wil's gaze as they rode on. "We fight for a world where we don't have to watch our saviors kill the ones we love."

Wil kept his focus on her, even as she turned back to the direction they rode toward. Although more of an impassioned battle cry, this was the first insight into herself that Elizabeth had let on. Her words struck close to home. Had Ella told her about Marco? Either way, her words rang true. Perhaps he had found a place where he belonged in this twisted world after all. Of course, that would all depend on how this ended.

Elizabeth rode up to a man at the front of the group. "What's your status?"

"Most of the residents have put their fate with N'ara underground," he answered. "To be honest, without weapons, they're probably safer there. We have eight groups roughly this size of men and women surrounding the city, ready to keep them at bay for as long as possible. Malachi's got some Community members setting up on the Strip, and we have our new laser cannon set up a few blocks away. There are also a few of the men who went to see if they could bring life into the old tanks that have been rusting on the south end, but after two hundred years, I'd be surprised if there's any way to start them up. I told them they'd probably been stripped for parts decades ago."

"I'm sure you're right. See if you can pull them out of there. We're going to need all hands on deck once the Onyx show up."

She turned to him and Ella. "If you're continuing on into the city, you can leave your horses here. I'll have a couple of our people use them to communicate with each other between the groups."

"Thank you," he answered. They dismounted their rides, Wil not so gracefully, and handed the reins to the man Elizabeth had just been talking to. "Once we have found our friends," he continued, "and have figured out our plans with them, I wouldn't be opposed to joining your cause."

Ella grabbed Wil's shoulder and whispered in his ear, "Careful."

He shrugged her off and waited as Elizabeth met his gaze once again, studying him as if judging the sincerity of his statement. "You would be a great ally to the cause. Your skill would come in handy if you can learn to control it. I hope you find your friends. When this is done, if we are both left standing, seek me out. The Resistance lives as long as one is willing to fight."

Wil walked away with Ella, making their way toward the Inn, leaving the group of Resistance fighters to forge their own plans. As they reached a distance out of earshot, Ella once again pulled him close.

"Don't be too hasty jumping into the Resistance, Wil. Their intentions may sound good, but their goal is foolish. The bots cannot be defeated. Not through force."

"We shall see," he said.

"For each bot they take down, another is created in its place. The ancients created a number of bots they wanted in the field at all times. They are programmed to recreate themselves to always maintain this number. There always exists the same amount, no more, no less. The best we can hope for is to be able to work together to avoid, evade, and outsmart their programs."

He had no interest in sitting back and letting the bots destroy these people or in playing along with their deception. The Resistance seemed to think their fight was worthwhile. He was willing to at least find out why. He pushed ahead a half a pace faster to let her know he wasn't interested in continuing the discussion. She kept up, but got the hint, and the two walked in silence.

Ella couldn't understand Wil's passion. Couldn't understand the need to see each and every one of these bots brought down. She could drone on about aiming for peaceful living. But how could there be peace when threat of destruction always loomed in the distance? And now that the Silent Zone had fallen, that destruction was headed for their doorstep. He meant what he had said to Elizabeth—this was no way to live. This was just trying not to die. He would make sure Marco's life meant something and do his best to put an end to the bots. Each and every one.

ELLA DIDN'T BLAME Wil for feeling the way he did. How could she? Joining the Resistance had crossed her mind when she first realized the truth around her, but she didn't have time to harbor those feelings for long. Before she'd had a chance to process the evil that the bots caused around her, she had been betrayed by a person she thought she knew, sold to the Prowlers. She had escaped that living hell with the help of Malachi, and since then, dedicated herself to helping his cause. She had traded revenge for helping her fellow humans, who were doomed to struggle by their ancestors.

How could she seek revenge on the bots, when it had been humans who had caused her the most pain?

Still, Ella worried for Wil. He was basically a newborn in this strange world and didn't understand the power struggles at play. Jumping in headfirst was a good way for him to get himself burned, probably taken advantage of, like she had been. She didn't trust Elizabeth either. Something seemed off about her. She was wary about Wil having been a member of the Sphere, like that made him part of the Guardian Order or something. Yet she also seemed to want him to join the Resistance so they could utilize his ability.

They approached the Rio Grande just as Malachi was leaving the building. Ella couldn't believe their luck. Leo was with him, and the two were engaged in an intense conversation.

"Malachi!" she yelled, ignoring whatever conversation he was engrossed in. She closed the distance between them to him and wrapped her arms around him.

"Ella! You're safe!" If she didn't know better, she would have thought he was about to cry. "We've been looking for you and Wil!"

Malachi looked at her and then to Wil as he spoke. He put a hand on Wil's shoulder as well. "I'm glad to see you both. How did you escape the Prowlers?"

"You know?"

"Yes, and about Oscar. Leo had some of his men track down what happened the other night. We searched into the belly of the Underground, where . . . well, things didn't go so well for us there either."

"It's okay. We managed," Ella responded. "We had some help from the Resistance. Though with bot killer here we may not have needed it."

"Bot killer?" He looked to Wil. "The Resistance? I wish we had the time for you to tell me more about it."

Ella nodded. "We will have time yet, but there are more pressing things to concern us."

Malachi looked to Leo. "Thank you once again my old friend

for everything you have done. I'd ask you to join us, but I know you have your own matters to attend to. Do you know where you will go?"

Leo shook his head. "I've already closed the Inn. Most of my guards have decided to join you or the Resistance to try and hold them off as long as possible. I'm too old. I'll just get in the way. There are underground passages beneath the Inn—ones not connected to N'ara's realm-where I'll probably wait out the initial attacks. If some of your people are unable to fight and need a place of refuge, I have more than enough space."

"I'll send those with children and those who are unable to fight here. You've been too kind to us."

"You treat your people well. They are your equals, and I respect that. It gives me hope for the future. N'ara would replace the tyranny of robots for that of her Prowlers. I'd rather see the Community thrive."

"Have you heard any word from the Order since the field dropped?"

"They've been strangely quiet. Not that I mind, but they seem to be waiting things out somewhere else."

"Ella, Wil, I know you're probably tired of travel, but there are still some of the folks from a few Outposts who have yet to arrive. I am heading out to make sure they are on their way and get them here and prepared for battle. You're welcome to join me, but you can wait here if you prefer."

"Do we have a chance at protecting the city?" Ella asked. "There could be hundreds of Onyx here at any moment."

"To be honest, chances are slim, Ella, but what choice do we have? Hopefully we can at least buy people time to get to safety."

"I'm going to stay here and prepare with the Resistance," Wil announced. "I don't think you need me to join you. I'll be of more help here."

Ella scoffed. The fool was going to get himself killed. If he was going to blatantly ignore her warnings, there was nothing else she could do for him. Malachi turned to face him. His face betrayed his fatigue, but there was also sadness in his eyes.

"I don't know if Sierra would forgive me for leaving you behind so soon after finding you."

"She'll understand," he answered. "I need to do this."

Malachi nodded. "Very well. I have no hold over you. You are free to choose your own path."

"Is Sierra with the other Outposts? What about Rhys and Ed?" Ella asked.

"Sierra is still on her quest to find this Terre fellow. She thinks he'll have a solution for all of this. Ed and Rhys went with her. We may take different paths during this battle, but we're still on the same team. Our journey with our new friends is still not done." He looked to Wil, but Wil was barely paying attention, if at all. Wil nodded, but he was eyeing up the battlements being set up farther down the road.

Malachi motioned for Ella to come with him, and they turned toward their new destination.

"Wil." Malachi turned to look at Wil. At the mention of his name, Wil looked back and returned his gaze. "The road to revenge is a treacherous path. At the end is never what one expects to find."

"Sometimes the path we're on is chosen for us," Wil replied.

30

———

DESPITE THE GLARING heat of the sun, Oscar had his hood pulled down. A breeze had picked up slightly and was cool against his shaved head. His skin didn't burn easily, so he wasn't worried about it being exposed. He was just happy for the relief.

He hung back. It was hard not to be seen in the flats of the desert, heading to the north, but he didn't want Malachi's charge to know he was following. He didn't know how they'd react, but he needed to make right what he had done. He didn't know how he would do so, but he was willing to wait.

Last night he had packed up his tent as the alarm was sounding, filled a backpack with all he could reasonably carry, and started to head toward the mountains. Then he sat and watched, waiting to see how the Outpost would handle the situation.

He had thought they would degenerate into chaos. He had waited for them to show their true colors, an every person for themselves mentality hidden beneath the guise of cooperation. N'ara also promised her subjects riches and sharing, but in the end the spoils went to herself and those close to her. Those willing to make a deal ended out on top. The rest were left fighting over scraps.

That was Malachi's game. Oscar had been so sure—so sure that he was willing to sacrifice the lives of two strangers for his own gain, and then, when things didn't go as planned, to sacrifice the life of someone who probably considered him a friend.

Last night, after the alarm sounded, he had watched as the Community members worked together to clean up the site. It was not that surprising. It wasn't the first time they'd had to move because of a Silent Zone fluctuation. They tried to keep their camps close to the edge of the protected areas, so that they could easily access nearby resources. Each of them a cog in the machine. This was just one part they played.

But Oscar knew better. He had seen that orb fly right into the heart of the city. There was no Silent Zone any longer. Once they found that out, their instincts would kick in. Malachi's farce would be on full display, and he'd take his spoils and run.

Why did he doubt Malachi? The same reason he doubted everyone. He had never met someone who wasn't shaking your hand with one arm and picking your pocket with the other.

Every man had a price. Malachi was resourceful, charismatic, a leader. Oscar had met men like him before. Been burned by men like him before. Nobody in Vegas put the needs of others ahead of their own. Nobody. It was a quick way to end up dead. Or sold to an interested party. Like those he had betrayed to the Prowlers.

But tonight had made him question his thinking. If only he could have seen it earlier.

First Sierra had greeted him like they were best friends from long ago. Happy to see him. Happy he was okay. She didn't know, couldn't have known. But she had thought he was among those missing. And even when she had seen her beloved Wil wasn't with him, she had still been grateful he was okay.

Oscar had written it off as the naivety of the Sphere. Sure, it was nice to be missed, but that kind of thinking was what made the few who escaped the Sphere easy targets. Ella had already been tricked into slavery once because of it.

But then he had seen the reaction of Malachi and his followers when they learned the Silent Zone had fallen completely. They had rallied together, packed up, and traveled directly into the city. Directly to where the bots would be descending when they realized so many souls were outside of their jurisdiction.

That was when he knew he had misjudged Malachi.

Malachi could have run. He could have taken his stock of weapons, food, and supplies and disappeared into the night. Just as Oscar had.

But he didn't.

Malachi loaded up the caravans. He gathered the provisions and rallied people to protect each other.

That was when Oscar had decided he needed to help. He just didn't know how. If he were to approach Malachi now and offer, he'd be locked up. Malachi knew the truth. He wouldn't take him at his word of redemption. He had no reason to. He had given Oscar every chance to be part of the Community, and Oscar blew it, because of greed, because of mistrust.

So Oscar stayed behind, sat in the mountains, and watched as they packed up.

Oscar watched as Sierra left with Edgar and Rhys, the two men who had called him their friend. Whose trust he had betrayed. Who had probably been the only true friends he'd ever had. He watched as they began their journey toward the north, and he knew it was his chance. He didn't really know where they were going, and it didn't really matter. He was going to help them. Somehow. He just had to prove himself. Maybe if he could help them, Malachi would see he had changed.

That was how Oscar ended up in the middle of the desert, sweat streaking down from his shaved head, across his face. The breeze still provided relief, and he tried to fan himself with his robe to allow it access to the rest of him. His nose wrinkled as he caught a whiff of his own odor. It had been days since he had had a proper shower. He should have taken the opportunity at the Outpost when he had the chance.

Blasters hung by his side. He'd be ready in case of an attack—and they were likely to be attacked, crossing in the open desert like this. The fall of the SZ almost guaranteed there would be more bots out than normal. It was only a matter of time. Where could they be going? There was nothing of interest in the direction they were headed.

Hot and sweaty, he followed them from as safe a distance he could manage without being spotted or completely losing them. He managed to luck out as he came across the remains of an old building. He ducked behind a partial brick wall, just as a bot jogged past.

He had never seen a bot like this one. He almost didn't realize she was one. That hair, though. No human had hair like that. Except Sentinels didn't have hair at all, so what did he know? The bot appeared to be shaped as a woman with bright red hair. Her skin bone white.

He watched. Watched as she joined up with Sierra and Ed and they started chatting like old friends. The bot was with them. He wasn't sure why, but she was.

Oscar continued to follow, waiting for his chance.

31

"YOU KNOW, we haven't had much time to talk." Sierra looked up at Rhys as they trekked alongside the base of a cliff face. The small range was more a group of hills than what Sierra would have called mountains, but it gave them some cover should they run into trouble. Ed had gone ahead a few hundred yards to act as a scout. He held the map to get to the Cursed Lands, despite Rhys claiming they didn't need one.

A few Sentinels occasionally passed in the distance or a solitary drone would fly overhead, either circling or entering the city. Ed had told her they were still just patrols. These areas had been off the Guardians' map for so long, the bots needed to update and adjust their parameters.

Still she was on edge. They were too close for comfort. She believed that the Scanners may be doing the updates. The Sentinels looked like they were looking for someone.

At one point they came across the remains of a group of travelers. Nothing was left but a smoldering pile of carcasses. It made Sierra wonder who these folks were and where they were heading before the Guardians found them.

The Guardians protect us.

"It seems life has gotten more interesting since you came along." Rhys flashed a smile as they carried on. His demeanor had changed so completely since their first encounter, she still wasn't sure how to act. Or what his true intent was.

"You mean you're not usually relentlessly attacked by bandits, Sentinels, or Prowlers?" She flashed her best smile back at him. But she imagined she looked ridiculous.

"Well, we are. Among other groups. But this week has been a little extreme."

"Hah! Probably just another day in the life."

"And you? Life in a compound? I've only ever heard stories from Ella. But I'm sure you never had a dull moment, being tormented and controlled by the bots."

Ella had been in the Sphere? There was so much about these people she didn't know. Maybe it wasn't the same one as she had been in. She did recall Malachi telling them there were more. Ella seemed so well adapted to life out here. It gave her some hope that maybe she'd start to feel more comfortable on the outside as well.

"I don't know what she told you, but life was pretty uneventful. My sister and dad died when I was young. But the Guardians instilled in us they were there to protect us. They told us they saved humanity from destroying itself. They never went into many details about how. The most we could ever get was that the ancients let their love of technology get away from them. That they developed war machines to destroy each other and succeeded, with the exception of the small Sphere that the Guardians were able to maintain. I didn't know anything existed, or even could exist, outside of the Sphere until a week ago. I grew up believing that the Guardians were there to protect us. They took care of us and had since the time of the ancients."

Rhys looked at her and raised an eyebrow. "You didn't know there were people outside the Sphere?"

She shook her head. "We were told that nothing survived, that nothing *could* survive. We were told the planet was uninhabitable."

"Why do you think they would do that?"

"You'd probably know better than me. I guess if there is nowhere for us to go, we're easier to control. Why keep us alive though? They seem pretty willing to eliminate people."

Rhys nodded, pausing briefly before looking at her and asking, "How did your dad and sister die?"

She blinked, not expecting such a direct personal question.

"I'm sorry. That was rude. I am just curious. You don't have to answer that."

"No, no, it's okay. You just surprised me. It was a long time ago." She took a deep breath. It was a long time ago, but the pain was still fresh.

"My dad had taken Izzy to work at the Core one day. That's the center that most people in the Sphere work at. They help keep the Sphere running efficiently. He wanted to show her what he did. It just so happened there was an accident that day. I was young, and Mom never liked to talk about it. So I don't know too many details about what happened. Only that neither of them came back. After that day, my mom had to go work in his place. Each family is expected to contribute. Ember was sent to watch me as my Keeper, since my mother had to be away from home for weeks at a time."

"I'm sorry, Sierra." He looked at her with sympathy. "I know it's hard to lose someone that close to you. My mother left me when I was young. My father . . . well, we didn't see eye to eye. He was content with the way things have been, with the Guardians and all. I never believed that this was the way things had to be. I wanted to make a difference. I left home when I was quite young. After that, I lived on the street, just trying to stay alive. I lost many friends between hunger, sickness, fighting through bots, bandits, and whatever else stood in the way of finding our next meal. It was a normal part of my every day to hear of someone else who didn't make it."

"I'm sorry too. I never realized how easy I had it."

"Life can be easy and still steal your soul. I hope that you can understand that's why we fight."

"Do you have a choice?" Sierra asked.

"Sure," Rhys responded. "Some have given up. My father had. He resigned himself to hiding instead. Some choose to live in the Sphere. They have to go through reeducation. Someone that once claimed to be dear to me made that decision. They can only allow so many in, so more often than not those who ask are just killed."

"So not really."

"No, not really. But to be honest, I'd rather live each day out here fighting for my next meal than have it handed to me by one of the bots. I'd rather fight for a world that can be ours than pretend an easy life is a good life.

"From what we understand, those who live in the Sphere are nothing more than their slaves. Working every day just to keep them going. Doesn't seem like much of a life."

"And life out here is so great?" Sierra snapped.

"Hey now! Didn't mean to offend." Rhys put his hands up. "All I'm saying is out here, you can be who you're meant to be. Can be your own person."

"Ha!" she exclaimed. "If someone doesn't kill you first. And that's if you stay within the blessed Silent Zone. If my plan doesn't work out, what then, Rhys? Now that the Silent Zone has fallen? I saw those who were hungry and depressed in the Underground. Don't tell me they were living a more fulfilling life than I had been in the Sphere. I don't buy it."

Rhys sighed. "Things aren't perfect out here, Sierra. But I'd rather die from hunger knowing the truth of things than locked up in a bubble working for a day that will never come."

Sierra shook her head. "This can't be all there is. Death by man or death by machine. I refuse to believe more isn't possible."

She clung to the medallion that hung from her neck. "I think that's what Greata would have wanted."

Rhys scoffed, then grew very quiet.

"What's that about?" she asked.

"Nothing," he responded, shrugging her off. "Let's catch up to Ed. I think we're almost there."

Rhys ran ahead without further explanation.

Movement in the distance caught her eye. A swarm of beings dotted the surface of the desert, as if a large colony of ants were marching in unison toward their ant hill.

Behind her, a figure of a woman skirted the edge of the mountains on the same path they had followed. Her white body was in stark contrast to the shadowed stone that she walked along. Sierra had forgotten that her friend would be able to sense them, now that the Zone had fallen. It hadn't even crossed her mind to try to connect with her to let her know about their quest. She paused to let Ember catch up to them.

"Sierra, what is happening? Why are you out here?"

"We have someone we need to find. You are welcome to join us."

Ed and Rhys noticed their encounter and came running back to meet them.

Ember carried on. "The Guardian network is showing me the Silent Zone has fallen. They're in the process of mapping the area. Are you okay, Sierra? Do you know why the Zone fell?"

"Your guess is probably better than mine. Malachi said it had been fluctuating for some time. I'm not sure if anyone really knows though. The Guardians don't know?"

"The Zone has been an empty space on our maps for two hundred and thirty-seven years. Their sensors haven't been able to penetrate the field. I am unable to access the databases that discuss the histories or technological aspects of the Zone. I'm afraid I possess no answers."

Ember's eyes were meant to replicate human ones. Sierra had

always thought they did a passably good job, but they had the same glossy look of the Guardian orbs. The irises of her eyes were orange, which she could tell sometimes startled people when they first saw her. She was young enough when she first met Ember that it didn't bother her much. As she looked at Ember's eyes now though, they were going wide as if surprised by something. She had often emulated human emotion. Even in the Sphere they knew that bots didn't experience emotion, but she had always thought Ember did a good job making her feel comfortable by expressing what she believed to be an appropriate emotional response. However, she had never seen Ember look surprised before.

First a sigh, now a surprise—it had been quite the emotional couple of days for her robot friend.

"What's going on, Ember?"

She looked at Sierra, shock still plain on her face. "Sierra, there are so many people here!"

"What are you talking about?"

"The scans the Guardians have completed. They are showing thousands, tens of thousands, of people living here." Her mouth moved silently, as if struggling to find words.

"Did they not know before?" Sierra asked.

"They had no idea." She was looking at Sierra, but not really seeing her. To Sierra, it looked like she was lost in thought. Was that possible? Maybe she was just reviewing the data being sent.

"So what happens now?"

"They're going to exterminate them all. They are an anomaly to the system."

"Well, I can't say we're surprised," Ed commented dismissively. "Look, the bots have never been out to help us with anything. You don't really think they'd start now."

"Ember, you did know that was how the Guardians handled people out of the Sphere, right? They exterminate or send them for reeducation to integrate."

Didn't she know? She was hooked up to their network. Why was this a shock to her?

"I have had very little reason to connect to outside activity," she said. "I knew that they dealt with people in and outside of the Sphere that posed a threat to the order of what has been established. Like Greata, who brought questioning authority into the Sphere, like Marco who destroyed a Patrol. But thousands of people? They are all showing up as targets for elimination."

Rhys had been hanging back a bit, but he stepped forward, brow furrowed.

"You're a bot. How did you not know this is what bots do?" His voice grew louder as he spoke. Sierra put a hand on his arm to try to calm him down, but he shook it off. "For hundreds of years you have been killing us. Eliminating those just trying to find food, to survive in the aftermath of the world left behind." He threw his hands in the air and started walking to the north in a huff.

Was she going to be the only voice of reason here? She had less of an idea of what was going on than any of the others did.

"Rhys! Wait!" She called after him, and surprisingly he stopped. He shook his head, putting his hands to his hair like he was going to pull strands of it out, but he stopped. He took a deep breath and stayed, staring at the desert before him.

Good, at least he was trying to calm himself down. At least she hoped that was what he was doing.

"Ember, how did you not know this was happening?" she asked.

"I was designed for a very specific reason. To take care of my charge. To take care of the one who showed great potential and was left alone. This is what I've done since I was created by the ancients. I didn't need to know much about the world outside. I didn't need to pay attention to much even within the Sphere that didn't affect you or your mother. I'm sorry, Sierra. I didn't mean to deceive you for all of these years. I meant to protect you.

That's what I was designed for. Guardians are here to protect you . . ." Her voice trailed off on the last part. She sounded apologetic and lost. Was that even possible?

"The Guardians protect us . . ." Ember said again, as if pondering the implications of the statement.

Even Rhys had turned around, and his demeanor had relaxed. He was studying her. Sierra realized he was just as lost as she was.

"What do you mean, you are sorry?" he asked, less defensive than before, definitely softer.

"My goal was to protect Sierra. It appears I misled her. If Guardians are willing to eliminate thousands of people . . . I don't understand how we can also be charged to protect. There's no empathy here. They've calculated how many people are sustainable. Anything beyond that number is a threat to be eliminated."

"I've never heard a bot talk like this before. Are you saying you don't agree with them?" Rhys asked, not completely dropping his guard. "Or is this a deception to bring Sierra back to your Sphere?"

Ember didn't answer. She was staring past them. Sierra turned to see if she could follow her gaze, but there was nothing within her line of sight except the open desert.

"Ember?" She put a hand on Ember's shoulder. "Ember, what's going on?"

Ember jerked so violently, it caused Sierra to reflexively jump back a couple feet. Ed had a blaster drawn and poised, as if he expected the Keeper to attack.

"It's okay. It's okay." Ember had her hands up and backed away. "I've disconnected myself from the network. They detected there was an anomaly within the system."

"You can do that?" Ed asked.

"Apparently."

"Why have I never heard of a rogue bot disconnecting from them before?"

Ember, for the first time, looked directly and intently at Ed.

"It's never happened before—well, not until a couple days ago."

"I don't understand, Ember," Sierra pushed. "What did they detect?"

"Me," she replied. "When I probed about the casualties, I got flagged with a bug error. We're not supposed to be able to question the actions we've been assigned. Each Guardian follows its own set of programming. My programming and questions triggered a response like someone was trying to hack into the system. They would have tried to reprogram or shut me down like a virus or faulty program. I disconnected to avoid being overridden."

"How were you able to go outside of your programming? Are others capable of doing this?"

"I don't know. My strongest desire is to protect Sierra. I have bent my protocols before for Sierra, and I was able to utilize this primary function to overshadow what I was doing. Leaving the Sphere, for example. A Keeper has never done this before, that I know of. Once a person leaves, they are marked as off the grid until they can be reintegrated. My protection protocols allowed me to follow you despite this norm. It's what allowed me to save you yesterday.

"I don't think I realized until today, but I am able to make my own decisions. Apart from the network. Once the system realized I was questioning the overall programming, it flagged me as undesirable. I had to disconnect, or they would come to reclaim me. They still might."

"How long have you been able to think for yourself, Ember?" Ed questioned. "If you search your memory banks, how long has it been since you first made decisions outside what you were originally programmed for?"

The distant gaze came back momentarily, and then she looked at Sierra. "Ever since I became Sierra's Keeper. I didn't think much of it. But my decisions have existed outside of the network since I came to her. My program had just always been consistent with my decisions. I don't know. Why did I not see this before?"

"You had no reason to," Sierra answered.

Ember shook her head. "Guardians can't think for themselves. I . . . I'm conscious. This must be. . . Sierra, do you remember when I said these malfunctioning bots were after you?"

"That's a hard thing to forget," she admitted.

"From what I can tell, there was a Sentinel that you came into contact with. He too has disconnected from the network."

"What are you saying?" she asked.

"I think it's you." Ember's eyes were wide, and her mouth agape as she processed what she was saying. "You're the cause of my consciousness. And this Sentinel, you caused him to become self-aware as well. He now has choice."

"So you're on our side now?" Rhys reluctantly asked, free hand gripping the backpack strap looped over his shoulder.

Ember nodded. "I've always been on Sierra's side. But, yes, I'm completely separated from the Guardian network, and you have my full support."

"So this other Guardian, is he on our side as well? Should we look for him?"

Ember's face went from wonder to fear, her red lips pursed as she struggled to compute what she needed to say.

"He's calling himself Titan. He was probing the network to look for weaknesses. The network was designed to defend against such attacks. A byproduct of when the ancients used to try to hack into our systems. He should have been quarantined from the system and deactivated, but the attempt was unsuccessful. That was when we lost contact with him. Before that, he left a clear warning. He wants to gain control over the Guardians, and he wants to kill you, Sierra."

"WHAT ARE YOU TALKING ABOUT, Ember? Why on earth would he want to kill me?" The only Sentinel she had directly come into contact with was the one that had tried to imprison Wil, right after they had left the Sphere.

"Something you did sparked their interest. What are you planning?"

Sierra took a deep breath. Ed made a motion to try to stop her, but she ignored him.

"We need to activate the machine I saw in my dream. This . . . EMP." She was unsure if this was going to work, but everything had been pointing her in that direction.

Had Greata known about the dream? Was that why she had sacrificed herself? Was that why she had sent her to find Terre?

The man had been in her visions. Finding him was integral to locating the device. If she was successful, Greata's death would serve a greater purpose. If she could stop the Guardians from invading Vegas, stop them from taking the lives of thousands of innocents, this wouldn't be in vain.

She looked to Ember, wishing her friend hadn't traveled so far for her. Another innocent life.

"What are you talking about?" Ed asked.

The time had come. She had to tell her companions the reason for the quest they had been on. She told them everything, about her visions, her conversation with Greata, and the events that had led her to leaving the Sphere. She described what her last vision had entailed, from meeting Terre in the ancient city to the device that was supposed to be launched but was disabled.

"You don't know if this is going to work, do you?" Ed asked when she was done.

"How could I know for sure?" she replied. "But Greata sent me to find this man before she died. My dream connects Terre with this device. The device has the capability to take out those

Guardians that are about to descend on Las Vegas. If this EMP was meant to establish the Silent Zone before it was attacked, then maybe we can put it back in place."

"Why you? Why these visions?" Ed asked.

"I've been searching for the answer. The only thing I can come back to is something Greata said to me before she died. My sister Izzy had visions as well. Something in our genes maybe? I don't have a clear answer for that yet."

"Aren't those who are born in the Sphere programmed?" Rhys asked. "Bred for specific jobs?"

Sierra blinked, taken aback by the statement. "We have genetics labs. The Guardians work with scientists at the Core to ensure those of us who are born are fit enough for survival." She realized Rhys had just answered the question she had been pondering the day of the exam. Confirmed what Greata said. The test was rigged. They were predestined at birth for their roles. But why go through the charade of choice?

"You said the device was deactivated by the Guardians. Why do you think it's going to work now?"

"Because of the gun at the Outpost. Because of her." She pointed to Ember. "I'm the key. The reason for my visions at precisely this point in time. Guiding me to help those out here."

"I'm not following, Sierra," Ed questioned.

"It appears I can activate technology. The gun wasn't supposed to fire in the Silent Zone. Malachi said it was me. Ember has gained self-determination because of me. This EMP, it's the whole reason I'm here. The Guardians knocked it out two hundred years ago. My bet is I can activate it."

"Well," Rhys said, shrugging. "It's no worse than any other option we have. If it doesn't work, nothing's changed. But if these rogue Guardians are after you, my guess is you're on to something. We best get going. How much time do we have, bot?"

"The rest of the scan of the area was estimated to take another four hours. I imagine attack units will be approaching soon after."

"We need to get going if we're going to stop them then." Ed appeared on board with the turn things had taken. "We have another few hours to get to the location Malachi marked out. And we're going to have to go cross country soon. This next stretch is straight north. We'll have no protection."

Ember stared at her for a while. Silent. Agonizingly silent. She'd figured it out. Of course she did.

"Ember," she started. "I . . ."

"Don't." Ember held a hand up. "After what's happened today, I see no other path forward. I can help you find this device. Just know, those in the Sphere are going to need help. They will no longer have Guardians to look out for them."

"What's she talking about?" Ed asked. He looked between her and Ember, not connecting the dots.

"If I understood the men in my vision correctly, this blast will take out the Sphere. They'll be free from the Guardians, but also helpless to the elements. It will take out all technology creating a bigger Silent Zone."

Sierra grabbed her Keeper's hand, holding it in both of hers.

"It will also kill Ember."

32

INVISIBLE BARRIERS. The Outside was full of them. Unseen, yet effective. Sierra had lived behind a barrier her entire life. A fake surface that made the outside look poisoned, a constant reminder of what had been keeping them trapped. A visible barrier meant to keep people inside. Here, the barriers were transparent, sometimes unmarked. Before it fell, the barrier of the Silent Zone had no visible markings. The decay of the Underground was marked by levels and guards, and nothing but a door separated those beneath the squalor from those who had built their homes out of it. Even the Guardians, it seemed had barriers they weren't allowed to cross. Networks, firewalls, secrets within secrets. Secrets and barriers the ancients had left behind, all standing in her way. Standing in the way of humanity.

The Guardians were blamed for the barriers they put up, for keeping humanity enslaved and trapped. But in reality, the ancients were holding them captive too. The barriers they set up determined whether a person lived or died. The Guardians— another effect of the world they left behind.

They were about to cross another invisible barrier. This one did have markings. Signs posted read "Do Not Enter" and

"Danger." Other symbols marked the signs that she didn't understand. But nothing distinguished the dirt on one side of the signs from the other. They could walk right through and have no idea. Until they died.

The sun was waning low.

"You sure you know where we need to go?" Sierra asked Rhys. He nodded. "I do."

"Do we go in now? Or wait until morning?" she asked.

"We don't have until morning," Ed responded. "The bot said four hours, nearly five hours ago. The attack units are probably already in the city. We need to go in now. Maybe we can find Terre before sundown."

Shots fired. A beam of light blasted past her head and exploded a nearby rock. Sierra spun around in time to see another ray of light headed for them. Diving out of the way, she pulled the blaster from her side. She hit the dirt, scrambling to find any sort of cover. There wasn't much to be had.

A group of eight Sentinels lined up before them. Sierra lifted her weapon as she caught a glimpse of Ember. She was still standing where they had been a moment ago. She hadn't moved. Ed had jumped in the opposite direction as she had, lying in the dirt, blaster up with the Sentinels in his sights.

"Defective unit," one of the Sentinels spoke. "Please come with us. You will be repurposed."

Nice of them to ask first and shoot later.

Ember wasn't moving. She had no weapon to defend herself with. Sierra could see she was calculating what her best course of action would be. Her friend was exposed because of her, but she had reacted instinctively. She imagined Ember's instinct would have been to push her out of the way even if she had tried to help.

"She stays with us!" Sierra yelled back to the Sentinels. She got up and moved toward Ember. She was going to have to pull her out of harm's way.

"Unacceptable," the nearest Sentinel replied. The lights on

their frames were nearly identical to Ember's. They were blue instead of orange, which seemed like it should be less intimidating, but the jagged, formidable patterns of the display didn't translate that way. Despite their similarities in appearance, their differences were even more pronounced. Their creators had made the Sentinels appear to be large, muscular armored men. With blasters pointed at the group, the intimidation factor was on point.

Shots fired, and Sierra dove for Ember. They both hit the ground, and she managed to roll around Ember and not damage her in the process. She skidded over a couple of sharp rocks before she gained a sense of balance. With a mouthful of dirt, she aimed her blaster toward their attackers.

Sierra paused. They had turned around. Blaster fire was still going, and she realized they weren't firing at her anymore. Following their new aim, and their weapon fire, she saw a solitary figure running toward them. Bald head, except for a long brown ponytail trailing behind him, tall and skinny . . . Oscar.

Oscar's robe flew behind him in the wind, making him an imposing figure, almost like he was flying into battle. In each hand he had a small blaster, firing wildly at the Sentinels before him. Sierra stayed low. His aim didn't seem to be all that precise, and she didn't want to get caught in a misfire.

Three of the attackers went down. Oscar's aim was maybe better than it appeared. The Sentinels fired back at him in full force. Five bots to one human was no match, and several of the shots made contact with him before he fell in a heap.

"Oscar!" she cried out. What was he doing here?

Ed used the confusion to fire on the backs of the guards. Two more dropped. It was now five on four.

Sierra fired back as best she could. She thought she made contact a couple of times, but her aim was horrible. Another went down. She couldn't tell if it was her shot or Ed's that delivered the blow. Probably Ed's.

Rolling in the dirt, she tried to avoid being shot as best she could.

She positioned into a half squat, attempting to gain her balance before taking another shot. Before she was able to, a wall of muscle came crashing into her, pinning her to the sand.

It took her a moment to realize Rhys was on top of her, his body like a tank. She looked up into his green eyes with question, and then to the spot where she had been standing a moment before. A plume of sand and smoke wafted into the air. She had nearly been hit.

She ran a hand along his shoulder, surprised to feel how solid it was. Sweat coated his arms as well as hers.

"Don't get too comfortable." He smiled and brushed her cheek with the back of his hand as he stood, then turned back to the guards.

Sierra shook herself and stood up, trembling. What had gotten into her?

Rhys had run over to Oscar. A Sentinel stood over him as he lay flat on the ground. Rhys had his gun trained on the machine, but the bot wasn't conceding.

Both of the remaining Sentinels focused their attention on Ed.

Ed fired at them, missing his mark. They moved in. Two of the shots fired from each of the Sentinels hit him.

He fell backward. Time stood still as Sierra watched him fall, fire landing on his chest, his thigh, and he hit the ground with a solid thud. She heard a loud, agonized scream, and started racing toward the last two standing Sentinels before she realized the scream was her own. Her blasters fired, and one of the metal beings fell right away, sparks flying from the contact with its armor.

Then, mid-stride, Sierra's blasters went dead. She was still moving, still pulling the trigger on each device, but neither did anything. She was too close now, moving too fast, to adjust her trajectory. She was going to take the final machine out, one way or another.

A flash of orange and white flew before her. The Sentinel was down. Ember had come at it from behind. Ember, on top of the being, smashed it in the face with the back end of its own weapon that she had somehow stolen from it. The Sentinel stopped resisting after several hits. Bits of artificial flesh and ceramic hung from its face, revealing the circuits and metal beneath.

Sierra flew to Ed's side. He lay still, face up toward the sky, eyes open but unseeing. He wasn't breathing. Tears filled her eyes as she knelt down beside him. A hole burned through his chest. He was scorched in several places, but one blast had gone straight through him. There was no blood, but the smell of burning flesh was enough to make Sierra want to vomit.

"Ed!" she cried. Tears streamed down her face, falling and running onto his, as she held him close to her. "Why?"

Ember was soon by her side.

"Sierra, we need to go. There will be more coming."

Through tear-soaked eyes, she looked up and could see orbs in the distance. They looked to be heading toward the city, but it was probably only a matter of time before more came for them.

This was too much. Too many people around her were dying. Ed didn't deserve this. She set him down and closed his eyes with the tips of her fingers. Ember helped her to stand up.

"I barely knew him," she said, wiping away the tears that now covered her face. "He was a good friend though. Loyal, he came all this way with me, not knowing what he was getting into."

"I'm sorry, Sierra."

Rhys came from his battle and rested a heavy arm on her shoulder. She looked to him, but he turned his face. She was sure she saw tears in his eyes.

She glanced over to where he came from. "Oscar too?" she asked.

Rhys nodded, giving her shoulders a final squeeze before stepping away.

Sierra wrapped her arms around Ember, tears freely flowing down her face. Ember embraced her back, not too tightly. Always the perfect comforter.

They stood like that for several moments before Ember broke the silence.

"Sierra, we need to go," she said, giving her a final rub on the back. "We don't have much time."

"Ember, please." She looked up at her robot friend and pushed her away, tears still in her eyes. "I have been dragged across this wasteland over the past week, from one catastrophe to the next. Within the past few days, two of my friends have died, two more have been kidnapped, and I'll probably never see my mother again. And for what? I had a dream of a device that may or may not exist. Give me one damn minute to grieve. Is that too much to ask?"

She hurled her dead blasters into the desert, then bent over to pick up a Sentinel leg that had become dismembered during the skirmish and used it to dig into the dirt.

"What are you doing?" Rhys asked. His voice had a slight tremble, but he was keeping it together.

"He was a good friend," she stated, sniffling. "We can't take him with us, but we should at least give him a proper burial."

Rhys nodded, grabbed his blade, and worked the soil with her. It wasn't an easy task, but it didn't take long before they had dug a small pit to lay Ed in. It wasn't deep enough, but they didn't have time for much more. Sierra said one last goodbye and began covering him with the earth.

"Safe journey, my friend," Rhys said once they had him covered. He opened and poured the content of his canteen over the mound they had created. "May your thirst in the next life be ever quenched."

She looked to Rhys. She was unsure of this ritual, but only

hesitated a moment before following Rhys's lead and dumping her canteen onto the mound and repeating the blessing.

As she stood up and stepped back from her lifeless friend, she looked over to Oscar, lying in the dirt. Sprawled out. Why did he show up? The man who had betrayed her friends. Sold Wil and Sierra. What an ass. And he had the nerve to show up here!

She could sense worry coming from Ember as the clock ticked forward, but she needed to know why. She walked over to him. Despite everything, if he hadn't shown up, perhaps another one of their party would be lying in his place. He had taken out nearly half of the guards before they had a chance to know what was happening.

As she approached him, his head turned slightly, eyes meeting hers. He was still alive!

She knelt down beside him. "Why did you come here?" she asked, tears still in her eyes. A mix of emotions flowed through her. He had betrayed them and then saved their lives. How was she supposed to react?

"Sierra," Oscar whispered. He was alive, but not in good shape. "Sierra, I'm sorry. Tell Terre and Ella . . . and Wil. Tell them I'm sorry. I didn't believe their vision. I do now."

Oscar's eyes closed as he lay his head back down and breathed his last.

Rhys looked to the horizon and cursed under his breath. "We've got more company."

33

———

WIL FELT a little ridiculous holding a sword and watching the sky.

It wasn't just that he didn't believe it would do anything against a flying bot, which it wouldn't. He still wasn't confident handling the weapon, and he had learned enough to know it wasn't as easy as it looked. If he could keep his composure enough to avoid swinging wildly at whatever came near him, he'd consider it a win. Unless he died in the process. Of course, he hoped it didn't come down to that. He was sure he'd have a blaster hole through him before he could take a swing.

He also had a large two-handed blaster, but based on his previous experience, he wasn't sure how much he was going to be able to count on the weapon firing. Plus, he had been told not to touch it unless he had to.

Other than the first time he had picked the blaster up in the desert, he had yet to fire one successfully. He was coming to terms with the fact that there was something more to technology failing around him than just bad luck. However, the blaster was proving to be rattling to his nerves before the battle. If only he knew how to control it. If he could make it work when he wanted it to, maybe he could be of use in this battle after all. Assuming it didn't knock him unconscious.

He had been trying to put the pieces together. Knocking out the group of Sentinels in the desert had rendered him unconscious. When the orb had fallen to the ground in the Sphere, he had only felt a little disoriented. The size of what he took out must have some relation to his physical reaction to it. Was there any way to minimize that impact? He could only guess or find out if it happened again. And what would happen if he took out something too large? Could this power kill him?

At first Elizabeth didn't believe him. But he tried to fire a couple of blasters and rendered them completely useless. Not only did they fail to fire for him, they failed to fire at all, for anyone, after he had handled them. She was reluctant to let him carry one at all after that. But there was only a finite supply of weapons to go around, and she said she still didn't feel right leaving him weaponless. So she made him promise not to touch it if it wasn't necessary.

A robot invasion is coming—define necessary.

She had given him a few quick lessons on how to properly wield a sword, but there was a lot to prepare for before the bots came, and so she had to settle for giving him just enough instruction so that he wouldn't stab himself. Though Wil hoped he could have at least figured that much out on his own.

He was delegated to helping those who were injured on the field, as best he could, until the ground troops arrived. Once the Sentinels started marching in on the city, during the second wave, that was where he would get more time in on the fight. Elizabeth gave him a bit of instruction on their weak spots. Joints, eyes, a power pack that could be reached by stabbing between their neck and body armor. Otherwise the sword was essentially useless against them. It wouldn't even dent their body armor. That was if he could get close enough to them without ending up as firewood. He just hoped he would live through the experience.

Resistance members stood in windows of some of the ancient hotel buildings. They had been warned the buildings may not stay standing for long, but the hope was they could take out a few of the bots before they got close to the city. Wil watched them position themselves in the remains of the crumbling towers, aiming at the sky in front of them, waiting. He wasn't sure the buildings were going to stay standing, even without the incoming attack.

Other members of the Resistance were evacuating residents of the tents, set up across the street from the Rio Grande. They were being moved into the Underground that they had tried so hard to live apart from. This Queen of Vegas sounded like a horrible leader, but somehow the Resistance had convinced her to allow the refugees in. Others were heading into the Rio Grande itself. Leo and some of his remaining staff were out on the street, helping those who were having a hard time head into hidden underground chambers attached to the hotel.

A group of men, women, and carts pulled into the alley beside the Inn. One of the people with the caravan was Malachi. Wil was surprised to see him back so soon and with so many others. He left his post—nothing was happening yet anyway—and half jogged up the street to catch up with him before he could disappear into the Inn.

"Malachi!" he called out.

Malachi turned toward him, gave him a simple wave, and carried on unloading people who had been riding in one of the carts. That must have been quite the workout for those who had to do the pulling.

"Wil, good to see you," Malachi said, glancing in Wil's direction while offering a hand to an elderly woman stepping off the cart. "Leo's offered to let Community members stay beneath the Inn. We should be safe there, at least until the initial waves pass through. We don't think the Sentinels will venture beneath the surface. At least not until later. If it comes to that, it won't matter much anyway."

Bags under Malachi's eyes betrayed his fatigue. He was giving these folks the best chance he knew how.

"Sierra and the others haven't returned?"

Malachi shook his head. "You're welcome to stay with Leo as well if you'd like."

"Thanks for the offer," Wil replied. "But I'm not going to hide while these people die to protect me."

Not so long ago, Wil would have been skeptical of Sierra's visions. He still was unsure, but with everything that had unfolded in the past few days, Sierra was one of the only people he would count on. He thought about how the weapon had fired at the Outpost. Perhaps that was the key to this entire thing.

Malachi nodded. "I didn't think so. I see you're suited up. I'll meet you out in the battlefield once I get these people inside."

"You're fighting too?"

"Damn right I'm fighting too. We may not be the Resistance, but we're not going to just let these bots walk in here either. There's a time to fight, and a time to let be. This, my friend, is a time to fight."

"Do you think Sierra's plan has a chance of working?"

"It doesn't matter what I think," Malachi answered, lowering his voice so those around couldn't hear. "If it doesn't, it won't matter if we win or lose this battle. With nothing to keep the bots at bay, they won't give up until we're all annihilated."

Malachi grabbed a few bags off the nearest cart and started waving a few young children into the entrance to the Rio Grande.

Wil wasn't going to give up either. Not if he could help it. He glanced at his sword. He just had to figure out what he was going to do.

Since he was unable to fire any of the powered weapons, he

was delegated to distribute blades and armory to those who needed them. Nearly each member of the Resistance had their own, though, so it seemed like a bit of a silly task. Still, he wasn't restricted to those in the Resistance. Many of the inhabitants of Vegas were willing to fight as well. Some were crawling out of the Underground for the first time in years, maybe ever. Some weren't strong enough to carry a sword, malnourished as they were. It was an effort for them to be out on the street at all. He was also in charge of trying to round the weakest, though good-intentioned, people off the street and get them somewhere safe.

It was designated as a secondary task, but Wil thought it was what they really wanted him to focus on. The weapon supply was just a decoy to get him moving around the city perimeter as much as possible. He was also to be on the lookout for Prowlers causing trouble. He expected there to be more of them trying to take advantage of a bad situation, but as it turned out, many of them were jumping in to help the Resistance. Being in danger of absolute destruction seemed to give purpose to even the criminals in the city. Most of them, at least.

A man carrying two children over his shoulders was running toward the outskirts of the city. Wil stopped him and asked where he was going. The man said he was taking his children to avoid the coming destruction. He had a sister on the coast and they were going to head there.

Wil wasn't an expert with kids, but he was pretty sure that the man wasn't going to get very far with two screaming kids on his back. When pressed about the children's names, the man couldn't answer.

"Couldn't even make something up there?" Wil challenged the man, and pulled the children down to safety. He then called a couple of nearby members of the Resistance over to handle the man, expecting them to haul him somewhere else. Instead they dealt with the man right there. After pulling him off to the side of the road, one of them ran a sword through his belly.

The man looked Wil in the eye as he collapsed, mouth open in as much, or probably more, surprise as him. He fell into the dirt, blood soaking the earth around him and flowing onto the road.

"We don't put up with children being traded," the Resistance member who had done the gutting said. He was a large burly man who wore a dark zippered vest and burgundy pants that were a little too tight. Wil wondered how his wardrobe didn't restrict his movement. Greasy hair pulled into a ponytail hung midway down his back. The man grabbed the dead kidnapper's dagger and hung it amid multiple weapons that already decorated his belt. This wasn't the first man he had killed. Maybe not even today.

"Trading adults is okay, but not children?" Wil's stomach dropped as he asked. This wasn't the man to pick a fight with.

The man with the ponytail drew a serrated knife from his belt and held it to Wil's throat. "I didn't say anything was okay, did I? I said we didn't put up with it."

"Dex! Stand down! Your fight isn't with this man!"

Wil had nearly forgotten about the other member who had stood off to the side. She was a smaller woman with wavy silver hair, and he would have easily mischaracterized her as timid until she spoke. The authority of her command made the man named Dex step back and put his knife back in its place.

"Sorry." His demeanor completely changed as he sheathed his blade. "It's been so long that we've had to hold our own, I forget most of us are on the same team today. Thanks for bringing the bastard to our attention. Next time, don't be afraid to deal with one of these yourself. Nobody's going to hold it against you."

The woman waved and followed Dex back to what they had been working on. It looked like a large weapon of some kind. Bolted to the ground, the barrel of it was nearly as wide as he was. He would love to see that thing in action. He probably would, he supposed.

"What is it?" He pointed to the weapon as he approached the woman.

"Laser cannon," she answered. She was wearing a white shirt with khaki shorts, and both were now streaked with dirt and sweat from the day's work. She lit a small cigar and gave it a puff. She didn't seem too interested in his questions, but he couldn't help pressing on.

"That looks like it would take down an Onyx."

"It better. That's what she's designed to do. Wish we'd more time to smooth the bugs out, but we take what the desert gives us."

"It hasn't been used before?"

She shook her head. "No, an' it won't ever be if you don't quit distracting me. Less than an hour before those killin' machines are here. Sure you got better things to do." She flicked the ash off her cigar and went back to Dex and their weapon.

Wil continued to make his journey around the city. It was hard to believe a city so large could exist. What was left of the ancient city was still far larger than the three villages combined, and to think it was only a fraction of what the ancients had built. Unimaginably larger. Even as it was, it took him about an hour to walk from one end to another. Metal heaps of transport vehicles still lay in ruin along the roadsides. Ghosts of a time that once was. Destroyed because of the same beings that sought to destroy them now.

The remaining shells of the past screamed of the disaster coming. A two-hundred-year-old warning of destruction and chaos.

Sierra better know what she's doing.

All he could do now was keep those here alive long enough for her to find Terre and this bot-destroying machine.

Alarms were sounding throughout the city. He looked to the sky. Six Onyx were right on top of them.

The machines somehow slipped past them undetected. They

were supposed to have an hour!

Six. Only six.

We can handle six, right?

Wil ran deeper into the city to gain cover, and images of Marco's death flashed through his mind as the same dark orbs flew through the sky. How many of these death machines were there? Ella had said there was no end. But they had to try. If they could bring these ones down, at least those here could fight another day.

One step at a time. The first step was to defend the people in this city. A voice in Wil's head told him they were attempting to do something even the ancients hadn't succeeded in, something that may be impossible. He was willing to die to avenge Marco. To avenge every innocent who had fallen or been destroyed by these death machines.

With the black orbs' arrival, the city had grown silent. The hum of the incoming attackers was the only audible noise. The entire city held its collective breath, waiting to see who—or what—would make the first move.

Blaster fire from out of the hotel windows flew overhead. The Resistance members had been instructed to wait. Damn it! Nerves were getting the better of everyone.

The shooter may have been nervous, but his aim was true. The weapon's fire made contact with one of the machines, to no visible effect on either. Lights around the lead orb pulsed, before it returned fire on the attackers. Stone and debris flew from the building, enough dust thrown from the impact that Wil couldn't tell if those inside escaped the line of fire in time. Three more blasts from the Onyx to the same building caused a chain reaction. The center of the building collapsed in on itself.

Nobody would have survived that.

"Now!" Elizabeth yelled. She stood in the middle of the street that led through the center of the city. Weapons fired all around her aimed at the droids closing in. Dozens of shots landed on the first Onyx sphere, all their efforts focused on taking down one at a time. Smart.

A large piece of glass shattered and fell to the ground before the orb itself dropped from the sky. A shower of dust and debris billowed from the earth as it crashed into the dirt.

One down.

Unfortunately, the other five were continuing to reign down destruction on the rest of the city. People ran in every direction, trying to avoid the assault.

Wil stood off to the corner of the Resistance, hanging in the background like he was told to do. His time would come when the Sentinels did. But for now, he would wait. He wasn't the only one. Reserve troops stood around him, watching the mayhem. There weren't enough laser weapons to go around, and he felt bad for having one strapped to his back not in use.

Beams of light streaked down the street as the remaining Onyx focused their laser fire toward the Resistance members. Pavement ripped up through the sand. Vehicles long abandoned turned over as their weapons' fire uprooted everything. People did their best to dodge the path of destruction, haphazardly firing behind themselves if they could.

Wil jumped as a body landed next to him, bleeding, burned. Dead. Fallen from the sky, tossed aside from an uprooted part of the battle. Without thinking, he reached down and grabbed the blaster from the body, trying not to look too close at the face of the man who was now staring at nothing.

Now Wil had two weapons.

Well, here goes nothing.

Lifting the weapon, he aimed at the sky. Orbs fired at another of the remaining taller buildings. He pulled the trigger and the kickback nearly pushed him over.

It worked!

This time Wil braced himself and fired again. The Onyx he targeted was also taking heavy fire from others surrounding him.

It began to spark, falling out of the sky into the foundation of a nearby building, bringing the whole thing down on top of it.

Four more to go. If this was only the first wave, Wil wasn't sure how much of the city there would be left to protect.

Another orb fell from the sky, this one farther out. He didn't think that one would have inflicted any damage to anything inhabited. He wondered how much those in the Underground would feel of these impacts.

More explosions in the distance, and a wide beam of light lit up the sky, taking down a fourth and then a fifth Onyx, one right after another. The laser cannon was working. Maybe that would give them a fighting chance.

Drawing all of the remaining fire, the sixth Onyx didn't last too long before it fell from the sky in a fiery explosion. It remained on fire as it lay in the dirt within the city's boundary.

Wil took a deep breath and surveyed the damage around him. Smoke rose from various buildings, fresh rubble now piled among the old. Bodies were being dragged out from under much of it. Some were alive, others not.

"Sentinels are next! We have less than ten minutes before they are here! Regroup!" Elizabeth shouted over the chaos as people searched for loved ones among the ruins. Others tried to hurriedly rebuild some sort of fortification that they could use against the imminent Sentinel attack. One thing was for sure, the city had suffered heavy casualties.

He caught a glimpse of Dex and his companion working on the laser cannon. It didn't look like he was having much luck. Smoke billowed out of it, as Dex sweated profusely and fiddled with some of its parts with a cloth. After burning himself, he picked up a small rock off the ground and hurled it at the device.

So much for the cannon.

The sound of Sentinels marching in the distance rose as the city once again quieted down. A calm before the storm. Wil tightened his grip on the blaster he had salvaged and waited.

34

"THESE ARE TITAN'S GUARDIANS," Ember whispered, almost to herself.

Three Sentinels, two orbs, and a human approached. Other than the human among them Sierra couldn't see anything else that would set them apart from the group that they had just fought off moments before.

The woman walking toward them wore a dark gray cloak with a glowing red pattern that appeared to be behind a crack in the garment. The cloak was similar to the ones the Order members wore back home, though she had never seen them a color other than green.

"Ember?" Sierra asked.

"Stand back, Sierra," Ember ordered. "They are only here to kill you."

"And let you be put in harm's way for me?" Sierra grabbed the blaster from her belt. "No way." The weapon had fully charged from the last encounter, and she made a mental note to make each shot count.

She shuddered to think that she'd have to kill the woman in

front of her. But she wasn't going to let them stop her from getting to Terre and activating the weapon.

In the distant sky, Onyx flew toward the city. They didn't have much time. The first wave of attacks would have launched already. If Malachi and the others had managed to fend those off, they'd have only a short breather before the Sentinels reached them. They needed to get moving.

"How far is it to get to Terre?" Sierra asked.

"Not far. Maybe half an hour if we hurry."

Too far to try to outrun the party coming their way.

Ember and Rhys were the last of her group left standing. Rhys knew the way. Ember knew the consequences.

Three Sentinels. The two orbs were Scanners—which would explain how easily they had found them, but at least they weren't likely to be armed. It was a risk Sierra was going to have to take.

The woman carried the same staff Sierra had seen Claudia and others carry. The stone on its head glowed red in unison with her robe.

Sierra took a second blaster from her belt. This one she had taken from Oscar's lifeless body.

Rhys did the same thing beside her. His giant grin let her know he was thinking the same thing.

"Ember, wait here."

Before the Keeper could respond, they were off running, charging full tilt toward the bots intent on their destruction.

The woman stopped in her tracks. She was younger, likely not much older than Sierra. Though with the Order it was always hard to tell. Long dark hair framed her face and flowed onto her robe. She had a look of bewilderment on her face at the two maniacs hurling themselves toward them.

A smile stretched across Sierra's face. She was bewildered as well. But this was for Greata. This was for Ed. This was for every damn lie she had been led to believe. This was for being told she wasn't capable of more. Look who was capable now.

The Sentinels raced ahead of the woman and the orbs. But by the time the bots had pulled out their weapons, it was too late. Blaster fire ricocheted off their metal bodies. One went down. They each picked a bot and fired relentlessly.

The bots fired a few shots. Beside her Rhys went down in a heap, somersaulting in a plume of dust.

Not Rhys too! Tears began to well in Sierra's eyes, but she pushed the fear she felt for Rhys down. She would persevere. She could not let it distract her, or she'd end up fallen as well.

At the same time, the bot Sierra had been firing at flew backward, sparks flying from its head as it shuddered and collapsed.

One left.

Sierra broke out in a full sprint toward the bot, screams filling her lungs, a war cry as she approached. It fired back, but it was already injured from Rhys's assault and limping on its right leg.

It didn't give up though. Not falling back, just as Malachi said.

Blaster fire made impact on the bot's chest, neck, and head. Smoke from the impacts lifted from the machine as it too collapsed from its wounds.

Still farther back, the woman in the white robes lifted her staff in the air. Its ruby-red hilt now flashed like a beacon in the evening sky.

Sierra hesitated. She didn't want to fire on a human if she didn't have to, no matter the side they were on. But she'd defend herself if she had to.

Sierra slowed her pace and locked eyes with the woman, whose dark-brown irises seemed to flash as a sinister grin cracked across her face. The woman shook her staff, and a blinding red light burst from its ruby gem. Sierra held her hands in front of her face, trying to protect her burning eyes.

It was only moments before her vision returned. But by then, the woman, the two Scanner orbs, and even the bodies of the fallen Sentinels had disappeared.

SIERRA RUSHED OVER TO RHYS, who was still lying on the ground, covered in dust.

Because of her, Ed and Greata were both dead. How many more were going to die trying to protect her? Dead. All because they tried to help her find the answers to riddles she received in a dream. And what if her visions weren't real?

And now Rhys. Rhys who had resented her at first. Rhys, who had slowly seemed to be warming up to her. She had spent the night dancing with him back at the Rio Grande. He had stuck his neck out for her despite his hesitations.

And she still didn't know why he had been so cold to her. Still didn't know how he knew Terre. And now they would be lost. How would they find Terre without him?

Sierra's heart raced. The adrenaline of the attack was still coursing through her veins. She wanted to pick Rhys up and carry him the rest of the way. If only she knew where they were going. He didn't have to do this. Didn't have to get himself killed on behalf of a girl he barely knew.

Ember reached him at the same time as Sierra. Sierra threw herself on top of him and wrapped her arms around him.

He startled as she landed, thrown into a coughing fit.

He's alive! She pushed herself off, giving him room to breathe.

He sputtered for a few moments and then started gasping for breath.

"Rhys, stay with us." Sierra didn't know what else to say. She grabbed his hand as he composed himself. Strong and calloused, it was the hand of someone who had worked hard his entire life. He gave her hand a squeeze making it feel soft and small in comparison.

"I'm okay," he finally said, his voice hoarse, but confident.

"You're injured," Ember said. "You've been shot in the leg."

Sierra looked to his leg. A burn mark had seared through his robe. She lifted it, revealing the burn mark continuing into his pants and onto his leg, his skin peeling back to reveal flesh and blood. She winced.

"I'll be okay," Rhys said, grimacing as he attempted to stand. He almost toppled over when he tried to put weight on the injury.

"You can't walk on that," Ember admonished. "We have to get you aid."

"Well, I sure as hell can't stay here," he replied. "We're not too far from where we need to be. If you can help support me, I'm sure I'll make it."

Ember looked uncertain, but Sierra gave her an approving nod, and the bot propped Rhys up on an arm.

Sierra circled the man, now standing, the smell of burning flesh rising in the air.

"Let me at least wrap that up for you," she offered. "You don't want to get sand in the wound."

She removed his robe. It wasn't going to do him any good anyway. But the material was too thick to use as a wrap. She began searching through her bag for something suitable.

Finding nothing, she removed her own robe and started attempting to rip a piece of her own shirt.

"Hang on, Sierra," Ember admonished. "There's no need for that." Ember took her white cloak, much thinner than the heavier desert robes the other two wore, and tore a piece of it with her hands. "Use this." She handed Sierra the fabric.

"Thank you," Sierra replied, and tied the piece around Rhys's leg.

He grimaced and hissed as it touched the injured flesh.

"We'll have to clean this once we get there, if possible," she said. "But for now, this should keep more sand and dirt from getting in and infecting it."

The smell of the wound was putrid, but Sierra was happy she didn't have to stitch anything up.

She reached up and ran her fingers through his hair. His green eyes stared into hers, questioningly.

"I'm glad you're okay," she said, before retrieving her hand. "I hate to force us to push onward so soon, but we're not done yet. Lead the way, Rhys."

Rhys was okay, but for her plan to succeed, one more close to her needed to die. Ember had been her closest friend since Izzy had died. Izzy, Greata, Ed. Wil was missing, maybe dead as well. And she would be the one to end Ember's life, intentionally.

As they began to move, the wind picked up, and the sun continued to descend from its high point in the sky. Sand blew into Sierra's brown hair, and she had to tuck her face behind her sleeve to keep it out of her eyes. There were only a few hours until dark now.

Mountains rose in the distance, toward the Sphere. She knew it was out there, past the horizon, filled with people going about their daily lives, working at the Core, attending class, living in a home the Guardians had made for them. In between her and that life was Vegas, where people struggled to meet their daily needs because the Guardians had kept them prisoners in a land they themselves hadn't been able to enter in two hundred years. How could two worlds, so different, both holding their residents captive to some degree, exist so close to one another? How many in each had no idea that the other existed?

Over the desert, black orbs filled the sky, only small dots over the hills, but there was no mistaking what they were. Dozens of Onyx were on their way.

Below them, a little farther ahead, a few dozen Sentinels marched toward the city. From where Sierra stood, it appeared as if they'd make it there within the hour.

How many would die if she didn't succeed? Thousands. The sacrifice of two suddenly became dwarfed by the immense burden that would be placed on her conscience if she didn't do anything. She would always wonder if she could have stopped it.

The Cursed Lands stood before them. The dirt on the other side of that sign looked no different than where she was currently standing.

"Are you sure you want to join us?" she said to Ember. "This could damage you."

"I've completed some scans while we were sitting here. I won't be any more affected than you. I'll probably have more time than you will. If anything happens to you, you'll need me to carry you out of there. I have twelve hours before I'll suffer irreparable damage."

Sierra nodded. She'd have to take her at her word on that one and hope for the best. "All right. Let's go then."

They crossed the barrier, past the signs that were the only signal that there was danger. She expected to feel something. Something that would tell her she was in a place harming her body, in a place that would kill her. It reminded her of when she had left the Sphere. She kept expecting a reaction, kept expecting something that would indicate to her that she wasn't going to make it.

There had been nothing lethal about leaving the Sphere, despite having been taught the air of the world had been poisoned, that it couldn't support life. This area, on the other hand, had an unseen death sentence. A land so toxic that not even the machines chose to enter. Ember had told her that the area was filled with something called radiation. A force that would harm them both if exposed for too long. An invisible force.

Ember also told her Terre wouldn't be able to live behind this field. No human could make it more than eight hours without experiencing a lethal dose of radiation. Less than that would make them severely ill. Malachi had been adamant—this was where Terre could be found. Rhys seemed to agree. Could they be wrong?

"You're sure Terre lives this way?" she asked Rhys. He had

been unwavering in his adamancy that he knew where the man was. "How can he survive in this place?"

Rhys sighed. "I'm sure," he said. "There are many things he can survive that would kill the rest of us. But he lives in a weakened pocket of the field. Any one of us could survive there for ages. It's the in-between bits that are lethal. A natural defense to the place he decided to call home. But we'll be okay as long as we keep moving. As for how I know where he is, let's just say I knew him once. But that was a long time ago."

HALF AN HOUR PASSED with nothing more than an empty road in front of them. The terrain was no different than the rest of the path they had traveled on from the mountains. But the road wasn't as hard packed, which made it apparent traffic had been lighter here, and smaller, even less used trails branched off from it, providing an infinite number of directions for them to go. How Rhys could tell they were headed the right way was beyond anything Sierra could see.

After their hike had continued for some time, a brick building appeared on the landscape before them. Nothing else was visible for miles amidst the flat rocky terrain. This must be where he lived. There wouldn't be any other reason for a building out here, not one that appeared to be in decent condition.

Movement caught Sierra's eye. A figure walked toward them, nearly silhouetted in the setting sun. He was a few hundred yards away, but clearly heading in their direction. She nudged Ember and nodded toward the other soul that had dared enter the Cursed Lands. It had to be him.

Ember nodded back, understanding. "My scanner is being distorted by the radiation levels. I can't tell you anything more than what you can see."

"It's him," said Rhys. "It's definitely him."

As they approached, the flat, gray design reminded Sierra of something that would have been constructed in the Sphere. Except this building was massive. Although it appeared to be all one floor, the building covered a lot of ground, and it was still twice as tall as anything they had in the Sphere. Did the ancients build nothing small?

The man was wrapped in a lightweight green robe. Flowing in the wind, it was designed to keep the sand off him, but it also masked his face.

They got within a few yards and he stopped. His eyes were intense. Intense in a way that made Sierra realize if this wasn't the man they were seeking, they were likely in trouble. Maybe they were in trouble anyway.

Would he remember her? Had he really even seen her during her vision? She attempted to catch her breath, trying to not make it obvious, but she was panicking.

The man paid her no attention though. His eyes were locked on Rhys. His face betrayed no emotion.

The man hadn't moved, which didn't ease Sierra's racing heart. He stood standing in silence staring at them, waiting. The wind had picked up, and his cloak flapped in the wind behind him. Still she couldn't see more than his eyes. Straining her memory, she tried to recall if the eyes in front of her matched the man she had seen in the vision. She couldn't tell. How would two hundred years change a person? Would he even be recognizable?

The eyes above the veil squinted. He pulled the mask down below his chin to reveal his face in its entirety.

Sierra let out a gasp. It was Terre, all right. He looked exactly the same as he had in her vision. Exactly. He hadn't aged a day. She didn't realize until that moment, looking at a man who appeared to be in his thirties, maybe twenties, that she had been expecting to encounter an old man. She was skeptical enough that a man who was alive during the wars of the ancients could still be alive and living in the wilderness. Seeing this man, an echo of youth still on his face, brought a whole new level of skepticism. Was this a trick?

"I am surprised to see you here," he said, eyes not leaving Rhys. "I didn't know if I'd ever see your face again."

"And you wouldn't have," Rhys spat, the same vitriol he'd expressed when he had met Sierra sparking anew. "It was only for her sake." He motioned to Sierra. "She needed to find you. Claims to see you in her dreams."

"Her?" Terre asked, a smile on her face. "She's from the compound."

Was it still so obvious?

"You've gone and fallen for someone that you left here spitting hate for. Do you think she'll bring your mother back? Why did you bring her here? Is she pregnant?"

"What! Wait. Pregnant?" Sierra interjected. "No, nothing like that! I have been seeking you out."

Terre's eyes never left the boy.

"Mother's dead," Rhys cut in. "My friend here, Sierra, she bears her medallion. Mother told her to seek you out."

Terre looked at Sierra for the first time. But Sierra was too busy staring incredulously at Rhys to even notice.

Mother?

Suddenly it all made sense. Why he looked so familiar. Those green eyes. They were just like Greata's, only . . . nicer. Why his demeanor softened when he saw the medallion. Greata was Rhys's mother.

"Let's see it," Terre said to Sierra.

"Excuse me?" Sierra answered, her mind spinning from Rhys's words. The boy was staring at Terre, arms crossed, very purposefully not looking in her direction.

"The medallion, let's see it."

She pulled the pendant from beneath her robe, removed it, and handed it to the man she knew only from her vision.

"This is it all right. How did you know Greata?" Terre asked, seeming agitated.

Sierra hadn't been sure what to expect upon meeting the man, but of all the possible scenarios she concocted, this had not been one of them.

"How did I know her? How did *you* know her?"

"She was my lover."

Terre said it so matter-of-factly that it took a moment for her to register what he had said. It shouldn't have surprised her.

"She was what now?"

He continued on, without missing a beat. "Probably twenty years ago, maybe more, they all ran together. Greata was a Traveling Person. They crossed back and forth between the mountains looking for items they could reclaim, recycle, and trade. She was the daughter of one of their elders. Without going into too much detail, suffice it to say we fell in love." He smiled.

"She left them to be with me. We were together for ten glorious years. We'd help those in the city collect food and goods to trade. She was a strong-willed woman with a heart of gold."

"What happened?" Sierra asked, engrossed in his tale. "How did she end up at the Sphere?"

"I was stupid. Her father didn't want her to be with me. He swore I was a member of the Order. No matter what I did I couldn't do anything right in his eyes. We spent a few glorious years traveling together. We were building a life. We had a son together." His eyes darted to Rhys for a split second.

"But we were always under the watchful eye of her father. I had asked him for his blessing to marry her and he turned me down. That night it just so happened that a couple of orbs found our camp and started attacking us. He thought I had brought them there to get even with him. He chased me out of the camp and forbid me to ever see her again.

"She fled the campsite late that night to find me. I don't want to go into too much detail, but she stumbled across a couple of

Sentinels on a routine patrol. They captured her and forced her to be put into reeducation."

"And you just let her go?"

He let out a long, deflated sigh. "Like I said, I don't want to go into too many details. But let's just say I had no choice."

"No choice? You didn't try? You didn't go after her?"

"What was there to go after?" Rhys interjected. "My mother was a coward who sought only comfort for herself. And my father . . ." He rolled his eyes and scoffed. "My father was no better."

"What choice did she have? What choice did I have?"

"She could have escaped. This one did." He dismissively pointed at Sierra. "You could have gone to get her."

"There was only so much I could do. Your mother lived a comfortable life."

"Until she died at the hands of the Guardians! And what of us? What of me? Instead of being here with us, she chose to stay away. To be a dirty Spherian. Lazy and pathetic."

Sierra cleared her throat at the implication.

"I did the best I could," Terre repeated.

"The best you could? Keeping us locked away in the Cursed Lands. Never seeing another living soul? How was that for the best? You have lived for over two hundred years, and you waste everything you know of the world. Everything that could be done to stop them from reigning over us."

Sierra was floored. There was no way this man in front of them could be two hundred years old. No way he was even old enough to be Rhys's father. And to have had a relationship with Greata twenty years ago, he would have been a mere child.

"I should never have come here," Rhys said, shaking his head. "I'm sorry, Sierra. This was a mistake." He stomped off toward the building and slammed the door as he entered.

"Rhys will come around," Terre said, shrugging off his son's behavior.

"How long has he been away?" she pried.

"Five years." Terre sighed, shaking his head. "I tried to keep him safe, but he wanted more. Wanted to help save the world."

"So, what he said is true. You've chosen to avoid the world instead of trying to help make it better."

"When you've lived for as long as I have, you begin to question if there is anything that has ever been worth saving."

"I think your son would disagree."

"Hope is a gift for the young. One day he'll understand."

"My hope is that one day *you* will," she answered. "Someone once told me I was at the heart of mankind's redemption. I've had visions. Visions of you. And visions of how we can help. At least in the present. Help to stop the Guardians from attacking Vegas."

The day was growing short, and Sierra hadn't really prepared herself for this meeting, so she spilled out everything. Greata, the visions, the Silent Zone falling. She rattled off everything about her week-long journey and took a deep breath when she was done.

Terre stood silently, eyeing her up and then Ember. She wondered if he was going to dismiss her like a crazy person. Had she told him too much? She should have started out slower.

The stubble on his face said he hadn't shaved in a couple days. Sierra watched him for any sort of reaction. He was rigid, holding himself with a calm confidence she was sure she was not mirroring.

Moments passed and she wondered if he was waiting for something more. Maybe he wasn't sure what she expected of him.

She realized he was eyeing up Ember suspiciously. It was probably best to try to convince him of the task at hand. "We need you to help us find this machine. We think we can activate it to reinstate the Silent Zone."

A deep sigh briefly destroyed the confident, bold demeanor

he held. She blinked, and his confidence returned, as if the momentary lapse never happened.

"I knew about the Silent Zone. It was only a matter of time. Like you said, we don't have much time to save your friends. To save Vegas. Let's get Rhys. He may not want to see me, but if he was willing to bring you here, he must see something in you."

They entered the building Rhys had disappeared into only moments prior. Her eyes had to adjust to the shift in light. The nondescript brick was the same on the inside as it was out. The building was just as monstrous from within. A large bay filled with ancient vehicles. Not like the shells of vehicles that were outside. Real vehicles. As if they hadn't been touched in two hundred years. Between Terre and the vehicles, she wondered if she had stepped into some sort of portal where time stood still. As the door closed, the light disappeared. There wasn't much light let in from the outside because there were no windows. Toward the back of the bay, a few lanterns revealed a small area with a small bed, a couple couches, and a few other belongings. Maps hung on the wall with giant x's crossed through various locations. A few ancient relics were huddled in a corner as if put there in hopes of better days and forgotten long ago. Otherwise the small lived-in corner seemed quite plain.

Terre removed his desert robe. His clothing below reminded her of Malachi's. Rough, dark dress made for combat. Though unlike Malachi's, his garb was cleaner and had likely never seen a day of fighting. A pendant fell out of his own cloak. A robot, another piece of ancient treasure. The same artifact she had seen him wearing in her vision. The item showing more age than the man wearing it.

One poster stood out on the wall among all the others. The identical symbol that was on the medallion Greata had given her was painted in gold on a life-size display: An open circle with three wavy lines beneath.

"What does it mean?"

"It once stood for hope," Rhys answered, stepping out from the shadows. "A promise of freedom and a people united. Now we're split into factions that can't even agree among themselves. The Resistance is a shell of what it once aimed to be. Now they are simply another tribe seeking vengeance at the expense of all others. My mother once had such a hope. But sold it all to waste away in the Sphere."

"Your mother was a good woman. If it helps you to know, she died helping others."

"Who was she to you?" he asked, seeming annoyed at her defense of a woman who had abandoned him.

"I know it was hard not having her here," Sierra began cautiously. "But, other than Ember, your mother was the only true friend I had. The only one who helped me see that I'm capable of more than what the Guardians prescribed for my life."

At the mention of the Guardians, Terre suspiciously eyed Ember once again.

"How did you hack her?" Terre asked, seeming eager for a change in topic. "I hope for your sake she's disconnected from their network?"

"Hack her? I don't understand."

"Well, either bots have taught themselves a whole new level of subterfuge, or you've hacked this one to be able to function and think off the grid. You're not connected to the network, are you?" Out of nowhere he had produced a blaster in his hand, pointing it at Ember. No alarm in his voice, just casually holding a weapon toward her friend. It could have been his finger with the nonchalant manner he held it.

"I am not," Ember replied, still calm. "But Sierra had nothing to do with my disconnection. I've disconnected myself."

"Disconnected yourself, huh? Well, I don't believe that, either." He turned to Sierra. "Are you sure you can trust her?"

"She's the only one I trust," Sierra responded.

"Bots don't disconnect on their own," he said. "But, then again, if she were connected, she'd have reacted when threatened." He reluctantly put his weapon back in a holster on his belt. "Well, I still don't trust you," he said to Ember. "But this kid has told me some things that nobody but me has known for nearly two hundred years. So, I'll believe that she trusts you at least."

"Look, Ember's loyalty isn't in question here," Sierra snapped. "We need to find this machine, and we need to find it now. The city is likely already under attack. Thousands of lives are counting on us."

He snorted. "Listen, kid, I know this is tough. I have seen millions of people come and go over the centuries. There is always something threatening a city or a group of people somewhere. A new plague, robots, bandits, civil war, rogue militias. Hell, I've seen the aftermath of a village destroyed by feral dogs. This can wait until morning. There will be another disaster right behind it."

"There may not be a tomorrow for them. Do you know where this detonator is or not?"

"The detonator," he said, "was just a mechanism to release the pulse. But yes."

It was the first time he had acknowledged anything in Sierra's visions had been real. His connection to Greata and Rhys had thrown her so off-guard that she had hardly realized that her farfetched request had gone unanswered. She breathed a sigh of relief. Maybe her instincts would prove to be correct after all. If she could convince him to cooperate.

"The Guardians are descending on the city as we speak. We need to act now!" She stepped in front of the man, staring into his dark brown eyes. It was the first time she really got a good look at them. He appeared so young, but his eyes, they hid decades, centuries worth of pain and struggle. They were the eyes of an old man resting in a young man's face.

Terre still hesitated.

"You're wasting your breath," Rhys exclaimed. "He lost his

nerve centuries ago. He's barely lived for the past two hundred years—merely avoided dying."

Terre's resolve hardened at his son's words. Anger flashed in his eyes. She was going to lose him if she couldn't ease the tensions.

"Please," she said. "Greata believed in me. I need you to as well. All I need from you is to show me where the device is. I need to at least try. You've had your chance to live two hundred years. If we don't do this, the rest of us—me, your son—we won't make it to twenty."

Terre looked to the poster on the wall, then back to the medallion, once again hanging freely from Sierra's neck.

"All right," he said. "I haven't seen someone believe this much since. . . well since Greata. If she believed this much in you, well, who am I to argue?"

35

DIM LIGHT SURROUNDED HIM, but Wil couldn't make out much else as he opened his eyes. Light chatter somewhere roused his senses as his mind slowly woke before his body.

That metallic feeling, raw in his veins, was there again. He was sore, stiff, he wasn't sure that it wouldn't be painful if someone brushed up against him. He could feel every movement of air against his skin, and it wasn't a pleasant sensation. Then the memories came. The events that had inevitably led him to this position. It had happened again, whatever it was. The fire and fury that somehow unleashed from within him to disable those bots.

SENTINELS HAD BEEN POURING into the city. It looked like there were hundreds of them, but with their depleted fighters and fatigue of battling the Onyx, there were probably closer to a few dozen. They moved fast though. Faster than he would have ever guessed a man made of metal, plastic, and lights should have been able to.

Wil had gotten cocky after the first Onyx wave. His blaster firing had made contact with the flying beasts. Inflicting damage on the bastards aroused a feeling of satisfaction and pleasure. His destiny was to stop each and every one of them. He'd avenge Marco. Avenge every human these bots have lied to and killed for the last two hundred years. He'd make them pay.

If only he could control the force that he seemed to possess.

As the Sentinels approached the city, he unleashed the blaster he had stolen. Taken from the body of another life the Onyx stole. Three shots landed on their targets. One bot went down. Twenty more came, then twenty more.

Wil had stood at the edge of the city. Bold and brazen in his newfound ability to operate the blasters that had denied him before. And then, with Sentinels approaching, they failed him again. He pulled the trigger, and nothing. He looked at the display, dead. The bots within a hundred meters now, he tossed the gun aside and grabbed the gun strapped to his back.

Dead. He wished he knew how to control whatever it was that was draining these weapons. He tossed the larger weapons and reached for the sword he'd been given.

Wil had his doubts that the sword would do anything against an army of Sentinels with blasters. But it was too late now. He had been foolish enough to push his luck and end up on the front lines. Blaster fire echoed all around him. Snipers had regained some of their positioning in buildings that remained standing. The cannon was operational again, but it wasn't made for ground fire. So Dex and his colleague were focused on protecting it until the next wave of Onyx made their appearance.

Sentinels were firing into their midst. He was able to shuffle off to the side of a building to avoid most of what was coming at them.

Elizabeth was against an adjacent building, firing a larger, two-handed blaster in between the shots coming at them. It took longer to charge than the smaller pistols Wil had held earlier, but the punch it packed sent any robot it hit flying backward, sometimes taking out one or two additional bots behind the one impacted.

Bots were falling left and right, but so were men and women, and the Sentinels just kept coming.

And then they stopped firing. Silence . . . and then a high-pitched noise flooded through the street and Wil was on his knees with his hands to his ears. A quick look around showed that his fellow fighters were experiencing the same reaction. Many doubled over, as the Sentinels marched on. Whatever it was, the bots were causing it. A few of the Resistance were fighting through it, firing back, but they were having a rough go of it. Wil looked to Ella, who had taken the opportunity to step out of her hiding spot and fire on the bots as quickly as her weapon could recharge. Several more went down as a result, but soon they resumed firing back at the Resistance fighters.

The stream of bots entering the city was endless. Streams of white metal and flesh flowed through the streets.

It was a massacre.

Blood painted the road red, and bits of Resistance members, Community members, and those from the Underground, were splattered against the walls of the buildings. The bots were indiscriminate. He jammed a sword into the neck of a bot about to descend on an unsuspecting soldier, but it was only replaced with three more.

Where was Sierra? Had her plan failed?

Blaster fire surrounded them. Some friendly, most of it not.

The bots were creating too many casualties; the city wasn't going to be able to hold on for much longer.

A group of Sentinels ran into a building nearby. The first of the Underground entrances, blown open by the Onyx, exposing hundreds of those unable to fight. They had moved farther into the belly of the city, but the Sentinels saw their opening.

There weren't enough men and women to fight in the streets

and protect those underground as well. Those in the bunkers were sitting ducks.

A laser beam struck Ella and she went flying into the dirt and against the building that had previously been sheltering him.

Enough was enough.

Wil had to do something to keep the bots at bay until Sierra could complete her task, and swinging a sword around wasn't going to do that.

Anger rose in Wil as he stood up, fighting the waves of nausea the noise of the Sentinels was causing. He grabbed his sword and hurled himself into the midst of the fighters. Familiar heat coursing through his body told him what was coming next. This time he didn't fight it.

Something within him was drawing power from what was around him, igniting within him. He leaned into the feeling until he couldn't hold any more of it.

He embraced the surge that coursed through his body and let it flow out of him in an explosive blast. Darkness surrounded him, and the last thing he remembered was his head hitting the ground.

THE NEXT THING WIL KNEW, he was lying in a bed with dim light overhead, barely conscious but knowing that he shouldn't be in a comfortable bed.

He sat up, a little too fast, and had to hold on to the mattress in order to not fall back over.

"Easy there, don't hurt yourself," a familiar female voice spoke to him, but he couldn't quite figure out who it was. He struggled to see, but everything was a blur.

He closed his eyes and tried to let his head adjust to being awake. He opened them again, hoping for his vision to be a little less blurry.

Slowly the cloud lifted, and Wil could clearly see Elizabeth standing in front of him. Her hand rested on his shoulder, though he was sure it was there more to ensure he wasn't going to stand up than it was to reassure him of her presence.

"Once again, we owe you for saving the lives of many, but it takes a great toll on you. Rest. There's no threat for the moment."

Wil struggled to find the words for what he was thinking. Questions formed just out of reach, and he realized he wasn't able to voice his thoughts. But Elizabeth was alive. Where was Ella?

As his vision continued to clear, he realized Elizabeth's shoulder was bandaged up.

"Glad . . ." He managed to get out after a concentrated effort. "Glad you're okay."

The concern on Elizabeth's face faded into a smile that touched her purple eyes, for the first time he had seen. Those eyes seemed familiar somehow.

Maybe the blaster fire softened her up a bit. It only lasted a few moments, though. The pleasantry didn't fade, but the softness did. Her guard was back up.

"Don't you worry about me, bot killer. I told you before you need to learn to control that power of yours before it kills you. We weren't sure if you were going to come out of this one."

"I meant to use it this time. Had to—" Wil paused to swallow. His mouth was so dry. "Had to slow them down until Sierra can finish her mission. How many did I get?"

She looked at him like it was the stupidest question in the world. How was he to know? He was unconscious.

"All of them."

"All of them?"

"We counted two hundred and fifty, though we could be off by a handful. They're calling you the bot killer. Some are acting like you're a savior come to free us from them."

He rubbed his temple as he tried to shake off the pounding in his head. Not to mention the fire in his insides that wasn't fading. "I wouldn't count on it."

"That's what I told them." Elizabeth laughed as if she'd told a great joke. He couldn't figure this woman out.

"Thanks." Wil gave a small laugh. It was nice to be able to laugh, but it hurt.

"I saw you running into them like a crazed man. You were lucky they didn't kill you before you took them down."

"I saw Ella get shot," he said, staring at the edge of the bed. "I couldn't handle someone else I know being blasted away. I had to do something. I didn't think. I just acted. By the time I realized what I was doing, I was in the middle of them."

"Well, you better start thinking. Next time you may not be so lucky. You don't know how valuable you are. You have the ability to change the course of our fight, and I'm not going to have you dying because you're upset that someone got shot in the arm. Keep your head on straight."

Wil laughed to himself. "And what if I had? Would either of us still be here? How many of the Resistance would have fallen? I am more than a weapon for you to manipulate. It may have been a rash decision, but it saved your ass. Somehow, I'll find a way to control this so it doesn't take me out with it, but right now, I'm working with what I've got."

Elizabeth glared at him and stormed out of the room.

Half a dozen other beds with men and women lying in various states of injury surrounded him. Judging by the decor he was back in the Rio Grande. There were no windows, just brick walls.

Wil forced himself to stand. He had to shake this off and find the others. He wished he had a better sense of what was happening. Was the city still under attack? Elizabeth had said there would be multiple waves. Surely the bots wouldn't have been defeated already, but she wouldn't have been down here with him if they were still under fire either. His legs complained and shook as he held himself up. He refused to stay in bed though.

It didn't look like anyone else in the room was in good enough shape to be up and about. Every one of them was asleep. He cringed at the thought that he had yelled at Elizabeth while these people were resting. Nothing that could be helped now.

Wil opened the door and stepped out. The hallway was empty. He didn't have a plan, but he wasn't going to be left lying in a bed while others were putting their lives on the line.

Two steps out, an earth-shattering alarm sounded. He nearly fell over on his shaky legs, using the wall to hold himself up. A lot of help he was going to be.

At that point he realized he was unarmed and didn't have a shirt on. He would have to find a way to defend himself once he was outside, but someone was going to have to point him to where they left his shirt. He expected the alarm, still blaring to the point of being deafening, would send people flying into the hall, but it remained empty.

He got to the end of the hall where a door was opened a crack. Peering inside, he could see people pouring up into a stairwell. He poked his head in and happened to see Ella.

"Ella!" he called out.

Ella whipped around at the sound of his voice and pushed him back into the hall.

"Wil! What are you doing up? You should be resting."

He was trying his best not to sway at the force of her pushing him. "I'm fine! There's no way I could be resting with this bloody alarm going off. What's happening?"

"Third wave, more Onyx parked outside of the city. There was a pause in the battle while the Guardians gathered their units, but they're starting to move. Everyone's being called to battle stations."

"All right, well, let's go then." He made his way to the door, almost falling into Ella.

"Wil, you're in no shape to be fighting! Please stay here. There will be plenty of opportunity to help." Her eyes were wide and her hands were on his waist. He was grateful for the extra support but had to consciously try to not surrender all of his weight into her.

"I can fight."

"Half naked and without a weapon? Wil, you can barely stand!" She looked into his eyes and visibly softened. "Please. You'll be no help if you're dead."

He knew she was right. Oh, how he hated that she was right.

"I'll stay here if you promise not to die out there. I can't help you down here."

Ella leaned in and gave him a quick kiss on the lips. "I promise I'll do my best." She let him go and stepped back into the stairwell. "Besides, someone needs to look after you the next time you pass out."

"Just pray Sierra can find what she thinks will take these bots out," Wil said. "I don't think I'll have enough stamina in me to knock another round out for a while."

"If she doesn't come through," Ella replied, "there won't be much of a city left to save."

36

MORE WALKING THROUGH THE DESERT, Sierra thought as she left the building, heading after Terre. Staff in hand, he had a lantern hanging from its hooked top. He was already a good dozen yards ahead of her, Rhys, and Ember. All this walking and running around was growing tiresome and her legs were killing her. She didn't think she had ever walked so much in her life.

They caught up to him as he approached a set of outbuildings, a few hundred yards from where they started.

"How far do we need to go?" Sierra asked, trying to catch her breath, and also apprehensive about what his answer might be.

"We're here," Terre answered, pointing to a doorway that was in a small sub-building about a hundred paces from where they stood.

"This is it?" she asked. "We're right here?"

"This has been the perfect location for me to stay. Nobody comes this way and the radiation scrambles the bots' sensors. They leave me alone. People leave me alone. I quite like it that way."

Sierra shook her head. So much of this man was a mystery. She needed to press for more answers.

"How is it that I saw you in my vision? How can you possibly remember the ancient wars?"

Rhys rolled his eyes, but Sierra put a hand on his shoulder. This was important and she needed to hear it.

"I was there when the wars began," Terre started. "I was in one of the first attacks where the bots started acting on their own. We didn't know what was happening yet. Attack drones circled around the base I was stationed at. We never expected an attack in America. That's what this place was called. They don't teach you that in the Sphere.

"Again, the details don't matter. I was injured, and they injected me with a type of bot. Nanobots, they're called. They were designed to heal. They work with my body to heal damage that's been done. They are biologically based, not made of the metal and circuitry like the bots you recognize."

She nodded as if that made sense, although she wasn't sure she understood.

"So, you can't die?"

"Well, I wouldn't go that far. But they've kept me alive this long."

"Why did the bots turn on us?"

"We programmed the drones to attack our enemies. Then we programmed them to learn, to adapt. Pretty soon they figured out they would be more efficient if they cut us out of the equation. At some point, they decided to talk to each other. All of them, not just ours. China, Russia, Europe, Iran, countries and regions in the old world—every nation had its own drones. In our haste to outdo each other in the race to develop better AI—artificial intelligence, they used to call it—they took on a life of their own. Our networks were still all connected, and they started sharing programming, and before we knew it, their mission evolved to kill not just a single enemy on the battlefield, but everyone.

"Only through dumb luck were we able to install part of an

override. A separate protocol from our space program, designed for AI to protect us on the Mars colony expeditions. It was incomplete, but it stopped the entire annihilation of the human race. The bots started to form colonies, like they had done on Mars. The problem was, the attack protocols were still in place, and anything that stood in the way of or on the outside of the biodomes were considered a threat to be eliminated. They calculated how to best preserve humanity in a world with limited power and resources. Anyone who didn't serve their best interests or fell outside of their direct control was to be eliminated."

Sierra struggled to process what she had been told. She barely understood any of it. "So, it was us," she finally said. "It was our fault. The Sphere, the Silent Zone, all of it."

Terre nodded and looked up at her for the first time since he had started talking, eyes filled with regret. "We programmed them to kill. We programmed them to protect. We should have been able to see it coming. We should have been able to stop it. I should have. It's my fault."

"What? How could it possibly be your fault?"

"We better go." He placed a hand on the door. A low hum made him pause.

"They're here," Ember announced.

THE ORDER WOMAN WAS BACK, this time with more Sentinels. Over a dozen, standing a few hundred yards away. They didn't have much time.

"You three get inside," Terre barked to Sierra, Rhys and Ember, opening the door. "I'll hold the bots off. Buy you enough time to activate the weapon. If you can."

"What do you mean, if we can?" Sierra asked incredulously.

"You saw in the vision for yourself. The bots knocked out the power. No power, no weapon."

Sierra smiled. "Don't worry. I've got that covered." She stepped toward the entrance.

"I'm staying here with you . . . Dad," Rhys said.

"What? No, get underground. I'll handle this."

"Look, there's no way you can distract that many bots, and there's no way even you'd survive that much blaster fire. We need to hold them off for long enough to let Sierra complete the mission. Otherwise, none of us are making it out of here."

"Rhys!" Sierra cried. She didn't want him to get killed, not for her sake. The snarky kid who had stared daggers at her when she had first arrived at the Outpost had turned into something more. Someone she cared deeply about. She fought back the tears that welled in her eyes. Too much bloodshed. Too much killing. She was about to lose Ember. She didn't want to lose him too.

"Please," she whispered as he approached. "Please be safe . . . I . . ." She couldn't finish the thought. Not even if she wanted to. She didn't know how the sentence would end.

"It's okay," Rhys said, putting a finger to her lips. "You just do what you need to do. Go save the city, Sierra."

He smiled the most beautiful smile, and his green eyes lit up as she pulled him close to her. Before she knew what she was doing, she was on her tiptoes, leaning into him as her lips met his. Electricity flowed through her as she held Rhys close.

"I'm sorry," Rhys began. "I know we got off to a rough start, but . . ."

"It's okay," Sierra whispered.

People here have a past that comes out in unpredictable ways. Malachi's words from her first encounter with Rhys echoed through Sierra's mind. Rhys had lost his mother to the Sphere. He had a right to be bitter.

"I hate to be the one to break this up, you two, but whatever

Sierra's going to do, she needs to do it now!" Terre pushed the lantern into her hands and shooed her and Rhys apart.

Sierra nodded, glad the man finally saw the urgency. She gave a final glance to Rhys and disappeared with Ember into the chamber.

A lantern in hand, Sierra led the way down the otherwise pitch-black cavern. The walls along the shaft had the same gray brick that the larger structure outside had been built with.

They passed through a doorway and entered a large room. Nothing had changed from the room Sierra had seen in her vision. The screens were off, the room had been eradicated of all furniture and other people, but otherwise it was exactly the same.

She looked in front of her and steadied her breath. This was what she had come here for, the room from her vision. But now that she was here, she didn't know where to begin. She circled the room, taking note of the screens, the control panels, trying to recall something from what she had seen that would give her the answer she needed. A short set of stairs led to the center of the room, and at the bottom lay a smaller circular inset. Guard rails surrounded a small tablelike structure with a metal orb on top. That had to be the key.

Sierra reached out and touched the orb. It was cold, metallic, exactly how she expected it to be. "The detonator."

Ember stood beside her, her silent confidence encouraging Sierra to continue. Not once had she interrupted or protested.

Sierra took her hand from the metal ball and walked over to Ember, whose orange eyes were glowing in the dimly lit room.

"Ember, I'm so sorry. If this works . . ."

"If this works, you'll be saving a city of people. You'll be giving thousands a chance at life. The chance to start over. This needs to be done." Ember smiled and embraced Sierra.

"I can't do it. I don't want to lose you too." Sierra shook her head, pushing Ember away. "I can't." She collapsed into a nearby chair. Her head fell into her arms, which rested on a nearby control panel.

"Sierra, listen, I knew what the risk was when I came here with you. What you are doing is more important than keeping me online."

Sierra shook as she sobbed into her arms, taking deep breaths to try and regain control of herself. It took several moments, but finally she looked up. "I know it's selfish of me."

She stood up and walked over to her friend. "Thank you for being brave when I wasn't. Thank you for everything you've done for me. Taking care of me all of these years. I don't think I ever told you how much it meant to have you after Izzy and Dad died."

"I know, Sierra. You have given me more than anyone could ask for. You gave me self-awareness, and in reality, the gift of life. A life protecting and growing with you. I couldn't have ever asked for anything more, and I'm so happy that I have had the honor of calling you my friend."

They embraced briefly again, tears streaming down Sierra's face. Ember smiled a reassuring smile.

Sierra sniffed. Time to do what they came here to do.

"There's a control panel on the second floor." Sierra wiped a tear from her eye as she pointed to the balcony above them. "If I'm able to activate the detonator, you'll need to flip the switch to launch it."

Ember nodded and gracefully walked up the stairs, blissfully coolheaded for someone about to push the button that would cause her own demise.

There was no more time to shed tears now. If Sierra didn't do this, there would be more loss than just her one friend. Greata had claimed she was meant for greater things. She was about to find out. To find out if she was capable of more than what the Guardians had planned out for her. She walked back down toward the ball in the center of the room.

"Well, here goes nothing."

Sierra placed both hands on the ball and waited. She had managed to maintain some control of herself, but the tears still rolled down her cheeks. Her hands began to feel warm against the metal ball, but still, she couldn't stop thinking of Ember.

Memories of Ember flashed through her mind: their walks along the Sphere, her healing touch when Sierra scraped a knee.

Warmth began to spread up Sierra's arms.

Late nights, especially early on after Izzy had died. Ember had filled that void. Sierra had grown to love Ember as the sister she never got to grow up with.

The heat traveled into her chest, then her whole body grew warm. Then hot. Sweat poured down her face, but she was unable to let go of the device.

Lights in the room flickered and then came to life. Control panels turned on, and the screens around the room started to hum.

Ember leaned over one of the consoles, pushed a few buttons. Sierra shivered. The orb turned to ice, and the entire room went black once again. An icy chill ran through Sierra just as the warmth had, until she collapsed, and her vision went dark.

37

—————

RHYS STOOD ready for the fresh attack. The bots would be upon them any minute. He steadied his breathing as he prepared. They didn't have to take them all out. They just had to stall them long enough for Sierra's plan to work.

If it would work, that is. They had nothing else to go on other than Sierra's visions and a hunch that she could willingly manifest the power she possessed. Rhys's father had confirmed that which Sierra had seen from two hundred years ago had occurred. She had gotten them this far. He hoped the rest played out as she imagined. Even if his father was involved.

"I am glad you came back, son." Terre looked at Rhys after the newcomers descended into the bunker. "All these years I've wondered how you've been. Wondered if you were all right."

Rhys stared at his father, not sure if he should answer.

"I didn't come back for you," he said. "Sierra needed your help. I agreed to show her the way."

"I did the best I could to protect you. I'm sorry that I pushed you away."

Fury burned inside of Rhys. He pushed it down as best he could. *Save it for the machines.*

"I didn't need your protecting. I needed your strength, Dad. I needed your will to fight the Guardians and to try to bring about a better world. One *I* could live in, could eventually raise a family in."

Terre looked away from his son.

"During the last ten years, you wondered how I was, yet you never came looking for me? Never thought it worth your while to help me to turn the table on these robots. Take back the world for humanity."

Terre shrugged. "I tried to save the world for two centuries before you were born. We never made any progress. I watched friends die in battle. The ones that didn't I watched grow old and die. I watched their kids and grandkids and great grandkids grow old and die. While I tried. When I met your mother that all changed. She inspired me. She had such hope. The hope of youth.

"When the Guardians captured her, I was devastated. Mortified that I would never see my wife again, that she would abandon all we had here, all we had worked for. But she did it to protect you. My number one priority was to keep you from harm." He grabbed the robot medallion around his neck. "I had already lost one child, centuries ago, to the metal demons. I didn't want to lose you as well. I wanted to give you a life, a safe life. But I held on too tight, and I lost you anyway."

His dad had another child? Why had he never mentioned it before?

"You kept us in a remote bunker in the middle of nowhere. We saw no people. I had no friends. I had just lost my mom, and I was stuck for hours alone while you went to gather supplies for us. I was only eight! You were keeping me alive. But we definitely weren't living."

Terre pulled out a blaster from a strap around his back, readying himself for the group of bots coming nearer.

"You deserved more," he said. "I didn't know how to be a

father. Your mother would have been proud at how you've turned out. Fighting for justice. Fighting for freedom."

"Sierra has brought me fresh hope. When I saw Mom's medallion—" He shook his head, smiling. "I knew there was something about her that would change the world. Mom wouldn't have given that medallion away to anyone. And you should have seen Sierra coming into the Outpost." He let out a laugh. "She was so green. I knew it hadn't been stolen."

Terre started laughing as well, but it was cut short as the group of robots neared. The same woman from before, dressed in white with red-lit cracks glowing from within, approached, leading the pack.

"If it isn't Terre. *The man who remembers the wars.*" The woman looked to him with amusement.

Rhys raised an eyebrow at his father in bewilderment. How did this woman know his dad? He had to remember over the course of two hundred years he would have met a lot of individuals. But this woman looked barely older than he was.

If he wasn't so preoccupied with Sierra, he would have thought the woman beautiful. Her dark brown hair was accentuated as it hung against her white robe. Her eyes were so blue they were almost white.

"Elana," Terre answered. "It's been quite some time."

Behind her over a dozen Sentinels stood at attention. Was this woman controlling them? That would be a new development. Guardians were known to leave the Order members alone, but never had they controlled them. It was typically the other way around.

A couple of Scanner orbs and several smaller attack orbs hovered above the group. One thing was certain—they were well outmatched.

"Where's the girl?" Elana asked.

"What's it to you?" Rhys piped up. "Why are you going to so much effort to find her?"

"The Guardians finally have a leader. Titan has risen from the ranks of the Sentinels and pledged to lead both Guardians and humans into a new world order. The ancient texts have proven true once again. He will lead us all to a better life under the Guardians' reign. Even for you, Terre!"

"Rule of tyranny and decay, or have you not seen what they've done to the place?"

"Out here in the barren lands, they control the only way they can. Pockets of rebels hiding in their protective bubbles foiling their efforts. But without the Silent Zones, their rule would be absolute. These zones are a scourge on the Guardians' plan. In the Spheres, we are provided with food, shelter, safety. All in exchange for only dedication and hard work."

"The Guardians don't have a plan, Elana!" Terre replied. "They're just machines. This is all part of an ancient program."

"That was before Titan. He has brought with him a new age of Guardian rule. But that girl is a scourge on his plan. She must be stopped!"

"And how do you know of her plan?" he asked.

"Titan has his ways," she answered. "We know she's trying to resurrect the Silent Zone. We've waited too long to allow that, and we have our orders."

She lifted her arms, and the orbs above her rose, blue lights spinning across their surface as they built up power.

Rhys braced himself. Against three attack orbs and a dozen Sentinels, they wouldn't even be able to put up a fight.

Light sparked from the closest of the orbs, and Rhys lunged toward his dad, knocking him to the ground before the beam could hit its target.

Searing pain flashed across Rhys's shoulder. The beam had clipped him, burning a mark through his flesh. He did his best to ignore the sting, but it burned as the skin curled and peeled. Along with the already searing pain in his leg, the injury was more than a little distracting. With his good arm, he aimed back and fired at the orb that attacked.

The beam made contact, sending sparks flying, but it was going to take a lot more than one shot from his handheld blaster to bring the beast down.

The Sentinels lifted their weapons in unison. There was no way Rhys and Terre could dodge them all. More than a dozen robots had weapons aimed at them.

Elana let out a cackle, a grating and horrendous noise considering the pretty face it emanated from.

Terre lifted his weapon toward their aggressors, and Rhys followed suit. If they were going to go down, it wouldn't be without a fight. He just hoped they could stay alive long enough for Sierra.

The earth rattled beneath them. It started off slow then turned to a full-blown earthquake, sending both him and Terre to their knees.

Elana continued laughing, taking a moment to realize something was amiss. The orbs stopped midair and fell dead to the ground, landing on the Sentinels, crashing metal on metal, causing sparks to fly.

Sierra did it. She actually did it.

By the time the dust had cleared, Elana had disappeared once again, leaving only a pile of decommissioned robots behind.

38

____

WHAT HAD ELLA BEEN THINKING? Wil thought as he made his way back to the room he had come from. They had discussed this. He wasn't ready to be involved with her. Not yet. Not so soon.

He opened the door to the chamber he had woken up in. Bedridden casualties. Bandages everywhere, blood soaking through some of them. These people were in rough shape.

If he wasn't going to be fighting, he could at least have a look at what was happening. He didn't want to be cooped up in the basement with those already dying.

Back at the stairwell, Wil opened the door slowly, peering around to make sure no other Resistance or Community members were funneling up toward the surface. He wondered briefly what lay below him. How deep did this cavern go?

Shaking off the thought, he started up the stairs. It was a harder task than he thought it would be. His legs struggled to push him up each step, and he had to lean on the wall for further support. Ella had been right—he wasn't ready for battle.

The stairs seemed endless, though in reality, it was only a couple floors that he needed to climb. As he reached the surface, he could hear blaster fire and explosions bleeding in from the outside. The attack had begun.

Wil stepped outside and nearly fell over. His already shaky legs would have given out completely if he didn't hold on to the wall of the Inn. Shadow covered the city, dozens of sphere patches slowly moving across the street and buildings. Some firing, others scanning. Blaster fire littered the street, lighting up the sky. One thing was certain: They weren't going to win this one. They had barely managed to hold off six without destroying the city in the process. How were they going to manage ten times that number?

There was nothing he could do to help, not in his condition. He couldn't risk having another sudden blast of . . . whatever it was that happened to him. If he even could knock out this many Onyx, he had no doubt the effort would kill him.

In the distance, sparks flew as the occasional Onyx hit the ground. Some collided with ancient metal structures that still had remnants peeking through the earth. Dirt and debris flew everywhere as they kicked earth into the air, clouding his view of their attackers. Through the haze, laser fire lit paths between the humans and bots. The air was thick. He wondered how they'd be able to manage if they lost all visibility during their assault.

"Wil? What the hell are you doing out here?' Malachi had his back pressed up against the wall behind him. He was dressed in a brown outfit that made him nearly blend into the wall and fully decked out in weapons and the same metallic protective gear that many of the Resistance members wore.

"I just came out to have a look," he said. "Sorry, I should go back inside."

"Forget that. You're out here now. Can you find Ella? I need her to run supplies to some of the other units. They need fully charged weapons."

That was the last person he wanted to find. She'd kill him herself if she saw him out here.

"I don't think that's the best idea."

He didn't have time to explain further. Fire from one of the Onyx split a line up the middle of the street toward a nearby group of fighters. Dirt and debris kicked into the air. Wil choked as he breathed and tried to spit out the dirt that invaded his mouth.

Malachi forgot about him and proceeded to fire back at the machine doing the bulk of the damage. His handheld blaster cannon managed to split the glass of the Onyx. It started sparking but flew off. If the damage took it down, it wasn't immediate. It may have been a good thing that it wasn't right on top of them.

Malachi ran off. Wil wasn't sure if he assumed he was going to fulfill the request to find Ella or had just forgotten about the ask. Malachi hadn't told him where she was, and he wasn't about to stagger around the battlefield trying to find her.

If things were chaotic during the first two waves, they were devastating now. Much of the city that had remained standing lay in ruin. Gaping holes in the earth revealed members of the Underground, once sure their location was safe, now scrambling like ants to get deeper into its belly or out into a new location before the next strike could hit. Some of them made it; many didn't.

Wil began to feel a warm sensation within him and started to panic. This couldn't happen again. He grabbed the door behind him and pulled the handle. It didn't budge. He tried again, putting the little strength he had left into forcing the door open. It still didn't move. Locked.

He skirted the edge of the building, trying to find another way in. A few steps away and a blast from an Onyx hit the door he had just been standing in front of. He leaped to avoid the debris. Something collided with his leg, and he hit the ground. A chunk of the building, no bigger than his head, but made of solid rock had landed on him. He couldn't move without a blinding flash of pain coursing through his leg and up into his hip. He was dead in the water. Other fighters scurried past him, trying to fire at the Onyx attacking the Inn, but there were so many of them floating above it was hard to actually tell which one it was. And really it didn't matter. It could have been any of them.

Wil cursed himself for leaving the underbelly of the Inn. Now he was a sitting duck, waiting for the rest of the building to fall on top of him or the Onyx to blast a hole through his middle.

The warmth returned. Would it be worse to die by blaster or in a final blaze of glory? He tried to hold it down, but what better time to learn how to control this? He might not have a choice. This sensation was different, so maybe his conscious effort was working. Before his veins burned like boiling water coursing through him. This was warmth, not fire. Like a warm hearth was growing within him. Either way, he tried to focus on isolating it so it didn't spread. Then it disappeared.

He had been so distracted trying to sort out the sensations within him that he hadn't noticed that the hum of the machines above and the fire of blasters around him had stopped.

Silence.

Wil looked to a group of fighters next to him and realized their gaze was turned skyward. He looked up as well. The Onyx were hovering. Dark. Silent. What was happening?

He barely had time to ask himself the question before they started to fall. Dozens of giant balls of black glass and circuitry plummeted to earth. He let out a cry and managed to roll himself toward the building, bracing himself among some of the rubble.

The ground around him shook violently. His face was toward the wall, but he imagined the chaos of giant black glass orbs embedding themselves in the earth, along with the buildings they were colliding with collapsing on impact. Clouds of dust and debris enveloped him. He closed his eyes as bits of rock, metal, and concrete rained down. Somehow he remained unscathed.

The roar of the frenzy around him died down. The world had

gone nearly silent, with the exception of the pitter-patter of smaller pieces of debris hitting the ground.

Wil opened his eyes and looked behind him. He couldn't see much. Dust and smoke hung thick in the air. Men and women covered in dirt stood in the street, standing among giant black orbs embedded in the ground and the remnants of buildings. Bodies lay scattered, many half-buried in rubble. Flames licked the edges of what was visible around him, rising through some of the buildings that remained. Sparks from falling bots had ignited anything flammable upon impact.

It couldn't have been him that did this. He had started to feel warm before, but there was no fire, no explosion from within. And he felt fine now. The warmth that had been within him was gone as well. This was something else. Had Sierra found what she had been looking for? Wil could only hope.

There was work to be done, and with the threat of being shot now eliminated, he thought he may be able to help with the cleanup. It was an absolute bloodbath around him. Fighters who hadn't been lucky enough to avoid the sky falling lay everywhere. Whether the cause had been an Onyx or a piece of a building, the result was the same. Some hadn't been able to get out of the way in time.

How many had died in this destruction? Had there been another way that would have saved them so many casualties? Perhaps not. Even while they were trying to take them down one by one their descent had been causing destruction.

Wil wondered how much of a dent this had made in their numbers, and how accurate Ella's warning was that the Guardians would just rebuild more. There had to have been over fifty of them in the sky. Today should have at least slowed them down.

A man and a woman walked by on what remained of the street before him. They shuffled around chunks of building that littered the ground, covered in dust from head to toe. Eyes wide at the remnants of fallen orbs, they almost didn't notice him lying in the dirt. He imagined the dust made him blend in with the rest of the debris.

"Excuse me!" Wil called out. "Can you help me get this boulder off my leg?"

Surprised to hear his voice call out, they looked in his direction, and he waved his arms trying to grab their attention further.

"Damn, man! You betcha!"

They ran over toward him, bent over the rock that had immobilized him, and lifted with a great deal of strength. The pair heaved and managed to move the rock only slightly, but it was enough for him to work his leg out.

Wil moved slowly. It was painful, but his limb didn't seem to be broken. The pair lifted him up, and he tested the amount of pressure his leg could stand. It seemed to hold his weight. He tried walking and managed to limp. It was sore. It would probably swell, but he could stand. He'd survive, for now.

"You sure you're okay? A rock like that on your leg, you're lucky it ain't broke!"

"I'll be okay, I think." He winced as he limped forward. "I won't be carrying anything heavy, but I'll live."

The city was starting to come to life out of the wreckage. Silhouetted figures moved about, picking up casualties who were in worse shape than he was.

Out of a billow of smoke, a soot-covered woman emerged before him, eyes hollowed and worried. It was Ella. As she limped toward him, the look on her face told Wil that she'd had the same initial thought as him. Did he cause the bots to fall?

Tears streamed down Ella's face, leaving streaks of mud along her cheeks. Her pants were torn. One pant leg had ripped right off, and wet dirt streaked down her leg, caked with blood. She was injured but still rushed to see if he was okay.

Wil hobbled forward, and embraced her, somehow finding

the strength to hold her up as she collapsed into him. Audibly sobbing.

"Wil, I thought . . . I thought you . . . " she managed to spout out between sobs.

He interrupted her, trying to calm her down. "I know. It wasn't me. It wasn't me. Sierra must have found the weapon she was seeking."

"Wil," she sniffed. "I'm sorry about before. I didn't mean to . . . I just wasn't sure if I'd ever see you again. I want you to know . . ."

"Shhh. Don't worry about that now. It's okay."

"No, you made your feelings clear to me. I . . ."

"Let's get you to the infirmary. You're losing a lot of blood. I'm okay. I promise. We're good."

She didn't say anything else, but she did continue to sob. That unnerved Wil more than anything. Up until then Ella had seemed so strong, so confident. Everyone had their breaking point, it seemed.

He realized he had no idea where he was going, but he hauled her toward where the main entrance of the Inn had been. Surely someone would point him in the right direction.

39

THE DUST HAD FINALLY SETTLED as the sun began to dip below the horizon the following evening. There was still so much work to be done. It would take weeks, maybe months to sort through the rubble. Wil lifted another dead body onto a cart being hauled by a couple of larger men from the Community. They would take the bodies out into the desert to bury them.

His leg was feeling better. It had been a minor strain that worked itself out as he walked on it for a bit. He could still feel the bruise where the rock had hit it, but he was more than capable of helping with the aftermath of the attack.

After he brought Ella to the Inn, he had come out to see what he could do and ended up helping to load bodies of the fallen onto an old cart. Wil didn't know a single one of them. He had no way to document who they were. Between members of the Underground, members of the Community, and members of the Resistance, they had lost more souls than they were willing to count. Hundreds for sure, probably more. So many missing. So much death. So many nameless faces. They spent all night and all day sorting through rubble. Trying to save any who were still breathing, and cleaning up those who weren't.

Wil made himself look at each face as he pulled them from where they had fallen, before he tossed them with the others. They had already made several trips into the desert. With too many dead to give each a proper burial, mass graves were being dug outside the city. One last injustice for people who had never known anything but.

It was hard for him to celebrate their victory. Others were jubilant and didn't hide their revelry. He couldn't blame them. The bots could have completely wiped them out. The fact that any of them were left standing could be considered a triumph. Many of them lived to fight on another day. But the stench of death only reminded Wil of the cost. This was only one small victory in a much larger fight. One pocket of humanity with a temporary achievement, allowing them to breathe another day while the chaos of the Guardians and the struggle of the day-to-day hung over each of their heads. One pocket that was safe for now, but others remained. Possibly hundreds, in Silent Zones of their own, hiding, waiting for their protection to fall. Who knew if they had already? He tried not to dwell on the negative but looking into the faces of countless dead skewed his perspective.

"This will be the last load for tonight." Malachi had been working tirelessly. He made his rounds, helping where he could, but mostly trying to bring some order to the otherwise directionless survivors. Getting to work right away gave them a sense of purpose and unity, but it also gave them a distraction from the grim reality they had just suffered.

"We can get one more in before the sun sets," Wil said.

"There will be many loads over the next few days. We have been through enough for today. Too many of you haven't slept since the attack. Leo managed to salvage some ale from his cellars. Everyone who isn't tending to the injured will rest and relax this evening. This is more than anyone should have to bear. A rest and a pint will ease our souls. The work will still be there tomorrow."

"We can manage this," said one of the burlier Community members who had been pulling the carts all day.

He nodded to Wil, "We'll take this out. You head back and rest."

Wil didn't argue further. He hadn't fully recovered from yesterday's attack. But he knew he wasn't the only one. Malachi had been running all day, with what was probably a broken rib. He didn't complain once. The only thing that gave away that he was in pain was the occasional wince if he turned a certain way.

Wil was eager to check on Ella. After he had brought her into the Rio Grande, she had passed out. He carried her to a bed and helped bandage her leg up to stop the flow of blood. Malachi had managed to talk Leo into giving Ella a private room. However, with so many injured, nobody was really checking in on her. Leo's staff certainly had their hands full trying to help some of those located on the side of the Inn that had been struck by an Onyx blast.

Thankfully, aside from some minor bumps and bruises, most of those who had taken refuge under the Inn had fared okay. As bad as Ella's leg was, she would survive now that the bleeding had stopped and she was getting rest. It was amazing nothing had been broken. From what Wil had understood, part of a building had fallen on top of her. Ella managed to free herself and run on pure adrenaline until she got to Wil. Her leg was swollen from the impact, and she wouldn't be walking for weeks.

He lifted one last body onto the cart and watched as the men made their way toward the mountains.

As the men left with their cart, Wil noticed three figures walking toward the city. He stopped to watch the travelers, coming in from the west. What appeared to be a man with a green cloak wrapped around him, a muscular man with an arm in a sling, and a woman with a white cloak and bright red hair. Ember.

He started in their direction. He would have run if he could, but his legs were so tired even walking was a challenge. He wasn't going to just sit and wait though. Who was the man in the green cloak, and where were Sierra and Ed?

Wait.

Ember?

After the Onyx had fallen, the survivors had checked to ensure the Silent Zone was indeed back in place. No weapons or bikes were working. Wil stopped in his tracks.

"Malachi!" he shouted. He was already making his way to his next stop of the cleanup.

Wil, finding a sudden burst of energy as panic coursed through his body, sprinted toward him.

"Is your blaster working?" Wil panted as he caught up. It wasn't a far sprint, but it had taken most of what he had left in him.

"What? No, of course not," he said as he pulled the weapon out and double checked. "Why?"

Wil simply pointed in Ember's direction.

"Shit."

"How is it possible?" he asked.

"Whatever blew out the Onyx must have been a one-time deal that also took out our gear. Shit! We were too quick to think the Zone might be back up."

Malachi took off running toward the three walking into the city. Wil was still trying to catch his breath from catching up to Malachi, so he followed behind at a much slower pace.

Malachi caught up and started to talk to Ember, Rhys, and their strange companion. Wil wasn't close enough yet to hear what they were saying, but he watched as Malachi's posture completely relaxed. He looked down at something behind the pair, and for the first time, Wil realized they were pulling a small wagon behind them. Malachi had a new sense of urgency and urged the pair to continue.

Wil realized that if he kept walking toward them, he'd

eventually have to walk back. He wasn't sure if his legs were going to make a round trip, so he stopped and waited. It wasn't long before they caught up with him and he realized why Malachi had suddenly been in a hurry to get them to the city. Sierra was in the wagon.

WIL HELPED Rhys move Sierra into a second bed in the room where Ella was resting. Ember was sure that after some rest Sierra would be okay, but the process of powering up the machine to trigger the EMP had significantly drained her. It seemed similar to what had happened to him when he knocked the machines out. He wondered how he and Sierra had both ended up with such similar, yet opposite abilities. Both born and raised within the Sphere under the eyes of the bots, yet something had been awakened within them. Something that had helped those on the Outside, people who weren't supposed to exist, escape the fury of the bots for at least another day.

He had been relieved when Terre had told them the Silent Zone, or something similar, had in fact been reinstated. After Sierra activated the device it created a pulse that was just as strong, if not stronger than the original weapon the ancients dropped.

Why Ember hadn't deactivated was a mystery. Terre had no explanation for it and neither did Ember. By her calculations her circuits should have been fried.

Sierra's eyes fluttered. They slowly opened, and she smiled as she saw them all in the room with her.

"Ember?" Sierra's voice was somehow filled with both relief and despair. "It didn't work." She sunk into her bed. Wil could tell she was trying to move but was unable, panic building on her face.

"It's okay," Ember's voice smoothed over as she ran her fingers through Sierra's hair, visibly relaxing the girl as she lay in her bed. Her eyes held tears, but her body had stopped its urgent desire to thrash around.

"It did work," Ember continued. "You stopped the invasion and reinstated the barrier. But sleep now. We'll let you in on all of the details later."

"You're injured," she addressed Rhys. The makeshift sling he had created himself had blood seeping through.

"I'm fine," he answered. "Thanks to you. If it weren't for you none of us would be here right now."

Sierra nodded. "The danger's not gone yet. We need to find this Titan Sentinel before he does more damage. We also need to help those in the Sphere. They won't be protected any longer."

"There'll be time for that later. Right now, rest." Rhys ran his fingers through her hair as she closed her eyes.

The End

SIGN UP FOR MY NEWSLETTER

**Stay up to date on upcoming releases, promotions and more
by subscribing to my newsletter.**

Thank you once again for supporting me as an author!

Secrets of the Sphere

Lies of the Guardians | Book Two

Coming April 2021 – Preorder Today

ACKNOWLEDGMENTS

A huge thank you to everyone who made my debut novel possible.

Thank you to my developmental editor Chersti Nieveen. You helped my take this story to the next level. Thank you to my copy editor, Sandra Olga, for your clear concise edits. Thank you to my friend and proofreader David Warriner as well as to Blair Thornburgh for giving this a final polish. Thank you as well to Miblart for the cover design.

To my beta readers, Margie Viers, and Chris Stokes, thank you for your initial insights into the early manuscript.

Thank you to my wife, Nettie, for always being the first to look at my mangled first drafts. It is a wonder that you can see the diamond within the rough.